THE

DARKNESS

COMES

The Second Book of the Small Gods

By

Bruce Blake

Also by Bruce Blake

The Books of the Small Gods:

When Shadows Fall
The Darkness Comes
And Night Descends
When Ravens Call
The Twilight Fades
And Kingdoms End

Khirro's Journey epic fantasy:

Blood of the King
Spirit of the King
Heart of the King

The Icarus Fell urban fantasy series:

On Unfaithful Wings
All Who Wander Are Lost
Secrets of the Hanged Man

Prologue

Am I ready to kill?

A cloud of swirling mist sighed out between Kuneprius' lips, rising into the night to smear the glow of the winter moon. He watched it dissipate, then exhaled another long plume, blowing it out the way he'd seen the Brothers do when they smoked their pipes filled with sweetweed. Instead of swirling like the wreaths he'd watched them create, his breath came out a ragged column.

"Shh."

Kuneprius cocked his head toward the urgent sound, an apology teetering on the tip of his tongue. At the last instant, he remembered himself and said nothing, pressing himself flatter against the side of the hill. Fildrian lay less than ten man-lengths away, but the Brother's black hood and robe hid him in the darkness; despite his proximity, empty loneliness ached in Kuneprius' chest.

The lad grasped the short sword's hilt tighter, testing its uncomfortable weight. Though he'd seen the seasons turn but twelve times, he'd trained with this very sword for six of them. The temple blacksmith formed it with him in mind, the grip molded to the shape of his fingers. Its length and weight had proved too much for him when he first held it, but he'd grown into it, its size ideal for a boy of his age. He shifted minutely, searching for comfort and understanding that the prospect of swinging the weapon to wound rather than in practice caused his unease, not the sword itself.

Will I be able to wield it when the time comes? Can I

kill if I need to?

He'd never been sent on a hunt, so the sword's edge hadn't tasted blood other than his own when he got clumsy or distracted while sharpening the blade. He shifted his grip on the leather-wrapped hilt, hand slipping with the slickness of the sweat on his palm. For so many seasons, he'd trained for this moment; he knew he'd kill if the need arose.

I hope it doesn't.

The rattle-clunk of wooden wheels on dirt track rolled along the shallow valley and up the hill to Kuneprius' ears. Soon, he'd need wonder no more.

The apprentice angled his head to peer down the weed-clogged road, squinting as he attempted to pick out the wagons in the darkness. The lanterns hanging at the front of each, bobbing and swinging with the horses' gaits, made it easy. He counted them silently.

One, two, three...four?

His heart lurched. Brother Fildrian had said to expect three—two carts and a covered wagon. Kuneprius' gaze flickered to the spot where he expected to find the expedition leader's dark shape, but he saw nothing. He glanced back to the track, the horse-drawn vehicles drawing closer and, in the glow of their lanterns, he counted two covered wagons.

Which one?

A horse nickered and a high-pitched voice spoke words to calm the animal, their meaning lost in the rumble of the wheels, but the intent clear in their timbre. This must be the tone of a woman's voice, the first he'd heard.

Kuneprius wiped his slick palm on the front of his coat, hand pressing against the hard, smooth surface of the leather chest piece hidden beneath. When he breathed in through his nose, he inhaled the tang of the oil used to keep it supple.

"Psst."

Brother Fildrian faced Kuneprius, his pale cheek a faint smudge beneath the dark hood. Moving precisely, carefully, the expedition leader stood and gestured for the apprentice to do the same. Kuneprius obeyed. Around them, cloth stirred against skin and sandals scuffed in frozen grass as the others rose, as well.

Fildrian descended the hill deftly, traversing from one narrow tree trunk to the next, leaving Kuneprius to wait as the other Brothers followed. A thrill of fearful excitement stirred in his gut. He tightened his grip on the short sword's hilt, licked his lips, and swallowed the excess of saliva flooding his mouth.

Tonight, I become a Brother. Tonight, I become a man.

When the last of the ten robed men passed him, Kuneprius followed, concentrating on the placement of his feet, moving with the stealth he'd learned from Fildrian during training. Truthfully, the racket made by the clatter of horses' hooves and wheels on stones and dirt would have hidden the tuneless din should he break into song and dance a jig. He'd do neither, but the thought made him stifle a nervous chuckle.

Brother Fildrian arrived at the bottom of the hill and crouched in the tall weeds beside the cart track. The others arrayed themselves on either side of the leader and Kuneprius stopped well back, secreted behind a tree. He hefted the sword, ready to fulfill his role to catch any who got through his companions in an attempt to flee.

But which wagon contains our prize?

He shouldn't concern himself—Fildrian knew. Twelve turns of the seasons before, the expedition leader had been involved in the raid which brought Kuneprius himself into the Fatherhood; one of many times he'd liberated male children from a Goddess' caravan. If anyone knew the ways of the Mothers, Brother Fildrian did. Kuneprius passed the time by counting his heartbeats.

Eight. Nine. Ten.

The lead cart drew close enough for him to see the sleek lines of the horse pulling it. Beyond the animal, the lantern hanging beside the cart's driver shone on her face, reflecting in the woman's eyes and outlining her features in its warm glow. Kuneprius swallowed hard.

He didn't expect a woman to be so different from men.

Her hair—the deep red-brown of a chestnut in the moonlight—hung well past her shoulders in a manner not permitted of a Brother. Many of the apprentices, like Kuneprius himself, wore their hair longer, but not so long as hers. Small nose, smooth skin, full lips. The sight of her caused a flutter in the lad's gut he'd never experienced.

What's wrong with me?

His inexplicably dry lips parted and his sandpaper tongue brushed their surface. As he gazed upon the woman—girl, really; she didn't appear many turns older than Kuneprius—the stirring in his gut spread. It spilled into his chest, speeding his breath, and crept into his loins. His man-thing began to harden, the way it often was when he woke in the mornings, prepared to make his offering to the Small Gods. He glanced at his breeches, then back at the girl, who was closer now, and noticed gentle curves hidden beneath her smock. His confused feelings grew. He crossed his legs to hide his confusion, but doing so increased his discomfort.

The girl's cart rumbled past the spot where Brother Fildrian and the others hid, and the men remained secreted in the tall grass, waiting. The wheels of the first covered wagon clattered past; the second drew even with them. Brother Fildrian raised his hand, signaling the attack party, and they sprang out of the weeds.

Horses whinnied, one of the drivers screamed—not a shriek of fear, but a signal, Kuneprius realized. At the sound of her call, two armed warriors of the Goddess burst out of the first covered wagon, four more out of the second, catching the Fatherhood's raiders by surprise.

Kuneprius' eyes widened as he watched the women pounce on his companions. Metal clanged against metal, horses pranced and neighed. A tall Goddess warrior with a shaved head knocked Brother Imir's sword from his hand, then skewered him. She pulled her blade free and a gout of dark blood spilled from the young man's gut before he slumped to the dirt.

Hand gripping his sword's hilt tighter than it should, Kuneprius took one step toward the fight, then hesitated. In his head, he heard Fildrian's instructions: guard the flank; let no one pass; do not desert your post. But did he foresee the women bearing weapons? Was this the way it always happened?

Kuneprius slid forward another step. A woman screamed and fell, a gash on her leg; Brother Xeoru swung his sword two-handed and split her skull. Kuneprius flinched and looked away, found the cart driver's gaze upon him. She climbed out of her seat, pulled a long dagger from a fold in her smock.

Panicked, Kuneprius returned his attention to the fight and realized the other drivers had abandoned their seats, too. Weapons filled their hands as they stalked toward the skirmish. Their addition to the warriors of the Goddess evened the numbers, swung favor away from the Brothers and squarely to the middle.

Until an axe separated Brother Xeoru's head from his shoulders and a spear poked a hole through Brother Ategar's chest.

For a space of heartbeats he forgot to count, Kuneprius watched, feet acting as though frozen to the ground. Blood spilled on the frosted dirt, painted the weeds beside the track the color of rust. One after another the fighters fell, Brothers and women alike, until three remained: Brother Fildrian; the tall, bald warrior woman; and the pretty cart driver.

The two Sisters stalked Fildrian, spinning him in a tight circle. One lunged, setting him off balance. He flailed and the tip of his sword caught the young one, opening a slash across her forearm. Kuneprius gasped. The girl dropped her dagger and clutched the wound, a pained expression creasing her smooth brow.

Finally, Kuneprius wrested control of his feet back from the grip of fear. He took a step toward the fray as Fildrian engaged the bald woman, his back turned toward the injured cart driver.

The warriors' swords met, the clang of their blades reverberating in the chill night air. Kuneprius forced himself another pace, his sandal-clad feet whispering in the tall grass. His heart pulsed in his ears, loud and painful, distracting. He blinked hard to dispel the discomfort. When his eyes opened, the cart driver had retrieved a sword from the ground and crept up behind Brother Fildrian.

"Brother," Kuneprius called, but his voice caught in his dry throat, cracked and fell to pieces.

Fildrian parried an attack from the warrior and lunged, running his blade through her gut. They stood frozen for a heartbeat, the two combatants staring into each other's eyes as though sharing a final moment, a sliver of respect, then he wrenched his sword free with a twist. The woman's knees buckled, spilling her to the ground. Fildrian turned, a smile on his lips.

And the cart driver slashed his throat.

"No!"

Kuneprius rushed forward, realizing he'd waited too long. When he needed it most, his courage failed him, and now ten Brothers lay dead with no one to blame but him. He gritted his teeth and growled in the back of his throat as he raced for the girl, using anger to drown his fear.

She spun at the sound of his approach, Fildrian's blood dripping from her borrowed blade. Kuneprius swung for her head, driving her back, and the girl's feet tangled. She stumbled, heel catching on dead Brother Ategar's arm, and she went to the ground.

Kuneprius growled again, the end of it fading to a squeak of sorrow and loss. The girl scrambled away, hands and feet digging furrows in the dirt track, but the bodies cluttering the road trapped her from getting far. The young lad caught up to her, put the point of his short sword to her throat. Staring up at him, she froze, the fear of death shining in her eyes.

He hesitated, blinked. A tear ran along his cheek and he sniffed back the snot threatening to spill out of his nose.

"You killed him."

"Please," the girl said. It surprised him she spoke the same language as he did, though he knew of no reason for her to speak any other. "Please."

The point of the short sword wavered and Kuneprius struggled to keep it from drooping. The anger burning within him after watching Fildrian, Ategar, and the others die melted away, dissolved by the blue of her eyes, the smoothness of her pink cheeks. Kuneprius' mind flashed away, wondering why Brothers were permitted only to spill their seed on the ground when such beauty existed in the world. An out-of-place sound brought him back to the moment.

They both heard it—a mewling from within the first covered wagon. The girl's eyes flickered toward it; Kuneprius raised his head. The small sound grew—a whimper to a whine, then to the full-throated cry of a tiny mouth that reminded Kuneprius why he was there.

A yell broke from the girl's lips and she swung the sword tainted with Fildrian's blood. Her grip slipped, the weapon twisted. The flat of the blade bounced off the leather chest piece hidden beneath the apprentice's robe.

Time stopped for an instant, the baby's siren cry filling the night. They stared at each other, each knowing what must come next. Kuneprius gulped around a lump solidifying in his throat and leaned forward on his sword. The tip sank into the girl's neck.

She gasped, coughed. Blood burbled over her lips, ran along her cheek and into her ear. Her eyes found the young lad's, a last plea shining in them, quickly fading. He turned away, unable to gaze upon her sorrow.

When her body went limp, he released his grip on the sword and stumbled away to retch on the ground beside the covered wagon. The baby wailed, beseeching him to come to it, take care of it. Kuneprius knew he needed to do just that, but his heaving gut and clenching throat prevented him.

Bent at the waist and breathing hard, he leaned against the wagon wheel. Sweat and snot and tears dripped from his nose and cheeks, the droplets pattering on the frozen dirt the same way as the blood of the Brothers as they lost their lives.

I should have aided them.

He coughed and spat bitter chunks of spew, wished for water to wash the horrid flavor off his tongue. The baby's crying continued, assaulting his ears and rattling in his head until he could bear it no longer. With a shuddering breath, he forced himself upright and dragged his aching body to the back of the wagon.

Kuneprius pushed the flap aside a crack and peeked inside.

The babe lay on the wagon's floor, a blanket tucked under its chin. Alone.

He clambered up, arms and legs exhausted as though

he'd crawled here from the temple. On his second attempt, he struggled his way in and flopped on the deck beside the child. The baby ceased bellowing, eyes wide with wonder finding him. A few seconds passed as Kuneprius stared at the child's tear-stained cheeks, its plump lips, and thin wisps of hair, then the wailing began anew.

Kuneprius wrestled himself to his knees and pulled the blanket off the baby, revealing a cloth wrapped around its groin and tied on either side. He fumbled with the knots, his numb fingers slipping until one knot came undone. If it wasn't the right child, Fildrian and the others had sacrificed themselves for nothing. The thought weighing on him, Kuneprius hesitated a half-dozen heartbeats before pulling the diaper aside.

The stink of the baby's soiled cloth made him gag. He raised his arm to cover his nose and undid the other knot. Beneath, he saw the baby's tiny man-thing, and Kuneprius breathed a sigh of relief.

The Brothers were dead, but he'd accomplished what they'd come for: the babe was his.

***

Kuneprius attempted slinging each Brother over their saddle, intending to lash them in place and return them to the temple for burial, but they proved too heavy for him. He struggled Brother Fildrian up, the effort leaving him drained and panting, and worried that, if he took the time to do the same for the others, he'd be discovered. So it was the young Kuneprius rode through the gates of Teva Stavoklis with a child in his arms, four horses on leads, and a dead man lashed to a saddle.

Brothers and priests were already gathered in the square, though the leading edge of sunrise had just grazed the horizon. The sky perched on the cusp of the earth was crimson as the blood he'd seen spilled; the Small Gods swam in the ocean of darkness above that, waiting to surrender to the light of day.

Hands took control of Kuneprius' steed, offered him help out of the saddle. He accepted, his sore and weary backside sliding off the smooth leather. When his feet hit the ground, his knees threatened to buckle, and another hand grabbed him by the elbow, helped him keep his feet. He glanced from one man to the next, realizing he knew each of them, but not recognizing any. A priest with his face hidden by a drooping cowl stepped forward and Kuneprius extended his arms, ready to hand over the child. The priest didn't take the babe. Instead, he led the apprentice away from the throng of Brothers occupied with unlashing Fildrian from the saddle.

Three priests followed as the man led Kuneprius on a winding journey through the streets, past stone abodes and empty fountains, to a low building with no windows. To those unfamiliar, it appeared more storehouse than place of worship.

They crossed the threshold, as Kuneprius did every morning to pray for the return of the Small Gods, but didn't stop to kneel on one of the threadbare prayer carpets. The hooded priest led him through the sanctuary room to a wide, stout door at the back, where they paused.

Kuneprius' head spun and his belly churned, though his body had taken steps to ensure nothing remained inside it during his return. The scent of melting fat hung thick in the sanctuary room, given off by the squat tallow candles flickering and hissing on stands in each corner. For an instant, he thought his stomach might rebel again at their odor, but he forgot his beleaguered gut when the priest raised his hand and rapped on the door.

The baby, who'd been miraculously sleeping, shifted in Kuneprius' arms, as though sensing the lad's discomfort. He'd often wondered what lay hidden behind the short, wide door but now, as he stood on the precipice of finding out, he decided he'd prefer not to know. Unfortunately, the choice didn't belong to him.

"Enter," a voice within said, and a shiver ran along Kuneprius' spine.

The priest pushed the portal open. Beyond, the chamber appeared similar to the sanctuary room, except much smaller. Bundles of herbs hung from spikes driven into the beams supporting the ceiling and thin tapers flickered in the corners. A table sat in the center of the room, a roll of yellowed parchment atop it. Beside it knelt Kristeus, the high priest.

In his twelve turns as an apprentice, Kuneprius had never laid eyes on the man or even heard of the door being opened. Seasons of wondering if someone truly lived behind the door had come to an end.

He hesitated in the doorway, gaping and waiting for the priest who'd led him there to enter, but he didn't. A moment passed, expectation hanging in the air, before one of the other hooded priests behind Kuneprius laid his hand on the lad's back and ushered him across the threshold.

The door clunked closed and the apprentice turned to find the others had left him alone with the high priest. The baby wriggled in his arms, then settled. Kuneprius gulped.

"This is the babe?"

Kuneprius knew the hooded figure spoke the words, but they seemed to float down to his ears from the ceiling. Before answering, his eyes flickered around the barren room, noting the lack of honey pot or personal items—only herbs, tapers, table, scroll, high priest.

"Y...yes."

The hood moved minutely, as though the invisible head inside nodded.

"And the others are dead? Killed by the women?"

The words dropped on Kuneprius flat and monotone, except the last: women. It came out twisted and skewed, spat more than spoken. Kuneprius' throat tightened with the urge to sob, forcing him to nod rather than attempt speaking. A dozen heartbeats passed and he thought the high priest might not have seen the gesture.

"Yes," he said, his tone quiet.

Kristeus tilted his head back, revealing a chin and mouth, but nothing further. Lips pale to the point of transparency moved, the yellow teeth behind them clicking together twice before he spoke again.

"Bring him to me."

The High Priest held out his arms, the sleeves of his robe falling away as he extended his hands. Skin as pallid as his lips; nails long, curved, yellowed, and cracked. Kuneprius hesitated. The baby stirred again, squeaked in his sleep.

"Come, boy."

Kristeus gestured with his fingers and Kuneprius found his feet carrying him the short distance to the middle of the room, despite not having asked them to do so. He passed the baby into the High Priest's hands and the child's eyelids fluttered open. Kristeus regarded the babe for a moment, then lay him on the floor and bowed his head, words whispering from within the hood. Kuneprius resisted the urge to fidget.

Time crawled. The apprentice glanced away from the child, saw the herbs hung on the spikes were fresh, the floor swept, the walls free of soot from the tapers' greasy smoke.

Someone comes in here.

The baby gurgled and the air in the room grew warmer on the lad's skin. Kuneprius snapped his gaze back to the High Priest and found the man looking at him instead of the baby. He shivered despite the rising temperature.

"You have done well, apprentice. I have seen the coming of this child and you have done what needed to be done to make it so. Henceforth, you are Brother Kuneprius."

The boy's eyes widened and a flutter of pride pushed aside the nausea gripping his midsection. Never had an apprentice been named Brother before reaching their fourteenth turn. Eight seasons yet remained before Kuneprius reached that age. He thought it must be expected of him to respond, so he parted his lips to thank the High Priest, but Kristeus raised a hand, stopping him before he spoke.

"You will no longer be part of the liberating expeditions." He slipped his hands under the baby, his long nails scraping on the wooden floor. "From this time forward, you have a much more important role to fulfill."

Kristeus picked the babe off the floor, held him up as though examining a ripe melon rather than gazing on a living thing. Kuneprius wondered if the High Priest viewed everything in this manner, but put the thought from his mind. The air in the room prickled against his skin, standing the short hairs on the back of his neck on end. His sight wavered and, for an instant, he saw flames raining from the sky, trees burning, a river boiling. The hallucination disappeared as quickly as it came.

"Henceforth, you will be caretaker to the child," Kristeus said, raising the baby into the air. "For you have brought to me Vesisdenperos, the sculptor. The one born to ensure the return of the Small Gods."

The sweat on Kuneprius' brow went cold.

I Horace - Pig and Small God

Once upon a time, Horace were a Seaman, and a First Man to boot. One in a long line o' men what spent their lives plyin' the dangerous waters off the Windward coast. But Horace had enough o' sailin' and stopped bein' a First Man, stopped bein' a man o' the sea, and called himself Tailor, but that weren't really him. Now, ol' Horace weren't nothin' but porthole clenchin' afraid for his life with a lump o' shit in his breeches.

The small gray man scowled at the one-time sailor, his bony arms crossed in front o' his narrow chest. If it weren't for his talkin' and movin' 'round, a thin' such as him might've been mistook for a hunk o' clay.

Horace's lips opened and closed in a manner resemblin' a fish yanked outta the sea and left on deck to suffocate. Life givin' breath didn't come no easier to him'n it'd do for that fish neither, with a creature escaped from the Green standin' in front o' him and a broken rib pokin' him ev'ry time he drew air. Instead o' words, he merely gasped and tasted the singed flavor o' his burnin' pig leg and the embarrassin' odor o' fear soilin' his britches.

"Where is Thorn?" the gray man demanded.

"Th...th...th..." Didn't make no sense, but Horace couldn't manage nothin' else at that partic'lar time.

The angry and distressed expression on the miniature man's gray brow deepened, his voice grew louder.

"Where is Thorn?"

Horace cast his gaze 'round the small clearin' what served as his temporary home, searchin' for the thorn the gray man were speakin' 'bout. Weren't no thorns anywhere to be seen—flowerin', poisonous, or otherwise. The sailor raised his shoulders and let them fall, the pain in his chest makin' him regret havin' done so.

"Wha...What's a thorn?"

The bird-dropped man's skin faded to pink, more likened to the color o' Horace's own. A heartbeat later, it deepened to red as if he'd been too long o'er the flames, like the poor ol' pig leg what Horace'd stole. His lids narrowed over his eyes and the sailor noticed a lack o' lashes on them.

"Thorn." The gray man said, pointin' his finger at his own chest. "Where is Thorn?"

Not knowin' what else to do, Horace raised his shakin' hand and extended a quiverin' finger, addin' his pointin' to the man's chest, too. "Thorn's right there?"

For a second, Horace figured the feller'd go so red, his head might pop off in a spray o' blood what'd cover the sailor in gooey brains and fill the air with steam. Might be a relief, too, because at least he'd be dead then and Horace'd be free to eat his crispy pig leg and wash his fear-filled breeches. Instead, the small man's red skin went back to gray and he laughed so hard he fell over onto his backside.

Horace gaped, not seein' anythin' funny in the proceedin's. The little feller rolled back and forth with his mirth, rockin' side to side akin to a rowboat caught in a storm. Even thinkin' 'bout rowboats caused a knot in the back o' Horace's throat what made him suspect he might lose them few mouthfuls o' stew he'd stole.

"What're you laughin' at?" Horace demanded, his fear forgotten in favor o' a good bit o' righteous anger.

The gray man chuckled a little more and wiped a tear offa his cheek with a long finger before sittin' upright and fixin' Horace with his gaze. Fear trickled back in.

"Oh, the look on your face," the gray feller said.

"Thorn scared you."

Horace frowned and his belly gurgled at the burnt piggy aroma what were overpowerin' even the stink o' dirt in his britches. The thought o' puttin' a bite o' tasty pig meat in his mouth maybe gave him more courage'n what he might normally've possessed.

"Who are you?" Horace growled, tryin' his best to sound more frightenin' and less scared'n he actually were on both counts. "Where'd you come from?"

"Thorn," the gray man said, slappin' both his hands against his chest with a clap. He followed it up by wavin' his arms o'er his head, in the general direction o' sunset. "Thorn is of the land behind the veil. Is it far from here?"

Horace stared at him, findin' himself unable to string together enough words to make any sense. They stood facin' each other in silence awhile, the fire poppin' and spittin' at Horace's back. They might've stayed that way for a while longer, too, if a crow sittin' in the trees hadn't've cawed. The sound jerked the gray feller what called himself Thorn's gaze away.

He glanced up, searchin' above his head with his eyes, and Horace looked up too, but he didn't see nothin' but branches full o' jackpine needles and jackpine cones. By the time he lowered his peepers, Thorn'd taken off for one o' the trees.

The little feller pulled up when he got to the bottom, raised his arms and jumped toward a branch what hung at least two dozen handspans over his head. He missed it by a good dozen-and-a-half handspans. It weren't no surprise to Horace that were the case, but it sure appeared like it caught Thorn off-guard. He looked first at his hands held up high, then down at his feet, an expression on his kisser like them appendages'd left him disappointed. His head shook back and forth a couple o' times and he gave it another try, gettin' the same results.

When it didn't work the second time, Thorn took to scuttlin' up the side o' the tree like one o' them sailors who enjoyed the peace and privacy o' the crow's nest. Horace weren't one o' them; he didn't have no love for bein' up so high.

The one-time sailor and now shitter o' pants watched for but a moment before the succulence o' blackened pig flesh beckoned him away from the spectacle o' a gray man shinnyin' up a jackpine tree. Horace turned his back to the feller and paced toward the fire, wonderin' what he meant by 'the land behind the veil'.

The fire'd done a fine job charrin' one side o' the pig leg to a dry, cracked bit o' charcoal, but the other side what faced away from the flames looked worth chokin' down. Horace wrapped his fingers 'round the knobby exposed bone end, then pulled away right quick. He weren't no cook, so it didn't occur to him the fire's heat might've made the bone hot enough to burn him. Now he knew.

Horace shook his hand as though doin' so might loosen up the pain. It didn't do nothin' to take away the burnin', so he blew on it instead, puffin' his cheeks out like one o' them spiny fish when he did. Blowin' didn't help, neither, so he decided to resort to cursin'.

"Fuckin' pig," he said, castin' a glance 'round for somethin' to protect his hand while he pulled his dinner offa the fire. When he didn't find nothin', he settled for usin' the tail o' his shirt. He wrapped it 'round the bone and grabbed it with both hands this time.

"Ow, ow, ow," he said, dancin' across the clearin' with a chunk o' burnt pig in his hands. He dropped the bastard on the mess o' firewood before it had the chance to burn him anymore.

The hammy leg laid there starin' up at him, temptin' him to take a bite. Horace's mouth filled full o' saliva beggin' for them savory piggy juices. He licked his lips and reached out to rip himself off a piece from the not-so-charred side when a sound like a wild animal crashin' through the brush scared him into whirlin' 'round. He completed the turn in time to see the little gray feller thump in the dirt at the foot o' the tree.

"This Thorn likes hittin' the ground, it seems," he said aloud.

The gray man lay motionless at the bottom o' the pine. Horace crept forward a couple o' steps, careful the way he'd been when he snitched the pig leg from the inn. He weren't thinkin' 'bout cookin' the man, though.

Thorn didn't move. Horace went closer, muscles tensed and ready to flee, his body achin' from when the little feller'd fallen on him. He took a breath what made the rib what'd been botherin' him bother him more.

Least he missed me this time.

Horace were close enough to stick out a leg and poke the gray man with his toe when the feller finally moved. He jumped back, glad he didn't stick that toe into Thorn's side. The gray man sat up, wobblin' as though somone'd spun him 'round in a circle a few times too many.

"You all right, Mr. Thorn?" Horace asked, tentative.

The little feller's eyes fell on Horace's face, but it didn't seem like he were really seein' him. They kinda fluttered 'round for a short time before findin' their focus.

"Thorn couldn't see it," Thorn muttered once he'd regained a portion o' his senses—not enough, it seemed to Horace. His eyes went off to the side, lookin' at nothin'.

Horace raised a brow. "Couldn't see what?"

Thorn shook his head real slow, like he might be worried somethin' got knocked loose inside, then dragged his gaze back to Horace. "The veil. Thorn couldn't see the veil. How far away are we?"

"I ain't ever heard 'bout no veil." Horace reached 'round and scratched his ass, then immediately regretted it. "What is it?"

"A magical barrier," Thorn said, climbin' to his feet. "It separates the land where Thorn and the rest of our kind live from," he gestured wide with his arms, "this."

Despite not wantin' it to happen, Horace felt his eyes get big, the lids pullin' away in fear and shock.

"You mean the Green."

The place above Thorn's eye where one'd normally find a man's brow wrinkled upward. "The veil shines with the brilliance of an emerald. An emerald is green, yes?"

Horace's head tilted forward and back slowly, confirmin' Thorn's statement and because it felt like it weighed more'n his neck wanted to hold.

"You really are one o' them Small...one o' them gods, aren't you?"

"Thorn is Thorn," the gray man said. He brushed pine needles off his arm what had stuck to his skin. "A part of nature, a piece of the world. Thorn always was, Thorn always will be."

Horace gulped a mouthful o' fearful spit. "Do you mean you can't die?"

Thorn tilted his head as though he didn't understand. "Die? Everything dies. Not Thorn, but everything else."

"Really?" Horace raised his arm and felt embarrassed by the shakin' in his hand, but there weren't nothin' to do 'bout it. "What 'bout that? Don't it hurt?"

Thorn's lowered his head to gaze at the branch stickin' outta his side, a few pine needles and a cone still hangin' from it. His mouth crinkled up and he grabbed it with both hands. When he pulled it out, it made an unpleasant suckin' sound what caused Horace's stomach to clench. A gout o' bright red blood followed the chuck o' wood.

"Hmm."

Thorn touched one finger to the flow and held it up in front o' his face, peerin' at it like a man what didn't know anythin' 'bout blood. After a second, he popped the finger into his mouth, which didn't bother Horace because he might've done the same thin' with his own.

"Can I help?" Horace said, takin' one step forward.

Thorn waved a hand at him, his gaze returnin' to the hole poked in his side. His brow furrowed, then he laid the fingers o' one hand beside the wound on one side, the other fingers on the other side. His face cinched up like Horace's when pushin' out a dump didn't work the way he wanted it to, but he didn't think the little feller were makin' the expression because o' constipation. He had somethin' else in mind.

Every muscle in Thorn's body tensed up, veins and such showin' through his thin, gray skin. A drawn-out grunt escaped his lips. Half o' Horace wanted to take the opportunity to put as much distance between him and this feller as his achin' legs'd carry him, but the other part desired findin' out what he were attemptin'.

The blood flowin' from the wound slowed to a trickle, then stopped. Horace opened his mouth, his brain disbelievin' his eyes. An instant later, the hole where a branch'd been stickin' out puckered up; Horace's porthole followed its example.

"That's—" Horace began, but his incredulous exclamation got cut off by the little gray feller collapsin' to the ground.

Horace stared.

Nothin' happened for a time. Horace eventually remembered to breathe—the broken rib pokin' into him, protestin' when he did—and his heart continued beatin'. He weren't sure the same could be said o' Thorn's, though.

"Hello?" He took a step. "You all right?"

Blood discolored the ground 'round the gray man. Horace stepped real careful to make sure he didn't get any on the boots Birk'd loaned him. When he were close enough, he poked his toe into Thorns ribs the way he'd been tempted to do before. No reaction. He did it again, and the same nothin' happened.

Without hesitatin' or stoppin' to worry what he might step in, Horace took off into the forest, jumpin' o'er logs and thrashin' through underbrush, intendin' to put a great deal o' distance between him and the gray man. He'd made it ten long paces, his chest hurtin' and his legs wishin' to do anythin' but runnin', when he stopped.

"I can't go like this," he said aloud. A crow cawed in response.

Horace 'bout-faced and went back to his camp where he grabbed hold o' the bone end o' the pig leg, happy to find it'd cooled off. He rested the chunk o' meat on his shoulder, took one more look back to be sure the gray feller hadn't moved, then took off into the forest as if one o' them Small Gods were after him.

Because if he waited, one o' them just might be.

II Teryk - Dead Weight

The beating Teth and his thugs laid on the young man was difficult enough to watch, but when he drove the fancy sword into the boy's guts, Elishbieta put her hand over her mouth to keep from gasping.

Bieta and Stirk sank back into the shadows as Teth and his boys stalked away with the sword, coins, and clothes they'd stolen. One of them kicked the torn backpack, but the ripped fabric wrapped around his foot and stuck. If not for her rescuer lying bleeding in the dirt, Bieta might have laughed at him for it. The fellow shook his leg like a dog dislodging a flea, and the satchel fell off.

When the group of men was halfway along the block toward the corner, Bieta straightened and took a half-step, but Stirk's hand on her arm stopped her.

"Wait," he whispered, all urgent-like.

Bieta glared at him, but did as he said. Getting themselves killed alongside the young man wouldn't help the lad.

Cheek pressed against rough stone, she peeked around the corner and watched them leave with her one good eye. Viewing things was always easier with the scarred and empty socket hidden behind something. When her head didn't expect input from the eye unable to give it, it fooled her into thinking she saw the way everyone else did, though she knew it a lie.

The men rounded the corner, a burble of laughter following them, and Bieta pulled away from Stirk's grasp. Truly, he'd released his grip, but it came out the same result, either way.

She hurried to the fallen man, rocks and chunks of broken flagstone pressing into her feet through the worn-thin soles of her shoes. Upon reaching the fellow, she meant to fall to her knees dramatically but noticed a pool of blood seeping out around him, so searched for a better spot before kneeling. Stirk skidded to a stop beside the poor man, spraying him with a shower of dirt. Bieta shook her head at how stupid her boy could be, but bit back any admonishment. No point giving him hell if the guy was dead, anyway.

The man neither moved nor made a sound. Bieta's tongue found the space once occupied by her two front teeth and the tip chafed against the ragged gum. She pressed hard enough to feel the bone beneath as she leaned forward and pried one of the lad's eyelids open with her thumb and finger.

"Why d'you think they took his clothes?" Stirk asked, staring at her.

Bieta shot her son the admonishing look she'd been holding back. "Must have thought they was worth taking, dummy."

"Don't call me that."

"Then stop acting the part."

She peered back into the injured man's eye, but it stared unfocused at the night sky without seeing the Small Gods twinkling in it. Nothing under his lid let her know for sure if he still lived or not.

"Is he dead?"

Bieta shook her head. "I think he might be living."

"I ain't got a good feeling about this, Ma. Let's leave him and head on home."

She moved her hand to pry the other eyelid open. "He helped me, Stirk. Can't just let him be if there's any chance of returning the favor."

The woman leaned in close, the tip of her tongue grinding into her gum, and aligned herself to match her one eye up with his. The coppery scent of his spilled blood found her nose, so she held her breath to keep it out. She bent low and peered into his peeper, saw the way the white had gone pink, and hope seeped out of her the way his blood leaked out onto the ground. She couldn't imagine any way he'd still be alive.

Until he groaned.

Bieta jerked her gaze toward her son. "You hear that?"

Stirk shook his patchy-haired head without lifting his eyes from the lad.

"He made a sound," she said, standing. "Groaned."

"Didn't hear nothing."

"We can't leave him."

Stirk raised his wide-eyed stare to her. "Well, it don't look as if he'll be walking nowhere."

"You gotta carry him."

Her son raised one brow and lowered the other, fixing her with a disbelieving expression. Bieta crossed her arms and glared at him.

"Carry him? I'd get his blood on me. And he ain't going to make it, at any rate."

She let her gaze trail down Stirk's grubby, gray shirt with the rip in the sleeve and the front bulging open over his generous belly where two buttons were missing. One leg of his breeches ended just below the knee in a jungle of dangling thread where it had torn off after the hole in it got too big.

"You afraid to get your clothes dirty?"

Stirk shrugged. "Don't wanna get blood on me, is all."

"We're taking him, so pick him up or you won't be getting any of this." Bieta cupped her ample breasts and jiggled them; Stirk sagged like a man beaten.

"Alright, but you gotta help me."

Bieta shook her head. Her son was strong as a horse—and near smart as one—so didn't need her help, but she obliged to keep him happy. She took up a position at the injured man's head and grasped him under the armpits, leaning him forward for Stirk to reach under. A moan shuddered in the fellow's throat when she propped him up, startling her so she nearly let go. She fixed Stirk with a hard gaze.

"Yeah, yeah. Heard him that time."

He bent and hooked one arm around the lad's back, the other under his knees, and picked him up as though he weighed no more than a sack of grain. Bieta pushed on the injured fellow's back to make it appear as though she helped; her palms came away smeared with his blood.

"You got him?"

"Yeah," Stirk grunted. "I got him."

They started along the dimly lit street, following the same path as Teth and his mates because it was the quickest way home. The next closest bridge would take them too far out of their way and through parts of the city Bieta wouldn't want to go even when Stirk wasn't carrying a load.

"What was he doing here?" she mused. "Don't everyone know to stay out of Thieves' Alley?"

"Don't think he's from around here, Ma."

"That's the truth."

"And he wouldn't't've been here if you hadn't been screwin' around with Teth."

She glared at Stirk, lips pressed together tight, tongue working hard in the gap between her teeth. He was too busy concentrating on keeping one foot moving in front of the other to notice.

"Someone's gotta make money, or how're we going to eat? You getting a job?"

"Ain't no jobs."

"That's right. And you ain't willing to put some fellow's cock betwixt your lips for a coin or two, are you?" This time, Stirk didn't respond. "Didn't think so."

She stopped him short of the corner and Bieta stuck her head out to peer around. The street was empty, so she signaled Stirk to follow as she continued.

"Hurry."

Stirk grunted and increased his pace, the young man hanging limp in his arms, weighing him down with the worst kind of load. Bieta wished there was more she could do to help—by reason of wanting to get home quicker, not due to caring about the strain on her son's back—but there wasn't. Being lookout for Teth and his boys would have to be her contribution.

They stopped to rest halfway along the next block,

Stirk leaning against a wall with its daub chipping off the wattle, though he likely didn't need the pause. He sucked a few heavy breaths to give his mother the impression he'd done some hard work, tilted his head and wiped sweat from his brow off with his shoulder. Bieta rolled her eyes and peeked over her shoulder, surveying the street ahead.

Empty.

Not much traffic at this time, but they'd pass The Dented Cup on their way to the bridge. Day or night, people frequented the tavern, and there'd be a good chance Teth and his thugs might stop in on their way by.

"Come on," she said, snagging Stirk by the ripped sleeve of his shirt.

"Can't we leave him? I think he's dead. He's getting cold."

Bieta touched the back of her hand to the lad's forehead and found it warm and moist. A faint breath caressed her fingers when she held them in front of his mouth.

"He's alive." She started out again, expecting her son to follow. "Just his blood on your shirt cooling off."

"Great."

Around the next corner, they walked into the busy tavern's noise spilling along the street. Bieta hesitated and Stirk lurched to a stop beside her.

"If we're gonna do this," he said, feigning panted breath. "Let's just do it."

She knew his strength would last and he just liked to play at getting tired to illustrate his contribution, but she worried about being discovered toting a blood-covered fellow through the streets, especially if one of the rarely-seen city guards picked tonight for an evening stroll. No See-Gee would believe for a second they weren't the ones who poked him with a sword.

They hurried up the street, Stirk's feet dragging in the

dirt and broken cobbles, sending rocks skittering across the ground. Had it been quieter, Bieta might have hushed him, but the tavern's clamor was louder than usual. Loud enough it made her nervous.

Stirk was busy concentrating on hauling his load, but it didn't take Elishbieta long to realize it wasn't normal tavern sounds seeping out through the door. The harsh clash of swords cut through the crowd's chatter, followed by a man's pained cry. As they drew even with the building, the place went deathly silent. A hush fell like a fog bank appearing out of nowhere to swallow the shacks along the river and Bieta stopped in her tracks, grabbed Stirk's arm.

"Something's wrong," she whispered.

Stirk grunted. Bieta tugged his sleeve, pulling him toward the alley opposite the tavern's entrance.

They melted into the shadows as best a big man with another fellow in his arms can hide. Bieta held her breath, both to keep from being heard and to prevent the stink of garbage and offal invading her nose. Her tongue rubbed back and forth against her gum, her one eye hard on the door as she wondered what might cause the drinking house's normally giddy crowd to go quiet. Were Teth and his cohorts menacing them? He wasn't the biggest thug in the outer city, but maybe the fancy sword he'd stolen from the young man was enough to make the others take note.

A few seconds later, the door swung open. Bieta pushed Stirk and his load deeper into the alley, their feet squelching in damp refuse.

The one-armed man who exited the tavern and the young with him were strangers to her, but she recognized the sword in his hand. Even her untrained eye couldn't mistake the value of that sort of weapon. The pattern etched along its blade caught the light, twinkling and flashing, a beacon signaling this sword was different from all others.

The two strangers backed out of the public house, acting tense and wary. Through the open door, she glimpsed the faces of some of the tavern-goers watching them with eyes opened wide with shock. A path split between them led back into the room, and she spied bodies lying on the floor, recognized Teth amongst them. Her gut jumped at the sight, part of her pleased he'd paid for what he'd done to the lad, another part distressed she'd have to find a new man to pleasure for money. She decided to be pleased—men loved the feel of her gap on their cocks, so it shouldn't be difficult to replace the meager coin Teth provided.

The door swung closed and the man and girl turned away from the tavern. He glanced up the street, but her gaze fell on the alley in which Bieta and Stirk hid, the bleeding man draped in his arms. The injured lad chose that precise moment to groan.

They froze.

The girl stared right at them, not seeing them in the dark, and took a half step their direction, but got no farther. The one-armed man rested his hand on her back, directing her away down the avenue. Bieta watched until they disappeared around the corner.

"Let's go," she whispered, dragging Stirk by his shirt sleeve once more.

At any second, the tavern crowd might come rushing through the doors. She didn't know what'd happened, but she could make a good guess. With men lying dead on the floor, someone within might come out seeking vengeance, and they didn't want to get caught up in it. And if no one had retribution on their minds, then one of them might decide to find a See-Gee and report the incident. Not that the city guard would care nor do anything about it, but they'd for sure take an interest in Bieta and Stirk and the man bleeding on Stirk's shirt.

She yanked on her boy's arm, urging him to put aside his theatrics and increase his pace. Two more blocks remained to the bridge, and two more beyond to the stinking room behind the tanner's where they made their home. If they didn't dally, they should be able to get well-hid long before any lazy-assed See-Gee showed his face.

They hurried through the next intersection and Bieta took a peek to her right. The two they'd seen leaving the tavern stood in the middle of the street far enough away to be no more than black shapes in the distance. With them heading that direction, she assumed they must be going to gather the city guard themselves. She pulled harder on Stirk's sleeve.

"Hurry up, dummy."

"Shut it, Ma, or you'll be carrying your friend."

One Way Bridge loomed ahead, so named for the fact its breadth only allowed one wagon to cross at a time. For this reason, most carts and wagons found their way to another bridge rather than get caught in a jam. The old One Way Bridge saw mostly pedestrian traffic, and this easier use had left it in better condition than the other paths over the river, save those reserved for nobles. Flagstones worn smooth by boot heels paved the bridge, but their edges remained unchipped by horseshoes and steel rimmed wheels. Since she was a young girl, Bieta had liked coming to the bridge and leaning over the edge to watch the swirling water flow by.

Not tonight.

She ran her hand along the crown as they crossed, fingers grating on the rough bricks, their corners worn smooth by innumerable hands over the course of a thousand of turn of the seasons. They reached the far side without notice, but figures milled about on the street ahead. Bieta leaned close and whispered in Stirk's ear.

"We'll have to go the back way."

"No," he groaned. "Ma, I—"

"Shh."

She tugged hard on his ear and he bent toward her to release the pressure. The lad moaned again, a sad, pained sound that brought Bieta back to the task at hand. This wasn't just about sneaking back to their humble abode, but saving the young man's life, too.

She held on to Stirk's ear as she led him down the side street running alongside the river. A block along, they took a right into a narrow lane. The mingled smells of murky river water, the sausage factory, and the tanner's shop made her stomach grouse and complain.

Along the alley, they side-stepped broken crates and a man she presumed to be sleeping before finally arriving at the tanner's. Here, the river's smell and the sausage aroma faded, overpowered by the stench of the tannery. As much as she despised it, the stink was the only reason they had somewhere to live—no one else wanted to reside where the shopkeep used dung and urine in his work.

"Get him in," she said, releasing Stirk's lobe and ushering him ahead of her before glancing along the alley to ensure the man they stepped over hadn't awakened.

Stirk went through into the storeroom that provided them shelter and she followed, shutting the door behind him.

"Ma! I can't see."

"Hold on to your breeches."

She reached up to the shelf mounted beside the door, found the taper and lit it. The dancing flame bounced light around the small room, across the disheveled blankets spread in the corners upon which Bieta and her son slept. A table with splintered edges sat in the middle of the room, a wooden crate and a chair with one leg too short pulled up to it. An empty pot hung over the cold hearth.

"Put him there," Bieta said, waving her hand toward the far corner.

"But that's where I sleep, Ma."

She raised her hand, showing him the back of it. Stirk made a display of flinching, but they both knew the days of the mother striking her son had long since passed.

"Do as yer told and stop arguing. You can sleep somewhere else."

With a frown on his lips, Stirk stalked the few paces to the corner.

"Put him down gentle."

Her son grunted and crouched, setting the man on the heap of blankets with all the care a man his size could muster. The fellow groaned and Stirk jumped back a step, staring at him as though he thought a Small God might burst out of his stomach.

"Why do you wanna keep him?" he asked finally, satisfied no creature intended on finding its way out of the man's gut. "We ain't got enough food for the two of us."

Bieta dipped a cloth in a bowl of cloudy water set in the center of the table and wrung it out. She kneeled beside the lad and drew the damp cloth across his forehead; breath sighed out between his lips.

"You didn't see him, Stirk," she said. "Didn't see him when he saved me."

Her son's feet scraped on the dirt floor as he shifted, dissatisfied with her answer.

"You wanna give him my bed and food because he acted brave? What kinda—"

"No, you fool," she snapped and fixed him with a gaze that was always more effective at straightening him out than the threat of a backhand. "Yer only seeing a fellow in his underpants. Before they got to him, he wore fancy clothes, like a merchant. And you should have seen his sword."

"Aw, Ma. You don't have to tell me about his cock."

"Not that sword." Bieta laughed despite herself. "His *sword* sword. Its blade was etched and it had gold on the handle."

"It's called a hilt, Ma."

She shook her head and returned to wiping the greasy cloth across the lad's forehead.

"Don't matter what it's called if it was made of gold."

"Gold, huh? What happened to this gold sword?"

"The one-armed man had it, but that don't matter, neither. Don't you get what it means?"

Stirk scratched his stubbly chin, long nails grating in the tough hair.

"Not only do I lose my sleeping place and half my meals, but a fellow with one arm got himself a nice sword?"

"It means he has money, and people who have money have friends."

Bieta raised her eyes to her son and saw his blank expression. Stirk had never been one for planning or figuring things out, which explained why he lived in a tiny storeroom with his mother and had to sleep facing the wall when she brought her work home. She stood and went back to the table to dip the cloth.

"People who have money and friends will be missed," she told him, watching the turbid water run between her fingers. "When people with money are missed, someone's willing to pay to get them back. Understand?"

Bieta raised her head and watched comprehension creep across Stirk's expression. He grinned and nodded once.

"We're gonna ransom him."

"Aye, we are." Bieta leaned over the poor lad,

dabbing the wound in his gut with the cloth and prompting a near noiseless groan. "But he won't be worth nothing if we let him die."

III Horace - A Change o' Mind

While runnin' through the forest—walkin' fast, really, because Birk's too-small boots was pinchin' his feet— Horace kept thinkin' 'bout Dunal. The big oaf's face refused to leave his head, but he weren't sure why. A bush resembled his misshapen head, its straw hair stickin' out at cock-eyed angles. A saplin' reminded him o' the simpleton's mop handle what he always held in his hand.

Seein' them thin's made Horace remember other thin's: Dunal not understandin' a fuckin' thin' what anyone said to him; Dunal hittin' Horace in the head with the filthy mop; Dunal slappin' him in the back and knockin' him overboard; Dunal threatenin' to tell if he didn't get back to the ship. He saw the swabbie lyin' on the bed on wheels in the doc's shack, eyelids closed, pretendin' to be unconscious. He recalled the feller's eyes openin', lookin' at him all disappointed and angry. Then he pictured his fingers wrappin' 'round the swabbie's throat, eyes bulgin' and tongue danglin' out the side o' his gob.

Horace held up in his runnin', the pig leg bouncin' against this shoulder, the broken rib in his chest pokin' somethin' what it shouldn't be pokin'.

"It ain't Dunal what's makin' me feel this way," he said to the trees and shrubs 'round him. "Dunal deserved what he got."

The ol' sailor rubbed a hand across his mouth,

smearin' the fat left by grippin' the pig leg across his lips, stirrin' his stomach to growlin'. Despite the tasty meat leanin' on his shoulder, he ignored the bellyachin' and glanced back the way he'd come.

"Dunal deserved it, but the little feller ain't done nothin' to me. Ain't no one deserves to die alone in the woods just for bein' small and gray."

He inhaled the aromas o' the forest and the pungent scent o' burnt pig, and shook his head as though disappointed with himself. Whether it might be for leavin' in the first place, or for goin' back, Horace himself weren't sure.

The trip back he undertook at a slower pace'n when he'd left, lettin' his tired legs and his painful rib dictate how fast he walked. It didn't take him long to get back, though, because he hadn't gotten quite so far away as he'd hoped.

Horace stood at the clearin's edge, peerin' in at his fire still burnin' in the middle, the messed-up pile o' wood, and the little gray man sittin' on the dirt under the boughs o' an ancient jackpine. His shoulders was hunched and his head hung so low, his chin touched his chest. His gray skin appeared grayer'n before—a color like ash left in a firepit when the flames've been out for more'n a day.

"Ahem." Horace cleared his throat, not wantin' to scare the feller. After bein' dropped by a bird, fallin' outta the tree, and bein' skewered by a branch, he prob'bly didn't need no more tribulations.

Thorn looked up and a grin crossed his lips what were colored a patchy shade o' blue.

"You came back for Thorn," he said and winced like speakin' caused him pain.

"Yeah," Horace said, stalkin' into the clearin'. He hefted the pig leg. "Figured you might be gettin' hungry."

Thorn's smile increased for a couple breaths, but melted to a grimace. His head sagged again.

Horace went a couple paces closer, lettin' the chunk o' pig swing at his side, but careful not to drag it in the dirt. The poor pig leg'd been through enough, too, after bein' tossed out a window and cooked to shit o'er Horace's fire.

The flesh 'round the wound in the gray man's side puckered up like whatever gods what made him'd put his porthole in the wrong spot. There were a scab in its middle, but it didn't look nothin' like the place where someone'd pulled out a tree branch. Thorn's chest heaved with his breath as he sat cross-legged, his slack man-thing lyin' in the dirt, a couple browned pine needles stickin' to it.

Nothin' 'bout the feller made Horace suspect he might want to hurt him, so he moved closer, sat in front o' him with the pig leg set across his lap. He squirmed at the uncomfortable feel o' his packed breeches while the prospect o' tasty meat made his mouth produce almost too much spit for it to hold, but politeness demanded he deal with Thorn before puttin' his attention to eatin'.

"Are you all right?"

Thorn raised his eyes, but not his chin. "Thorn is getting better."

Horace blew air out between his lips noisily. "Pppptt. Helluva tumble you took outta that tree." He looked up into the branches. "Second one today."

"Yes."

Neither o' them said anythin' more for a bit. Thorn sat all slack like he might topple o'er at any time. Horace looked from the gray man, to the tree, to the pig leg, repeatin' the circuit until the quiet felt more like disquiet.

"What happened?"

"A branch broke when I stepped on it."

"That'll happen when you're gettin' near the treetop." He'd never been anywhere close to the top o' a tree, but even from the ground he saw branches were skinnier and flimsier up near the top.

"None have ever broken before."

The ol' sailor nodded because he didn't have no other way to answer. They both fell quiet again, but for shorter this time, and it were Thorn what spoke first the next time. He raised his hand and held it out, palm facin' Horace. The blood smeared across it from the wound in the gray man's side were startin' to dry out and darkenin' to the shade o' bricks.

"What is this?"

"Your hand?" Horace didn't imagine that were what he meant.

Thorn wiped his hand along his side, smearin' the dryin' blood across his ribs, then held it out toward Horace again.

"This."

"Blood?" Horace said. He tilted his head to the right. "Ain't you ever seen blood?"

"Not Thorn's. Thorn doesn't bleed."

"I'm thinkin' the poke in your side might be disagreein'." Horace waved a finger at the gray man's wound, the movement waftin' another sniff o' cooked pork up to his nose. His stomach grumbled again and he wondered it Thorn'd heard it. "But how come you ain't bleedin' no more?"

"Thorn healed it."

"Thorn what?"

The gray feller raised his gaze and some o' his normal gray color'd come back to his face and lips. "Healed it."

"How'd you do that?"

Thorn shrugged, the muscles under his gray flesh flexin', and it reminded Horace he weren't speakin' with no reg'lar man what happened to be a diff'rent shade'n him. This feller were somethin' diff'rent. Somethin' magical. Thinkin' it made Horace want to shiver, but he wanted to know more, too. He leaned forward, lessenin' the distance between them as if they was makin' plans to mutiny. Horace even looked o'er his shoulder, though weren't no way anyone'd be listenin' in on them sittin' here talkin' in the middle o' the woods.

"You healed it cause you're a—"

"Because Thorn is from behind the veil."

Horace swallowed hard 'round a lump what decided his throat were a good place to reside. He looked away from the gray man and at the pig leg lyin' in his lap, then the redness on his palm where the bone'd burned him. Not very long before, he'd cared 'bout gettin' that tasty meat into his mouth and runnin' from this monster sittin' before him, nothin' more. But Thorn didn't strike him as monstrous now. In fact, the ol' seaman found himself wantin' to know more. Scared though he might've been—and some o' that continued livin' in his belly and ticklin' through his limbs—he couldn't help himself.

Horace scooted his ass forward, cringin' at his own dirt squishin' between his cheeks. He looked from the pig leg on his lap up to Thorn's face and found the little gray feller watchin' him. Horace held up the chunk o' meat.

"Want somethin' to eat?"

Thorn leaned forward and sniffed, his nostrils flarin' with the inhalation. "What is it?"

"Roast pig."

The gray man wrinkled his nose, looked at the meat, then up at Horace.

"Pig," Horace said. "You know, like a boar."

Thorn's mouth tightened in disgust and he leaned away. "Thorn doesn't eat living things."

"Really?" Horace pulled a chunk offa the bone and

popped it into his mouth. The flavor flooded his tongue—a bit charred tastin', but piggy enough to make him want to eat more. "Isss good," he said through a mouthful. "You never ate it before?"

Thorn shook his head and his gaze returned to the pig leg. A faint growl rumbled in the gray man's midsection and he glanced at his stomach as though the grumble'd startled him.

"See? You're hungry. Try a chunk."

Horace grabbed another piece between his thumb and finger to tear it off, but it slipped out as he pulled it.

"Ha. It's kinda greasy," he said, wipin' his hand on the front o' his breeches, "but it tastes like heaven come down to the forest."

He gripped the chunk again and this time were successful in liberatin' it from the bone. It looked as though it might be too big to fit in the gray man's mouth, but he offered it to him, anyway. When Thorn didn't take it immediately, he pushed it nearer. The gray feller examined it for the space o' a few breaths until his belly gurgled again, coaxin' him on, so he took it. He held it between his fingers, inspectin' it for a moment, then sniffed it, then his little mouth opened wider'n Horace'd've guessed it'd be able and he inserted the whole chunk.

Horace watched him chew, his face goin' from disgusted, to curious, to surprised, and finally ravenous.

"Thorn likes it," he said after swallowin' the chunk. "Can Thorn have more?"

Horace smiled and nodded; Thorn scooted closer to tear bits and pieces off the bone himself. Turned out he paric'larly liked the charred bites, which suited Horace just fine, because his opinion were they tasted too much like shit.

They sat in silence for a while, no sound passin' between them but the noise o' their chompers grindin' away at their meal. Thorn kept eatin' long after Horace'd stuffed his belly full enough to make him uncomfortable. After days with nothin' to eat, stuffin' himself were exactly what he'd hoped to accomplish.

"What's it like?" Horace said, watchin' Thorn open his mouth impossibly wide to insert a chunk o' charred pig flesh between his square, flat teeth.

The gray man tilted his head, the muscles in his jaw flexin' as he chewed. One eye opened wider'n the other, his face askin' what his otherwise occupied mouth couldn't.

"The Green," Horace said. "What's it like in the…what's it you call the place?"

Thorn finished chewin' and swallowed. "The land behind the veil?"

"Yeah. That place. Sounds nicer'n what we been callin' it."

"It is beautiful. The trees are…" He spread his arms o'er his head, tilted his head back, but the sentence laid in the air, incomplete. He let his arms fall and lowered his chin. "The hills are…"

Horace lifted a brow, not knowin' what was goin' on with the little feller. He considered askin', but the expression on Thorn's face kept him quiet, waitin'. The gray man's gaze flickered 'round the clearin', settlin' on nothin', then came back to Horace.

"The beasts…" His voice trailed away and his face drooped, a shadow fallin' across his expression. His head shook side to side. "Thorn doesn't…Thorn doesn't remember."

Horace scrunched his face up. In all the turns o' the seasons he spent aboard them accursed ships, he'd been to more'n a few places along the coast, and a bunch in Leeward, too. He'd tell 'bout them all if asked; he might not recall much beyond the dock, the inn, and the local whorin' establishment, but at least he remembered it.

"What do you mean you don't remember?"

Thorn's head continued shakin' and his shoulders sagged, his hands fallin' into his lap, pig fat and his own blood smeared across the palms and fingers. Them few jackpine needles still stuck on his man-thing, too, but Horace tried his best not to look at that.

A surge o' despair crossed the space between them, strikin' Horace in the chest as surely as if someone'd bounced a rock off him. It coaxed a pain where the rib were pokin' him, but also squeezed his heart the way it might've been squeezed if he lost somethin' precious. His throat started closin' up and he suspected if he gave in to it, he might find a tear squeakin' outta his eye. He coughed into his fist, snorted and spat into a nearby bush. His snotty saliva hit a leaf and hung there, droolin' its way down.

"Thorn...Thorn doesn't remember his home."

Horace reached out with the unconscious intention o' layin' his hand on the little feller's for comfort, but caught himself before his finger's touched the gray flesh. He pulled away, unsure what'd happen if he on purpose touched a Small God.

"It'll come back to you," Horace said, curlin' his fingers up and sittin' his hand back in his lap by the pig leg. "You prob'bly bashed your head when you fell, is all."

Thorn raised both hands and put them on either side o' his head. He held onto it for a while, like he were keepin' it from poppin' off, then lowered them again. They left faint marks behind, faded imprints o' his fingers in blood and grease. He stared at the puckered scar on his side before raisin' his eyes to Horace, an understandin' expression dawnin' across his face.

"Thorn's magic didn't work the way it should," he said. "Things are different this side of the veil. That's why Father Raven stopped talking to Thorn. Why he didn't understand."

"Father Raven?"

"That's why he threw Thorn off," he continued as though he hadn't noticed Horace speakin'. "Thorn must get back to the land behind the veil."

This time, the gray man reached out his hand, but didn't stop short. Horace jerked back, but the little feller's fingers touched his knee. The ol' sailor tensed, halfway expectin' a jolt, or at least a tinglin' along the surface o' his skin. Turned out there weren't nothin' but the light touch o' skinny fingers. Horace stared at the gray man's hand, noticin' for the first time he didn't have nails on the ends o' them lengthy digits. When he raised his gaze again, Thorn were lookin' at him, eyes shinin' like tears might be comin', an implorin' aspect to his face.

"Will you help Thorn get home?"

Horace gazed at him, unblinkin', unbreathin', close to forgettin' ev'rythin' what his body should do to keep him alive until his lungs let him know they wasn't happy with the decision. He sucked a deep sigh through his nose—the scent o' trees and roast pig strong, the stink o' the dirt crushed into the inside o' his britches floatin' underneath, embarrassin' him. Before he had a chance to consider it, his head bobbed in a gesture no one'd misconstrue for anythin' but the affirmative. After that, his mouth got to talkin'.

"If I'm gonna help you, we have to get you a pair o' breeches." He nodded to the space between Thorn's legs. "I ain't traipsin' all over the kingdom with that little snake o' yours danglin' in the wind."

The Small God smiled and Horace shuddered, wonderin' why his mouth'd agreed to somethin' so foolish.

IV Kuneprius - Murtikara

Kuneprius woke with a start, the young woman's gaze haunting him as it did every morning when his sleeping ended.

He sat up and jammed the heels of his hands into his eyes hard enough to hurt, attempting to rub the vision away. Some nights, her eyes glistened with sadness and tears; others, they held an unfamiliar expression his dream-self knew to be desire. This night, hatred and a thirst for vengeance shone in their deep blue.

Kuneprius inhaled noisily through his nose and let a prolonged sigh escape his lips.

"Are you all right, Brother?"

"Everything's fine, Ves." He lowered his hands and glanced across the room at the empty bed. "A nightmare, that's all."

This marked the third sunrise since he and Vesisdenperos last engaged in their morning ritual, yet he carried it on, his friend's voice heard only in his head. He swung his legs around and set the soles of his feet on the threadbare rug, flexed and released his toes four times to encourage the blood to flow. Another breath, filled with the scent of the room's dirt floor and clay dust hanging in the air.

He stared at the other bunk, pretending Vesisdenperos had risen early, eager to get to the day's tasks, though they were the same as every other day. Kuneprius wondered if his friend still performed his task, perhaps with someone else assisting him, replacing Kuneprius.

No. That wouldn't be.

He stood, knees popping from over-use, not with age, he insisted to himself. A sliver of dim light squeezed through the crack around the shutters, indicating dawn crouched just below the horizon, waiting to creep into the sky at its usual languid pace. Everything about the day was the same as every other day, except for the absence of the man he'd raised as his son.

Kuneprius found his way across the room to the washing bowl. The water he'd filled it with the night before was clear, unlike most mornings. Normally, after filling it in the evening, Vesisdenperos would return from the cave, fingers curved into useless claws caked with clay. It fell to Kuneprius to wash him, unbending his gnarled hands and leaving the water silty and tinted gray, then change his clothes, feed him, and put him to bed. It had been this way every day since Ves came of age and began his training.

This was the third sunrise he'd woken to unclouded water, and the sight of it set his chest aching with loneliness.

He cupped his hands and submerged them in the cool water, splashed it on his face. Once. Twice. Three times, then stood leaning over the bowl, letting drops fall from his nose and chin. As tiny waves rolled across the surface, he wondered what had happened to his friend. None of the Brothers of Murtikara had uttered a word, and the priests who'd come from Teva Stavoklis had disappeared in the dark of the night, leaving behind no answers for Kuneprius.

Was he alive? Dead? Caught somewhere in between?

Hands gripping the table in either side of the bowl, Kuneprius leaned forward and plunged his face into the water. The chill touched his nose, his cheeks. He shut his eyes and counted.

One. Two. Three.

As happened every time he closed his lids, he saw the girl begging for her life, heard the cry of the baby Vesisdenperos, inhaled the coppery tang of her spilled blood.

Forty-nine. Fifty. Fifty-one.

He drew out each number as he counted, making them each a uniform duration. When he reached eighty, he opened his eyes and stared at the bowl's flat, white surface. A single dark fleck sat in the crease where the bottom bent upward into the bowl's sides—a tiny speck of clay. The last remaining sign of Vesisdenperos.

One hundred eight. One hundred nine. One hundred ten.

The air captured in his chest threatened to set his lungs on fire and bubbles spilled out of his mouth, rolling along his cheeks and up past his ears. He pressed his lips together, determined.

One hundred twenty-eight. One hundred twenty-nine.

He threw his head back, splashing water down his back and across the floor. Vesisdenperos' voice laughed in his head.

"How many?"

"One hundred twenty-nine," Kuneprius said as he wiped droplets off his face with his hand.

"That's not many. Haven't you done one hundred eighty before?"

"One hundred eighty-eight. Once. In my youth."

He pushed his wet hair back from his forehead and peered over his shoulder at the other bed, its blankets and sheets tucked in around the edges as they'd been these last three sunrises. The emptiness and order of it made Kuneprius shake his head. He took a cloth from the stand, dunked it in the water. After wringing it out, he washed his body, anxious to get to the seed garden and commence his day, though it promised nothing more than waiting.

Alone with his thoughts.

Kuneprius donned his robe and went to the door, pausing to consider the empty room once more before he stepped across the threshold.

Sunrise hues of pink and orange smeared across the distant horizon and bled away into a still-dark sky where the Small Gods continued to reign. Kuneprius closed his eyes and bowed his head, saying a silent thanks to the gods for whom he lived—for giving him this day, this life. He didn't thank them for taking away his friend.

With his morning thanks complete, Kuneprius made his way across the courtyard toward the seed garden, thankful to find it unoccupied. Many of the other Brothers did their seeding in groups, but Kuneprius preferred to offer his tribute alone.

Pebbles pressed into the soles of his bare feet, but they didn't bother him. Unlike the priests and most of the Brothers, Kuneprius rarely wore sandals, for his job didn't require foot protection. With the passage of seasons, he'd developed thick calluses on his heels, toes, and the pads of his feet. In fact, he rarely wore more than the simple robe.

A robin perched on a low branch in the tree beside the seed garden, the bird's breast the same color as the arbutus tree's trunk beneath its peeling bark. Kuneprius stood at the edge of the garden, watching the bird singing its morningsong, letting its melodic strains calm him. Upon noticing him, its twittering ceased, and it hopped to a higher limb.

"You're right. I best get to it before someone else comes."

Kuneprius settled his feet and inserted his hand between the folds of his robe, taking his manhood in his fingers. He began manipulating it, closing his eyes and counting each short stroke. In his mind, he pictured the Small Gods—their struggle, their sacrifice—as he'd been taught from the time he became old enough to produce seed.

Nothing happened.

He opened one eye and peeked back over his shoulder at the courtyard. It remained deserted. At least he had time.

His eye closed again, Kuneprius increased the pace of his strokes and shortened his breathing. He abandoned counting to concentrate on his tribute, his stomach knotting at having done so. The images he'd been trained to hold in his mind faded and reshaped themselves until he saw the young girl's face.

Her eyes gazed back at him, but they didn't shine with hatred as in his most recent dream. They were soft and caring, filled with emotion he'd been taught since childhood that women didn't possess.

In his hand, his manhood trembled and grew.

Kuneprius thought of her lying on the ground, staring up at him, but he didn't see blood and death around her. Instead, he pictured a field of grass and flowers and her curves hidden beneath the plain gray smock. He imagined what the coarse, gray fabric might hide.

His staff hardened and Kuneprius stopped stroking, opened his eyes.

He couldn't seed the garden of the Small Gods with such blaspheme in his mind; to do so would be sacrilege—an act he'd perpetrated too often. Now that his friend's fate rested in the hands of the gods, he'd take no chance he might offend them.

The robin sang overhead. Kuneprius scanned the courtyard once more and, finding it still empty, snorted hard through his nose, drawing its contents into the back of his throat. He spat the wad of mucus into the garden where it spattered against the side of a rock, the viscous fluid sliding toward the dirt. Not exactly the right color, but it would pass a cursory inspection.

Kuneprius let his robe fall closed and tilted his head back to view the bird again, slowing his breathing while in wait for his erection to deflate. The robin twittered and sang, letting its brethren know it had survived another night, but this time its tune didn't ease the man's concern. He'd made it through the night like the robin, but what of Vesisdenperos?

The sun climbed above the horizon, sending the Small Gods fleeing to their dens to hide from the day, and Kuneprius felt the pressure of their gaze lift from his soul. Perhaps today would be the day he'd have news of his friend.

Before pivoting away from the seed garden, Kuneprius adjusted his robe, lining the seams up in a symmetrical pattern, then he made his way toward the meal shack.

It sat at the end of the compound and looked no different from the other buildings but for the near-constant column of gray smoke swirling skyward from the ovens and cook fires. As he approached, he detected the scent of the meal meant to break his fast and his stomach grumbled in anticipation.

"Probably gruel again this morning," he said.

"Maybe fruit today," Vesisdenperos' voice responded. "Or berries."

"Or maybe they've slaughtered a pig and they'll have a rasher of bacon for all."

He chuckled at the morning ritual, but his laughter burbled across his lips alone. It was always gruel, seldom fruit, and bacon touching a Brother's plate was unheard of, but the repartee wasn't amusing without Vesisdenperos walking beside him.

The meal shack's door opened on creaking hinges and Kuneprius entered to a clatter of clay mugs and plates, the odor of milk and cereal boiling in great pots. He counted the Brothers in the room—eighteen, not including the cooks—and made his way to his accustomed place on the bench to the far left. His plate sat exactly the way he'd left it, chipped edge at the top, facing sunset, and his cup flipped upside-down to keep spiders out. He retrieved both, straightened the woven place mat that shifted as he picked up his plate, and started for the front of the room to await Brother Ytheriod to scoop a ladle full of porridge from the pot for him.

Halfway to the short line, he stopped.

A robed man he hadn't counted stood at the serving table, a hood pulled low to hide his face. Kuneprius glanced at his own tan robe, then up at the man's black one.

A priest of Teva Stavoklis.

He stared at the priest, unable to make his feet move any farther, but he didn't need to. The black-robed man's head tilted in his direction and he strode toward him. Kuneprius struggled to prevent his hands from shaking.

"You are Kuneprius," the priest said—a statement, not a question, "keeper of Vesisdenperos, the sculptor."

Normally, Kuneprius would have nodded his head three times to indicate agreement, but this time he struggled to move it once.

"You are to come with me."

The priest glided past without awaiting a response, his sandals silent on the dirt floor of the meal shack. Kuneprius stood frozen for a moment, noticing the Brothers around him sneaking glimpses as they scooped spoonfuls of flavorless gruel into their mouths or sipped their juniper tea. Their gazes touched his soul like fingers poking him, coaxing him to follow the priest.

"Better go," Vesisdenperos' voice whispered in his ear. "This is your chance to see me. You might not recognize me."

Kuneprius spun around and followed the priest. On his way past his seat, he set his plate and cup back on the table, the chipped edge left askew and the cup upright, inviting spiders to enter.

***

The color of the dirt beneath his bare feet faded from brown to gray as they approached the mouth of the cave.

Kuneprius had been here once, on the day Vesisdenperos saw the seasons turn for the sixteenth time—the day the priesthood revealed to the boy his calling. Season after season before that day, he'd knelt in other caves, manipulating clay into different shapes, building his skills until a priest came from Teva Stavoklis and showed him where he'd build the man who'd change the world. He'd been so excited, he couldn't wait to show Kuneprius the cave. That day, they'd stood outside and peered into the darkness, not daring to step within.

The priest ducked his head and entered the cave, but Kuneprius halted after his three thousand, eight hundred and thirty-first step, stopping precisely in the same spot where he'd squinted into the cave with Vesisdenperos that day so long ago. Then, as now, he'd known the task meant for the boy, because wasn't it he who'd condemned him to it? He'd liberated him from the Goddess' caravan; he'd brought him before Kristeus; he'd taken care of him every day since.

The early morning sun peeked over the top of the cave's mouth, its rays warming Kuneprius through his robe and making it impossible for him to see beyond the entrance. A bead of sweat rolled down his chest; he did nothing to stop it.

He knew what to expect inside the cave, but he didn't want to enter. Was he supposed to? The priest had disappeared within and not beckoned him to follow. Kuneprius shuffled his feet, felt a pebble pressing against the arch of his foot, shifted away from it. He inhaled a breath filled with the scent of clay and nothing else, then released it through pursed lips, readying himself to discover his friend's fate.

Before he took the first step, the priest reappeared. He strode out of the cave and into sunlight, his shadow stretching in front of him. Kuneprius looked at the front edge of the dark shape—the shadow of the priest's hood—falling across his feet, the black outline connecting the two men.

Another shadow joined the first. It flowed across the gray ground like water, joining the priest's at his feet, then continuing past. Without meaning to, Kuneprius let his mouth fall open and tasted clay on his tongue. He raised his head.

The biggest man Kuneprius had ever seen stood beside the priest. If he was a man at all. He didn't move, and it was difficult to tell where the ground ended and the man began, for they were both of the same color, molded of the same substance.

This is what Ves sculpted.

He dragged his gaze along the clay man's imposing figure of bulging muscles and impossibly smooth skin. Its broad chest heaved with breath, its lids blinked like any man's.

Its eyes gazed upon Kuneprius.

"Today, your duties to the sculptor resume." The priest's voice sounded as though it came from a great distance. "Tomorrow, you leave to acquire a Small God from the Green."

The words should have thrilled and excited Kuneprius with the promise of danger and adventure, but they barely registered in his mind. He could do no more than stare at the monstrous figure standing before him.

A figure he knew without asking had once been his friend.

"Vesisdenperos," he said when he regained control of his lips. "It is you."

V Danya - Spokes Market

When days of peace approach their end,
 And wounds inflicted are too deep to mend,
 A sign shall come, a lock with no key,
 Borne by a man from across the sea.
 A barren Mother, the seed of life,
 Living statue, treacherous knife.
 To raise the Small Gods, a Small God must die,
 When stars go out, the end is nigh.
 One must die to raise them all,
 Should Small Gods rise, man will fall,
 One can stop them, on darken'd wing,
 The firstborn child of the rightful king.

What a horrible dream.

Danya rolled onto her back, eyes closed against the light shining on her. A sense of emptiness filled her belly, a residual feeling of her dream of a strange scroll, a mysterious prophecy, the death of her brother. This last made the nightmare most disturbing. What would her life be without Teryk?

She stretched her arms over her head and felt hardness press against her back. It jarred her senses, and she became more aware of her surroundings—sounds, textures, smells.

An overpowering stench.

It wasn't a dream.

Danya's eyelids snapped open.

The trash heaped around her had settled during the night, covering her legs with a stinking blanket of rotted food and torn and soiled fabrics. She scrambled back, pulling herself out from under the pile, hands sinking into other slimy substances she preferred not to identify. The princess wiped her palms on the sides of her breeches and rushed out of the lane before the fetor caused her to lose the contents of her stomach.

He's dead. That was a memory, not a dream.

The weight of the realization landed on Danya as though someone had thrown it onto her from a third story window. She lurched away from the alley, drawing disapproving looks from passersby as she leaned against the wall gulping fresh air into her lungs and fighting the urge to weep.

She spit to clear the sour taste of bile from her mouth, wiped wetness from her cheeks on her sleeve. When she'd regained some composure, she straightened, put one hand on the hilt of her sword and the other on her knife—the first thing she should have done upon waking in unfamiliar surroundings, according to Trenan's teachings. Both hung where they should be, but knowing so comforted her little.

She tilted her head back to judge the height of the sun in the sky and saw the day remained young. Men with bent backs and gnarled hands shuffled along the streets, making their way to begin another day of hard labor on the docks or in warehouses or a blacksmith's. A few glanced at her furtively, but their gazes disappeared when she met their eyes.

The events of the previous day came back to her: blackmailing Trenan, the fight in the tavern, leaving the master swordsman so she could take up her brother's quest to fulfill the prophecy. She recalled standing on the bridge and gazing into the river, half-dazed with shock as she tried to decide where to start, how to decipher jumbled lines inscribed on the scroll.

One thing I'm sure of: I'm not the firstborn child of the rightful king.

Beyond that, the stanzas seemed no more than nonsense. Man from across the sea; Small Gods; darken'd wing. Only the barren Mother meant anything to her—some of the members of the Goddess Sisterhood were called Mothers—but she couldn't be sure the prophecy referred to one of them.

I can't be sure it refers to Teryk, or even to our time.

She started down the street, allowing her feet to carry her away from the stinking alley, though she knew not where to go. If the Mother to whom the scroll referred was a member of the Goddess' order, she might find help at one of the temples, but still didn't know where to find one. She thought the city's outskirts, but knew no more.

The street she was on intersected with a wider avenue and the princess stopped and attempted to orientate herself. If she faced left, it put sunrise and the inner city somewhat behind her. The direction of sunset was the quickest route to the city's edge. Not much, but somewhere to start.

The outer city was a foreign place to her, never visited and rarely spoken of, but she knew that when she'd crossed the river, she'd moved into the part of the city called Evenside—a place where she'd want to take care. Hands on her weapons, she went left and put the inner city and Draekfarren castle at her back.

A wagon rumbled past, heading toward sunset, like her. It clattered and bounced on the chipped and broken cobbles, and Danya stepped back lest a loose rock be spat out from under its wooden wheels. She glanced up at the driver, who wore a cowl pulled up over his head, then directed her attention to the man's cargo.

Three corpses lay stacked in the back of the wagon.

Her breath caught in her throat. Might one of them be Teryk?

The princess set out after the wagon, heels grinding in the loose pebbles and dirt strewn across the road. She quickened her pace, hurrying to glimpse the faces of the dead. In ten hurried paces, she'd caught up to within an arm's length of the wagon.

One face she saw clearly—a woman of many turns, her face wizened, mouth open to reveal yellowed, toothless gums. Beside her lay a man with a wound across his face and white maggots spilling out of his nose. Green and black rot around the edges of the gash suggested he'd been dead for some time.

Danya gulped back the nausea rising in her throat. One more corpse remained for her to see before she'd allow herself to succumb to emotion or sickness, but the third had been stacked the other direction, head at the front of the wagon and feet sticking out by the others' faces.

The princess inhaled a breath to steel herself and regretted it—the stench of the rotting man inhabited her nose and brought the threatening lump back to her throat. She turned her head away and reached out, setting her hand on the edge of the wagon to steady herself. She wiped her arm across her eyes to clear the tears the reeking corpse caused in them. When she could see again, she returned her attention to the corpses, her breath held.

Pink flesh showed through the holes in the soles of the boots worn by the third corpse. The sight encouraged her—Teryk's boots weren't in such disrepair.

What if the thief swapped with him?

She doubted the likelihood of a criminal taking the

time to replace boots on a dead man, but she needed to be sure. Danya increased her pace, moving alongside the wagon. Her gaze followed up the corpse's leg clad in dirt-caked breeches tied at the waist by a length of frayed rope. His shirt front lay open, his belly smeared with blood. A few more steps would bring her to a place where she'd see his face, and then she'd know, then she—

"Hey! What d'you think you're doin'?"

The driver's harsh cry cut through her thoughts, startling her. He jerked back on the reins, wrenching the horse's head and pulling the animal to a halt. Danya's feet skidded in the loose chunks of broken cobblestones and she grasped the side of the wagon to keep her balance.

"I'm sorry, sir. I'm looking for my brother."

The man threw back his cowl to reveal a face with a twisted nose and sunken cheeks.

"Ain't nobody's brother in the back of my wagon," he snarled.

"Can I just have a look?"

Danya stretched up on her toes and caught a glimpse of dirty hair sticking up, but the legs of the rotting man hid the corpse's face. She cursed under her breath.

"No, you can't," the driver said and whipped his crop on the edge of the wagon, slapping the wood a few handspans from Danya's fingers. She jerked her hand away. "If you're that interested, I'll sell him to you."

The princess stared at the driver, her mouth open. "Sell him to me?"

"Where d'you think I'm taking them? To the market at the Spokes. They'll be for sale whole or in pieces, I don't care which. Do you want him or not?"

Danya faltered back a step, head shaking. She'd never have imagined people sold corpses, let alone entertained the thought someone else might want to buy them.

"What...what would someone do with a corpse?"

"Don't know, don't care." The driver pulled his hood back up, throwing shadow across his twisted nose. "If you don't want him, someone else will."

He snapped the reins, prompting the horse to whinny, and the wagon pulled away leaving Danya standing off to the side of the road. She stared after the wain rattling along the avenue, hardly believing the driver's words. Did her father know such things went on in his city? Surely not, or he'd put a stop to it.

When the wagon was far enough ahead, she started out again, determined to follow it to market and find out for sure if the other corpse belonged to her brother.

***

Danya followed the wagon for a dozen blocks before the city changed around her.

Where she'd woken had been awful compared to the castle and the inner city—garbage everywhere, buildings falling apart—but the place yet held a sense of purpose. People went about their business as though they had business to go about. Blacksmiths and tanners lined the street, their shops beside carpenters and candle makers. All at once, the buildings in disrepair gave way to ramshackle houses and tumbledown shops. Men lay passed-out in alleys, drool dribbling from their open mouths and empty bottles clutched in their hands. Unwashed women leaned in doorways, tattered clothes hanging on their emaciated frames, asking for a coin in exchange for things Danya had never heard spoken of. She passed an open doorway and saw unkempt children sitting on the floor using chipped pestles to grind dried weeds into dust.

Selling corpses wasn't the only aberration her father should put a stop to happening in this part of the city.

Afraid of seeing worse—though she couldn't imagine

what that might be—Danya kept her eyes on the wagon rumbling along the avenue ahead of her. An unseen goat bleated pathetically; something hard crashed against a wall; a man cried out in anger or pain. The princess turned her head toward none of them.

They passed a few more side streets before a murmur of activity reached Danya's ears, clearly coming from somewhere ahead. She increased her pace, hands gripping the hilts of her weapons. The wagon driver reached an intersection and guided his wain to the right, disappearing behind a building. Beyond, the princess saw ragged awnings, their once colorful canvases faded to a near-uniform brown, and people milling around, moving from stall to stall.

The market.

She halted at the crossroads where the wagon driver had turned—a spot where four avenues intersected, forming a star of eight arms. The middle of the broad intersection gave home to the market's tents and lean-tos, any traffic from the streets redirected into a roundabout on the outside edge instead of running through the center.

Danya caught sight of the wagon aiming its way around to the far side. Rather than following, she bolted across the roundabout and into the market, cutting across the middle of the square. At the first tent she came to, a man grabbed her arm and spun her toward him. Danya loosened her dagger in its sheath.

"You're a pretty one, ain't ya?"

The rotund man wore a once elaborately embroidered vest missing thread and buttons both, the red fabric darker where gold thread had once been. His patchy beard surrounded lips that parted to show a golden tooth. The princess pulled her arm away from his grip, but his expression suggested he hadn't noticed her offence at his touch.

"A pretty girl like you needs herself jewelry, she does."

He stepped to the side and waved an arm toward a gray awning under which sat a table littered with rings, necklaces and bracelets. Danya glanced at them and saw they'd been fashioned of teeth and bone strung together to form hideous adornments the likes of which she'd never seen. She took a step back without taking the time to identify what type of animal they may have once belonged to.

"No. Leave me alone."

She turned her back on the man, ignoring his words as he called after her, imploring her to come back for a better look. Lips pressed together hard in disgust, she made her way deeper into the market, doing her best not to view the wares for sale, but occasionally giving in to morbid curiosity.

One bent old woman stood beside a table holding devices made of leather that looked as though they belonged in a torture chamber, not a market.

"Enhance your love life," the woman said. She brandished some sort of harness, its many buckles jingling.

A skeleton-thin man selling powders derived of crushed bones and herbs; a butcher in a blood-stained apron hawking meats of questionable origin; a robed woman offering to view the future; a man with coal-black skin wanting to cure whatever ailed her. Danya scurried past them, determined to find where the man with the wagon set up shop to sell his wares.

Finally, she reached the far side of the market and stood on the edge of the roundabout, her heart beating fast. Never had she seen or heard tell of the things she'd encountered as she made her way across the Spokes.

How can the king allow this?

She put the thought from her mind and glanced to her

right, expecting to see she'd made it to this point before the corpse-merchant. The street stood empty but for a few men and women hurrying to and from the market. Danya's forehead creased and she looked the other way, wondering if the merchants who accosted her had slowed her enough the wagon had already gone by.

No. She saw a wagon in the avenue, but drawn by two horses, the seat occupied by a tall, thin man and a stout fellow wearing a disgruntled expression. Danya stepped back as they passed, the weapons they carried rattling and clanking in the back of the wagon. She watched them go, a sliver of panic starting in the pit of her gut. Did she lose the corpse-merchant?

A moment later, the familiar wagon came around the bend in the roundabout. Danya let out her breath but didn't relax. She reached across her body and gripped her sword's hilt, ready to draw it as she stepped into the street directly into the wagon's path. The driver reined his horse in and flipped his hood back from his head, one brow raised.

"You again?"

"Yes," Danya said taking a purposeful stride forward. "And I mean to look in your wagon."

The man shrugged. "Go ahead, if you want."

Suspicious, Danya stepped forward. She skirted the driver, staying carefully out of range in case he should produce a spear from some hidden place, and made her way to the side of the wagon. Once there, she stopped, her gaze on the man watching her, a bemused expression on his face. It angered her. Who was he to dally as though she was a child?

She peeked into the wagon, then quickly back at the driver to make sure he didn't move. He smiled. An instant later, Danya realized what she'd seen and stretched up to peer over the side of the wagon.

It was empty.

Dried blood stained the floorboards and a stray boot lay in one corner, but all three corpses were gone.

"Told you someone else'd buy him if you didn't."

The steel of Danya's sword hissed against the leather scabbard as she yanked her weapon free and pointed it at the driver. His eyes widened and he raised his hands, dropping the reins in his lap.

"Where is he?" Danya demanded. "What have you done with him?"

"Sold 'em."

"To whom?"

The driver shook his head. "Don't know. It ain't polite to ask the name of those buying the dead."

Danya stepped forward, the blade steady. The point hung in the air close enough to the man's throat she could pierce it if she lunged, and the expression on his face suggested he knew it.

"Who bought him?"

The driver swallowed hard, the prominent lump in his throat bobbing. He shook his head slowly, then his gaze flickered to something beyond Danya's shoulder. Her heart jumped.

Be aware of your surroundings.

Trenan's voice spoke the words in her head, one of the many lessons he'd taught them.

"Everything all right here, Zel?"

The voice, deep and menacing, came from not far behind her and a pace or two to her right. She flicked her gaze over her shoulder and back, caught a glimpse of a long and tangled beard, the glint of sunlight on a short, curved blade.

"No, it ain't all right. This whelp's got a sword at my throat."

"Want me to take care of that?" the deep voice asked.

"Tell your friend not to move," Danya said, forcing steadiness in her voice, "or he'll have a corpse to sell on your behalf."

The man behind Danya laughed, the sharp, barking sound bursting through the morning air and drawing attention to them. She heard feet shuffle as others gathered; a smile crept across the corpse-merchant's lips.

"You might want to take a gander about," he said, smirking. "We take care of our own here in Sunset."

Against everything Trenan ever taught her, Danya glanced back over her shoulder—four men with bare steel in their hands had joined the fellow with the tangled beard.

"I suggest you put down your sword or it'll be your corpse I'll be selling."

Danya inhaled a slow breath through her nose, ignoring the scent of horse manure and sour herbs, using the air in her chest to calm her, prepare her. If she laid her sword aside, these men might not kill her but, if they didn't, whatever they did might be worse. She wasn't going to let that happen. And if she were to die, she'd do it with a sword in her hand.

She spun around, sword raised, knowing the armed men behind her presented a greater menace than the corpse merchant. The man with the tangled beard fell into a defensive stance—a trained fighter. The others around him bared their teeth and tensed their limbs. Danya scanned them, assessing the threat each posed, and read in most of their eyes they'd rather not risk their lives. She needed to worry about the bearded man—his presence gave the others courage. If she disposed of him, the rest would likely flee.

She glared at him and moved to the ready position Trenan had trained her again and again. In this pose, she waited for him to accept the challenge.

A heartbeat passed, then another and another. The man didn't move until his eyes widened; his mouth opened as though he might speak, then he took a step away, hands raised in surrender. The other men did the same.

A thrill of excitement pulsed through Danya. She'd never expected her first real sword fight to go so well.

"Leave the girl alone," a woman's voice said from behind Danya. She cursed herself for making the same mistake twice. "She is with me."

The man backed farther away, and the princess took the opportunity to see who'd seemingly come to her rescue.

A figure wearing a dull green robe stood off to the side of the corpse merchant's wagon, her stance not in any way threatening. When Danya's gaze found the robed figure's face, her own eyes widened, mimicking those of the men.

The woman's cheeks and forehead were of white wood, a black mustache painted above red-painted lips. Dark eyes gleamed through round holes.

She's wearing a mask.

The green robe fell away from delicate fingers and a small hand as the figure raised her arm.

"Come."

Danya lowered her sword but didn't replace it in its scabbard. Her instincts told her not to go with the woman—girl, judging by her hands and the sound of her voice—but the alternative was far less appealing. She strode toward the figure.

"Go back to your business," the girl said with a wave of her dainty hand, then she led Danya away.

The princess didn't look back, but she sensed the gazes of the men upon them, watching, ensuring they left the market. She could imagine the amazement in their expressions, because she felt it herself.

"Who are you? Where are you taking me?"

They hurried along the avenue, choosing the arm Danya thought would take them toward the setting of the sun. The stranger didn't answer so, when they were out of sight of the market, Danya stopped.

"Who are you?" she demanded.

Unafraid of the sword Danya held, the girl reached out and wrapped her fingers around her hand.

"Come," she said. "We have been waiting for you."

VI Ailyssa - Rescue

Once, the woman who'd been known as N'th Ailyssa Ra relished the caress of wind on her cheeks and the warmth of the sun touching her skin. The woman known only as Ailyssa despised how the breeze cooled the fearful sweat on her brow, the manner in which the sun-dried tears on her cheeks, tightening her skin.

Another careful step, one hand leading the way, groping, her blind eyes unable to see more than the glow of the sun. The aroma of baking bread that encouraged her when first she woke had been replaced by the scent of trees and dirt. The burble of the creek she sought to follow also eluded her, gone from her hearing, usurped by the drone of insects, the songs of birds.

When she resided at the temple and possessed the ability to see, she considered being alone in nature as being closer to the Goddess. Now, blind and lonely, lost and afraid, it seemed the Goddess had forsaken her.

Ailyssa blinked hard, wishing for the thousandth time to reclaim her vision as her other senses had returned. The world remained a blur of light without shade or shape. Was this how it was for every woman cast out from the Goddess' bosom? Had the woman once known as N'th Sylla Ra wandered blindly until the elements or an animal ended her existence?

Ailyssa shuddered.

She stopped, shoulders shaking with a sob she could no longer contain. Her hands covered her face. Tears moistened her palms—anguish at both her current situation and for having been forced to give up the only life she'd known.

Without the Goddess, do I have any life at all?

"No." She sniffed, attempting to stem the flow of tears. "They took my children, and now my Goddess, too. There is no reason to go on."

A sigh filled her chest and she resumed her trek, finally with a destination in mind, but unsure how to reach it. Blind eyes kept her from finding a cliff to throw herself off, or from weaving a noose of vines and grasses. If she found a sharp rock, might she find the courage to open her veins?

The soles of her bare feet rubbed on what she suspected was a carpet of dried needles, fallen from the trees that were so pungent in her nose. Her toe caught on a root, sending pain through her foot. She yelped and stopped again.

"There's no reason to go on," she sobbed.

"There's always reason to go on, sister."

The voice held the timbre of a young woman, and it startled Ailyssa. She jumped back, hands extended in front of her, fingers splayed.

"Who's there?"

A rustle of feet on the ground, the whisper of fabric. Ailyssa took another step away and her foot struck a rock; she tumbled to the dirt. Before righting herself, a hand touched her arm. She scrambled away.

"Who are you?"

Ailyssa wanted to be hopeful, to believe she'd been discovered by someone willing to help. In her heart, she wanted it to be a savior sent by the Goddess to rescue her, but after her expulsion, and being administered drugs that left her blind, faith failed her.

The hands didn't seek to touch her again.

"My name is Creidra," the voice said, and its tone gave Ailyssa the impression the woman might be smiling. "I won't harm you."

Ailyssa blinked rapidly, attempting to discern a shape amongst the bright glow, a distortion to show where the woman was; she saw nothing but the blurred light. She shook her head, staring at blank whiteness.

"Are you all right?" the voice asked.

"I...I can't see."

"Oh my."

Ailyssa heard cloth brush against cloth—the woman kneeling beside her. She still didn't touch her again.

"What happened to you?"

"I...They..." Ailyssa's words cracked with emotion, her throat clogged with the words she wanted to speak. Without knowing this woman, the urge to tell her everything nearly overtook her.

"There, there." This time, the woman patted the back of Ailyssa's hand; she didn't pull away. "Take a deep breath. Everything will be all right."

Nodding, Ailyssa did. She opened her mouth and inhaled, air shuddering into her chest. It tasted of the forest, and the threat of rain.

"Better?"

Ailyssa let one corner of her lips curl in an awkward thanks.

"How do you come to be here?" Creidra asked.

An insect buzzed past. "I was left here."

"Left? How awful. Who left you?"

Ailyssa's lips trembled, wanting to answer, but she found herself unable to. She shook her head; her chin dipped toward her chest.

"You are of the Goddess, aren't you?"

The question surprised Ailyssa and she raised her head, directing her sightless gaze toward the voice.

"Why...why do you say that?"

"Your hair," Creidra said, fingertips brushing the side of Ailyssa's head by her ear. "The Mothers of the temple in Olvana shear their hair in the same manner when they prepare to couple."

Ailyssa sat up straighter, her chest loosening at the mention of her order, allowing hope to enter.

"You know Olvana? Are we near?"

"Oh, no. Olvana is leagues upon leagues away. But you are of the Goddess, yes?"

How am I so far away? How long was I unconscious?

Ailyssa's chin sagged again. She let her arms go limp and fell back, a rock jabbing her in the ribs. She ignored it and threw one arm over her forehead, drew a breath heavy with regret.

"I was. The order cast me out. The Goddess has deserted me."

"That's a silly thing to say. The Goddess does not desert her subjects. She simply provides new opportunities."

"You don't understand." Ailyssa squeezed her eyes shut, blocking out the blurred glare.

"But I do. I am a Daughter."

Ailyssa's breath caught in her throat and she pushed herself up on her elbows again.

"A Daughter? What are you doing so far from Olvana? Can you take me back?"

"I am not of the Olvana order. Did they leave you here?"

"Yes. I am too old to bear children. I am of no use to the Goddess anymore."

"Nonsense," Creidra said and Ailyssa heard the stirring of fabric again as the other woman stood. "Let me help you.'

Ailyssa could do nothing more than nod.

"Give me your hand."

Blindness prevented her seeing Creidra holding her hand out, awaiting the opportunity to help her up, but Ailyssa sensed it. A heartbeat passed as she hesitated, unsure why this woman was here. If the Goddess had forsaken her, shouldn't she be left alone to perish, to starve to death or succumb to the elements?

Maybe the Goddess has not turned her back on me.

"Come," the woman prompted. "I'll take you to my temple. You will be welcomed—the Goddess holds a place for everyone."

Ailyssa raised her arm. Creidra grasped her hand and Ailyssa found the woman's skin smooth with the barest hint of calluses from performing work. She tugged on her arm, pulled Ailyssa to her feet.

"You've cut your toe. Can you walk? My wagon is on the other side of the hill."

Ailyssa nodded, the warmth of the sun on her skin bringing hope to her heart, the caress of the breeze on her cheeks gentle and loving. Creidra put her arm around Ailyssa's waist to guide her; Ailyssa supported herself on the young woman's shoulders.

"They left me to fend for myself, cast out by my order. But why are you here, Creidra?"

"I am gathering herbs and roots, but I didn't expect to find a new sister in the forest."

"You are a herbalist?"

Creidra giggled. "No, I am helping out. My duties in the temple are much more...pleasurable."

Ailyssa's brow furrowed at the young woman's choice of words, but she didn't inquire further. The elation in her chest at having been saved, brought back into the Goddess' arms when life appeared most bleak, made her ignore its significance. Excitement at returning to a temple, even one that wasn't hers, set her head buzzing with possibilities. Perhaps she'd find her own

Daughter, Claris, or her Mother, Pedra—if she was still alive.

Creidra led her up a gentle rise, guiding her carefully around rocks and roots, steering her away from prickle bushes and dense shrubs. As they reached the top of the hill, the nickering of a horse floated to Ailyssa's ears; the sound made her think she might one day get her sight back.

"Where are you taking me?" Ailyssa asked as they made their way toward the woman's wagon. "What temple do you belong to?"

"I am N'th in the Goddess' temple of Jubha Kyna."

Ailyssa's feet stopped moving, nearly pulling Creidra over.

Jubha Kyna. The Goddess' brothel.

VII Teryk - Horse Doctor

The beads of sweat on the lad's head popped back into being as quick as Bieta wiped them away. He breathed so shallow, it forced her to lean her ear close to his lips to be sure he still drew air. Through the night and morning, it had been the same.

"This isn't good, Stirk."

"What's not good, Ma?"

Bieta shook her head, partially at the state of her rescuer, partially because her son needed to ask.

"Lad might not make it 'til we can ransom him."

Stirk kneeled beside her and scratched the rough stubble on his chin with dirt-clogged fingernails. He tilted his head, watching the young man and pondering the situation.

"What should we do? We won't get no gold for him if he's dead, will we?"

"No, we won't," Bieta said instead of slapping him in the side of the head like she wanted—jarring his brain might knock loose whatever little sense he may yet possess inside his skull. "You need to fetch Enin."

"Enin? The horse doctor?"

Bieta nodded.

"Why don't I find a real doctor? This feller ain't no horse."

"Because we can't afford a visit from the surgeon. Enin might not be a real doc, but he'll accept the kind of payment I can give."

The man lying on the stack of hay moaned in the back of his throat as though agreeing with Bieta's plan. Both mother and son turned their attention toward him; his brow was sopping again and his cheeks glowed an unhealthy red. Bieta planted her tongue firmly against the space between her front teeth and wiped his sweat away with the grungy cloth.

"Fever's got him," she said without looking at her son. "You need to hurry and get Enin before it's too late."

Stirk stared a moment longer, then nodded so hard his brain might have smacked against the inside of his head. When he left, he neglected to shut the door, leaving the dim light of the overcast day to shine into the room. Not many people used the alley behind the tanner's, but anyone who did would see in—and it might be someone who'd recognize their prize. Bieta huffed an annoyed breath, climbed creakily to her feet, and went to close the door.

With her shoulder leaning against the lintel, she scanned both directions along the lane. There seemed more traffic than usual on the streets beyond, but she saw no one in the alley. Bieta's brow crinkled at that, but she shook her head and put it out of her mind as she swung the door closed, shutting out the day. She returned to the lad's side, wringing out the cloth as she did.

Shallow and irregular breath whispered between his parted lips. Once in a while, the pause between inhalations lasted longer, and Bieta worried the young man had expired, but then he'd draw another hitching inhalation and the rise and fall of his chest returned to its broken pattern.

During each of the elongated intervals, guilt prickled through Bieta's chest. The lad ended up here because of her—and she didn't mean because she made Stirk carry him. If he hadn't come upon her and Teth arguing, he'd never have had his own sword plunged through his gut.

"He wouldn't've hurt me. Not bad, at least." She wiped the cloth across his forehead. "He just wanted a free one."

If he'd truly saved her when she was in need of aid, she doubted she'd have the same feelings nibbling at her brain. Maybe she'd be more concerned for him than full of guilt. But she could have stopped him before he embarrassed Teth—a man who didn't take kindly to embarrassment. If she had, he likely wouldn't be lying on a pile of straw that smelled of Stirk's sleep sweat, breathing ragged breaths, and perspiring enough to fill a pitcher.

"We'll make sure you live," she said to the empty room. "Soon enough, you'll be home, and a few pieces of gold in my pocket'll make me forget everything."

She rubbed her scarred-over eye socket with the back of her hand, digging at a phantom itch that scratching never satisfied. Time crept by, and Bieta glanced over her shoulder often, expecting the door to open and Stirk to return with the horse doctor in tow.

"Where is that boy?"

An instant later, the door opened as though Stirk had been waiting outside for an invitation. He crossed the threshold, his wide frame blocking out the late morning gloom, and Enin followed. The horse doctor was skinny as a stick but stood taller than Stirk and had to duck to enter the storeroom, his head appearing huge on his spindly body. Bieta didn't think his scrawny neck and sunken chest contained the gumption to straighten him up again, but they managed.

Enin surveyed the room, a shadow crossing his face.

"I should've guessed you a liar. When have Stirk and Elishbieta owned even a flea-bitten nag?"

Bieta scrambled to her feet, one knee popping as it unfolded. She went to Enin, grasped him by the front of his shirt and looked up at him. Often, she'd thought his large head and long nose made him resemble the animals on which he worked.

"Had to, Enin. We need your help and you wouldn't have come if you knew the truth."

He glared at her for a time, then raised his gaze to see past the woman. His brows cinched, the two bushy things meeting over top of his nose, and he pushed past Bieta, strode across the room in two floor-gobbling steps.

"What—?"

Enin stood over the lad, staring at him for the space of more than a couple breaths. He crossed his arms in front of his chest and redirected his gaze to Bieta.

"What happened to him? Did you do this?"

"No," Bieta said, hurrying to him, head shaking all the way. "Teth did it."

Enin raised a brow. "Teth's dead, y'know."

"I know. I think he's dead because of what he did to this fellow."

The horse doctor stared at her a moment longer before finally turning back to the poor, sweaty lad. He kneeled and pulled a pouch from where he had it tucked into the waistband of his breeches.

"I've known Teth a long time," he said, putting the pouch on the floor and unrolling it. Metal things inside it clinked against one another. "The man had it coming for a while."

Bieta nodded to herself and stepped up behind Enin, peeking over his shoulder. The light flickered on the blades of a variety of knives, each a different size or shape than the others. In a pocket beside them were an array of needles, the smallest looking as though it might be intended for sewing tiny buttons; the largest may have counted varmint killing among its uses.

Instead of pulling out one of the shiny instruments, Enin leaned in for a closer look at the wound in the lad's belly. He laid his hand next to it, pressed down. The young man groaned.

"It's got to be cleaned, Bieta. Don't you know anything?"

"I cleaned it," she said, gesturing toward the bowl of murky water on the table.

Enin glanced over his shoulder at the vessel. "That didn't help clean it. Made it worse, more like."

Bieta's cheeks went warm. Her mouth opened to defend her actions, but Enin interrupted and she was glad of it.

"I gotta have something better at killing infection. Do you have any alcohol?"

"No, I—" She stopped and canted her head to find Stirk standing in the corner, hands clasped in front of him. His eyes strayed to the nearly empty sacks of grain and rice near his feet, then back to his mother. "Stirk?"

"Ain't got any. Drank it."

She frowned, put her hands on her hips. Her head tilted to the left and her eye fell on the sagging bags. She raised her hand and pointed but said nothing; she didn't need to. Stirk slouched across the room and stuck his wide hand behind the rice sack, pulled out a clay jar with a loose lid and handed it to his mother. She glared at him for a few seconds longer before giving it to Enin, the contents sloshing.

"Will this do?"

Enin removed the top and inhaled a deep sniff of the liquid, then jerked his face away, nostrils flaring and eyes pinched.

"Smells like it'll kill anything."

"I know what I wish it'd kill sometimes." Bieta scowled at her son again.

"Ma..."

"Be quiet."

Stirk fell silent in the face of his mother's anger, and she looked back to the horse doctor. Enin was still on his knees, holding the jar of hooch a safe distance from his nose, but he peered up at her instead of tending to the poor lad.

"Ain't you going to help him?" she asked, hands on hips.

"It's going to cost you, Bieta."

"You know I can pay the way you like." She smiled, pulling her lips back far enough to show the space her front teeth once occupied, and plunged her tongue in and out through the gap. One corner of the horse doctor's mouth twitched.

"Gonna cost more than that." He lowered his eyes to the front of her dress.

"You'll get what you're owed. Can you fix him?"

Enin sighed and regarded the young man again. "It's bad. I'll clean and stitch the wound, put a poultice on like I'd use on a horse, but I'd be worried about the bruises." He raised his hand and pointed at the dark patches on the lad's face and chest. "Could be they broke something inside him. Only a surgeon can fix it if they did, and I don't think any of them'll accept the kind of payment you're offering."

"You'd be surprised."

"You'd still need to convince one to brave the outer city. Good luck with that."

Bieta opened her mouth to say more, but the horse doctor tilted the jar over the injured lad's wound, splashing the clear liquid onto his belly. His body jerked and he groaned louder than he'd done since they got him to the tannery. Bieta gasped and covered her mouth with her fingers.

"Sorry, boy. It's going to get worse before it gets better."

Enin sloshed another generous dollop of hooch over the hurt, and this time Stirk moaned. Bieta slapped him on the forearm.

"Guess that'll have to do," Enin said. He took a swig of the alcohol, pulled a face, then set the clay jar aside and reached for his pouch.

His thick finger brushed along the tops of the needles arrayed in the pockets of the satchel until they came to rest on the second smallest. He plucked it from its place and reached into another, smaller pocket with his thumb and forefinger and pulled out a spool of black thread.

"Might want to hold onto him," the horse doctor said, nodding toward the lad. "I don't imagine he'll do much squirming, but you can never be sure."

Bieta crouched on one side, hand resting on the lad's shoulder, and directed Stirk to do the same. As they moved into place, Enin expertly threaded the needle, finding the eye on his first attempt. He pulled the fiber through, tied it, and snapped it off the spool with a practiced flick of his wrist. After dipping the needle in the hooch, his hand hovered above the lad's gut, the point poised to pierce his flesh.

"Ready?"

Bieta nodded and turned her gaze toward Stirk. He faced the wall, refusing to watch.

"Stirk?" Bieta prompted.

"Just do it." He swallowed hard, the lump in his throat bobbing with the effort.

"Here we go."

Enin plunged the needle into the skin at the edge of the lad's wound and the fellow jerked again, the way he did when the horse doctor cleaned the gash in his belly. Bieta leaned forward putting more of her weight on him and then watched Enin work.

He pulled the needle through the other side of the cut, then brought it back and repeated the process. After each time he put in a suture, he pulled the thread taught the way a seamstress might when sewing together the panels of a dress. Bieta counted the loops of thread as Enin worked, but stopped when she reached fifty-nine because she couldn't recall what came after that—she'd never been given reason to count any higher. The fellow ceased his groaning long before she lost count.

The horse doctor worked quickly and efficiently, pulling the two sides of skin together until they became a puckered line held together by black stitches that stood out against the lad's pale flesh. When he finished, Enin tied off the thread and took one of the small blades from his pouch to cut it.

"That'll keep his blood from seeping out, but he's probably bleeding on the inside," he said replacing his tools in the pouch. "I'll put a poultice on, but he'll need a surgeon or a healer."

Bieta pursed her lips, tongue working against the space between her teeth behind them. Surgeons were rare in the outer city and, if the stories about them were true, no healer would have any interest in the type of payment she had to offer. All she'd be able to do was hope to keep him alive long enough to collect their ransom, then his life would be someone else's concern.

Instruments stowed, Enin pulled another, smaller pouch off his belt, this one bound by a length of twine. He undid the tiny knot, his large fingers proving more dexterous than Bieta remembered, and flipped open the flap. With the same thumb and forefinger he'd used to take the spool of thread out of his other pouch, he removed a large pinch of dried brown leaves from the pocket. He stuck the wad into his mouth and chewed, his face screwed up in an expression of disgust. When he decided he'd softened it enough, he added a sip of the hooch to the concoction and ground it between his teeth some more.

"This, my friend," he said to the lad around the mouthful of herbs, his face twisted by the foul flavor, "is going to hurt you more than it hurts me."

Enin took the pasty mixture from his mouth and leaned forward, allowed his dark saliva to drool from his mouth onto the sutured wound. The lad's body tensed, his hand involuntarily clawing the air. Bieta pinned his arm under her knee.

The horse doctor took another mouthful from the clay jar and sloshed the liquid around inside his mouth. Satisfied he'd collected the residue, he spat it onto the wound.

"Arrrr." The elongated sound spilled through the lad's lips. "Nooooo."

The fellow jerked in Bieta's grip, but she held fast. His other arm slipped out of Stirk's grasp, fingers slapping the floor.

"Hold him, Stirk," she demanded.

Her son grabbed the lad by the wrist and pinned him the way his mother was. When his eyes fell on the stitched wound, now discolored to the hue of mud by Enin's spit, his face blanched. Stirk jerked his gaze away.

"Don't you pass out on me, boy," she said.

"I won't, Ma." He belched, cheeks bulging.

"No honking, neither."

He nodded but didn't look at her as he swallowed with great effort.

"Make sure you hold him tight," Enin said, his fingers caked with the pasty mixture hovering over the wound. "This will hurt him more than anything else, but it won't last too long."

Bieta shifted her weight again, ensuring his arm remained trapped beneath her knee. She looked to Enin again and nodded.

The horse doctor touched the tip of his fingers to the lad's injury, smearing the near-black paste along its length. Nothing happened for a second, and Bieta thought maybe Enin had exaggerated for effect, but then the fellow's body went rigid. His spine arched, lifting his back off the straw, and his face pinched up like a raisin, the veins in his neck standing out.

"Arrrr," he cried again between clenched teeth. "Daannnyyaaaaa."

Enin's head snapped to the side, staring at the lad. Bieta watched him, but found nothing to say as she struggled to hold the young man while he thrashed.

"Trennnnannnnn."

The fellow's body went limp as quickly as it had tensed, but Bieta continued holding on in case he convulsed again. While she was holding him, Enin jumped to his feet, eyes wide enough they might have bugged out and bounced across the floor.

"Wh—what did he say?"

Bieta's gaze darted from the horse doctor to the lad who saved her from Teth and back again. She shook her head and shrugged.

"Sounded like 'trenan' or something," she said. "What's a trenan?"

"And what did he say before that?" Enin asked, acting as if he hadn't noticed Bieta asking him a question.

"Arrrr," Stirk replied.

"Not that. He said another name. What did he say?"

Bieta rubbed the itch on her empty socket with the back of her hand, releasing her hold on the fellow—he'd played himself out and wouldn't be moving again, in her estimation. Stirk continued holding on, face still toward the wall, eyes closed tight.

"Something with 'ya' at the end," she said. She hadn't heard clearly because she'd been concentrating on keeping the young man from moving, like Enin had asked. "Tranya? Sendya?"

"Danya," Enin whispered and backed away. His thigh banged against the table, slopping cloudy water tinted brown with blood out of the bowl.

Bieta got to her feet with a wince, tongue rubbing the skin between her teeth. She squinted her one eye at the horse doctor, but he was too busy staring at the lad to notice the dirty look she had for him.

"Who's Danya?" she asked. "Someone you know?"

With an effort, Enin dragged his gaze away from the fellow and met Bieta's eye. She didn't understand the expression on his face—he appeared fearful and worried. Why be scared of a practically dead man?

"He said Danya," Enin confirmed.

"Guess so."

"Don't you know who that is?"

Bieta shook her head, a tingling of embarrassment in her gut at not recognizing this name the horse doctor so obviously thought she should. Her mind whirled through the faces and names she encountered in her daily life: the tanner, the men she serviced, the whores with whom she competed for coin. An examination of her mental list of acquaintances came up empty, so she continued shaking her head.

Enin's gaze flitted to the lad's face. "Danya. *Princess* Danya."

Bieta didn't understand for a moment, her mind grasping to find the meaning in the horse doctor's words. He must have seen the struggle on her face, the lack of understanding.

"Don't you see? You've kidnapped Prince Teryk. The heir to the throne."

VIII Danya - Temple of the Goddess

"Where are you taking me?"

The girl didn't respond—and Danya harbored no doubt she was indeed a girl. With the imminent threat looming at the Spokes, she hadn't really observed her rescuer. Now, with more time, she saw the slightness of her stature, the smallness of her hands. She recognized the girlish nature of her voice on the rare occasions she urged the princess to keep pace. Though she had yet to see the face beneath the mask, she thought the girl had seen the seasons turn no more than ten times.

Despite the fearful reaction of the men at the market when they saw the girl, she appeared determined to skirt any potential confrontations. Rounding corners and cutting through alleys, she kept her pace steady as she led Danya by the hand. They followed a lane narrow enough it forced them to turn sideways to fit. In one particularly tight section, the wall scraped against both the princess' chest and back before they emerged into a small courtyard created by the back walls of different buildings.

Danya planted her feet, nearly unbalancing the girl as she stopped.

The stench in the courtyard made the princess cover her mouth and nose with her free hand. She surveyed the tiny area, feeling the girl's inquisitive eyes peering at her from behind the mask. The source of the malodorous fumes became quickly apparent: two moldering bodies lay against a wall, the skin dried and shriveled to the look of ancient parchment. Their eyes had been pecked out by birds or gnawed by vermin, and scabbards hung empty at their waists—taken by a different type of scavenger. Danya wondered if it was by the masked girl.

"Why do you take my through a place like this?" Danya demanded, refusing to continue despite the girl tugging on her hand.

"So, no one will recognize you."

Danya pulled the girl closer and raised a brow. "Do you know me?"

"You are Princess Danya."

"And where are you taking me?"

The girl released her hold on Danya's hand. "You are searching for a Mother, aren't you?"

The princess' mouth fell open, the putrid stench of the rotting bodies touching her tongue. "How do you—?"

Before she completed the question, the girl hurried off, squeezing through another narrow space at the far end of the courtyard. This time, Danya needed no prompting to follow.

She emerged into a section of the outer city that looked different again from the rest, with narrower streets and taller buildings. Many looked to have begun their existence with one or two stories, but they'd been added to as the seasons turned, growing toward the sky haphazardly until they resembled a pile of over-sized children's blocks placed slightly askew. Above them, gray and white gulls wheeled, the upper levels of the buildings smeared with their droppings.

We're close to the wharves.

Beyond these taller buildings, closer to the shore, they'd find squat warehouses. She'd seen them once when her father took her out upon the sea for the maiden voyage of a ship he'd named *Devil of the Deep*. Danya had been young at the time, and found the ship's name frightening, but the network of docks and warehouses set against the backdrop of the city and the water's salty scent had served to quell her fears. The memory was one of the few pleasant ones she could readily find in which she stood at her father's side.

"Hide your face," the girl said over her shoulder, then turned onto a busier street.

The princess pulled her collar up beside her cheeks, peering over the top at the people and wagons flowing along the avenue, ferrying workers and wares between Fishtown and the docks. A wagon heaped with fish, some still flopping, trundled past, three men armed with spears walking on either side, gazes fixed on the rest of the crowd.

Ahead, the girl slipped between a group of men and their wain and disappeared from Danya's view. She hurried her pace, trying to get around the wagon stinking of sea water and scales, but one of the spear-bearers blocked her way.

"Step back," the man commanded, scowling at her.

Does he think I'm here to steal his fish?

Danya frowned, but slowed as he'd asked. If she meant to discover why this girl said she'd been looking for her and how she knew about her search for the barren Mother, she'd best not get herself impaled on the man's pike.

She stood on her toes and craned her neck, attempting to peer around the slow-moving obstruction and locate the dull green-robed girl before she got too far ahead. No color moved amongst the uniform drab browns and grays of the working class. Danya considered revealing her identity to them, demanding they let her by, but that would draw unwanted attention. Surely her mother and father had people searching for her by now.

The princess sighed, resolved to follow the wagon and hoping to find the girl once she could pass. The wagon rattled past an alley on the left and a figure called to Danya from the shadows.

"Psst."

The princess stopped and peered into the dim space between a two-story building with a roof sagging in the middle and another building that sprouted six stories high. Its top level leaned precariously—the reason the alley lay in shadow.

In the dimness, she made out a shape that may or may not have worn an olive robe, but there was no mistaking the white face adorned with red lips and black mustache. Danya glanced over her shoulder before zipping across the street and into the alley.

The girl reached for her hand and the princess allowed her to take it. They moved along the alley— wider than the one which had led to the courtyard, but narrow enough her shoulders brushed the sides at points. Danya raised her gaze to the edge of the building looming above, which nearly created a tunnel for them to pass beneath. Beyond the girl ahead of her, the alley lay empty—of people, of trash, of anything. No doors opened onto it from either of the buildings, no windows peered out over it. And the narrow lane stretched on as far as she could see.

"Where are we going?"

Danya stole a glimpse over her shoulder. The mouth of the alley seemed impossibly distant, the people and wagons traversing the street beyond blurred.

How have we come so far?

She turned back just as the girl halted in front of a

brooding structure built of dull red brick that hadn't been there a moment before. A black wooden door as wide as the lane broke the wall's uniformity, no windows or decoration adorning the bricks. Danya stared.

"Is this...?"

"Our temple," the girl said, stepping forward. "Come."

The door swung open without benefit of her touch. She entered, still gripping Danya's hand and, once they both crossed the threshold, the portal closed. The princess glanced back at who'd opened the door, but saw no one.

Flickering tapers set into sconces mounted on the wall at regular intervals illuminated the hallway. Danya examined them as they passed and noticed each candleholder was fashioned of wrought iron and shaped to resemble flowers. Some of them she recognized— roses, tulips, daffodils—others were less familiar. Between each set of sconces was a door, and every one of them the same—dark wood, brass handle, unnumbered, no signs. Nothing to indicate what lay behind them.

Danya followed in silence despite the feeling of foreboding weighing on her thoughts. What if the girl meant to bring her to people who intended her harm? To a nest of brigands set on making their fortune by ransoming her? It seemed unlikely, but couldn't someone have recognized her and sent the girl to retrieve her? A sound explanation for the mask.

But it didn't explain how she knew about the Mother.

No matter why she'd been brought here, she'd carry on; her brother's death demanded it.

I will honor your name, Teryk. I promise.

As they walked, Danya counted her steps and kept track of each passage they traversed so she'd be able to find her way out. When they'd come upon the building, they'd been heading away from the docks—leeward, then. Through the door, eighty-six paces to the first turn—a left—thirty-two to the next—a right. Two more right turns and three more lefts combined with over five hundred paces and the princess had forgotten the first part of their trek. Realizing she'd be unable to escape the maze on her own, her hand found her dagger, its leather-wrapped hilt giving her a sense of composure.

After more turns and more paces Danya didn't bother keeping track of, the masked girl stopped in front of a door identical to the others. The identical dark-stained wood, its brass handle mounted in the same place. The girl faced Danya and held one finger up to the painted lips on her mask before reaching for the handle.

A shiver coursed through the princess. She didn't know what lay hidden behind the door, but as the hinges creaked, the air crackled and pulsed. The girl stepped through, her hand sliding out of Danya's, and the princess remained standing in the hall, the hairs on the back of her neck prickling. Her heart beat fast, but it wasn't fear that froze her step and increased her pulse—it was reverence.

Without seeing anything beyond the masked girl, she sensed what she'd find within the room would be capable of changing her life.

The girl wiggled her fingers, prompting Danya to follow, and the gesture released her hesitant feet from their spell. She crept forward three paces to carry her into the room and the young girl stepped aside.

The chamber was round instead of having four square walls like she'd expected. A dozen figures kneeled at regular intervals at the base of the curved wall, guttering tapers clenched between their hands. Each of them wore robes of deep purple and white wooden masks, every one painted with the same red lips, the same mustache and eyebrows. Despite the extraordinary scene, a bed set in the center of the room drew Danya's attention.

A woman lay upon the bed, a thick layer of blankets tucked in around her and pulled up under her chin. Her wispy gray hair, recently brushed, lay fanned across her pillow. The skin upon her forehead and cheeks was wrinkled and pruned as if she'd spent too much time in water. Her pale lips were closed, her eyelids drawn like shutters.

By far the oldest person upon whom Danya had ever set her gaze.

Is she dead?

She glanced at the woman's blanket-covered chest but saw no movement at first. When Danya faced the masked girl who'd guided her to the chamber, her escort waved her arm toward the bed. Danya swallowed and moved to the bedside, close enough to see the shallow motion of the woman's breathing. A moment later, the masked girl stood beside her.

"This is N'th Sylla Re'a Shi," she said, her voice a hushed and pious whisper. "The Mother of Death."

IX Ailyssa - Jubha Kyna

The Matrons of Olvana had spoken of Jubha Kyna in hushed words, proclaiming it an affront to the Goddess and a shrine to greed suited more to the Small Gods. As the wheels of Creidra's wagon rumbled along the rough track, Ailyssa longed to view the temple her Sisters had whispered of, the place capable of causing such a stir.

"We are close," Creidra said raising her voice to be heard over the sound of hooves tromping the ground.

Beside her on the wagon's bench, Ailyssa clasped her hands in her lap. Her chest ached with the emotions battling within her—nerves brought on by the rumors and hope at being brought back to the Goddess.

"Tell me about the temple, Sister."

"Oh, it's beautiful." Creidra laid her hand on the woman's forearm. "It sits outside the town of Farmland, surrounded by lush fields. Four floors rise above the plain, with Goddess sculptures watching over us from each corner."

"Statues of the Goddess?" The thought brought a shiver along Ailyssa's back. In Olvana, depictions of the Goddess were forbidden.

"Yes. Some are carved of marble, others of simple sandstone. In every one, she is triumphant and loving, though in each her face takes on a different aspect. Each sculptor shows her in a different light, with a different face, but they are all the Goddess."

"It sounds..." Ailyssa swallowed, unsure whether it sounded wonderful—the word clinging to the end of her tongue—or sacrilegious, which her mind told her to say. She chose neither. "Tell me more."

"The center of the temple opens into a courtyard, where the prayer gardens are kept. Every flower imaginable. The colors are breathtaking."

Ailyssa said nothing, staring straight ahead at the blur of light disrupting her vision, but the mention of the garden eased her concern. She relished the idea of being somewhere that held some familiarity, even if blindness hid it from her.

"Oh, I'm sorry, N'th Ailyssa Ra," Creidra said, squeezing her arm. "Am I being insensitive speaking of colors you cannot see?"

A smile crept across Ailyssa's face. Though she'd had her titles stripped and no longer deserved them, it warmed her heart when the young woman used them. She chose not to correct her.

"No, Sister. Do not interpret my silence as sorrow. I'm glad to be returned to the Goddess. Glad you found me before..." Her voice trailed off. She didn't want to imagine what she might have done if the young woman hadn't discovered her. She cleared her throat and changed the subject. "Did you mention a town nearby? There were no towns near Olvana."

"Your order is...extreme."

Ailyssa's smiled wavered and she sensed Creidra's gaze on her. "What of this town?"

Creidra took her hand off Ailyssa's arm and snapped the reins. Her horse whinnied and increased its gait, the faster pace enough to create a breeze against Ailyssa's cheek.

"Farmland is small. A surgeon, a general store, a banker—the essentials necessary to serve the farmers. The area is peaceful and quiet and filled with hard-working men who enjoy the opportunity to support the Goddess when they're not busy in the fields."

"Support the Goddess?" Ailyssa repeated, though she read the implication in Creidra's words and suppressed another shiver.

"Don't worry, Ailyssa. There is room for you to do your part."

They fell into silence for a while. Ailyssa concentrated on the jingle of the horse's harness and clatter of the wagon's boards to distract her from the bits and pieces of rumors she recalled about Jubha Kyna. Surely they couldn't be true. How could the Goddess hold a place of honor and love for women who sold their services to become with children?

Maybe it's a blessing my blood ceased.

Ailyssa's blurred vision dimmed for an instant, then brightened again, making her breath catch in her throat.

"Are we here?"

"Yes," Creidra said. "We've just passed under the gate into the outer courtyard. How did you know?"

"The light changed." The thought sparked hope in her

chest. Did this mean her vision was returning?

Creidra guided the wagon through the yard, angling left before yanking on the reins to halt the horse. They sat for a moment, the aroma of herbs the young woman had gathered reaching Ailyssa's nose now they no longer moved. She detected mint and doll leaf, but the others were unfamiliar; no surprise as she'd received no education in herbology. Not recognizable, but their odors pleased her, warmed her heart.

"Wait. I'll help you."

Creidra climbed out of the driver's seat, the wagon jouncing under her weight. Her sandals scraped the ground as she hurried around in front of the horse before skidding to a stop beside Ailyssa. An instant later, her hand rested on her passenger's arm.

"Take my hand."

Ailyssa nodded and groped in the foggy light of her vision until her fingers found the young woman's. She bent and placed her other hand on the edge of the seat, then stepped down tentatively. Despite her care, the jolt of her foot finding the ground clicked her teeth together.

"I will take you to N'th Adnine Re'a. She is high Matron of Jubha Kyna, the Mother of Mothers."

Creidra took her arm and led her away from the wagon, allowing her no time to respond. But what would she say? Her skin prickled with nerves at hearing the words Jubha Kyna, never mind being in the place. But if her choice was to wander alone and lost until death took her, it was no choice at all.

They paused and hinges creaked. New smells wafted to Ailyssa—incense, polished wood, the odors of a kitchen. Creidra tugged on her arm and pulled her across the threshold, then paused again as she closed the door with a solid thud of wood against stone and the thump of a metal ring.

The quality of the blurred light filling Ailyssa's eyes

dimmed. Without seeing, she knew they'd entered a building—the temperature dropped, the light faded, the sounds of the outside were muted. A few paces in, the stone floor ended and a thick rug began, silencing their passage.

Creidra led Ailyssa a dozen paces along what she assumed to be an entrance hall. They rounded a corner to the left, then continued around enough corners and bends, down passages and through sufficient doors for Ailyssa to lose any sense of orientation. Occasional whispers reached her ears—the hushed voices of women commenting on their passing or merely the rasp of their feet on thick rugs, she couldn't tell which. Creidra didn't speak, though, so Ailyssa chose silence, too.

As they walked, the scents of the building changed. The aroma of roses came and went as quickly as Ailyssa identified it, replaced by jasmine and lilac. The familiar smells fortified her; perhaps Creidra intended to take her to the prayer gardens, somewhere Ailyssa might feel less lost, less abandoned by the Goddess.

She hasn't abandoned me. She sent sister Creidra to rescue me.

The thought sat well in her head, but didn't fit in her heart. Ailyssa tried to force it, but found no room.

The garden scents disappeared and Creidra slowed their pace.

"Watch your step," she said, and the two women mounted a flight of stairs.

They climbed twenty steps to a landing, then bent to the right, where there were twenty more. At the top, they hurried along another hallway and Ailyssa had the impression it was narrower than the others they'd traversed. Even without the benefit of sight, she sensed the ceiling hanging overhead, the walls closer on either side. And the odors of the passage were so different from the lower floor—thicker, musky.

For the first time during their trek, she detected noises she could be certain didn't belong to the scuff of their feet on carpet, the rub of the fabric of their clothes. Voices spoke behind closed doors, muffled by thick wood so she couldn't understand their words, but she understood their tone and timbre. Many of them belonged to women, but men's voices rumbled amongst them. Recognizing this explained the odor.

These are coupling rooms.

"More stairs," Creidra said and they climbed another twenty steps, bent left and ascended twenty more.

Another hall followed, this one shorter than the others, and they mounted a third set of stairs. By the time Ailyssa counted the thirty-fifth step—there had been no landing after the twentieth—her heart pounded hard in her chest like a caged animal attempting escape, and her breath struggled to reach her lungs.

"How much farther?" she panted.

"Almost there," Creidra said with no hint of breathlessness in her voice. "Are you all right? Do you want to rest?"

"I'm fine. No need," Ailyssa said shaking her head and feeling the dampness of perspiration on her brow. Five steps later, they reached the top.

Despite her dissent, they paused long enough for her to catch her breath. When her breathing eased, she noted the silence pervading the floor.

"This is the great hall," Creidra whispered. Her voice echoed, providing evidence of her words. "The chambers of N'th Adnine Re'a are at the far end."

Ailyssa swallowed hard and nodded, waiting for the young woman to lead her. They didn't move, as though awaiting something, the silence pressing in around them. Ailyssa shifted from foot to foot, noted the small pain of the cut on her toe where she'd kicked the rock. Feeling it sent a shiver of relief along her spine—perhaps it was good to be alive, after all.

The emotion died when N'th Creidra let go of her arm.

"I am not yet Ra," the young woman said. "I cannot cross the Goddess' hall."

"But I can't see."

Panic jumped in Ailyssa's chest. A wave of vertigo gripped her mind and she groped blindly in front of her, reaching for Creidra to help steady her. An instant later, the young woman's hand touched her shoulder and the dizziness passed.

"You'll be fine," she said, her tone hushed and breathy. "The Goddess will guide you."

Ailyssa licked her lips, her mouth suddenly dry. She shook her head, remembering her stumbling journey after she'd awakened, the number of times she fell, scraping her knees and cutting her palms. Any of them could have been a tumble over a cliff, a fall that hit her head on a rock, a blind grope into the den of a bear.

But this is the Goddess' hall.

No bears' dens to wander into, no cliffs to plunge off, no rocks to stub on and stumble over. Judging by the way Creidra's whispered words echoed, the floor lay bare ahead of her.

What if there is no floor?

A foolish thought. Why should this woman rescue her and go to the effort of bringing her here to watch her fall to her death? The Goddess wasn't so cruel. Was she?

"It's okay," N'th Creidra said. "No harm will befall you. I'll guide you with my voice."

Ailyssa's lips quivered and she ran her tongue back and forth on the inside of her teeth. After a hesitation, she nodded once, and the young woman took her hand away.

"Go ahead."

Ailyssa lifted her right foot, extended it, and set it

down again. A step the same as any other, like the thousands upon thousands she'd taken in her life. She panted a breath out through her nose and took another step, another. Her bare foot's gentle slap on the smooth stone floor swirled around her like birds taking wing, fluttering past her head to alight on beams unseen in the ceiling high overhead. Ailyssa raised her head as if she might espy the wings of those echoes, but saw only the hazy light.

"Keep going," Creidra encouraged.

After wiping her brow on her forearm, Ailyssa continued. She crept across the room, sure with each step she'd topple and fall, relieved when her foot rested safely on the floor. She lost track of the number of paces she took, but when Creidra called out for her to stop, the young woman's voice seemed to come from a distance.

"What do I do now?" Ailyssa's words fell flat against a wall or door directly in front of her. "N'th Creidra?"

The young woman didn't answer. Ailyssa first thought to find out if she remained with her, but that would do her no good. Did it matter if the woman had left or fallen silent? It did—Ailyssa didn't want to be alone.

"Creidra?"

The creak of old hinges answered her call. A waft of warmer air scented with cedar incense and the hint of medicinal herbs beneath washed over Ailyssa's face. She tensed, expecting a hand laid upon her, but there was none.

"Enter, child," spoke a voice tinted with the passage of years. "Be not afraid."

She was, but Ailyssa extended her hand and took a step across the threshold despite the fear. The door swung shut behind her.

"You cannot see?"

"N—no."

"You are safe in the chambers of N'th Adnine Re'a. Come forward five paces so I can see you."

Ailyssa hesitated, the niggling feeling things weren't what they seemed pressing at the back of her mind. But hadn't N'th Creidra gotten her here safely? And guided her through hallways, up stairs, and across the Goddess' hall without incident? Why should this be any different?

She gave in, her hand sweeping side to side in front of her as she counted off five steps in her head. After the fifth, Ailyssa stopped and lowered her arm, standing stiff and straight, waiting.

"You are of the Olvana temple, are you not?"

Ailyssa ran her hand over her short hair, assuming it identified her to Adnine as it had to Creidra.

"Yes, Matron."

"What is your name?"

"Ailyssa."

A pause. "Just Ailyssa? You must at least be N'th."

"Once they called me N'th Ailyssa Ra, but no more." The words tasted bitter on her tongue, foreign. "They cast me out."

The woman drew a deep breath and let it out in a forceful sigh.

"I will never understand the ways of Olvana's order. How does banishing any woman serve the Goddess?"

Ailyssa assumed the woman spoke her thoughts aloud rather than requiring an answer, so she remained silent.

"What did you do to be cast out?"

"I gave birth to two sons and only one Daughter."

"That is enough in Olvana to be condemned?"

Ailyssa bowed her head, drew a shuddering breath. She considered keeping the truth from this woman so she might not judge her badly, but she couldn't. After so long living the Goddess' teachings, she knew untruths were always found out.

"My Daughter has produced no Daughters of her own to honor the Goddess. And..." She hesitated, blinked. "And I refused to couple when I was supposed to."

Silence. Ailyssa's mind drew a picture of the Matron: gray hair, face lined with well-earned wrinkles, eyes hard and judging. The longer the silence drew on, the more filled with contempt the expression of the woman in her thoughts became. After what seemed an eternity, Ailyssa decided not to wait for the inevitable question.

"I didn't couple because the partner they sent was my son. I knew him from a birthmark on his shoulder."

"The Goddess' order in Olvana couples with their own offspring? Sacrilege. It's no wonder you didn't honor our Lady with more Daughters. She likely didn't want them."

"N'th Adnine Re'a, I don't know if—"

"How old are you, Ailyssa?" the old woman interrupted.

"The seasons have turned fifty-four times since my birth."

"So your blood has ended?"

Ailyssa's chin sank to her chest. "Yes," she whispered.

"Hmm. Age is no reason to be cast out, otherwise we'd all end our lives wandering the wilds praying for the Goddess to take us back."

Ailyssa raised her head, wiped her hand across her lips, the knuckle of her finger lingering before her arm fell back to her side. The white blur of light was brighter in this room and she suspected it might be lined with windows.

"The order of Olvana may have banished you," the woman said. "But I see no reason the Goddess should. I hereby reinstate you, N'th Ailyssa Ra."

Ailyssa involuntarily raised both hands to cover her mouth. Joy swirled in her stomach, forcing out the fear and hurt she'd carried since she woke without her sight. The Goddess hadn't forsaken her—or perhaps she decided to forgive her. The only life she'd ever known would continue.

"Thank you," she breathed between her fingers. "Thank you, N'th Adnine Re'a."

"Tut, tut." Ailyssa imagined her waving her hand dismissively. "Get your rest today and tonight. Tomorrow we will set you to work to earn your keep in Jubha Kyna."

Her heart jumped, the rumors of how Jubha Kyna became the richest of the Goddess' orders returning to her. The Goddess' Brothel, the Sisters of Olvana called it. Ailyssa's hands dropped from her face.

"What will be my role, Matron?" she asked, a tremor in her voice.

"The same as everyone. You will be available to the men who come to pay their tribute to the Goddess." Fabric rustled as the woman stood. A joint popped. "At Jubha Kyna, we do not couple with our own sons and bring tainted Daughters into the world to disgrace the Goddess."

"But I bleed no more." Ailyssa took a breath, hating the words before they came out. "I can no longer honor the Goddess with Daughters."

"We all earn our keep, N'th Ailyssa Ra." The woman's feet scraped the floor and her hand touched Ailyssa's shoulder. "The men do not only pay tribute with children. In addition to their seed, they bring coin, food, services. If you could see the room in which you stand, its treasures would take your breath away and you'd understand why we all contribute. I still lay with men. We are all desired."

Desired.

Ailyssa flinched at the word as though an open hand slapped her across the face. She had never desired anything but serving the Goddess, never expected to be desired by anyone. Never *wanted* to be desired by anyone.

The old woman's fingers tightened on her shoulder—not enough to hurt, but enough to garner her attention. She raised her head to where the Matron stood.

"Rest tonight. If you are to remain in Jubha Kyna, you will take your first man tomorrow. If you refuse, we can send you back where we found you, if you like."

N'th Adnine Re'a guided Ailyssa toward the door; her heart squeezed and ached as though it had been crushed in the old woman's fist.

At Jubha Kyna, was rescue truly a better fate than death?

Goddess help me.

X Trenan - Before the King

The portrait of Erral and Ishla stared at Trenan from where it hung beside the other kings and queens of the Windward kingdom. His gaze lingered on it for a moment, but he soon turned away. He hated the glimmer of sadness the artist had captured in her eyes and often wondered if the sorrow was present when she posed, or if the portrait master added it.

If it was there, was it because of me?

The painting had hung in the reception chamber for more than twenty turns of the seasons—since not long after the king and queen married. Not long after Trenan lost his arm.

Not long after...

He shook his head and rested his hand on the hilt of his dagger hanging at his hip. The eyes in the painting possessed the same ability to penetrate his soul as did the very ones they modeled. And now here he stood with no news of Teryk, and Danya wandered off on her own. Today, he'd have no doubt the fault for the sadness in her expression would belong to no one but him.

The door opened behind him and Trenan straightened but didn't turn. Weapons and armor rattled—Cellin and Dansil, the queen's guards, entering first—accompanied by the tap of boot heels on the stone floor. The reception chamber was far smaller than the hall, so it only took two breaths before the king and queen swept past him. Ishla took her seat, but the king remained standing, hands curled into fists set on his hips.

"What news?" Erral's voice boomed, even in the small room.

Trenan bowed his head before speaking. "I am regretful to report I have found no sign of the prince...alive or otherwise."

"And my daughter?" The king made a show of glancing around the room, though no possibility existed he'd have missed her had she been present.

"She left to carry on the quest upon which Teryk set out."

"Prince Teryk. Mind your place, swordmaster."

"Yes, Your Grace."

Trenan had known the king since before the Leeward kingdom offered Ishla in peace and he'd lost his arm saving Erral's life; the king only insisted his friend use titles in dire times.

And that, they are.

The master swordsman glanced at the queen, who stared back at him with a stern countenance he understood she wore to hold back her tears. Her children were gone and he'd disappointed her.

The king crossed his arms and tilted his head forward, glaring down his nose at Trenan.

"How could this happen?" he growled. "How did my

children leave Draekfarren, let alone the inner city? Were guards not assigned to them?"

"Yes, my king," Cellin said. "Rile to the prince and Gerton to the princess."

"And where are they now?"

Cellin cleared his throat. "In cells in Dreemskerry, as ordered, my King."

Trenan felt a prickle along the back of his neck. It didn't bode well for the two men if the king had them imprisoned. Likely if the prince and princess did not return alive and unharmed, they'd forfeit their lives. Maybe if they did, too.

"These two soldiers should not shoulder the blame," Trenan interjected. "I have spent much time with the prince and princess. I realized their obsession with the scroll and should have been more aware."

"Don't worry, swordmaster. They will not accept the blame alone." The king gestured at him with his chin. "Were it not for your missing arm, you'd be keeping them company."

Trenan's teeth clenched and his lips pursed. Erral knew exactly what to say to provoke a reaction in one of his oldest friends.

"Enough bluster." Ishla sat forward on the edge of her decorative chair, one strand of hair falling out of the bun pulled tight at the back of her head. "What of my children?"

She glanced from Trenan to the king, both of them returning her gaze. For an instant, the master swordsman thought the king might reprimand her for speaking out of turn, as he had done in the past. Instead, he faced the master swordsman to continue their conversation.

"We do not know the prince is dead?"

Trenan held the queen's gaze an instant longer, trying to find a way to apologize to her without words before facing Erral again.

"Brigands claimed to have taken his life. They had Godsbane." He touched the sword's gold pommel, having forgotten it still hung at his side until mention of it. "But I have found no other sign of him."

"The prince must be found, no matter what state he's in."

"And Danya?" Ishla said.

"Be quiet, woman. The heir to the throne takes priority."

Trenan's gaze flickered to the queen, who glared at the king. Her mouth opened as though she meant to say more but, when she noticed Trenan looking at her, she thought better of it. She pressed her lips together and her expression no longer matched the sad mien on the portrait, but took on an aspect of anger.

"You will take Dansil and two others," the king continued. "Search the outer city. Find the prince, but be discreet."

"My liege, if you give me at least a squad, we will locate the prince more quickly, and then we can search for the princess, too."

The king's head swung side to side. "Conditions in the outer city are...tenuous. A larger armed force barreling through the streets might tip the scales in a direction I prefer it not be tipped. Four of you will be enough."

"But Erral—"

"I am your king," Erral roared in response. "Do as you are told, swordmaster. And come back with the throne's heir or that sacrificial arm will not keep you from seeing the inside of Dreemskerry."

The king stormed out of the room, brushing Trenan with his shoulder on the way by and forcing Cellin and Dansil to step aside for him to pass. The master swordsman swallowed and looked at the queen perched on the edge of her seat. The expression she wore hurt him far worse than anything that might be done to him in Dreemskerry prison.

Ishla stood as though it took great effort to lift her weight from the seat and padded across the floor to stand in front of Trenan. She stared straight ahead at his chest instead of raising her gaze to meet his.

"Bring back my children, Trenan," she said too quietly for the guards still in the room to hear. "Please."

She swept past, careful not to touch the master swordsman. Trenan's fingers twitched, aching to reach out and grasp her wrist, pull her back to him and hold her. He wanted to caress her hair, tell her it would be all right, but not with Cellin and Dansil present, and he doubted she'd let him if they weren't.

Sometimes he hated himself for falling in love with a woman he could never have.

He listened to her dress swishing around her legs as she left and remained a moment before he turned to find Dansil waiting by the door, one corner of his mouth tilted up in a cock-eyed smile.

"You and me, eh, swordsman?"

Trenan frowned and walked out of the room, leaving the big guard to follow.

***

They went out through Merchant's Gate, the flow of wagon and foot traffic thin at midday compared to other times of the day. Trenan led the way, followed by Osis—a sergeant of similar age to Trenan whom he'd chosen to accompany them—and then Dansil and Strylor—a young swordsman who Dansil had insisted would be handy in their search because he'd been born in the outer city and was familiar with its tangled avenues.

They passed through the barracks area housing the king's army, Trenan with his gaze focused straight ahead as they went. Soldiers watched them, brows raised or scowls upon their faces as they wondered what might prompt the king's swordmaster to visit the outer city twice in two days. He didn't explain and had told the others to stay quiet.

They reached an intersection at the end of the army's section and the beginning of the city proper and stopped.

"Where'd it happen?" Dansil said stepping up beside Trenan as if he intended to take charge.

Trenan waved his hand between sunrise and leeward. "I found the brigands at a tavern, but it's hard to say where they came upon him."

"Well that's where we'll start then, ain't it?"

Dansil took a confident stride forward, the axe strapped to his back bouncing with his gait, but Trenan caught him by the arm, stopping him.

"I've looked there. We'll start closer to here in case he tried to make his way back. We have to assume he is gravely injured."

Dansil frowned and stretched his neck to peer back at Strylor.

"Whatcha think, Stry?"

The young man shrugged. "Whatever. Could've got anywhere, I guess."

"Strylor don't care, you thinks here and I thinks there. S'pose it's up to the sarge here to break the tie."

Trenan gritted his teeth against the heat boiling into his cheeks. The moment Erral ordered him to take Dansil with him, the master swordsman knew trouble would follow. Here they were, one step into the outer city, and the idiot thought they should vote what to do.

"We are not taking a poll, Dansil," Trenan said through his teeth.

The burly man glared at Trenan, then turned his head toward the sergeant.

"What's yer vote, Osis?"

The sergeant shook his head. "No vote. If Trenan

says we search here, then we search here."

The master swordsman's thumb hooked into his sword belt, fingers poised to move for his weapon. Dansil dragged his gaze back from Osis to Trenan, the sour expression still painting his brow.

"All right, then. Vote says we search here." Dansil strode into the street, headed for the nearest building, Strylor following close behind.

Osis stepped up beside Trenan and waited for his word.

"Do me a favor, Osis," Trenan said staring after the other two men. "Don't let me kill him until we find the prince and princess."

XI Danya - The Mother of Death

A weighty hush of death hung in the air, the woman's small and rasping breath the only thing disturbing it. Danya wondered, if the old woman were to pass, would the chamber become her tomb? Around her, she sensed the masked girls, but none of them moved and she couldn't remove her gaze from the Mother of Death.

Small red veins snaked across the woman's nose and pallid cheeks; three short hairs grew from a dark patch on her skin near her ear. The princess couldn't imagine how many times this Mother might have seen the seasons turn. Danya leaned toward the masked girl who'd led her to the temple.

"Is this the barren Mother?"

The old woman's eyelids slid open as though the princess had spoken magic words meant to rouse her from her sleep. The clouded eyes beneath, gray with age, moved unerringly to find Danya's. When her gaze fell upon the princess, she drew a heavy breath in through her vein-covered nose and released it slowly. Her colorless lips parted in the middle, the corners remaining closed as though stuck together.

"I am not the Mother you seek, lass."

The woman's voice was no more than the sound of wind through dry grass, yet her words were clear. Danya's heart sank.

They brought me here for nothing.

"Not for nothing, princess—you're the one for whom we've searched."

A chill crawled along the surface of Danya's skin. What form of evil allowed this old woman to know her thoughts? And why had they been searching for her?

The Mother of Death's mouth curled ever so slightly at the corners, as though she intended a smile. Danya blinked once and it disappeared.

"Why have you brought me here?" she demanded.

Her voice—too loud for the quiet room—bounced from wall to wall. The masked girl at her side laid a hand on the princess' arm and leaned close to her ear.

"Sshh."

Danya shot the girl an angered look, then returned her gaze to the so-called Mother of Death. The old woman's eyes had slipped shut again, as though they weighed more than a woman of her age could manage to hold open for too long.

"A barren Mother, the seed of life." The words floated up from the woman's barely moving lips. "Do you understand what they speak of, princess?"

Before she thought about what she was doing, Danya responded by shaking her head. When she realized her mistake, she parted her lips, but the old woman interrupted.

"These are important words; words that may decide the fate of the world."

The icy feeling crept across her flesh again; the

princess stared at the woman's wizened face.

"You were right in coming here." The Mother of Death opened her cloudy eyes. "The barren Mother serves the Goddess, but she is not here. She is lost."

Danya shook her head, unable to accept that the woman knew of her quest. Did she know about Teryk's death, too?

"Your brother is not dead."

Mouth agape, Danya faltered back a step. The masked girl who'd escorted her grasped her arm to steady her. The room spun around the princess as though she'd been drawn into the swirl of a whirlpool; her stomach lurched and her breath fled. A gray fog crept into the edges of her vision and she reached out to support herself on the masked girl. Bent at the waist, she gasped for air, struggling to fill her lungs and come to terms with the words the old woman had spoken.

If he's alive, then I left him behind.

The thought echoed through her head like the toll of a death bell. It might have overcome her if she let it, but she clung to one word to find her center again: *alive.*

The vertigo passed and Danya straightened again, released her grip on the masked girl, though the girl's remained. She used her sleeve to wipe a chilling sweat from her brow and stepped back to the side of the bed to gaze upon the old woman.

"The brigand who stole Godsbane said they killed him. How could he be alive? How do you know?"

The Mother of Death didn't respond. Her murky eyes remained fixed on the ceiling above as though seeing visions in the grain of the wooden beams. Danya waited, her breath made small and quiet lest the woman spoke, but she didn't.

"I have to find him."

"No." A skeletal hand darted out from beneath the blankets to grasp her wrist, the skin stretched thin, the veins beneath prominent and blue. It was cold. "He has his own path, and is not meant to follow yours. Finding him would divert both of you. All would be lost."

"I don't understand." Danya shook her head, looked at the woman's long and knobbed fingers. "The scroll speaks of the firstborn child of the rightful king. If Teryk lives, there's no part for me to play but to support him."

"There's much you don't grasp."

The room fell into silence, save for the rattle of the woman's breath in her chest. The light of twelve candles flickered across her sallow cheeks sending tiny shadows dancing in her deep wrinkles. Danya stared, waiting for her to say more, to say something other than vague riddles meant to frustrate her. Enough time passed that the princess thought the old woman might have slipped into slumber, but still no one moved. Eventually, she spoke again.

"Searching for the barren Mother is the right path, princess. Your task is to find her. We will help."

"But how? You said she is lost."

"You were chosen for this for a reason."

The old woman's breath hitched in her throat. She gasped and coughed, spraying spittle across her chin. One of the masked girls kneeling near the curved wall shifted, handing her taper to one beside her, then stood. She drew a cloth from her sleeve, hurried to the bedside, and wiped the Mother of Death's chin before returning to her place and taking back her candle. Danya watched in disbelief—would the king be treated this well were he so ancient?

"What reason?" the princess asked when the old woman again seemed as though she'd volunteer no more information.

"Your gift."

Danya narrowed her eyes. "What are you talking about? I have no gift."

"No? What did you see while standing on the bridge and peering into the river?"

The princess' throat clogged and dizziness threatened to return, but she concentrated on the woman's frigid grip on her wrist to keep herself grounded. She'd put the hallucination from her mind, dismissing it as caused by the grief of losing her brother. Her lips parted to say what she saw was merely that, but again the Mother of Death spoke before her.

"It was no hallucination, princess, but a vision. If the evil already in motion isn't stopped, the river will run red as it did the night the Goddess banished the Small Gods, but this time with the blood of man."

Danya swallowed hard, remembrance of a disembodied head floating past on the river's current, dead eyes staring at her, then rolling away only to stare at her again. Then she remembered the body of a child.

"A vision?" she whispered.

"Your gift. It is what allowed you to read the scroll. The Goddess has blessed you, but with it comes responsibility."

The princess raised her gaze to the old woman's face and saw her head had shifted, her milky eyes fixed on Danya's. She didn't know if the Mother of Death saw her through those carapaced orbs, but it felt to her as though she did.

"Will you accept the blessed responsibility the Goddess has honored you with, Princess Danya?"

Danya continued to stare, her breathing shallow as her mind turned from the vision in the river to her brother. If he had a role to play and she didn't fulfill hers, what would happen to him? Would he survive? Would he save the kingdom from the return of the Small Gods? She waited for the Mother of Death to hear her thoughts and respond, comfort her, but silence engulfed the room. Its heaviness weighed on Danya like a mail shirt crushing her chest. When it became too much to bear, she nodded and whispered:

"Yes."

The corners of the old woman's lips twitched like she wanted to smile but no longer possessed the ability to do so. Her grip on the princess' wrist tightened, squeezing it in thanks, and then she released it and drew her twisted hand back beneath the blankets. A long exhalation sighed out of her chest.

"Make her ready for her journey, Evalal. You will accompany the princess."

"Yes, Mother," the masked girl who'd brought Danya to the temple responded.

She pulled on the princess' arm to guide her away from the bed and toward the door, but Danya hesitated, her head spinning with everything that had happened. Despite Teryk's faith, she'd continued to wonder if they should give any credence to the words written on the scroll. After all, they did not name Teryk or their father, nor the age in which its prophecy might transpire. She'd thought to continue what her brother started to honor his memory, not because she thought it might be real.

And now it is.

She was unable to remove her gaze from the old woman. The girl pulled more insistently and the princess finally allowed herself to be drawn away. Her stomach ached with shock and excitement, sweat moistened her palms. When they reached the door and the girl stopped to open it, Danya turned back toward the old woman.

"Why are you called the Mother of Death?"

No one moved or spoke and Danya wondered if the old woman had heard. Perhaps she'd fallen asleep, but after a few heartbeats, the same gaunt hand with which she'd gripped Danya's wrist slipped from under the blankets and one bony finger gestured. A masked girl kneeling by the wall passed off her taper and stood, went to the bed. Danya watched the girl grasp the blankets near the old woman's chin and pull them down, exposing the Mother of Death.

Naked beneath the covers, the flesh on her arms and legs hung loose from the bone. Her emaciated breasts sagged beside her chest and blue veins showed through skin as brittle as antiquated paper. The hallmarks of age, but the woman's protruding belly snatched Danya's attention and made her mouth drop open. Fly wing-thin skin stretched tight over her abdomen and the princess saw a hint of movement beneath.

The Mother of Death—the woman more ancient than Danya might imagine—was pregnant.

XII Teryk - Healer

An uncomfortable sensation tingled along Bieta's flesh, raising the hair on the back of her neck. She rubbed the heel of her palm against the smooth, pink flesh where once she'd had an eye, glanced toward the lad with the one she still possessed. His features held a familiarity, she had to admit, one she didn't notice until searching for it.

"Couldn't be," she said, breaking the heavy silence in the small room. "Not even a low-level noble'd be traipsing around the outer city. You're making this shite up."

Enin shook his head. "Ask yourself this, Bieta: why would a merchant speak the name of the princess?"

"Why does anyone speak anyone else's name?"

"Because they know them," Enin insisted. "When did you last utter the words 'Princess Danya'?"

She shrugged. "Not sure I have."

"Exactly."

"Doesn't mean no one else does. Could be he sold goods to her. Or she commissioned him to make a necklace and it's weighing on his mind that he ain't delivered it yet. Guilt's got him for lying around doing nothing other than bleeding instead of getting to the task at hand."

"Judging by the state he's in, I don't think he's too worried about work." The horse doctor scratched his sharp jaw. "No, he called out for someone he knows. His sister."

Bieta wiped damp palms on the front of her smock, her mind racing through possibilities. If the lad was a merchant, they could get a few gold for him in ransom—up to a hundred, she figured, depending on which family he belonged to and what he sold. But if he truly was the prince, the amount might be thousands...tens of thousands.

Enin took a step away, skirting the table. Bieta fixed her gaze on him, squinted her one eye.

"Where d'you think you're going?"

"I don't want any part of this," the horse doctor said before taking another step back. "This can't be anything but bad."

"Stirk," Bieta said over her shoulder, and her son was up and reaching for Enin in an instant.

The horse doctor made a break for the door, but Stirk snagged him by one sleeve, pulled him to a stop. The expression on Enin's face suggested he was considering to pull away, but the shorter man's greater bulk convinced him not to bother.

"You want me to kill him, Ma?"

They fell quiet for a handful of heartbeats, the injured lad's labored breathing the only sound as the horse doctor's gaze flickered from Stirk holding his arm to Bieta. Enin's lower lip quivered; Bieta rubbed her gums briskly with the tip of her tongue.

"You can't," Enin said finally.

Stirk yanked on the sleeve of his shirt, making the taller man stumble, but he didn't fall.

"Course I can," Stirk said, eyeing the tall, skinny man. "I'd break you in two like a twig."

"That's not what I mean." He nodded toward the injured man. "He's going to die."

Bieta stepped forward, rested her hand on Stirk's arm. Her son didn't release the other man, but he didn't rip any of his limbs off, either.

"What are you talking about? You sewed him up and put that gunk on him. Ain't that going to fix him up?"

"It'll stop the bleeding and heal his wound on the outside, but he's bleeding inside, too. If it keeps up, he'll die."

Bieta leaned closer to him, pressed her teeth tight together. "Well, fix him, then."

"I can't. The insides of a person and the insides of a horse aren't the same."

"Then you ain't no use to us," Bieta said. She glanced at her son. "Kill him."

A smile stole across Stirk's lips and he raised his hand, fingers curled into a fist. He cocked his arm back.

"I can get you a healer," Enin cried before Stirk swung his blow.

The stocky man hesitated, tilted his uncertain gaze toward his mother. Bieta jammed the heel of her hand into her eye socket again, its movement synchronized with her tongue darting through the space between her teeth.

"Why didn't you say so before?" She gestured at Stirk with her chin and he lowered his fist but didn't release his hold on the horse doctor's sleeve.

The fear etched into the lines on Enin's face dissipated and his expression morphed into a smirk. Bieta didn't appreciate this new look; it brought a shiver to her spine.

"I didn't realize how much he might be worth until I saw it was Prince Teryk," he said, his words measured. "Half that sort of ransom might set a man up for life. Two lifetimes, perhaps."

Bieta's brow creased, making the shiny scar on her eye tighten uncomfortably. "What do you mean?"

He shrugged. "I don't imagine you're planning to walk him back to the Inner City gates and hand him over, otherwise you'd have done it already. That means you see him as a money-making venture. You're a shrewd businesswoman, Bieta."

A tickle of pride at the horse doctor's words made the corner of her mouth twitch, but she kept it from breaking out into a smile. Better men than he had done their best to charm her and failed.

"Maybe I am, maybe I ain't. Either way, it's got nothing to do with you."

Enin raised one brow. "Except I'm the only one besides you and your oxen son who knows he's here. Am I right?"

"Stirk." Bieta frowned and nodded. Her son raised his fist again, but Enin didn't so much as flinch at the threat.

"He's going to expire without help. Then he's worth nothing but the trouble of disposing of the corpse."

"The river ain't so far away," Stirk growled.

"Shut up, Stirk," Bieta said.

Her son's threatening expression drooped while Enin's smirk remained. Bieta regarded him for a moment, resisting the urge to scratch her eye. She tapped her foot and crossed her arms in front of her chest.

"What is it you're suggesting?"

"I'll get you a healer to make sure he lives long enough to get your ransom."

Enin paused, looked at the injured lad. Bieta followed his gaze, saw the sweat dampening his brow, the sickly hue of his pale skin.

"And?"

"In return, you'll give me half the gold."

"Half?" Bieta barked. "Half? You're already getting this." She waved both her hands along her body.

Enin shook his head. "You can keep your wares. I can buy all I need with my share of the ransom."

Bieta pursed her lips, biting back an angry retort. The horse doc never minded her wares the times she put his too-small-for-his-body man thing through the space between her teeth. But with so much gold at stake this was no time for pride.

She glared at him, waiting for a sign that he'd relent in his demand. In the time she'd spent collecting coin in exchange for her favor, she'd gotten a good deal of practice at negotiating. No one wanted to pay what you asked, so you always asked for more than you wanted, and they'd always offer less.

"We'll split it four ways: one for you, one for Stirk, and two for me for thinking up the plan."

"Only one for me?" Stirk said. "But I lugged him here."

"And you'll likely have to lug him again. Just shut up."

Stirk gazed at his feet.

"Give me a third and you two can fight over splitting the rest," Enin said. "For that, I'll bring the healer and my lips are sealed on the matter forever."

She crooked a brow. "Why should I trust you?"

"The same reason I can trust you...there's a lot of gold to be had."

Bieta put her thumb in her mouth to rub the flesh between her teeth, but the sour taste of dirt and sweat made her take it out again. She peered at the lad, disappointment churning in her belly, but the truth of it was, two shares of a mess of gold was more than the whole pot of a little gold. Or none, if he died.

"All right," she said, nodding to Stirk to release the horse doc's sleeve. "You've got yourself a deal."

"I'll get the healer right away." Enin smoothed the wrinkles from his sleeve where Stirk's fingers had bunched it. He took two steps toward the door.

"Hang on," Bieta called after him, his hand halfway reached out to open it. "Stirk'll be going with you to make sure you don't come back with a squad of See-Gees instead."

"As you like." He dipped his head in a mock bow. "But I don't think the reward they'll offer is near as much as the ransom we'll get."

"No matter. I can only trust you when I can see you, and Stirk here is my other eye."

Stirk glared at him, but Enin only nodded again and pulled the door open a crack. He peeked out, saw no one in the alley, and went out, Stirk hard on his heels. The door closed again, throwing Bieta back into the relative darkness of the flickering taper. She crouched beside the lad, dabbed his forehead with the cloth still wet with his sweat.

"Prince Teryk," she cooed. "A pleasure to meet you, m'lord."

***

Darkness. Heat. A bolt of pain.

Teryk's throat wanted to cry out in agony, but he had no control over the actions of any part of his body. He felt himself twitch and jerk, shiver and quake. A ringing in his ears led to a pounding in his head. His blood scraped through his veins as though loaded with shards of steel swept up from the blacksmith's floor and emptied into his heart.

Sounds came to him through the ringing, voices he didn't recognize speaking words he didn't understand. He longed to answer them, to communicate, to beg for relief, but had no voice of his own. He trembled and occasionally moaned, the sound coming from his throat surprising him whenever it did.

After a time that might have been very long, the thunderous torment gripping him eased, the roar in his ears lessened to a hum, the hammering in his skull became a pulse. The shivering and trembling and shaking ceased, leaving him with the sensation of floating atop the pain, its waves licking at him like he was a boat and it was the sea.

The sea. The man from across the sea.

The thought came to him from out of nowhere—words he suspected he should recognize but didn't understand why. He focused on it, using it to distract him from the sensations in his body, and other words materialized, none of them making any more sense than the first.

Barren Mother.

Small Gods.

Darken'd wings.

First born child of the rightful king.

The last words sparked regret in his chest, a feeling of a task he was meant to carry out but remained undone. He didn't know what.

What child? What king?

The thoughts were the first of his own, made by him with purpose and meaning, unlike the words that appeared in his mind. Hazy images followed them: a scrap of blue paper, an ornamented sword, the face of a young woman.

Danya.

The name, the face. Warmth filled the prince's chest, spilled along his limbs. It comforted him, soothed his pains, eased the tension filling his body. Breath flowed more readily in and out of his chest. Danya's face drifted in his mind, smiling and laughing, taunting him to go for a swim. He saw himself jumping in the river, experienced the jolt of cold water on his skin, and the shock of it brought everything back to him.

The scroll. The prophecy.

If he'd had the ability to sit up or to cry out, he'd have done so but, though his mind was coming back to him, his body remained rogue. He concentrated on his limbs, but to no avail. His mouth refused to move; even fluttering his eyelids proved too much.

I have to find Danya. I have to tell her.

The thought came to him without understanding of what he needed to tell her. He abandoned his attempts at moving, focusing instead on the one thought.

What am I supposed to tell her?

Pain jarred him again, more intense than before, and the thought fled his mind, chased away by overpowering darkness.

***

Bieta watched the robed figure lay hands on the injured lad, wondering less about the ritual performed than whether the healer be man or woman. Silky hair flowed past narrow shoulders. Delicate features and high cheekbones showed not a hint of whiskers. Yet an energy surrounded the healer that made Bieta suspect a cock and balls dangled behind the robe.

"What payment will the healer expect?" she asked leaning toward Enin. Stirk stood by the far wall, facing away from the healer, eyes closed. "I don't want to give up more of the gold we'll get for him."

The horse doctor bent closer to Bieta, spoke in lowered tones. "The healer has no interest in gold."

She nodded, understanding his meaning. The payment she'd intended to give the horse doctor for stitching up the lad would be transferred to the healer, then Bieta would find out for certain if the robe hid the parts of a man or a woman. Didn't matter to her—she'd make payment either way.

The prince's body jerked under the healer's hands and Bieta gasped, startled by the sudden movement. His body remained tensed for longer than seemed possible, then the robed figure stood, breaking the connection with the prince. His back remained arched for two beats of Bieta's heart, then finally relaxed, settling back onto the pile of dirty straw. The healer stood gazing at the lad for a few breaths, then faced Bieta.

No one spoke. Stirk remained facing the wall and Bieta thought Enin might be holding his breath beside her. The healer's glimmering eyes held her attention as they regarded her expectantly.

"Done?" Bieta asked.

The healer nodded once.

"And he'll live?"

The healer nodded one more time.

"He's my nephew," Bieta lied. "My sister'd hate me if she found out what happened."

The healer's expression remained unchanged; his placid but intense gaze didn't move from the woman's face.

"Time for payment, I suppose."

No response.

Bieta crossed the short space between her and the healer and sank to her knees. She drew a deep breath, readying herself, and wondered which set of parts she'd find beneath the robe.

"Bieta," Enin said behind her, but she ignored him.

Her tongue rubbing back and forth on the skin between her teeth as though preparing it, Bieta reached out and grasped the front of the healer's robe.

"Bieta."

She waved her hand, signaling for the horse doctor to keep his comments to himself, and gripped the front again. The healer didn't move or react in any way, so she figured she'd made the correct assumption about the payment due. She parted the robe and gasped.

The flesh between the healer's legs was a puckered, pink scar, similar to Bieta's eye. The woman stared, surprised and sickened, but found it impossible to tear her gaze away. No hair grew through the shiny skin, and nothing left behind indicated whether the original equipment had been a man's or a woman's. The cauterization that had kept the healer from bleeding to death rendered the spot where his or her legs met unrecognizable but for a tiny hole left through which to piss.

Bieta finally dragged her eyes away and found the healer smiling at her.

"The healer has no interest in your sort of payment," Enin said.

Bieta let go of the edges of the robe, allowing them to fall back into place and hiding the hideous scar. As she stood and took a step back from the healer, she imagined she detected the scent of burnt flesh.

"What are you?" she whispered.

"It matters not," the healer said in a voice neither male nor female, possibly either. "The requested healing is done and payment is due."

Bieta's lips moved, opening and closing a few times, but no sound came out. Her tongue worked furiously between her teeth.

"What payment do you require?" Enin asked on her behalf.

In response, the healer raised one arm, extended one finger. Bieta followed it, found it pointing at Stirk standing with his eyes closed and his nose almost touching the wall.

"You want my son?"

"Not all of him," the healer replied. "One part."

Bieta looked at her son's back and shuddered.

XIII Danya - The Garden

The hallway's turns and switchbacks twisted Danya's sense of direction, making her feel she'd be hopelessly lost without Evalal's sure steps leading her. They climbed steps, descended flights of stairs, turned corners, went through doors and seemed to walk a great distance, though the building hadn't appeared so large on the outside. When the princess realized they'd passed no windows, she guessed they must be traversing an underground labyrinth. She might have been concerned about their destination if what she'd seen didn't consume her thoughts.

How can it be?

She had no doubt the woman had been with child—she'd seen tiny movement within her distended belly—but she was far beyond her childbearing seasons. The wrinkles on her face, the gauntness of her limbs, the wisps of gray hair, all suggested age greater than anyone Danya knew. If she was as ancient as she appeared, could this be a blessing from the Goddess, as the masked girls believed?

"How old is the Mother of Death?" the princess asked as they descended another set of stairs.

"No one knows for sure. Even she has forgotten." Evalal stopped before a wide door, hand poised on the ring. "I've been told she's been here more than fifty turns, and she was beyond the seasons of honoring the Goddess when she arrived."

"Where did she come from?"

"I don't know."

Danya swallowed hard as Evalal pushed the door open a crack. She put her hand on the masked girl's arm to stop her and asked the question burning in her mind.

"What happens to her children?"

The girl faced her, eyes peering through the wooden mask's holes alight with the tapers' reflected light. When she spoke, she did so in hushed tones.

"All are born dead. They go to the market to fund the temple."

She pushed the door open without waiting for Danya to reply and stepped through, leaving the princess on the threshold, mouth open and a sickened feeling throbbing in her gut. She stared at the back of the girl's head before movement in the room jarred her attention away.

Beds stacked three high lined one wall of the massive room, ladders leaning against the sides to allow access to the higher bunks. Near the other wall sat a line of long tables, plain wooden chairs tucked under them on both sides. Women in robes—some of them young girls in masks and drab green like Evalal, others bare-faced women clothed in a variety of subdued colors—went about their tasks.

Some sewed garments while others repaired chairs, painted masks, peeled potatoes, or partook of a multitude of other chores. At a glance, Danya counted at least sixty people in the room—the first they'd seen since leaving the Mother of Death.

"Is this where we're going?" the princess asked, finally stepping into the room.

"No. Come."

Evalal set out toward the far side of the room, Danya following close behind but watching the other women. Each one of them raised their heads as they passed, made brief eye contact with Danya, then lowered their gazes. Every masked girl and woman in the room repeated the strange ritual.

It took more than a hundred steps to cross the room and, when they reached the far door, Danya stopped and peered back, seeing the room itself for the first time.

Skylights overhead let in columns of pale sunshine. A few handspans below the level of the ceiling, intricate figures and scenes were carved into the stone wall, but they were too high for Danya to make them out. Now that the eyes of the women weren't upon her, she sensed a familiarity about the room, but couldn't place why. Before she had the opportunity to consider it further, Evalal tugged on her sleeve.

Beyond the door a set of stairs led upward, and the masked girl mounted them without waiting for Danya. The princess glanced back once more to see the girls and women return to their work, sewing and painting and chatting as though no one had interrupted them.

So many strange things here.

She hurriedly ascended the stairs to catch up to the girl, though the narrowness of the steps forced her to walk behind when she did. At the top, they stopped before another door different from all the others. It was fashioned of burnished bronze with the clear image of a woman's face set upon it. Evalal paused before opening it, taking a moment to bow her head and run her fingertips lightly over the forehead and cheeks of the image. Danya wondered if she'd be expected to do the same.

The answer came when Evalal leaned against the door with her shoulder, using her weight to push it wide. The hinges moved smoothly and silently, as though well-kept, and they entered a room filled with the light of the sun.

It streamed in through a wide opening in the far wall that led out onto a balcony. Danya wondered what lay beyond and suppressed the urge to rush over and see in favor of surveying her new surroundings.

The room was outfitted simply but well—a comfortable-looking bed with a mattress, a dresser, and a thin carpet covering most of the floor. Carvings similar to those in the large hall ringed the room below the ceiling and the princess determined to take a closer look at them later. Evalal started toward the balcony and Danya followed eagerly.

Despite the time she thought had passed as they traversed the complicated labyrinth of the temple, the midday sun perched directly overhead. Danya raised a hand to shield her eyes as they stepped out onto the balcony. She leaned against the stone rail and peered over.

The height of five tall men below lay a courtyard enclosed by walls, but not like the flower-gardened courtyards the princess was accustomed to strolling through in Draekfarren. Instead of trees and paths, flowers and shrubs, a mound of dark, moist earth sat in the center of this yard, surrounded by jagged rocks. Danya squinted, wondering why anyone would create such a bleak place.

"What is this?" she asked, facing the masked girl.

Evalal said nothing for a moment, but stared at the patch of dirt where one might expect a garden to grow. Her painted mask smiled, as it always did.

"This is why the Goddess brought you." She raised a hand and extended a finger. "Beneath that earth lies the seed of life."

XIV Ailyssa - First Visitor

A baby's mewling drifted down from the third floor where the Sisters kept their rooms. Ailyssa tilted her head, the strained cry squeezing her heart. The temple at Olvana was one single, sprawling level, with the nursing quarters away from the Sisters' chambers, the coupling rooms separated from both. Rarely did one hear the sounds of another.

At Jubha Kyna, the first floor housed the reception area and lounge, the dining room and kitchens. The second level's rooms were dedicated to coupling, the third to the Sisters' chambers, and the fourth to the Goddess. In one of the chambers on the second floor, Ailyssa perched on the edge of an over-stuffed mattress, the palms of her hands damp with perspiration as she waited.

When she met N'th Adnine Re'a, the Grand Matron had told her to take the day and night to rest and recuperate. The time passed with little of either. Exhaustion and worry weighed on Ailyssa's limbs, crushing the elation she should have felt at the reinstatement of her titles. What good were titles when forced to lay with a man with no chance of conceiving a daughter in honor of the Goddess?

Ailyssa curled her toes in the deep pile of the carpet beneath her feet. Another time, she might have marveled at its softness and guessed it worth a fortune; perhaps she'd have stripped off her smock and relished its caress against her bare skin. Today, it held the texture of coarse sand grating against her soles. The thickness of the mattress disappeared in her roiling emotions, as did the pleasing aromas of the scented oils N'th Creidra had rubbed on her back to encourage relaxation.

The word struck her as black humor. Relaxation. When did she last have the luxury of relaxing?

The last time I bled.

Ailyssa breathed a heavy inhalation and blinked for the thousandth time trying to clear the white fog from her vision. Like all the times before, it didn't disperse. The haze hung before her as it had since she opened her eyes, smearing her world into a colorless cloud without movement or shape. Perhaps it was better this way. If they meant her to couple for a more nefarious purpose than bringing forth a Daughter to honor the Goddess, it might be best she didn't have to gaze upon him.

What will it be like coupling with a man because he wants to, not because it's his duty?

A knife edge of nausea creased Ailyssa's gut. Lust and desire were things beyond the reckoning of a true devotee of the Goddess, yet here a temple full of Daughters, Mothers, and Matrons succumbed to the basest longing of the flesh to carpet the floor with thick pile and stuff the mattresses with goose down. The unease rose into Ailyssa's throat, and she swallowed it to keep down the food they'd brought to break her fast.

The babe's crying stopped—likely someone put a nipple in her mouth. Ailyssa closed her eyes that could not see and remembered nursing Claris, the euphoric sense of peace that began at the top of her head and cascaded over her as the babe suckled.

So many seasons have turned.

Despite the passage of time, a remnant of that long-ago rapture fell across Ailyssa, easing the tension from her brow and loosening the knot in her gut. She inhaled again, this time catching the fragrances hidden beneath the incense, oils, and perfumes—the smells no man would recognize: breast milk, the scent of a baby's hair, the essence emitted only by a new Mother.

The door handle rattled and Ailyssa's limbs tensed. She sat straight, her back rigid as a spear, her unseeing eyes staring ahead and away from the door. Hinges squeaked gently and feet scuffed in the deep carpet.

"N'th Ailyssa Ra? It is I, N'th Creidra."

She imagined the girl peeking out from behind the half-open door, a tentative smile on her lips. In Ailyssa's mind, her face belonged to Claris.

"Hello, N'th Creidra," she responded in clipped tones. Ailyssa admonished herself silently—Creidra shouldn't be blamed for any of this. She'd brought her here to rescue her, to give her back her life. The woman knew no other way of living besides that of the temple at Jubha Kyna; she couldn't have understood how it felt a death sentence to Ailyssa.

"You have a visitor."

"A visitor?"

Ailyssa's heart jumped with hope. Had N'th Adesi Re changed her mind and come for her? Maybe Claris learned of her presence and came to rescue her.

"Come in," Creidra said to someone other than Ailyssa.

The door creaked open wider and heavy footsteps carried another body into the room. From their sound, Ailyssa judged this person to be considerably larger than Creidra. An instant later, the musky odor of hard work wafted across the room and Ailyssa's hope sifted out of her like sand through a screen, leaving behind nuggets of fear.

"Allo." A man's voice rumbling deep in his chest.

Ailyssa nodded in response, though she doubted she'd done so anywhere close to the direction the man stood from her. Silence fell, the air filled with the cloying mixture of the man's sweat, the ginger oil on her back, and the scent of sandalwood incense. The concoction threatened to turn Ailyssa's stomach.

"Is she really blind?" the man whispered.

Ailyssa imagined him as taller than Creidra, hunching over toward her in a vain attempt to keep his question between them.

"Yes," Creidra confirmed.

"She can't see nothing?"

"I cannot see anything," Ailyssa said. "But I hear fine."

"Oh...ah...my apologies...hmm...miss. Just wanted to know what I was getting into."

The man giggled at his unintentional pun, his laugh higher pitched than Ailyssa might have expected from a man with a rumble for a voice.

"The bell is on the side table if you are in need, N'th Ailyssa Ra," Creidra said. "I will return when time is done."

Feet rustled in lush carpet, hinges murmured. A thought occurred to Ailyssa and she opened her mouth to ask a question, but the door clicking gently shut cut her off.

Where is the side table?

She pressed her lips together and sat with her hands clasped in her lap, the man's breath competing to be heard over the beat of her heart. Time crawled past and he didn't move. Ailyssa wriggled on the edge of the bed, the thick mattress uncomfortable as though she sat on a heap of pointed rock.

"This be my first time," the man said, finally breaking the silence. His boots scuffed in the carpet as he inched closer to the bed.

Ailyssa faced him and raised one brow, but said nothing.

"Not my *first* first time." He chuckled and Ailyssa imagined him bashful; glancing at his feet and shaking his head. "The first time here."

"It is also my first time." Ailyssa paused, swallowed. "Here."

Footsteps. The mattress shifted with his weight as he sat on the opposite side of the bed from her. The scent of his sweat intensified, other odors of life on a farm lingering beneath. Ailyssa suspected manure might be clogging the soles of his boots, maybe stray straws of hay poking out of his clothes and hair. He inhaled noisily and let the breath out the same way.

"I told them I didn't want no young girl," he said. "I wanted someone more mature."

Ailyssa bit her bottom lip, unsure how to respond.

"Didn't know they'd get me someone beautiful as you."

A lump crawled into Ailyssa's throat. She attempted to swallow it, but it proved stubborn. Did fear of what he might do to her cause it? Or was it because no man had ever called her beautiful?

He's a man. The Goddess says he is worthless.

His fingers brushed her back and she jumped, cowered away. The mattress jounced as he jerked back.

"I'm sorry. Did I hurt you?"

"No, I..." Her nerves jittered beneath her skin; blood rushed in her ears. "You startled me."

"Apologies. Can I come sit beside you?"

Ailyssa didn't think she had any choice but to agree. The man's weight lifted off the bed and she gripped the edge of the mattress, the muscles in her arms tightening into knots. His feet shuffled, carrying him around the end of the bed. A moment later, he sat to her left, his bulk pressing on the mattress and making her tilt slightly toward him.

"I'm going to touch you again."

Ailyssa swallowed and nodded.

His finger caressed her shoulder, trailed along the top of her arm to her elbow. It disappeared for a heartbeat, then reappeared on her ear, brushing it as though a butterfly flew too close to her lobe.

"So beautiful," he said again, leaning toward her.

His lips touched her neck, the coarse hairs of a week's worth of mustache and beard sandpapering her skin. She'd never been kissed by a man before, and it made her shudder, but her reaction didn't deter him. He drew his tongue along her exposed skin, up to the corner of her jaw. His breath smelled of mint leaves. Ailyssa clenched her jaw as he moved the neckline of her smock and nipped at the muscle leading to her shoulder. She endured without noise or comment.

The man's breath became short and hard. Teeth and lips and tongue made their way back and forth between her shoulder and her ear, a moan sounding in the back of his throat. His weight pushed more firmly on the bed, shifting her closer to him. Ailyssa held tight to the edge of the mattress. After a moment, his lips parted from her flesh with a wet smack and he leaned away.

"What's your name?" he asked, voice filled with breathy lust.

"Ailyssa."

"Well, Ay-lissa, it's your turn to put your hands on me. I didn't give up a perfectly good goat to see how your neck tastes."

Like any Mother, Ailyssa was no stranger to couplings. In fact, given her circumstances, she assumed she'd been subjected to the coupling ceremony more than most. Never had she touched a man to offer him pleasure in any way—the Goddess forbade it because men were not worthy of such treatment.

This is not Olvana.

She relinquished her grip on the edge of the bed and reached out with a tremorous hand, struggling to keep her fingers from shaking. The man held his breath, waiting as her hand hung in the air between them. Her mouth went dry and she licked her lips. He must have been watching her face because he moaned at the sight.

Ailyssa forced her hand onto a place where she expected to find the rough fabric of a farmer's breeches. Instead, her hand touched his bare thigh covered with a mat of thick hair. When he'd rounded the bed to sit beside her, he'd removed his clothes without her realizing. She jerked her hand away from his naked flesh, but he caught her by the wrist and returned her touch to his leg.

"That's right," he murmured, and she had the

impression he didn't truly mean the comment for her.

She fought against his insistence as he shifted her hand up his thigh, but his superior strength won out. The coarse fuzz grew thicker the higher he moved her touch until her fingernails caught in a forest of tangled hair.

"Yes," he breathed.

He moved her farther, her fingertips brushing his erect manhood. She jerked her hand open, stretching away and flattening her palm. The man said nothing, but grasped her fingers with his free hands, wrapped them around his shaft. Thick, short, and hard. The tangle of hair crawled up much of its length, dissipating before reaching the end.

Ailyssa gasped. Her hands had never touched a man in this manner. During coupling ceremonies, the man put his thing where it needed to be and nowhere else.

"Oh," the man groaned, moving her hand along his organ's meager shaft.

The lump in Ailyssa's throat grew larger, choking her with panic and threatening tears. She gasped shuddering breaths as the man worked her grip for her, stroking, caressing.

He let go and his hand found its way to her leg, under her smock. His fingers crawled up the inside of her thigh and she squirmed away, but he pushed her over onto the bed. In an instant, he'd climbed on top of her, his hardness pressing against her hip.

"I gave up a good goat for you," the man whispered too loudly into her ear. "You best be doing what you're supposed to."

He reached down with one hand, his fingers collecting the skirt of her smock, pulling it up. Ailyssa threw her free hand up over her head, reaching desperately for the bell on a side table she had no idea where to find.

XV Horace - Britches

Horace woke gradually, a dream's remnants clingin' 'round the edges—more a nightmare, really. He'd been dreamin' he were captain o' a ship sailin' away from the coast, leavin' the shore behind. Only it weren't his boat, but one what he'd stolen from the Water Kingdom. Instruments he'd never seen crowded the rails by the big wheel, all o' them made o' steel with scales inscribed on them in unrecognizable characters. Peerin' at them confused him, but he quickly forgot his bewilderment because he knew his ol' friend, the God o' the Deep, were lurkin' somewhere below the hull o' the stolen ship.

When his eyes opened facin' toward the darkened sky, the nausea o' seasickness he experienced in the dream the way he did in real life followed him into wakin'.

Fuck me dead. Can't get away from the sea no matter how hard I try.

He let his lids slide closed, thinkin' he'd aim for findin' himself more shut-eye what didn't involve water and waves and creakin' boards—and gods what shit hard-workin' sailors out on the shore. Near gettin' his wish, a gentle rustlin' made him open them up again. He peered at Thorn's face hangin' over him and did a startled jump, not rememberin' he were keepin' company with a gray man what came from the Green. When his heart's frantic pumpin' slowed, he resumed breathin'.

"Fuck me dead. You threw a scare into me."

Thorn responded by raisin' a finger, tellin' Horace to hush. The ol' sailor pressed his lips together, afraid if he didn't, words might slip out. His eyes darted, but he saw nothin'. He didn't hear any sounds, neither, 'cept the wind blowin' through the tree branches and his pulse poundin' in his ears.

He squirmed under Thorn's touch as the gray man looked away into the distance, an expression o' intense listenin' sittin' on his brow. His skin had returned to the same gray it'd been before he healed himself. Horace presumed this its proper, healthy color, though it'd've looked akin to death on any other man he knew. But this Thorn feller weren't a man, were he?

"What do you hear?" Horace asked, hissin' the words between his teeth.

Thorn blinked at him, a smile crinklin' up the corners o' his mouth and shinin' in his eyes.

"Breeches," he said.

Horace had barely enough time to raise a questionin' brow before the little gray feller took off into the woods. The ol' sailor pushed himself up on creakin' elbows and rubbed the sleep from his face with one hand, the specter o' his nightmarish dream hangin' o'er him the way too much ale drunk the night before has a habit o' doin'.

After climbin' to his feet and wipin' dirt and rottin' pine needles from the arse o' his britches—still on the damp side after a washin' in a convenient stream—he watched after Thorn, tryin' to see where he were goin'. Turned out easier'n expected as he'd stopped a few paces into the trees, waitin' not so patiently for Horace to drag himself after him.

"Come on," Thorn said, voice filled with excitement and arm wavin' Horace to follow.

"All right, all right," Horace grumbled and set out after him.

Crickets continued sawin' out their songs in the dark, but Horace caught a glimpse o' the horizon through the branches and leaves tellin' him sunrise weren't so far off. An owl sittin' on a branch somewhere high above his head *hoo-hooed*, but the ol' sailor paid it no attention. Thorn'd gotten on the move again and he didn't want to lose him amongst the trees and undergrowth.

"He hears breeches," Horace mumbled under his breath, his eyes watchin' the ground for roots and creepers what might want to snag his foot. "Prob'bly I broke wind in my sleep, is all. Likely reeked o' pig leg."

He chuckled to himself, the thought o' the tasty meat washin' saliva into his mouth. His belly growled.

Thorn stayed the length o' ten horses out front o' Horace, slowin' sometimes so he'd catch up, stoppin' others when he got too far ahead. Whenever he stopped to wait, he didn't really stop; he danced back and forth as though searchin' for a pair o' britches for him were the best adventure anyone might think to undertake. Horace didn't find pickin' his way through the woods in the dark quite so excitin'.

The horizon had brightened, though not enough to coax a rooster into crowin'—just shy o' sunrise—when Thorn halted and dropped into a crouch. Horace caught up and mimicked the pose.

"What—" the ol' sailor began, then cut himself short.

Ahead o' them, he spied a shack. Moss grew on its wood roof, so thick in places, one might've wondered if the moss were meant to be the roof. Shutters covered the windows and no lights shone through behind them. The place were either empty, or its residents didn't believe in gettin' themselves outta bed as early as the gray man.

Thorn raised his arm and extended a finger, so Horace obliged by lookin' where he pointed. Turned out to be a pair o' breeches hangin' from a rope strung between two trees.

"Fuck me dead," Horace murmured, eyes starin' in disbelief.

He gaped at Thorn and Thorn looked back at him,

wide mouth pullin' up in a smile what, were it talkin' might've said, "See? Told you so." Luckily, the smile didn't say anythin'.

The little gray feller jumped up and danced through the brush without so much as stirrin' a leaf. Horace considered followin', but didn't see no way through the tangle o' leaves and branches without causin' a ruckus, so he stayed put, content with watchin' Thorn cross the short clearin' to the clothesline. He snatched them pants offa the rope, spun 'round to face Horace, and held the pair o' britches up by the waist, triumphant and beamin' as the sun's leadin' edge peeked o'er the horizon.

A rooster crowed, just like it and the fiery orb'd got together in advance and planned it that way.

Horace jumped to his feet and waved his arms emphatically, callin' Thorn back to the forest. With the cock signalin' the dawn, it wouldn't be long before whoever were asleep inside the shack got themselves up and 'bout—and they'd likely be lookin' to put on their britches.

Thorn looked back o'er his shoulder, his action echoin' Horace's thought, then he pranced across the clearin', headed back toward the ol' sailor. He picked his way deftly through the brush again and came to a stop beside Horace, the wide, shit-eatin' grin still plastered across his kisser. His mouth opened to speak—prob'bly to boast, because that's what Horace'd've done were it him—but the former First Man grabbed him by the wrist and pulled him away.

They hadn't got too far when ol', rusty hinges signaled the openin' o' the shack's door, but enough trees and bushes separated them from the breeches' owner that the feller weren't gonna see them. They hurried away in silence but for the occasional giggle escapin' Thorn's lips.

The sun'd climbed a little ways into the sky by the

time they stopped, its rays shinin' through a mix o' branches and wispy dawn mist. The clearin' weren't the same one where they'd spent the night, but it resembled it. Breathin' heavy, Horace slumped onto a rock bigger'n his head, his legs tired from the jaunt through woods. Luckily, his broken rib weren't hurtin' him near as much as before.

Not near as much as before I met a Small God.

Thorn stood in front o' him holdin' the britches up by the waist. The wide, long things hid him near completely behind them, startin' at his head like they did. The frayed hems on the legs brushed the dirt.

"They ain't gonna fit you too well," Horace said between labored breaths.

The waistband drooped far enough for Thorn to peek o'er the top at his companion and shrug. Horace raised his brow—a habit he'd never possessed until this curious feller came into his life—as Thorn lowered the pants and stepped into them. The ol' sailor'd been doin' his best not to look, but now he had little choice, and he were glad to see no pine needles stuck to the gray man's trouser snake.

Thorn pulled the breeches up and buttoned them at his waist. Sure enough, they was big enough 'round his middle Thorn could've fit another o' his Small God friends in with him, and long enough for a second pair o' legs set end to end with his.

"Told you they wouldn't fit," Horace said, shakin' his head and feelin' satisfied at bein' right.

The little feller raised a finger, gesturin' for Horace to wait, then smiled and closed his eyes. The tendons in his neck went taut, a vein stood out on his forehead. His skin faded to a lighter shade o' gray and the air became palpable enough to make Horace shiver and glance 'round to be sure no one were creepin' up behind him. When he returned his gaze to Thorn, he gasped a surprised breath and nearly took a fall offa his rock.

The pants was shrinkin'. The waist, which Thorn gripped in one fist to keep the britches from fallin' down, drew in and the legs snaked their way back toward the gray man's feet. Shocked despite havin' seen how Thorn healed the hole the branch'd poked in his side, Horace got to his feet. He took two paces toward the spectacle, part o' him wantin' to touch the breeches and see if a pulse o' energy flowed through them, but the other part o' him were smart enough not to do somethin' he'd have to be simple as Dunal to've done.

A moment later, the britches fit perfect and Thorn opened his peepers. Horace stared, his mouth agape; the gray man spied Horace lookin' at him and smiled, but this one didn't glow like the last one—this one sagged wearily.

"How do you—," Horace began, but Thorn's knees wavered beneath him and the ol' sailor jumped forward, catchin' the gray man by the arm to keep him from hittin' the ground.

Thorn's skin were cold and covered in a sheen o' what Horace would've called sweat if his fingers grasped a man's arm and not that o' a Small God from outta the Green. The little feller's eyes slid back closed for an instant and he rested his hand on Horace's shoulder to steady himself.

"Are you all right?"

Thorn nodded with an effort. "Thorn needs to rest."

Horace gulped a mouthful o' spit what carried the now-familiar bitter tang o' fearfulness, then stepped in closer to put his arm 'round Thorn's waist. The gray man draped his over Horace, allowin' him to help him o'er to the rock seat. The ol' sailor lowered his unusual companion onto it and moved to take his arm away, but Thorn held on 'round his neck, refusin' to let go. Horace cranked his head toward him and their gazes met; fear-tastin' saliva flooded back into Horace's mouth.

"He is in good health," Thorn said.

Horace stared, his face creased up in a frown to hide the fact he were afraid o' what the gray man might do to him if he wanted. "Who's in good health? Thorn?"

The little feller shook his head, a portion o' the gleam returnin' to his eyes."

"Rilum," he said. "Rilum Seaman."

Horace's mouth dropped open like the muscles in his jaw had forgot how to keep it closed. Somewhere, rattlin' 'round in his head, he figured he should say somethin' in response, but only one thought occurred to him:

I didn't tell him 'bout my son.

"Horace hasn't heard from Rilum in a long time," Thorn said.

Horace's head moved minutely—not enough to deserve the title o' nod, but Thorn rightly took it as such and continued.

"He is fine. He thinks of you, too." The gray man looked at him intently; his eyes narrowed, one lid quiverin', then they opened again. "And he misses his mother."

A breeze rustled through the trees. Tiny feet scampered in the long grass. A cricket chirruped, a fly buzzed. The world kept makin' its sounds, carryin' on like ev'rythin' were normal, but silence nestled in between Horace and Thorn for a while. The ol' sailor's breath were so shallow, it didn't make a sound slidin' in and out between his lips.

"What happened to her?" Thorn asked finally, his voice soundin' loud even though he whispered.

Horace swallowed a lump too big to fit down his throat and started lookin' at his boots, head shakin' to let the gray man know it weren't no topic for discussion. Thorn understood and released his hold on the ol' sailor.

The little feller got to his feet.

"Thorn is sorry for bringing you sadness," he said.

"It's all right," Horace said. He cleared his throat, chokin' back the urge to tell Thorn ev'rythin', then stood. "You couldn't've known."

Horace wondered if that were true.

"At least your son..."

The ol' sailor nodded, hopin' doin' so'd put an end to the conversation before he couldn't stop himself tellin' the gray man 'bout his entire life. He didn't want to, but somethin' inside him longed to share it, and he didn't much like it. Luckily, Thorn smiled a shaky smile and walked away, endin' the matter before it jabbed a knife between Horace's ribs.

They made their way across the clearin' side by side as the sun creepin' higher in the sky burned off the last o' the misty dawn. The ol' sailor wondered if a half naked, angry feller might be huntin' through the forest in search o' the thieves what stole his britches, but the thought disappeared when Thorn stumbled. Horace reached out to catch him, but hesitated. The gray man righted himself without any help.

"You all right?" Horace asked.

"Tired still," Thorn replied. "Doing things expends more energy than before."

"Before? You mean when you was at...home?"

"Thorn is not tired after doing things like this," he gestured toward the well-fitted breeches, "when he is in the land behind the veil."

"Well, maybe you should stop doin' it while you're...ahem...out here."

"Thorn cannot stop. He must release the energy to live. If he doesn't, he will die."

"It seems like if you do let it go, you might end up with the same result."

Thorn didn't reply, only stared at his bare feet

whisperin' through the grass. His gait steadied itself and he returned to the kind o' pace what made Horace have to hurry to keep up. The ol' sailor sighed a breath full o' new day freshness, but it didn't seem so sweet to him, knowin' what they had to do.

"Guess we better get you back to the Green quick as we can, then."

They turned their backs on the sunrise and plodded into the forest, headin' for a place Horace'd spent his life tryin' to avoid.

XVI Teryk - Stirk's Hand

Stirk sat on the floor, elbows resting on his knees, the stump where his left hand had been the day before hanging in the air before his eyes. He didn't blink, just stared at it as though doing so might cause his missing appendage to grow back.

The stink of burning flesh had dissipated, replaced by the usual vile odors seeping through the cellar from the tannery. Bieta shifted where she sat on the floor beside the prince, watching her son, a sliver of guilt poking her heart the way her tongue poked at her empty gums.

"You okay, Stirk?"

He didn't answer. Bieta shifted again, her gaze falling to the shiny skin stretched tight over the end of her son's arm. She didn't know how the healer had done it, or why, but it explained the appearance of the flesh between his/her legs.

"It'll be worth it," she said, facing away from Stirk's blank stare to check on the injured lad. "Soon we'll have enough coin to buy you a golden hand if you want."

She touched her palm to the prince's forehead, found it had cooled considerably since the healer's strange visit. Though nothing appeared to have happened beyond the laying of hands upon the young man, his condition had improved markedly. It had been the same when the healer took Stirk's hand in payment—a grip around his wrist, a bright glow, the stench of burning flesh, and the hand came free.

Bieta shuddered. Seeing the healer leave their home holding her son's hand, fingers entwined as if lovers going for a stroll, brought nausea to her stomach then and it resurfaced as she recalled the sight. After swallowing around the sickly lump forming in her throat, she returned her attention to her son.

Stirk's eyes moved away from the stump for the first time since he'd sank to the floor under the force of the healer's grip. His gaze found Bieta's.

"Why'd you let this happen to me, Ma?" he said, a quake in his quiet, accusatory tone. "I liked that hand."

"W—we." Saliva flooded Bieta's mouth, spilled through the gap in her front teeth. She slurped it back. "The healer needed to be paid. The work was done."

"Couldn't you have paid with your hand? Or Enin's?"

"The healer didn't want mine or the horse doc's."

Stirk's bottom lip quivered; tears shimmered in his eyes. With a creak of joints, Bieta pushed herself up from her seat and went to kneel in front of her son. Her fingers touched his forearm above the spot where his hand had been and he jerked away.

"Does it hurt?"

A tear spilled along his cheek as he shook his head without taking his eyes from hers. He shrugged his shoulder up and bent his head to the side, wiping the wet trail away.

"Feels like it's still there," he said, his face hardening. "Feels like I could reach out and wrap my fingers around your throat for letting this happen to me."

A spark of fear ignited in Bieta's chest. Stirk outweighed her and would have no problem ending her life if he decided to do so, but she was his mother. He'd do no such thing.

She reached out and grasped the smooth end of his arm in both her hands before he could move away again. He jerked, but she held on, the scar warm against her fingers.

"I'm sorry, Stirk, but what else could I have done?"

"Could've said no."

Bieta shook her head. "Then we'd all be dead."

He glared at her, his lips pressed together, the bottom one protruding, pouting the way he did as a little boy. She took one hand from his stump and brushed her fingers against his cheek, making him flinch.

"Isn't it better to be rich with one hand than dead with both?"

"Guess so," he said, pouting lip still extended. "Must've been another way, though."

"No. The healer didn't want these old things." She removed her hands from Stirk's arm and held them up for them both to see the wrinkled skin and protruding veins. "And Enin's likely smelled too much of horse shit."

Stirk sniggered. "Does stink a bit, don't he?"

"What'd you expect from a man who lives in the stables?"

"Yeah. Bet his prick tastes like it, too, don't it, Ma? Probably been sticking it in some poor horse's arse."

The mirth in Stirk's eyes hardened into cruelty and Bieta saw that, despite the laugh they shared, she wasn't forgiven. Maybe she never would be.

"That ain't funny, Stirk."

"Neither's this, Ma." He raised the stump, waggled it in front of her eye. "But don't worry. I ain't gonna kill you."

"I know you won't."

"But that fucker..." He extended his arm, pointing the shining scar at the unconscious prince. Bieta peered back over her shoulder at their captive.

"That fucker is what's going to get us enough gold to make losing your hand worthwhile."

"It's all right, Ma," Stirk said, a devious smile creeping across his face. "I won't kill him 'til we get ourselves paid."

*　*　*

The sun had mostly set by the time Enin returned. He'd been in and out a few times through the day, tending his business but always coming back to ensure they didn't leave him without his cut of the ransom. Bieta wasn't sure where he expected she might go with an unconscious prince and a broody, one-handed man, but his feet were doing all the extra walking, not hers.

This final time he entered the storeroom, he only opened the door enough to slip his slender body through quick as he could, and he banged his forehead on the way. Bieta wondered at why he acted like someone was after him.

The horse doc cursed and rubbed his head, hand still on the door handle. Bieta parted her lips to ask what was happening, but he held up a finger to silence her, then cracked the door and peeked back the way he'd come.

Bieta wedged a knuckle into her eye socket and gave it a vigorous rub. Her good eye flickered between the horse doctor peering into the alley and Stirk crouched beside the prince, staring into the lad's face. He'd made no move on the young man, but Bieta didn't feel confident with what might happen should Prince Teryk awaken.

Finally, Enin shut the door and shrank back into the room, rubbing the spot on his head where a bump was forming and messing his sparse hair. When he turned,

Bieta saw sweat on his upper lip and staining his shirt front.

"What's happening?"

He gulped, the pronounced man-bump in his throat bobbing. His gaze flickered from Bieta to the prince and Stirk, then back.

"They're looking."

Bieta scrunched up her forehead. "Who's looking?"

"King's men came to my shop asking questions." Enin lowered his hand from the bump on his head and pointed at the prince. "Searching for him."

She followed his long, crooked finger to look at the injured man. Stirk raised his head. For the space of a dozen heartbeats, no one spoke. Bieta and Enin stared at the prince; Stirk stared back at them as though assigned to do so for the lad because he was unable to stare back himself.

"What do we do?" Stirk asked finally.

His words shook Bieta out of her mild state of shock. Did she really think the prince could go missing and no one would search for him? Had she believed holding the king and queen's son for ransom would be easy?

"How many of them?"

"I only saw a small squad—four of them. Might be others, though, searching the entire city." His hand returned to the bump on his forehead, swiping sweat from his lip on the way past.

Bieta shook her head. "The sun's set twice since Teth poked him," she said, working things through in her mind. "And your place ain't too far from where it happened. If there were lots of them, they'd have talked to you long ago."

Enin crossed to the middle of the room and sat on the edge of the table. It creaked beneath his weight.

"You might be right." His head-rubbing might have been to soothe the pain or a gesture of thought. "But they'll find their way here eventually."

"We have to move him, then," Bieta said.

"Or kill him and dump him in the river," Stirk added.

Bieta fixed her son with a chastising glance; he didn't divert his gaze the way he usually did. "Do you want to have lost your hand for nothing?"

"No," Stirk grumbled and went back to staring at the lad.

"Moving him's not a good idea," Enin said paying no attention to Stirk's comment. "Don't know where they might search. Staying here might be better. Can you trust the tanner?"

Bieta scowled. "He don't know anything."

Enin surveyed the room. "Does he come in here?"

"No. There's a trap door to the cellar, but it's the only other way in. You don't think they'll search down an alley, do you?"

"We have to be ready." He lowered his hand from his head to his lips, rubbed his finger briskly across them. Bieta mimicked the action with her tongue on her gums. "I have an idea."

"Better not mean me losing another body part," Stirk said.

"Hush," Bieta admonished then returned her attention to the horse doctor. "What's your idea?"

"I'll lock you in."

Bieta shook her head. "Won't work. Ain't a lock on the door."

"No, but I can get boards, a hammer, and nails."

The woman frowned. "You intend to make it so they can't get in, but we can't get out, neither?"

"They won't search somewhere inaccessible."

Bieta put her hand to her lips, glanced over at Stirk. He continued staring at the prince, attempting to burn holes in his flesh with his glare and ignoring the conversation.

"Suppose we can always go through the cellar if we have to," she said. "How long will we have to stay?"

Enin shrugged. "Until they move to another part of the city. A couple of days."

She put her thumb into her mouth, rubbed her gum, touched its pad with the tip of her tongue. Her eyes darted from Enin to Stirk to the prince. If the guards saw no way for anyone to get in or out, they'd search somewhere else. It made sense. She pulled her thumb from between her lips with a faint pop and nodded.

Enin didn't wait for her to speak. He jumped up from the table and rushed to the door, opening it a crack and peeking through the way he did when he arrived. Satisfied the alley was empty, he ducked lower than he needed to keep from banging his head again and hurried out, slamming the door shut behind him. Bieta had time for one heavy breath before hammering began.

"He had it planned," she said, scrambling to her feet. "He must've had everything he needed waiting outside the door."

Bieta limped across the room, one leg tingling with pins and needles from sitting in one position too long. She reached the door and thumped on it with the heel of her hand, the sound lost in the banging of Enin's hammer driving in another nail.

"Enin," she cried, the word as lost as her knocking. "Enin!"

After a moment's pause in the hammering, Bieta breathed more easily, expecting the horse doctor to respond to her calls. A heartbeat later, the hammering resumed, nailing a board across the door at a lower level. Bieta thumped on the wooden door again, shaking it with the impact.

"What about food, Enin? And water?"

She peered back over her shoulder at Stirk, who'd raised his head and stared across the dim room at her, his mouth curved into a frown. The prince lay unmoving, his breathing regular and smooth.

Bieta banged again. "Enin! Enin!"

The hammering stopped and she put her ear against the wood. She imagined the horse doctor's footsteps carrying him away, leaving them trapped in the storeroom behind the tanner's. The pins and needles in her leg loosened to an ache; she panted through her open mouth, the air whistling between her teeth. After a long moment, she abandoned her place listening at the door, knowing the horse doc really had left them. Her gaze fell on Stirk crouched beside the prince, murder flickering in her son's eyes.

XVII Trenan - Door to Door

They searched through the day and into the evening, going from one door to the next, street by street, block by block. At first, they stayed together in a group of four because Trenan didn't trust Dansil and his friend to be discreet if he left them on their own. He quickly realized the search would take far too long if they continued that way. Grudgingly, he split them up into pairs, sending Osis with Dansil one way down the block and keeping Strylor with himself.

He wasn't sure Osis could handle the big guard's bullish nature, but didn't think he'd be able to keep himself from running the big-mouth through if left alone with him.

When they got back together at the end of the day, neither pair had found any sign of the prince. They ate a quick meal and settled into spare bunks in the barracks after Trenan gave strict instructions not to speak of their task to anyone.

The next day dawned clear and warm again, as the days had for near on two full turns of the moon. It was the sort of day that should bring hope and joy to anyone's heart, but Trenan woke with a gray cloud hanging over him and an ache in his shoulder. Every time he'd closed his eyes through the night, he saw Ishla's disappointment and worry boring into his chest, heard the ice in her words. If ever things were to be right between them—as right as their stations might allow— he needed to find Teryk and Danya. Fast.

The four soldiers marched through the streets, arms and armor clanking as the early morning populace moved aside to let them pass. Tradesmen and workers on their way to their jobs eyed them warily. Trenan paid them no mind.

Dansil and Strylor walked a few paces ahead of Trenan and Osis, the master swordsman and sergeant striding in silence as the other two conversed.

"Helluva good job, protecting the queen," Dansil said.

"Better'n walking the walls like I gotta do," Strylor replied.

"Anything's better."

"You don't have to spend your days outside in the cold."

"Ha! When the temperature drops, the bitch never goes outside."

Trenan flinched at the guard's choice of words. "Watch your mouth, Dansil. You speak of the queen."

"Relax, swordsman," Dansil said casting a glance back over his shoulder. "She ain't here, so you don't have to protect your secret crush."

The master swordsman's fingers clutched Godsbane's hilt, but Osis lay his hand on Trenan's forearm, stopping him from freeing its steel. He looked at the sergeant, angry at first, then nodded his thanks—

no good killing one of the queen's guards over a few words.

"Know what the best part of guarding the king's whore from the Leeward kingdom is, Stry?" Dansil continued as though Trenan hadn't spoken.

"What's that?"

"Sometimes she needs to be guarded at the bath house, or when she's getting dressed. I don't care about my pay those days."

Strylor laughed and Trenan's stomach clenched with anger. He realized the guard's words held no truth—the queen's attendants helped her with bathing and dressing, not her guards—but it riled him, nonetheless. Visions of Dansil peeping through a door left ajar, or standing on a crate outside a window came to his mind, igniting a fire of jealousy in his chest. The heat spilled into his cheeks but he ground his teeth, biting it back.

"Ignore him," Osis said, leaning close to prevent the other two from hearing. "He's naught but hot air."

"I know," Trenan responded, but it didn't relieve his anger.

They continued toward the spot they'd finished their search the night before; Dansil and Strylor's conversation carried on, but Trenan paid no attention. His mind kept trying to find its way to thoughts of the queen, but he diverted them because the pain of unrequited love wouldn't serve him in his search for the prince and princess. He chose instead to replay the events that led him here, hunting through his memory for clues to what happened to Teryk, where Danya might have gone. He found no help amongst his recollections.

"Well? Where's it gonna be today?" Dansil asked as they reached the point where they'd stopped searching the night before. The tone of his voice might have been fingernails scratching the inside of Trenan's skull.

"We'll begin where we left off," the master

swordsman replied as he stared along the street. "What's in this part of the city, soldier?"

"Mostly businesses," Strylor said. "A few warehouses and such, too."

The master swordsman nodded. "Fine. We'll work our way toward sunrise." He faced Osis. "You head toward sunset and we'll meet back here at midday."

"Me and Strylor been talking," Dansil said, interrupting before Trenan took his first step. "Didn't seem me and Osis got along so well yesterday, so we thinks we should switch things up today."

Trenan glanced at Osis; the sergeant raised a brow and gave his head a tiny shake, indicating he'd given Dansil no cause for his words, though the master swordsman would have understood had it been true.

"Switch up the partnerships?" Trenan said.

Dansil stood straighter, poked out his chest. "That's right."

The master swordsman rubbed his jaw, hardly believing himself what he was about to say.

"Fine. Strylor, you go with Osis. Dansil, you're with me."

The big guard opened his mouth to protest, but Trenan spun in the direction of sunrise, his boot heel grinding in loose stone. Silently, the master swordsman wondered if they'd make it through the day without shedding each other's blood.

***

An apothecary, a blacksmith, a tailor, and two warehouses.

The large storehouses stacked with crates, barrels, and sacks had taken more time to search than Trenan expected, and the sun was creeping closer to its zenith and the time for he and Dansil to regroup with Osis and Strylor. Still they'd turned up no sign of the prince or princess, a task made more difficult by their inability to tell anyone for whom they searched.

Trenan closed the door of the last warehouse and marked it with the charcoal stick he kept tucked in his belt to avoid searching the same place twice. He turned and found Dansil standing close behind him, hands on hips.

"Why can't we just spread the word we're looking for the brats," he said. "Someone's bound to have seen them."

Trenan sighed, tired of explaining the king's reasoning to the thick-headed guard.

"It should be enough the king doesn't want the word out about the prince and princess' disappearance." He emphasized their titles. "But, if we let it be known, then every brigand in the outer city will be looking for them, dreams of ransom on their minds."

"Let them demand coin," Dansil scoffed. He reached over his shoulder and pulled his axe out of its sling, hefting it threateningly. "They'll get nothing but my steel for their troubles."

Trenan's face went stern. "And what if they see your offer and decide to kill the heir to the kingdom, you idiot?"

Dansil leaned toward the master swordsman, the corner of his mouth twisting upward in a nasty smirk.

"Then I suppose whoever was responsible for them going missing should have his head removed, shouldn't he?"

Trenan's hand found its way to the hilt of his sword, fingers wrapping around it with the familiarity of caressing a lover. Since that one time, one encounter that changed his life and ruined everyone else for him, it was the closest he'd come to laying his hand on anything in passion.

Past the big guard and a short way up the street, Trenan caught a glimpse of a tall, slender man as he opened a door. The fellow paused and regarded the master swordsman and his companion with the same suspicion as most of the people they'd encountered. He ducked through the portal and closed the door furtively, as though attempting to avoid notice.

Trenan nodded in that direction and released his grip on Godsbane, determined to return to the task at hand. If they found Teryk and Danya, he'd be free of the torture of Dansil's company.

"Put your over-sized meat cleaver away. We've work to do."

He pushed by the guard, senses prickling as he exposed his back to the armed man, and crossed the avenue toward the building the man had entered. Behind him, he heard Dansil turn to follow. Trenan waited as a wagon rattled past, the horse's hooves clopping on chipped and broken cobbles, then strode up to the wooden door. He raised his fist and pounded against its surface.

No immediate response. Trenan hammered on the door again as Dansil stepped up beside him.

"Open this door in the name of the king."

Before anyone inside had a chance to respond, Dansil thumped the flat side of his axe against the door, the sound obviously steel contacting wood.

"Open the fucking door," he shouted.

Trenan eyed him, ready to objurgate him for his lack of tact, when the door opened a crack. A gaunt face peered out.

"Can I help you, gentlemen?"

"We're here on business of the king," Dansil said before Trenan opened his mouth. "Open the door before I kick it in and then do the same with your head."

Trenan glowered at the guard, biting his tongue and expecting the man inside the shop to slam the door in their faces while telling them to go fuck themselves. To the master swordsman's surprise, hinges squeaked softly and the door swung inward. The tall, slender man with a large head that made him resemble a horse—the man Trenan had watched enter the premises—stood in the doorway.

"King's business, is it?" He eyed Dansil, his gaze lingering on the guard's bare axe, then turned his attention to Trenan. "Must be important if he's sent his swordmaster to visit me."

Trenan cocked a brow. "Have we met?"

"No. But everyone knows you." The man nodded toward the master swordsman's missing arm. "Bit of a legend, you are."

"Hmph," Dansil scoffed, pushing through the door and past the man. "He ain't the one you got to worry about."

The gaunt fellow stepped aside to allow them entry, but Trenan saw him peer out the door before closing it, gaze darting up and down the street as though watching for someone. Or ensuring Trenan and Dansil didn't have any other soldiers with them. The hair on the back of the master swordsman's neck prickled and he laid his hand on Godsbane's pommel.

"What can I help you with?"

"We be searching for someone," Dansil said, already halfway across the room.

Trenan surveyed the inside of the shop. They'd entered a small room with sundry items of riding tack and the like spread out on low benches set against the walls. If the man made his living selling horse equipment, he must only be scraping by.

"I haven't seen anyone unusual," the man said. He looked to Dansil, then Trenan and back again. "Except for the two of you."

Dansil spun on the man, axe half-raised. "You calling us unusual?"

Trenan rolled his eyes, but the man wrung his hands, nervous and believing the threat.

"N—no, sir. Just that it's unusual to see knights from Draekfarren in the outer city."

"Well, if who we're looking for don't turn up, you're gonna be seeing more of them," Dansil said lowering his blade. He returned to surveying the room, though its size prevented any possibility anyone else hid in it.

"Who is it you're looking for? Perhaps I can help."

"It doesn't matter," Trenan said before Dansil revealed the truth of their search. "If you've seen anyone you don't normally see, you need to tell us."

The man's dark eyes found Trenan and he shook his head, but the master swordsman didn't like the fellow's aspect.

"I haven't seen anyone."

Trenan strode across the shop toward a door in the back wall. "What's your name?"

"Enin, sir."

"And what do you do, master Enin?"

"I am a horse doctor."

Trenan nodded. Dansil picked up a bridle, examined it then dropped it. It banged against the wooden bench and slid off onto the floor; he didn't pick it up.

"What's through here, horse doctor Enin?" the master swordsman asked nodding toward the door.

"That's my shop," he replied and hurried across the room without prompting. "It's where I do my work when people bring their horses to me."

He grabbed the door handle and threw it open. Trenan grabbed Godsbane's hilt and loosed a sliver of steel; Dansil dipped into a crouch, axe raised. When Enin turned back to them from opening the door, he jumped visibly, surprised by their response.

"No one in there," the horse doctor said. "One horse with a cough, nothing else."

Trenan backed Dansil off with a look and crept through the doorway, the muscles in his sword arm tight and ready, his breathing smooth and controlled. Sunlight shone in through a window in a door set in the back wall, illuminating three empty stalls and one in which stood a medium-sized horse, chestnut in color. The horse raised its snout from munching on a pile of straw, regarded the intruder with a disinterested gaze, then returned to its meal. The master swordsman went past the horse's stall and peered into the others, aware of Dansil's footsteps close behind him.

Empty.

He surveyed the exit, noticed a fastened padlock on the inside. If anyone stole out the back when they entered, they'd have needed someone to lock it behind them.

"What's through there?" Dansil demanded.

"It leads to the alley behind the shop," Enin answered. His voice cracked with apprehension.

The big guard reached back and grabbed the horse doctor by his sleeve, shoved him toward the door. Enin stumbled and sprawled on the straw-covered floor, his long arms and legs tangling. With a shake of his head and a disapproving look to his companion, Trenan released his sword's hilt and offered his hand to help the man up. Enin gripped the master swordsman's hand in his own; the horse doctor's palm was moist with sweat.

"Sorry, I must have stumbled," Enin said with a nervous titter. "Thank you for your help, Sir Trenan."

Trenan nodded. "Open the door, please."

"Of course."

Enin fished in his pocket and pulled out a key ring, the three iron keys on it jingling discordantly. They all appeared the same, but he selected one confidently and unlocked the rear door, throwing it open and stepping aside for the two soldiers to move past.

As he'd said, the portal opened onto a narrow alley cutting behind the shops of this street and the next. Garbage and refuse clogged most of it—including a large pile of manure stacked beside the horse doctor's door. The stink made Trenan's nostrils flare.

Dansil pushed through beside the master swordsman, glanced one way up the lane, then the other. Satisfied there was no one there, he retreated inside. Trenan followed.

"Looks like you're clean," Dansil said leaning his axe against his shoulder. "But you'll tell us if you see anyone."

The horse doctor raised his brow. "And how will I do that?"

"Go to the barracks. Tell anyone." Dansil scowled hard. "Don't fuck with me, horse doctor, or you'll regret it."

"Of course, I beg your pardon."

Enin bowed deferentially, and Trenan shot Dansil another disapproving look. The big guard cracked a brief smile, then returned the scowl to his lips before the horse doctor raised his head.

"Anything else I can do you for you, gentlemen?" Enin asked, his gaze darting between the two armed men. "Perhaps a check up for your horses?"

"Won't be necessary," Trenan replied. Dansil had already stalked through the door into the horse doctor's shop. "Let us know if you hear anything."

Enin nodded, then followed the master swordsman past the paddock's lone resident and through the door. He hurried ahead, opening the outside door for them and bowing shallowly at the waist. Dansil swept past and into the street without a sideways glance, but Trenan hesitated at the doorway, looking at the tall, gaunt man; Enin didn't raise his gaze.

When the master swordsman's boot heels hit the

street's cobblestones, the horse doctor shut the door without so much as a word or a peek. Trenan paused and looked back at the shop, a sliver of suspicion niggling in his gut.

"Something wasn't right about that man," he said.

"Nothing a few good meals wouldn't fix. Have you ever seen a man so tall and bony?"

"That's not what I mean. Didn't he appear nervous to you?"

"Downright scared shitless." Dansil laughed and patted his hand on the side of his axe's polished head. "Can't say I blame him with me in the room. Maybe you should do the next place by yerself so the shop keep don't get so frightened."

Frowning, Trenan ignored the big guard's jab and followed his companion to the next door. The feeling of something more going on with the horse doctor than what they saw gnawed at his gut.

XVIII Ailyssa - Breaking Fast

In the bright glare of her blindness, sounds became more distinct to Ailyssa, even after the passage of only a few sunrises.

How many has it been since they cast me out?

She thought the sun had risen four times since she regained her senses, but how many while she was drugged?

Knives and forks tinkled together, scraped the smooth surface of clay plates. Around her, the Sisters of Jubha Kyna spoke in hushed tones as they ate, but Ailyssa paid no attention to their conversations. She sat waiting, stiff and straight and partially in shock, for Creidra to return with the food to break her fast. Against her will, her mind replayed her encounter with her first man from the night before, no matter how much she wanted to shut out the made-up images.

As he made her touch him in ways she'd never touched a man before—ways the Goddess never intended women and men to touch—her fingers had revealed much about the man. The thick hair covering his body but not his head, the cant of his nose, his angular jaw. Her mind filled in the details of his hair and eye color to complete a picture she didn't want in her head. His face took on an aspect of her son—the last man with whom she'd been meant to couple before her banishment. Ailyssa shuddered.

The things the man made her do—things she never imagined a woman might do with a man—might never leave her. He'd made her touch him with her hand, her lips, her tongue. And he'd put his hands in places on her that her own hadn't been for pleasure. In all her times participating in coupling ceremonies, she'd never touched or been touched that way. His rough tongue grated on her ear, her neck, and he'd put his... She doubted she'd ever wash his taste out of her mouth.

The tender flesh between her legs still throbbed with his pressure—always the way of it after coupling. This was worse, though, because she still felt his lips on her flesh, his grip on her hips; his harsh breath yet rushed by her ear, stirring her hair and stinking of mint.

"Here you are, Sister."

Ailyssa flinched away from the clatter of a plate and utensils being set on the table in front of her. The scent of ham wafted to her nose, setting her stomach grumbling, and she raised her face toward the sound of Creidra's voice. The young woman's presence helped calm her and distract her from her thoughts; she forced a smile on her lips and hoped it didn't appear as strained as it felt.

"Thank you, N'th Creidra. Will you be joining me?"

"For a short while. I have my first appointment soon."

"So early?"

The Sister sat on the bench across the table from Ailyssa in a rustle of skirts and the dull rattle of plate and silverware as she set her own meal down. She cleared her throat and the edge of her knife scraped against her platter as she cut herself a bite of meat.

"It isn't unusual to have visitors this early," Creidra said. "This man is one of my regulars. I hope he's starting a new day with me rather than finishing up yesterday. He'll smell better that way."

Creidra laughed and Ailyssa added her own fake chuckle to the sound. A heartbeat later, the young woman's fork scraped against her teeth and they fell silent.

Visitors.

The term used by the Sisters to describe the men who came to the temple to partake in their services grated in Ailyssa's mind. Visitors were people you delighted in meeting with, not ones who forced you into things you didn't normally do. These weren't visitors, they were rapists.

"Do you often couple with the same men more than once?"

"Yes. Many of my visitors come specifically to see me."

Ailyssa gulped back acidic saliva suddenly filling her mouth. Did that mean the man from the night before would return and she'd be forced to endure his touch again?

"How many..." She hesitated, the word sticking to her tongue. She cleared her throat. "How many visitors do you have in a day?"

The sound of chewing was the only answer for a

moment, then Creidra slurped from a cup. "Sometimes one, most often two. The most I've served in one day is four."

Four!

Ailyssa struggled to control her reaction, hoping her expression didn't give away her shock or offend her one friend amongst the Sisters. She turned her face down, but Creidra didn't act as though she'd seen.

"Today there will only be Edric. He sees me the twelfth of every moon." Cutlery scraped plate; Creidra chewed. "He pays in coin, but he brings me gifts, too."

"Gifts? Like what?"

"Oh, this and that. Sometimes a block of cheese, other times a jar of wine or bauble he carved of wood. He brought me a ring one time."

Ailyssa raised her head, surprised by the note of affection in the young woman's tone. Did she have emotions for a man? The Goddess couldn't be pleased with her if she did.

"It seems he thinks of me as a mate. Are you not hungry, N'th Ailyssa?"

Ailyssa opened her mouth, partly to respond, partly in shock at Creidra's words. Rather than speak her mind and question how the Goddess allowed this, she groped along the top of the table until her fingers found the handle of her fork. She used it to stir around the contents of her plate and wondered how much food she spilled over the lip if the plate

"What is it?"

"Side ham and quail eggs. Here, let me cut it up for you."

Steel scraped clay as Creidra carved the slice of ham into manageable pieces. Ailyssa waited, hating her need to be dependent on this young woman.

"How were things with your first visitor?"

"It was..." Ailyssa's voice trailed away, unsure how

to answer the question. Should she tell of her impatience for the opportunity to bathe and rinse the man's scent from her skin? "I think he left pleased."

The sound of knife against plate paused, and Ailyssa sensed the young woman's gaze on her, likely with pity in her eyes. An instant later, her fingers on the back of her hand confirmed Ailyssa's suspicion.

"It must be a bit of a shock for you, I know," Creidra said, a tone of understanding in her voice. "But you'll get used to it."

Ailyssa's chin dipped. "I'm not certain I will."

"I am." The young woman patted her hand. "You are not the first Sister of Olvana we've taken in. Everyone becomes accustomed after a time."

Ailyssa raised her head again, directing her gaze toward Creidra, wondering if she was looking into her eyes.

"Others of my sect live here?"

Creidra returned to eating. "Yes. I think so."

Ailyssa sucked her bottom lip, the fork in her hand and food on her plate forgotten. "Who?"

"Um." A mouthful of breakfast muted the sound. Creidra chewed thoughtfully for a moment before continuing. "N'th Nessina Ra is from your order, I believe. Do you know her?"

Ailyssa thought about it, but the name didn't sound familiar. The possibility two women from the temple didn't know each other existed, but it wasn't likely. Perhaps she'd been relocated, as had happened to Ailyssa's own Mother, and her Daughter. She shook her head.

"Are there others?"

"Yes, but I am out of time, Sister." Scraping fork, chewing, the rustle of skirts. Creidra stood. "Make sure you break your fast. You need your strength."

"Wait, Creidra. Who else is there?"

"I have to go. I'll find the Sister and send her to you."

The young woman took her plate and cutlery and left Ailyssa alone to poke around on her plate with the fork until she skewered a chunk of ham. Its smoky flavor spilled over her tongue as she chewed. Did one of the temple's visitors leave it as payment? She assumed so; she'd heard nothing to indicate the presence of men here taking care of animals to feed the Sisters like in Olvana. How long before the goat paid by the man who'd employed her the night before ended up her meal? Her nose wrinkled at the thought.

Garlic and rosemary seasoned the scrambled quail eggs—a stunning contrast to the plain cereal and dense bread she'd broken so many fasts with in the past. It seemed the differences between the temples of Olvana and Jubha Kyna extended far beyond their methods for honoring the Goddess with children.

Ailyssa put another piece of ham into her mouth, the savory flavor coaxing her to continue though her stomach remained uncertain if it wanted more. As she chewed, she pondered the other differences: the appointment of the bedroom, the size of the temple itself. Why did the Goddess allow it? If one sect's methods were right and another's wrong, wasn't one in danger of banishment from the world they way the Small Gods had been?

"Hello?"

The voice came from in front of Ailyssa, where Creidra had been seated. Ailyssa raised her face and blinked, but the bright blur remained, as always.

"Who's there?"

Feet shuffled on the floor as the unknown woman moved closer. Ailyssa's grip tightened on her fork.

"Are you N'th Ailyssa Ra? From Olvana?"

The question hung in the air between them as the sounds of eating and conversations continued. Ailyssa pushed her plate away, no longer hungry.

"I am. Did N'th Creidra send you over?"

"She did. May I sit?"

Ailyssa nodded. "Of course."

The legs of the wooden bench scraped on the floor as the woman pulled it out, then sat. She said nothing for a while.

"What is your name?" Ailyssa asked. "Are you of Olvana as well?"

"Yes."

Silence. Ailyssa waited, expecting the woman to say more. After five breaths, she still hadn't spoken.

"Are you still there?"

"Oh, yes. I'm sorry. Creidra told me you couldn't see. How long have you been here?"

"This is my second sunrise here." Ailyssa's stomach churned, though she didn't understand the cause of it. "Have you been here long?"

"I have seen the seasons turn more than once," the woman said, though she sounded distracted. "I never expected to see you."

Ailyssa's brows drooped and she chewed her bottom lip, the unease in her gut increasing. She thought about the women from Olvana who'd been relocated, wondered who this might be. Surely, none of the Sisters of Olvana had been be sent to Jubha Kyna.

It must be a mistake.

"Do I know you?" Ailyssa asked, tentative.

"It's been a long time."

Ailyssa inhaled a deep breath through her nose and set her fork on the table. It clinked against the edge of her plate.

"You have me at a disadvantage." She waved her hand near her eyes. "I do not know to whom I speak."

"I...I'm sorry," the woman said, her voice sounding as though tears threatened. "My name is N'th Claris Ra.

I am your Daughter."

XIX Teryk - A Visit to the Tanner

The sound of running water brought Bieta to the precipice between wakefulness and sleep. Out of habit, her tongue prodded the space between her front teeth, but the inside of her mouth felt sticky and dry. She smacked her lips, attempting to prompt saliva to life, but none came.

She opened her eyes.

In the flickering light of their last taper, she watched Stirk standing in the far corner, a stream of urine disappearing into the open trap door leading to the cellar. Bieta blinked, the tight skin covering her empty socket pulling uncomfortably, and tried to make sense of what she saw.

"Stirk. What're you doing?"

He looked back over his shoulder without interrupting his flow. "Honey pot's overflowing, Ma. Had to go and didn't want to piss on the floor."

Bieta pushed herself up to a sitting position, nostrils wrinkling at the stink in their room. With the materials of the tanner's trade stored in the cellar below their home, the place was always rank. After what Bieta judged by the amount of tallow they'd burned to be two sunrises trapped in the room, the stench was worse. Honey pot, sweat, and frayed nerves added up to an awful reek.

"Couldn't you stick it under the door?"

"You know it's too big to fit." Stirk chuckled, shook off the last few drops, and stored himself back in his breeches. Wiping his hands on his thighs, he faced his mother. "Hungry, Ma."

"I know. Me, too."

She stood and went to the prince, still prone on Stirk's messy pile of hay. The lad hadn't moved or made a sound since the healer's visit, but his forehead and cheeks were cool to the touch, and his bruises fading. Bieta poked the flesh beside his wound, the compound Enin had spread on it dried and cracked with the passage of time. The surrounding area had nearly returned to its natural pink hue rather than the sickly, angry red.

"The healer's work is helping," she said without looking up.

"Hmm," Stirk grunted.

Since he stopped glaring at the prince, he hadn't spared the lad so much as a glance. He refused to help keep him comfortable and clean—or the semblance of clean afforded when using a dirty cloth dipped in filthy water—and didn't even speak of him. Bieta gave up reminding him how much gold the young man'd be worth to them and worried Stirk no longer cared.

She smacked her lips again and dragged her parched tongue around the desert-dry inside of her mouth.

"We're going to need water."

Bieta went to the table and eyed the bowl they'd been using to clean the prince. The water—cloudy before they brought him here—was a sickly brownish-gray. Particles of dirt floated on the top of the mixture of water, blood, and sweat. The water was so dirty, Bieta doubted even Stirk'd drink it.

"How you going to get us water?"

"By sneaking into the tanner's through the cellar, see if he's got any."

Stirk's eyebrows met above the bridge of his nose. "You said we should never steal from old Flenge. Said it's like biting his hand."

"Biting the hand that feeds us," she corrected. "But this ain't a usual happening, Stirk. I don't know how long it'll be before Enin comes back. If we don't get water, we ain't going to be around to enjoy no gold."

Bieta went to the open trap door in the corner and peered into the dark. Beside her, Stirk looked over her shoulder.

"You didn't piss on the ladder, did you?" she asked.

"Naw. Careful of your step at the bottom, though. Had to shit before you woke up."

She rolled her eye. "Get me the taper," she said, holding out her hand.

Stirk hesitated. Bieta fixed her gaze on him.

"But it'll be dark in here if you take it," he said, a vague whimper hidden beneath his tone.

"I got to see my way through the cellar, Stirk. Plunk your ass down while I'm gone and stay in one place."

His lip quivered. "But it'll be dark."

Bieta's tongue darted back and forth across her gum, her teeth clenched tight. She glared at him and he diverted his gaze.

"Get me the taper."

Head hung, Stirk slouched across the room to the shelf and pried the candle holder out of the pool of melted tallow. The flame bounced and faltered but remained alight as he moved it away; he held it out for Bieta to take, the light reflecting on the shiny surface of the cauterized skin pulled tight across the end of his shortened left arm.

The tension in Bieta's jaw eased at the sight of the scar, her heart softened. She took the candle holder from her son and put her hand on his forearm.

"Does it hurt?"

He shook his head. "Not in my arm."

His gaze fell on the prince, hatred burning in his eyes. The muscles in his arm tensed. Bieta gripped it hard, jarred his attention away from the lad and back to her.

"Sit your arse right here and don't move."

His bottom lip protruded in the pout to which Bieta had become so accustomed. His eyes smoldered, but he nodded.

"Right, then. I'll be back quick as I can, with water and hopefully food, too." Her gaze flickered to the prince, back. "Don't move."

Stirk nodded once more and sank to the floor, his thick legs crossed awkwardly, elbows leaning on his knees. Once he settled, Bieta knew he'd do as she said— his fear of the dark outweighed his hatred of their captive.

The woman set the candle holder on the floor beside the open trap door and gathered her skirts so her feet might find the ladder's rungs without catching in her dress. After descending the first three steps, her knees quivering with nerves until she'd gone far enough to grip the top rung, she paused and peered back at Stirk.

"You going to be all right?"

He nodded but refused to meet her gaze.

Not exactly satisfied, but realizing it was the best she'd get out of him, Bieta picked up the taper and resumed her descent. She counted the steps silently, having traversed the ladder enough times to know it took twenty-two to reach the bottom. With each new moon, she descended the ladder and made her way to the tannery to pay Flenge the rent due for allowing them to live in his storeroom. Sometimes she worried about him getting too old to receive the kind of rent she paid, and that he might start looking for coin instead. If so, they'd need to find a new place to live.

Bieta reached the bottom rung and paused, craning her neck and holding the taper out to ensure she didn't step in her son's excrement. A rat squeaked and scurried away from the light. A drop of saliva squeezed into her mouth at the thought of it, but she wasn't willing to chase it around in the dark—that'd be a job for Stirk for later.

She stepped off the ladder into the tannery's worst stench. In the cellar, Flenge kept the urine and dung used for making cow hides into leather, along with the oak bark, stale beer, and lye—the raw materials needed for removing hair and softening the pelt. Bieta had watched Flenge work more than once, disgusted by the proceedings as she awaited the opportunity to make good on the turn of the moon's rent.

Bieta stepped away from the ladder, careful of her footing, and made her way along the narrow cellar. The scrape of vermin feet on the dirt floor scurried ahead of the taper's light, but she paid it no attention, fixing her gaze ahead without looking at the rows of clay jars lining the shelves on either side. As she approached the ladder leading into the tanner's, the vessels gave way to folded leathers, finished and waiting to be sold to an armorer or shoemaker, perhaps. In this section of the cellar, the tannery's stink relented, allowing the sweet scent of the leather in. Bieta inhaled deeply, enjoying the aroma. Her stomach rumbled.

Upon reaching the steps to the tanner's, she stopped at the foot of the ladder and gazed up at the bottom side of a closed trap door. Since a few sunrises yet remained before the new moon when rent was due, Flenge wouldn't be expecting her today. She hoped he hadn't set anything heavy atop the door in the floor. After setting the taper on top of a pile of folded leathers and gripping a rung above head level, she stepped up onto the ladder.

Up she climbed, the aroma of leather dissipating with each step, replaced by the mixed scents of the tannery itself. When the top of her head brushed the underside of the door, Bieta stopped. She stared at the boards. Normally, she'd have knocked and Flenge, who'd be expecting her, would open the door, happy to let her in and receive rent.

But she wasn't here to use the space between her teeth to pay the tab this time, and she didn't want the tanner to know of her presence since she planned on robbing him. She didn't expect to find any food, but Flenge used water in the tanning process, so it'd be plentiful in his shop, and that was her first priority. She needed it as badly as did their captive, and her throat ached at the thought.

Tongue massaging the space left by her missing teeth, Bieta released the rung held in her right hand and reached up until her fingers touched the underside of the door. Her fingertips brushed the rough wood and a droplet of sweat rolled along her temple. She murmured to herself, saying an unfamiliar prayer for nothing to be set upon the trap door, that no latch locked it in place, and in hoping Flenge wasn't nearby where he'd see her climb out. Bieta pushed lightly on the door and it shifted upward.

Thank the one God.

Bieta paused, lips pressed tight together waiting for Flenge to call out, asking what she needed, but he didn't. The tallow of the taper popped and sizzled, coming near to its end as she hesitated. The droplet of sweat from her temple caught at the corner of her mouth. She swiped it away with her tongue, its salty flavor making her throat burn with thirst.

The sensation encouraged her to continue despite her nerves. A firmer push raised the trap door a full handspan—enough to stretch her neck and peer through the crack.

Bieta looked along the surface of the dusty floor, at the bottom of shelves and the mouse droppings caught beneath them. Her eye flickered one way, then the other, but she caught no sight of Flenge.

Maybe it's closer to sunset than I thought. Or he

might've left to pick up more hides or supplies.

With a deep breath tasting of dust and leather, Bieta stepped up another rung on the ladder and pushed the trap door the rest of the way open. She knew a set of shelves stood close behind it, so didn't worry it might fall open and slam against the floor. Her foot moved up again, her head protruding through the floor.

The back of the tannery lay in darkness. Flenge kept the front of his workshop well lit during the day, with the door and shutters at the front of the building thrown open both for illumination and ventilation, but he refused to leave a lamp burning at the back, claiming it a waste of oil. Today, Bieta gave thanks for his miserly nature.

Hiking her skirts up high, she climbed the last few steps until she put her knees on the floor and pulled herself out through the trap door. When she did, she paused again, waiting for any indication she'd been heard. The sound of a voice stopped her.

Not Flenge's, she could tell, but a man's, and she couldn't make out what he said. Likely a leather worker negotiating the purchase of materials to make belts and scabbards, vests and cuffs. All the better for Bieta that Flenge be distracted while she liberated fresh water to sustain Stirk, herself, and their captive.

Bieta stood and let the hem of her dress drop back to the floor, then took one step before pausing. She searched her memory, recalling where Flenge kept the water. Most often when she visited, she paid little attention to the tanner's business as she wanted to get hers out of the way as quickly as possible.

A barrel by the wall.

Flenge collected rainwater in barrels, preferring to use it for tanning rather than river water. Bieta licked her lips at the thought of it, imagining its sweet flavor on her tongue, soothing her throat.

But she'd be unable to take a barrel down the ladder and through the cellar. She'd need a container in which to carry it.

The woman moved furtively amongst the shelves, her gaze flickering between the tools and supplies set upon them, then toward the shop with its voices floating to her ears. Whenever she came to a clay pot, she tested its weight but found most of them full or close to. Finally, near the edge of the shelves and a few paces away from the water barrel, she found one with only a few scraps of bark left in the bottom. She crouched to empty the rest of its contents but stopped when she saw a flash of movement between the shelves.

A man in armor.

Bieta leaned closer to the shelves, the pot in her hands momentarily forgotten as she concentrated on the goings-on at the front of the tanner's workshop.

"...haven't seen nothing," Flenge's croaking voice said. "Nothing unordinary, at least. Who you looking for again?"

Bieta's heart jumped in her chest.

"A young man of twenty turns," the other man said. "He may have been dressed in a merchant's garb."

"Nope. Ain't been no one of that description 'round here. No one I don't already do business with."

Bieta squinted her eye, staring hard through the space between a clay pot and a pile of hides, bits of flesh clinging to the pelts stinking of rot. She ignored the odor, concentrating on the man, instead. After a moment, he turned and Bieta saw he possessed only one arm.

The man from the tavern.

The one-armed man nodded toward the back of the workshop and the shelves where Bieta hid.

"What's back there?" he asked.

"Storage," Flenge said. "And there's a storeroom out back, too. I rent it out to a woman and her son."

Bieta didn't wait to hear more. She scrambled back toward the trap door, leaving the clay pot and its scattering of oak bark sitting on the floor. With her skirts held up from her feet, she scurried through the shelves toward the dim glow of the taper shining out of the cellar, hoping for their conversation to continue and give her time to get away.

What will we do?

Her mind raced. If the one-armed man found the prince in their room, she had no doubt of their bodies being relieved of their traitorous heads. She needed to get back to Stirk fast. They needed to figure a way to get the prince out of the room.

We could hide him in the cellar.

Bieta bent over and stuck her legs through the open trap door, located the third rung down with her foot and began to descend. Two steps farther, her sandal caught and she slipped, scraping her shin. She caught herself on the edge of the floor, saw the movement of feet in the space under the shelves, and reached up to grasp the trap door. Breath held, she swung the door shut, closing it quietly in a puff of dust.

The woman reached the cellar floor and retrieved the sputtering taper off the shelf, cold sweat trickling between her breasts. She spun and hurried back toward the storeroom, her mind considering options as she went.

We can't put him here; Flenge'll show him the cellar. And if he sees the cellar, he might come to our room through the trap door.

The possibility of telling Stirk to lay in wait for the one-armed man occurred to her. When the soldier poked his head through the trap door, Stirk could hit him, but she doubted the man was here alone. Enin mentioned two men visiting him at his shop, and maybe more. He couldn't stay where he was and they couldn't put him in the cellar. What, then?

"Stirk'll have to break down the door," she muttered as she reached the ladder leading to the storeroom.

She grabbed a rung as her foot slipped in something she suspected might be her son's shit and hurried up, the taper gripped precariously as she climbed. It sputtered and flickered, the wick burned near its end.

Bieta stuck her head through the trap door and pulled the candle holder through after her, heart beating hard in her chest. To her relief, Stirk remained exactly where she'd left him, legs crossed, elbows on his knees, leaning toward the door in the floor. As the taper's light washed across his face, his strained expression eased.

"Ma—," he began, but Bieta didn't let him finish.

"We have to get him out of here," she cried, pulling herself into the room and slamming the trap door shut. "They're going to find us."

Stirk leaned back, his eyes going wide. He opened his mouth to speak when the taper fizzled and went out, throwing the room into darkness.

***

Stirk froze, lips parted, a breath half-drawn. The dark fell on him like a blanket thrown over his head, suppressing the ability of his lungs as surely as it took his sight. His muscles—already aching from the strain of waiting for his mother's return in the dark—tensed again, clenching his joints and bones into an inert state.

"Stirk?" his mother called out, invisible in the blackness.

He wanted to answer, but the darkness stole his voice, too. He opened his eyes as wide as they'd go, hoping they'd suck enough light into his head to allow him to see, if just a little.

"Shit."

For a moment, he thought she meant the bowel movement he'd sent tumbling into the cellar earlier in the day, then he realized she was cursing. He knew he should understand why she was upset, but the unyielding pressure of the dark room squashed his thoughts, left him as dumb as the day of his birth.

"Stirk. We got to get the prince out of here. The one-armed man is in the tanner's looking for him."

Her words struck a chord in him.

One-armed man.

Did she mean him? With a huge effort, he raised his left hand and ratcheted his eyes toward it. Darkness kept him from seeing the shiny scar at the end of his forearm, but he did notice a sliver of light squeezing through the crack under the door. The slim slice proved enough to loosen the dark's hold. He wondered how he hadn't noticed it the entire time his mother had been gone.

"The one-armed man?"

"From the tavern. He's a See-Gee, or a man of the king. He's looking for the prince."

Stirk sensed his mother's presence near him. It spilled confidence into his chest and he climbed to his feet. "What do we do?"

"We got to get him out."

"How?" He paused, realizing there was but one way out. "I ain't going in the cellar."

"No, Flenge'll show him the cellar. You got to break down the door."

The whistle in his mother's words sent a shiver along his flesh—the sound only happened when she was excited or scared. If something frightened her, he should be afraid, too.

He shifted his gaze toward the splinter of sunlight shining under the door and closed his eyes, picturing what the room would look like were the taper still lit. The table set directly in the middle; the shithead prince laid out on his bed off to one side; his mother's things lying to the other side.

Stirk opened his eyes and the light sneaking through

looked even brighter. He gritted his teeth and stalked across the room, his right hand clenched in a fist, his left feeling as though it would be if he still had it.

"Stirk—"

"I got it, Ma."

He navigated his way to the door, avoiding the table and keeping from stepping on their captive no matter how much he wanted to do it. This was the little turd's fault. If he'd stayed in his castle, he and his Ma wouldn't have this trouble, and Stirk's hand'd be where it was meant to be instead of decorating some healer's mantle.

When he reached the door, he stopped, the light shining underneath illuminating his toe sticking through the hole in the end of his shoe. He laid his hand on the wood, struggling to remember how many nails Enin hammered in, recall how many boards he put across the door.

"Hurry, Stirk."

She was closer behind him, standing by the prince, he thought. Protecting him from her son. In a short while, he'd have the door open and it'd be up to him to take the captive away, find a place to hide him. She wouldn't be able to protect him then.

Stirk reared back then pushed forward, slamming his right shoulder against the door. It shuddered but didn't move, so he repeated the action with the same result. He stepped back and raised his foot, planted his heel hard beside the handle. Wood creaked.

"Hurry, Stirk."

"I'm hurrying." He faced toward the sound of her voice, saw the edge of her jaw dimly illuminated, recognized the fear in her expression. Seeing it churned his belly and he returned to his task.

Kick. Kick. Shoulder.

Nails squealed in the frame like pigs running to avoid slaughter. The door opened a quarter handspan, spilling more light into the room, fortifying Stirk.

"Good," Bieta cried, her voice straining, suppressed.

Stirk put his shoulder to it again and a board split with a loud crack. He kicked it once. Twice. The third time his foot struck it, the door flew open, flooding the room with mid-morning sun. Warmth touched Stirk's skin, light hurt his eyes, but he didn't squint or look away. He allowed it to fill him.

Bieta rushed past her son, leaning out through the broken door to survey the alley beyond. She looked right and left, then turned back to him.

"Clear," she said, and Stirk saw the strain and worry plain upon her brow. Her expression suggested the future held no gold for them, that this had all been for naught.

He'd lost his hand for nothing.

"Get him out of here," Bieta commanded.

Stirk obliged, stalking across the room to the unconscious prince. He grabbed him roughly by the arm and pulled him up, the captive's arms flopping in the manner of a rag doll's. When he had him in a vaguely sitting position, Stirk jammed his stump into the prince's armpit and wrestled him onto his shoulder, uncaring if he caused pain in the pissant's wound.

He made his way back to the doorway, face contorted in a scowl—not from the effort of carrying the prince, but disgust at having to touch him. Before he crossed the threshold into the alley, Bieta put her hand on his arm, stopping him.

"Be careful," she said.

Stirk's heart swelled. This was the first time she'd acted as though she cared more for him than the prince and his ransom since they found him bleeding in the street. His frown eased.

"Be careful with him. And be sure you hide him where we can find him after the one-armed man's gone.

Somewhere no one else will."

The muscles in Stirk's jaw balled up until they hurt. He sucked at his bottom lip to keep it from protruding and pushed past his mother into the alley, hurrying away without looking back.

XX Man From Across the Sea - Barn

He recognized the building around him as a barn, slivers of light shining through the gaps between its boards, but ascertained no more about his location. Or how he came to be there.

A vague recollection of water stirred in his mind, and a distant memory suggested a word used to represent him might exist, but it eluded him, too. The more he thought on it, and where he'd been before the poorly built barn, the more his head throbbed. He stopped trying. He was where he was, and he knew no more.

Outside the gap-toothed barn walls, a cow lowed; overhead, birds twittered and flitted in the dark rafters. He stood and tilted his head back to gaze toward the ceiling, eyes squinted to see the birds, but the boards of the roof fit tighter than those of the walls and no light filtered in from the sky. Their birdsongs brought a smile to his lips, nonetheless.

He brushed hay off the backside of his red breeches, the tough fabric stiff with dried sea water and too much time being worn. His white shirt clung to him, damp with sweat. The heat within the barn wasn't unbearable, but enough to keep his perspiration fresh and coax odors from every corner of the building.

Though he saw no animals, he detected the faint odor of livestock. Goats, he suspected, or sheep, but not the cow he heard, or horses. The dung of the larger animals possessed a distinctly different aroma, though he wasn't sure how he knew.

The stink of wetness and decay overlaid the sweet scent of stale dung. Though the roof looked sturdy enough to hold up to the weather, the gaps in the wall would certainly let in rain carried upon a stiff wind. He inhaled deeply and detected the briny aroma of the sea. Whether it simply emanated from his clothing or the barn sat near the shore, he couldn't be sure without seeing. If the building did rest by the ocean, then breezes brisk enough to turn the rain sideways and push it through the cracks in the walls were likely common, and decay, rot and mold inevitable.

He turned his attention away from the various smells and to the wide array of items around him. Some he recognized, some he didn't, others he thought he should but couldn't recall, much like his name and where he'd been before the barn.

A forest of long-handled tools leaned against one wall. Rakes; spades; hoes; a pitted and rusted scythe; three pitchforks; an instrument with a long, knife-like blade, sharp on only one side. He took a step toward the tools to gain a better view and a chain rattled, stopping his right foot from moving more than half a pace. His brow furrowed and he examined the cuff around his ankle, the chain snaking through the mess of dirty straw to a thick spike driven into the dirt floor.

He forgot the contents of the barn and dragged his tethered foot across the floor to the iron stake, the chain kicking up dust as it moved. When he reached it, he examined the plain, straight piece of iron and saw a device connecting his shackles to it. He grasped the end of the spike with both hands and pulled. It didn't move.

I am a prisoner.

He squatted shallowly and used the strength of his legs to pull up on the post, but it remained driven too deep for him to extract. With a sigh, he gave up and returned to his survey of the barn.

Rickety shelves built of driftwood and scraps of board rested beside the row of tools, jars and bottles of all shapes and sizes balanced precariously on their surfaces. A clay jug with a broken handle sat beside a squat jar with no lid, unfamiliar letters inscribed in it before it went in the kiln. He squinted at it, but the strange shapes made no sense to him, triggered no memory or recognition. None of the other vessels showed any markings.

He scanned the rest of the barn: piles of tattered furs, an apple barrel with the hilts of swords and hafts of axes protruding out the top, spears with broken shafts, oddly shaped chunks of wood, bricks, rocks, a heap that might have been a pile of rotting vegetables. Stacks of stuffed-full burlap sacks sat in one corner; angular corners pressed against the inside of a few, others looked as though they held feathers.

The spike pinning his chain to the floor had been cunningly positioned to keep him from reaching anything but the grubby straw strewn across the dirt floor. The weapons and armor were farthest from him, though he didn't have the sense he'd know how to use a sword or axe if he reached them.

He redirected his focus from the sundry items contained by the barn to the gaps in its walls. Sun shone through, but he saw little beyond the light: snatches of yellowed grass and dirt, a house not too far away, perhaps the green foliage of a forest. He crouched, attempting to peer through at different angles. When that showed him nothing further, he closed his eyes and listened.

A dull breeze rattled the tall grass. Birds flitted overhead, but others called and responded from the forest. The wind occasionally lifted something hanging on the outside of the barn, then dropped it back with a gentle thump. Beyond it, he heard the slosh and tumble of waves rolling onto the shore.

He recalled a vision of the sea, but not the view standing on the beach, gazing out over churning green water reflecting the sun's glow. Without intending to, he pictured waves washing over his head, felt the chilly sea biting into his body and tightness in his chest as though struggling for air. He sensed a shadow pass over him and snapped his eyes open, fear gripping him.

Nothing had changed in the barn. The tools leaned, the pots sat, the sacks bulged. He stood, dragged the chain in a circle as he scanned the corners of the wide-open room and searched the shadows. When he realized he remained alone, he released his breath and sagged to the floor again, limbs feeling exhaustion like he'd truly been in the sea treading water for hours. His eyelids fluttered and he allowed himself to tilt over, lying on his side, sleep sliding over him to push fear and confusion out of his head.

***

A noise woke him, but he didn't know what.

He pushed himself up to sitting and brushed away straw stuck to his cheek. Sunlight still found its way through the spaces between the boards, so he hadn't slept too long, but what had jarred him from his sleep?

"Giddup."

The man stood by the door, arms crossed in front of his broad chest, a dark and shaggy beast sitting at his side. How he'd missed the fellow and his dog, he didn't know—he resembled a barrel onto which someone affixed arms and legs, with a head covered almost completely in black hair. His eyes and nose and a sliver of cheeks peeked out, but the mouth uttering the nonsensical sounds hid deep in a thicket of facial hair. The dog growled and made its considerable teeth conspicuous.

"Giddup," the man repeated. This time, he waved both arms in an upward motion, palms facing the roof.

Still groggy with sleep but understanding the gesture, he wiped his hands on his red breeches and climbed to his feet, wary eyes darting between the man and his dog. The fellow crossed his arms again, his gaze unreadable in the dim light.

"Whadder yadoin onmaland?"

The man in the white shirt shook his head, hoping the burly man realized it meant he didn't understand his language.

Bushy brows lowered; he scratched an itch deep in his beard. "Wassername?"

He considered attempting to explain his lack of comprehension, but thinking of doing so made him realize he wasn't aware if he possessed the ability to speak. Or what words he might form if he did. He only knew he couldn't decipher this man's communications.

"Wassername?"

He shook his head again. This time the man didn't take as long to reply. The fellow uncrossed his arms and tapped his chest with both hands.

"M'name sjud ah."

His bushy brows dipped further. He tapped himself again, more insistently.

"Juddah. Wassername?"

The sounds were words, he realized, but their meanings were as mysterious to him as the contents of the over-stuffed sacks. He shrugged, wondering if it was a gesture this stocky man covered with hair might understand.

The fellow blew a breath out that slapped his lips together and fluttered the long hairs of the mustache draped over his mouth. He let his arms hang at his sides, the fingers of his left hand finding the fur at the back of the dog's neck. The beast looked up at him and stowed its teeth.

"Stay." He pointed and the dog whined in its throat.

The animal stayed put as the man walked closer, but not close enough for the two men to reach each other. The facial hair under his nose tilted as though a smile might be hidden underneath the tangle.

"Ayegot taname ferya." Sunlight glimmered in his eyes and he clapped his hands together once, the sharp crack startling the birds in the rafters. "Yername sgunnabee jakazz."

A barking laugh spilled out of the man's beard. He closed his eyes and rocked forward, one hand on his belly, the other slapping his knee. The man dressed in white and red watched, curious and more than a little worried. When the laughter ceased, the burly man stood straight, snorted and spat a wad of snot on the floor. He wiped his eyes on the sleeve of his shirt that looked as though it wasn't the first time things had been wiped on it.

The two men regarded each other. The rafter birds the stocky fellow's outburst had disturbed settled back on their perches, their whistles and coos the lone sounds interrupting the barn's heavy silence. The dog's front paws danced on the dirt floor like it couldn't stand remaining in one place but didn't dare to disobey its master.

Mirth disappeared from the stout man's eyes and he put his hands on his hips.

"Welliv yergunna stayear, yergunna dewsumwerk, jakazz."

He chuckled at whatever he'd said and took one step toward the spike in the floor, then stopped. The man in the white shirt watched, waited, unsure what to expect. He thought the other fellow—Jud-dah's—laughter might be a good sign, but his demeanor otherwise was unreadable.

Jud-dah raised his arm and pointed to a spot beyond him.

"Giddoverthar."

The white-and-red clad man peered over his shoulder at the pile of sacks. What did Jud-dah want him to do? He couldn't reach the sacks, had no idea what they contained. Didn't he realize that? He faced the stocky man again but did nothing.

A cloud fell across the small section of face visible through the shock of Jud-dah's hair. He stomped his foot on the floor, raising a puff of dust, and pointed again.

"Giddoverthar orall sikoojonya," he said, his voice raised.

The chained man flinched and faltered back a step. Jud-dah stabbed the air with his finger a third time, making him realize the stout fellow wanted him to move away. He obliged, the chain clanking with each step until it went taut.

"Goodnow staythar."

Jud-dah stalked across the floor toward the spike without removing his gaze from the chained man. The heel of one of his boots was loose, and it flopped and slapped every time he took a step. When he reached the stake, he stuck meaty fingers into a pocket in the bib of his overalls and pulled out a piece of metal with one round end and one long and straight. He crouched and grabbed the device fastening the chain to the spike, slid the slender end into a hole the chained man hadn't noticed, and the mechanism opened. Jud-dah slipped the device from around the stake and the chain fell slack.

"Donchoomoov," he said, pointing with his free hand. The dog growled.

He gripped the device in his fist and looped the chain twice around his wrist, then stood. A breeze lifted the whatever-it-was hanging against the outside of the barn wall and let it drop, rattling the boards and distracting the chained man. He looked back when he felt the chain tug against his ankle.

Jud-dah had moved toward the row of tools leaning against the wall, but the chain didn't give enough length for him to reach. He yanked on it again, hard enough to move the fellow's foot, prompting him to take a step, then another. Jud-dah reached the tools and stopped but the man kept moving.

"Yewstopwokken."

The words made no sense, so he took another step. Jud-dah snatched a spade from the row of tools and raised it threateningly.

"Stayritethar, jakazz."

The dog jumped to its feet, lips pulled away from sharp teeth, its ears laid back on its head. The man stopped, Jud-dah's meaning and the dog's threat clear in their actions. Any hope the stocky man's laughter meant he might not be a danger disappeared. He held up his hands, palms out in a gesture of surrender.

"Thasbedder." He turned to his animal. "Siddownkooj."

The dog sat and Jud-dah returned his attention to the tools. He selected a long spike similar to the one he'd fastened the chain to, and an instrument with a medium-length wooden handle and a lump of iron on the end. It was unfamiliar to the man wearing the red breeches, but it looked dangerous. Jud-dah held the three tools with the thick fingers of one hand and jerked the chain again with the other.

"Cumonan follame."

He headed for the door, the tether between the two of them pulling taut, giving the man no choice but to follow. Jud-dah's heel flopped as he walked, each step slapping it up against the faded leather boot.

Sunlight spilled into the barn when he thrust the door

open with his shoulder.

"Cmonkooj."

The dog trotted after his master as he continued through without pause. The chained man followed, noticing loops of thick, worn rope held the portal in place, not hinges—one near the top, a second near the bottom.

Jud-dah led him out of the barn and he squinted against the sunlight. Across a small yard of tall grass, a shack smaller than the barn stood, its boards fitted together no better than the outbuilding, but mud and grass plugged the cracks and gaps in an attempt to keep out the elements. A cow stood at the far end of the grounds where the yellowed grass ended and the tree line began. It looked up from its feast and regarded the two men with round, brown eyes before returning to the monumental task of taming the yard's vegetation.

The man waved his hand toward the shack. "Gosidd ona porchkooj."

The dog amended its path, heading for the front of the broken-down house, its tongue lolling out of one side of its mouth. It glanced back at them once before settling on a porch outside the front door of the shack.

The chain links clanked together as they crossed the yard, moving in a direction that took them between the barn and the shack, away from the forest and the cow. They went ten paces before Jud-dah halted and held up the hand with the chain looped around it.

"Stawp!"

The word was foreign, but the man understood the gesture. He stopped, waiting as Jud-dah jammed the tip of the spade into the ground and unlooped the chain from his fist. He put the device at the end of it down and set his boot on top of it, pinning it to the dirt.

"Donchew gitno eyedeas," he said before setting the point of the spike against the ground.

The iron end of the other tool clanged against the head of the stake, driving it into the dirt. Jud-dah hit it five times before he seemed satisfied it would hold. The chained man watched, curious why he'd moved him outside but thankful for the exposure to the sun and fresh air.

Jud-dah threw the tool he'd used as a hammer aside and crouched. The man couldn't see what he was doing, but he assumed he'd be using the device to attach the chain to this spike. The light breeze carried the click of metal against metal to his ears, confirming his thoughts. Jud-dah straightened and gestured with his finger.

"C'mere."

When the man didn't move, he reached down and grabbed the chain, yanked it hard enough he almost pulled his foot out from under him.

"C'mere, jakazz."

He stumbled his way through the tall grass that ended a few paces short of where Jud-dah stood. The dirt by the stocky man's feet was loose, as though it had been worked.

"Yergunna diggmeawel."

Jud-dah swept his hand toward the loose earth expectantly. The stranger looked at the ground but didn't respond, so Jud-dah huffed an exasperated breath and grabbed the spade's handle, pulled it out of the dirt.

"Dig. Dig, jakazz."

He sank the tip back into the soil, gathering dirt on its surface, then lifted it and deposited it on a shallow pile, then repeated the action.

"Dig. Yougotid?"

Jud-dah held the spade out toward the man, who looked at it for an instant. He pictured himself grasping its long handle, swinging it around to hit Jud-dah in the head with its wide blade. He imagined teeth and blood spewing from the mouth hidden within his beard, but the images brought a sickly wave rolling through his belly and he abandoned them. Jud-dah thrust the spade at him again and this time he wrapped his fingers around the handle, taking it from the stocky man. Jud-dah danced back a few steps as though he'd seen what the man had been thinking. He bent quickly and retrieved the hammer, held it in front of himself defensively.

"Dig, jakazz." He nodded toward the ground.

The man took the spade in both hands and scooped a blade full of dirt, then tipped it off onto the same small pile Jud-dah had. He repeated the process a second time, then a third. Doing so appeared to please his captor.

"Gud," Jud-dah said, walking toward his ramshackle dwelling. "Iffnya diggagudwell, maybel gitya sumfinta eet."

The chained man leaned on the end of the handle with the spade's tip buried in the dirt and watched Jud-dah push his way through the tall grass, then disappear into the leaning shack. With the stocky man gone, he returned to the task set out for him, pleased to be physically occupied.

As he worked, he found his muscles aching as though recently exerted to the peak of their abilities. He concentrated on his other worries to distract himself from the modest pain.

First, he wondered about Jud-dah's intentions but, as the size of the pile on which he dumped dirt grew, deeper concerns resurfaced, creasing his sweat-misted brow.

How did I get here?
Where am I from?
Who am I?

The scrape of the spade's metal blade on dirt and rock provided no answer.

XXI Teryk - Hiding the Prize

By the time he reached the end of the alley, Stirk realized sauntering through the streets with an unconscious man slung over his shoulder would draw attention.

He paused and glanced back over his shoulder. Bieta had disappeared back into their room, for which he gave thanks. She'd pulled the remnants of the door closed behind her and the boards Enin had nailed across it hung askew, one of them split in half, making their lodgings conspicuous.

Part of him hoped the one-armed man found her.

Stirk shook his head, remembering that wasn't why he'd looked back. He needed to find a way to conceal the prince while he took him to get rid of him.

For good.

Scraps of garbage scattered the alley's chipped pavers, but nothing he might use. He shuffled his feet, felt cloth brush against his bare ankle, and peered down at a burlap sack lying at his feet. Just what he needed.

He dropped the prince off his shoulder without care; his skull bouncing against the ground brought Stirk a sliver of satisfaction and a slender smile. With a lopsided smirk on his lips, he pulled the torn sack out from under his feet and set to putting the prince inside it.

The bag turned out to be one of the big sacks used for hauling loads of potatoes and such. Though a split along one side rendered it useless for holding turnips and whatnot, it'd do to contain a man the size of the heir to the throne. Stirk put him in headfirst and curled him up into a ball to make him fit. When he finished, he stepped back to admire his work. Other than a bit of pink flesh peeking through the rip, it might've been any old sack of veggies.

Stirk bent and stuck his fingers into a pile of what

might have been either mud or dung—he didn't care to find out which—and smeared it on the prince's leg showing through the tear. Camouflage, he thought it might be called.

Satisfied the next in line to rule the kingdom resembled no more than a sack of vegetables, Stirk reached to pick him up and realized the biggest challenge was going to be carrying him with one hand.

"If you weren't here, I'd still have two," he muttered and grasped the top of the sack. "And I wouldn't need to carry you."

He entwined the sack's opening in his fingers, pulling it closed, wrapped the excess burlap around his wrist, and heaved the sack up. His joints protested with the effort, but he got it over his shoulder. The prince hung uncomfortably against his back, a knee or elbow sticking into Stirk's spine. At least he might be able to get away without everyone knowing what he carried.

Where am I going to go?

At the end of the alley, he stopped and looked both ways. Workshops of various kinds lined the avenue and people bustled back and forth between them. No chance he'd find anywhere close by to hide the prince.

Could throw him in the river and be done.

Not a good idea. The cleaners constantly monitored the water, watching for things like this clogging the grate where the river flowed from the outer city to the inner. Probably they'd find the prince before he had time to drown.

A touch of panic stirred in Stirk's belly. His mother seemed convinced the one-armed man'd find them going through the cellar, but what if he didn't? What if he walked out the front door of the tannery and came around the end of the block to the alley's entrance? The soldier might show up at any moment to find Stirk with a lumpy sack of prince hanging over his shoulder.

Got to get out of here.

Where didn't matter, just that he got rid of the incriminating evidence. He struck out, heading left, away from the corner leading along the avenue to the front of the tannery. Stirk's feet dragged on the street's dirt-strewn broken cobble stones, but no one cast him a sideward glance as they went about their own business.

Two blocks on he'd find Sunset, the part of the outer city where the Horseshoe's brothels, pleasure dens, and drug houses did business alongside those that catered to the even less desirable element. Somewhere amongst the twisted mess of streets and desires would be the Guild of Healers, secreted away where only those meant to find it could. Stirk considered ditching the prince and searching out the healer who took his hand, demanding its return, but he wouldn't know where to start looking. He resigned himself to the task at hand, expecting he'd find a suitable place in Sunset to dispose of the prince. If not, the docks of Waterside lay beyond, and then the sea.

I'll get rid of him where no one'll ever find him.

A strained smile twisted his lips as he hefted the lumpy sack to ease the pressure on his shoulder and lowered his head, determined to complete his task.

***

Most of the streets of Sunset were behind Stirk when he caught his first whiff of the sea.

The sack stuffed full of prince dangled over his shoulder, the joint aching, his fingers knotted. On his stealthy trip, he'd passed women offering their bodies, men seeking to sell him stinkweed and powdered sea serpent bone to sniff up his nose, as well as a tiny woman no taller than his waist who offered him services the sound of which made his skin crawl. He stopped to speak to none of them, nor did he stop to find a place to let the prince off his shoulder and snap his neck to release himself and his mother from their problem.

He didn't stop because someone was following him.

Stirk wrenched his head to the left, looking back over his shoulder. No one behind him, but his ears detected the faint jangle of chain mail, the vague whisper of boots creeping across flagstones. The roil of worried nausea in his stomach increased and Stirk quickened his pace, the muscles in his thighs burning.

He swept past the last of the two- and three-story buildings at the outer edge of Sunset and crossed a wide boulevard into Waterside, with its low, flat-topped warehouses. A wagon driven by a tall, thin man seated beside a squat fellow rattled by, the driver yelling at Stirk to watch where he was going, but he ignored him, eyes fixed on the far side of the street.

The large buildings led toward the water, lined by the taller buildings of the shipbuilders, then the docks. Somewhere in these labyrinthine avenues, Stirk would be able to lose his pursuer—the one-armed man, to be sure—and get rid of his problem forever.

Part of him lamented they'd receive no gold for their troubles and he'd lost his hand for nothing, but he also relished the idea of wrapping his fingers tight around the whelp's throat, squeezing until his windpipe popped and his breath ceased.

Stirk tried to smile at the thought, but effort and worry kept the expression from his lips. Sweat ran into his eye and he wiped it away with his stump. Rather than leading a chase through the twisting streets and getting himself lost, he headed straight for the horizon, where he knew he'd find the sea.

Shoremen seated on crates set on end eating their lunches of pickled eggs, cured meats, or wilted vegetables, watched as he passed. Other men he guessed to be sailors waiting for their next ship wandered the streets in groups, laughing and singing, most of them intoxicated. The majority of them headed back the way

Stirk had come, doubtless to spend their recent pay on narcotics and whores, or the dark delicacies he didn't want to think about.

Every few steps, Stirk glanced back, searching the street for a man with one arm, or guards dressed in the garb of the See-Gees. Nothing of the sort. Only the backs of drunken sailors or the eyes of the shoremen staring after him, likely wondering his destination carrying a lumpy sack.

The thought made him worry the split in the side of the sack might have grown, that a princely arm or leg protruded from it. A sailor or shoreman might tell the tale of a fellow hurrying toward the docks with a man in a bag if a one-armed king's man inquired.

Stirk lowered his head and stopped looking at everyone he passed, pushing himself to go faster. Three blocks from the docks, he stumbled, wrenched his ankle. Twisting as he fell, he hit the ground hard with his left side, then cursed himself for not falling on top of the prince. He scraped his shoulder on the cobblestones spotted grayish-white with the shit of the gulls wheeling in the sky overhead.

"Shit on a stick," he cried.

With the sack lying in the dirt beside him, he sat up on the street and rubbed his throbbing ankle, eyes closed tight against the pain. Knots cramped his fingers; one shoulder breathed a sigh of relief for no longer lugging the prince, the other cried out in discomfort from being dragged along the street. Stirk rocked back and forth, holding his leg, wishing for the discomfort to disappear.

"Hey! Hey you!"

Stirk's eyes snapped open. The voice came from behind him, back along the street he'd just walked. He moved to climb to his feet, forgetting his missing hand and jamming the stump of his arm on a sharp stone. Breath whistled between his teeth.

"Hey, mister."

He didn't turn to find out who called to him—he knew. If he looked, he'd find the one-armed man hurrying toward him, ready to use his fancy sword to punish Stirk for carrying the heir to the throne in a torn burlap sack.

Stirk didn't want to be punished.

Heart racing from more than exertion, the big man gained his feet and jerked the sack, intending to pull it back onto his shoulder. The pain in his back and shoulder stopped him. Instead, he started out along the street, limping and dragging the sack behind him.

The buildings appeared the same on both sides of the street—plain wooden doors, no signs, bars on the windows. Narrow alleys clogged with refuse ran between a few, but they didn't offer enough room for Stirk to get away from the man chasing him. At an intersection, he took a right, then the next left, heading closer to the docks.

One block from the sea, the droppings of squawking gulls and terns painted the streets dirty white. Stray feathers littered the walks and birds perched on every roof top, calling out to each other, yelling at Stirk.

"Shut up," he cried and waved his stump over his head.

Another left, then a right onto a narrow street devoid of any other foot traffic. In the close space between warehouses, the sound of the birds weighed on Stirk's ears, blocking out any other sound. Did the one-armed man still follow him? Had he lost him? Did he give up?

The birds' cacophony continued, passed from one to the next as he progressed toward the docks. He spied the wharf now, a block ahead. Beyond, the sea sloshed and undulated, a froth of foam washing against pilings and the sides of boats at anchor.

Stirk paused to peek back, find out if his pursuer still

followed, and his breath caught in his throat. He didn't notice anyone, but the dragging sack had pushed aside rocks and bird shit to form a trail a blind man could follow.

"No," Stirk breathed.

His gaze flickered between the rut left by the sack and the last corner he'd come around, expecting a one-armed man to appear at any moment. The soldier must be close, biding his time, waiting for Stirk to make a mistake and reveal the contents of his sack.

I won't do that.

He hefted the bag, throwing it over his shoulder with a cringe of pain, and hobbled toward the docks.

The bastard won't see what's in my sack.

Stirk passed the end of the final warehouse and the bird shit-covered street gave way to a bird shit-covered wharf smelling of creosote and brine. Men moved about, shifting crates and loading ships. Stirk paused, scanning the docks for a place to hide, a spot to give him enough cover to kill the prince and be finished with the whole affair. If the one-armed man found the heir to the throne dead, but didn't know Stirk had done it, that would have to be sufficient payment for losing his hand.

Stirk wended his way between rows of crates labeled with words he didn't possess the ability to read. He assumed they named their contents, or said to what port they were bound, but he didn't know for sure. He'd never learned his letters or his numbers, same as his Ma. Amidst a maze of wooden crates of different sizes, Stirk stopped again, surveyed the area.

There's too many people.

He stretched up on his toes, his twisted ankle flaring pain along his leg, and a man came onto the docks along the same street he had. Stirk ducked before counting how many arms dangled at the man's side or what kind of sword he carried.

"It's him," he whispered and let the sack slip off his shoulder. "I ain't going to have time to kill you."

Forgetting his hurt ankle, Stirk planted a kick against what he hoped was the whelp's ribcage, then cringed at the pain it caused him.

"Damn you," he growled. "Everything you do hurts me."

Stirk stood, keeping his head ducked to avoid the man coming onto the docks, and glanced around. A tower of small crates was stacked to his right, larger ones to his left. He snagged the top of the sack and dragged it toward the big ones. If he hid it between them, at least he'd have time to get away.

A gull circled overhead, and a man called out. Stirk ducked again, breath shortening to harsh pants. This wasn't working how he'd planned. He dragged the sack into the midst of the larger crates, and decided this place would have to do. One more kick to the prince—with his uninjured foot—Stirk released the sack and started away.

He stopped when he located an unattached crate top leaning between two boxes. He crept up beside it and straightened, peered into an empty container large enough to hold a man.

Stirk laughed.

Another man called out, but Stirk didn't hear what he said. He wiped sweat off his brow with his stump and limped back to where he'd left the sack, grabbed it and dragged the prince to the open crate.

With an effort that sent a sharp pain jolting through his shoulder and into his chest, Stirk lifted the prince-laden bag off the ground. He slipped his stump under it for support and hefted the sack up and over the crate's edge. It balanced on the lip for a second before tumbling in, hitting the bottom with a meaty thump. Stirk wrestled the top into place, regretting he didn't have time to nail it down, then crept away without waiting to find out if anyone had seen him.

***

Stirk chose a different route home than he'd taken during his flight to the docks. He made good time, too, stopping only briefly to give the woman who came up to his waist a try.

Though his twisted ankle hampered him, the lack of the prince's dead weight made him feel lighter as he hurried past Waterside's warehouses, Sunset's pleasure dens, and back to Riverside. He breathed a sigh of relief when he reached the familiar streets with their broken cobblestones and stinking alleys.

Arriving home'd never been so good.

A block from the tanner's, he stopped and peered along the street, convinced the one-armed man would have left See-Gees behind to keep watch in his absence. He saw no one out of the ordinary. After a short time, Flenge exited his workshop, pausing to lock up before heading down the avenue.

Stirk took that to mean it was safe to return.

He peeked around the corner and along the alley leading to the storeroom he shared with his mother. The broken boards Enin had nailed across their door still stuck out at odd angles, but the alley lay empty otherwise.

Stirk hobbled toward home, relief filling his aching joints. He hadn't made the prince pay for him losing a hand, but he'd gotten rid of the whelp, and no one'd ever guess he and his ma had anything to do with the heir to the throne's disappearance. Bieta might not be happy at losing out on the ransom, but she'd have to be proud of her son for getting rid of the problem so well.

"I'm home, Ma," he called before reaching the open doorway. "You ain't got to worry about our problem no more. I got rid of him where no one'll find him."

He reached the broken lintel and stepped inside, the

interior dark and shadow-filled while his eyes adjusted. When they did, the prideful smile on his face melted away and a confused thought crept into his mind.

How'd he get here before me?

Bieta stood against the far wall wearing a frightened and concerned expression as one armored man held each of her arms and another peered down into the cellar. She looked like she might have been crying, but it was the other man in the room who concerned Stirk.

The one-armed man stepped in front of him, the tip of his fancy blade leveled at Stirk's throat, his eyes burning with anger.

"Where is Prince Teryk?"

XXII Ailyssa - Prayer Garden

Ailyssa detected the scent of lemon first. It floated along the hallway, coaxing her toward the prayer garden with her Daughter leading her by the arm.

Claris. My Daughter.

How long since the Matrons separated them in the name of the Goddess? Many turns of the seasons—she'd counted the deep scores in the wall of her chamber time and time again. Claris hadn't blooded until she'd seen the seasons turn fifteen times—a late bloomer—which meant nineteen summers since her Daughter had been taken from her.

Has she been here all this time?

Ailyssa gripped Claris' arm tighter but didn't ask. She didn't know who else might be nearby and thought such discussions better kept private.

"Are you taking me to the prayer garden?" she asked instead.

"Yes, Mother. The courtyard is beautiful, and few

Sisters will be there now."

The sense of relief filling Ailyssa at the idea of visiting the prayer garden surprised her. Since waking with a blur of white replacing her view of the world, she'd beseeched the Goddess, begged her, even cursed her, but her daily habit of communing with her had been the farthest thing from her mind. In her fear and distress, she hadn't noticed how abandoning a life-long ritual had left an empty ache in her chest.

Claris opened a door and a breeze touched Ailyssa's face, the aroma of flowers and shrubs carried on it. The perfumes combined into one rapturous fragrance, none of them easily identified on their own, and Ailyssa closed her unseeing eyes and inhaled, letting the scents that always reminded her of the Goddess fill her lungs.

Perhaps the Goddess hasn't deserted me. Jubha Kyna is not ideal, but I am alive, and now I have my Daughter.

Claris guided her across the threshold then paused; the door clicked shut behind them.

The glare of her blindness brightened with the quality of light, and the sun warmed Ailyssa's cheeks, calmed her spirit. Amongst the floral aromas, she detected a faint whiff of rain, as though a few drops had fallen overnight. Somewhere above, birds sang, and Ailyssa imagined them to be sparrows hopping from one branch to another branch of a magnolia tree, their brown and white wings standing out against the tree's faded pink blooms. The image soothed her as much as did the sun's rays.

Claris led her away from the door, their sandals scuffing along a dirt path. The gurgle of running water reached Ailyssa's ears and she gasped with delight—a stream or a fountain. The garden at Olvana had been peaceful, but hadn't had water.

"It does seem beautiful here," Ailyssa said, the sun's warmth on her skin fading then returning as they passed through a patch of shade. "Where are you taking me?"

"Somewhere we will be able to speak uninterrupted," Claris replied, her words terse.

Ailyssa's brow furrowed at this, then Claris increased their pace, hurrying them through the garden. The path climbed a shallow hill, bent to the left. The murmur of water grew louder, and the scent of gardenia filled the air.

"This will do." Claris drew to a stop. "You are standing beside a bench, Mother. Let me help you sit."

Ailyssa allowed her, the peace brought by wandering through a prayer garden dangling by a quickly fraying thread. What caused the tension in Claris' tone? Why must they be away from the other women?

Claris sat beside her Mother. She clasped Ailyssa's hand in hers, held it in her lap.

"I...," Claris began, but her voice cracked. She cleared her throat before speaking again. "I didn't expect to ever see you again."

Ailyssa shook her head in response, worried her own voice might not withstand the emotion swirling within her at finding her Daughter. Still, beneath it hung a sense of dread.

"It's been many turns of the seasons," she added.

"Yes," Ailyssa agreed. "Nineteen."

Claris squeezed her hand and sighed. Ailyssa imagined her face tilted toward the sun, a smile on her lips, but the woman in her mind had seen only fifteen turns, not thirty-four like the woman seated beside her in the Goddess' prayer garden. The urge to reach out and touch her cheek, trace her features with her fingers, nearly overwhelmed her.

"Have you been well?" Claris asked, her voice hesitant.

"They cast me out."

Awkward silence. Ailyssa clearly heard her Daughter

197

swallow before she spoke again.

"I'm sorry, Mother. I wasn't thinking. Did you..." She hesitated, though Ailyssa knew what the question would be. "Did you not have other Daughters?"

"No. There were only your brothers."

"I remember."

Ailyssa's heart cinched tight as she remembered the man she'd been meant to couple with, the unmistakable birthmark on his shoulder. So much time had passed since that child was taken—thirteen turns more than when she lost Claris—but the pain remained as bright as the midday sun.

Ailyssa inhaled a breath to calm herself, savored the gardenia's fragrance, and shifted toward her Daughter, facing her.

"What of you? Did you Mother any children?"

"Not at first," she said, sadness in her words. "Not when I was with your order. But I have become Ra since I came to Jubha Kyna."

"That's wonderful."

"Two daughters."

"How old are they?"

"The youngest has seen seven seasons, the elder ten."

Ailyssa frowned at the sorrow in her Daughter's words. She knew the sound of it because her own voice held the same note of lamentation when she spoke of her children. Though it was her Daughter sitting beside her, she didn't know how to comfort this woman she hadn't known for so long.

"I am relieved they didn't bring you here when they took you away from me. How long have you been here, then?"

"Almost four turns."

She opened her mouth to ask Claris how she came to leave the order of Olvana and end up a Sister of Jubha Kyna, but she found no words that might not offend.

Instead, she closed her mouth and looked away, as though gazing out at the prayer garden.

"I wasn't cast out, Mother," Claris said after a pause that became uncomfortable for them both. "I left."

Ailyssa shook her head. "Why?" she whispered, unsure if anyone else was around to eavesdrop. "Why leave to come here?"

"I didn't leave to come here. I left because I fell in love."

The word shocked Ailyssa in the same manner it might have had her Daughter struck her across the face with the palm of her hand. She cocked her head back toward her, wondered if she directed her eyes toward the younger woman's, if Claris could bear to gaze at her or if she diverted her face.

"Love? How...?"

Claris let go of her Mother's hand and stood, the abrupt lack of contact leaving Ailyssa feeling the emptiness she'd carried inside her so long. The brief touch had filled it. The younger woman's sandals scraped the dirt path, paused, then she turned.

"We didn't mean it to happen. A coupling ceremony like any other, but we connected in a way I never imagined possible with a man." She hesitated over the next words. "In that short time, we decided we couldn't live without each other."

Nausea stirred within Ailyssa. Every coupling ceremony she'd ever been part of flooded her memory with visions of rough skin, hair, the odor of sweat disguised by scented oils, deep-throated grunts as each man fulfilled his duty. Never did the possibility of having a connection with any of them crossed her mind—it was forbidden. Her thoughts whirled with what Claris told her, but the outcome didn't make sense.

"And your solution was to come here?"

Claris sighed heavily and returned to the bench. She

didn't take her Mother's hand this time.

"We meant to live a normal life together, away from the order. He came for me one night, and I left."

Claris fell silent, the quiet drawing out. The birds continued to sing, the water continued to burble, but now they were annoyances in Ailyssa's ears. She wiped her palms on the front of her smock, waiting for her Daughter to continue while not wanting her to do so. Her desertion explained why they'd banished Ailyssa with such little regard.

"Fewer than four moons later, he'd cast me aside for another. Love, it turns it out, is not real."

"Claris," Ailyssa said, intending to speak words of comfort, but she possessed no experience with this sort of thing. Rumors of women loving men existed, and she knew it happened outside the order, but she'd never heard of it happening to a Sister of the order.

My Daughter.

"I was despondent, Mother. My love was gone, I'd borne no children, and I knew they wouldn't have me back. I..." Her voice wavered again. "I considered taking my own life."

Ailyssa's body tensed. Claris' story—its ending, at least—sounded too familiar. Heartsick, sorrowful, alone; Ailyssa herself had been these things when Creidra found her, seemingly sent by the Goddess at her time of need.

"And when things appeared the darkest," Ailyssa ventured, "a Sister of Jubha Kyna saved you?"

"N'th Adnine Re'a herself," Claris said. "The knife was pressed to my wrist when she happened upon me. She said she could show me my path back to the Goddess."

Ailyssa shifted uncomfortably on the hard bench, suddenly aware of the way it pressed against buttocks. Could it be but coincidence she and her Daughter ended up in Jubha Kyna through such similar circumstances? Not long ago, she'd have assumed it the Goddess' will, but she was beginning to suspect there might be more to the brothel order than any realized.

"So she brought you here," Ailyssa said, abandoning her thoughts. "And you are happy?"

"I was."

"I don't understand. How could anyone dedicated to the Goddess be happy here? Doing this?"

"I enjoy the men."

The words dropped between them like a brick thrown from one of the trees overhead. Ailyssa opened her mouth, struggling to find the words to express the disgust she'd felt when the man touched her, made her touch him. How could anyone enjoy it?

"You enjoy it when they touch you with their hands? Their tongues? When they do those...those...things?"

"There's more, Mother. The longer you're here, the more the men will ask of you. I've been tied up and gagged, beaten—"

"Oh, Claris." She groped in the glow of her blindness and found her Daughter's thigh on which to place her hand, to comfort her after the horrible things she'd endured. "That's awful."

Silence for a moment. "No, Mother. I like that, too."

Ailyssa gasped and jerked her hand away. She stood abruptly and stumbled away a step. The ground tilted beneath her, a wave of vertigo spinning her head; she reached out, groping in the nothing of her vision, and would have fallen if Claris' hands hadn't grasped her. When she found her balance again, she shrugged off her Daughter's touch.

"I'm sorry to disappoint you so, Mother. But none of that matters."

"None of it matters?" Ailyssa cried and spun in the direction of Claris' voice. "How can you say that? This is an affront to everything the Goddess teaches. This is the reason the Goddess banished the Small Gods."

"Mother," she said, her hand brushing Ailyssa's arm. The older woman twisted away again. "There is more."

"Don't tell me." Ailyssa pressed her hands against the sides of her head, turning the chirping of the birds and the water's gurgle into a dull hum in her ears. "I don't want to hear any more."

Her heart raced. How could things change so quickly? When they'd entered the prayer garden, she wanted to find a way to reconcile her feelings, the Goddess, and this place. Not now. Would she eventually be expected to let men bind her? Stuff her mouth full of rags? She shuddered at what else those animals might be allowed to do to her—what they already did to her Daughter.

And she enjoys it.

Claris spoke again, her muffled words drowning out the birds and the running water, the rush of blood pulsing in Ailyssa's ears. She grabbed at her Mother's arm to pull her hand away, but the older woman spun from her, her feet tangling. Ailyssa went to the ground, barely catching herself. A rock cut into the heel of her right hand and she fell over onto her side. Before she considered righting herself, Claris kneeled beside her, gripping her shoulders.

"Mother, please," she cried, tears plain in her voice.

"No." Ailyssa struggled to get away but her Daughter held her, kept her from returning her hands to her ears.

"They took them away."

Ailyssa stopped writhing, unsure if she'd heard Claris correctly. She directed her gaze toward where she expected her Daughter's eyes might be, the disgusting things she'd said fleeing her mind. She pushed herself up on her elbows.

"What?"

"They took them, Mother." Claris collapsed against Ailyssa, her body racked with sobs. "They took my babies."

XXIII Kuneprius - Clay Feet

The bed creaked under his weight as Kuneprius pulled the boot on. The old leather was tough and hard, the sole worn, the heel lopsided. It hurt his foot. With a sigh, he repeated the action with the other boot, then stood. Not until he was up and staring at the hated footwear did he realize the reason for his discomfort—he'd put them on the wrong feet. He sagged back onto the bed and pulled them off again.

"It's been four sunrises, Ves," he said aloud, though he was alone in the tiny room. "Only four and I want to go back. Not much of an adventurer, me."

Leaning forward, he yanked the correct boot onto his right foot—always the right first, he'd decided—then did the same with the other. When he stood this time, they didn't hurt his feet so much. He still hated them, but the priest had said he needed to wear them to fit in.

He also detested the shirt binding his chest, the vest making him sweat, and the breeches chaffing his manhood.

Kuneprius inhaled through his nose. The room reeked of must and stale beer slopped on the floorboards over the course of many seasons. Worse, the inn hadn't been able to supply him with a bowl of water big enough to partake in his usual morning rituals. Not doing so placed a lump in the top of his chest, directly below his throat. He imagined that, should he put his hand on it, he'd feel its hardness beneath the surface of his skin.

"I'm all right, by the way, Ves. It was but a dream." He wiped his fingers across his lips. "But you forgot to ask."

The lopsided heels carried him out the door and down the stairs. The aroma of fresh bread wafted up to him, setting his mouth watering and his belly grumbling before he reached the bottom, but he headed straight out the front door instead of pausing to break his fast. They'd build a fire later and make his gruel.

"Come again," the woman who he'd hired the room from said as he passed.

Kuneprius glanced at her stirring the contents of a cast iron pot hung over a hearth behind the bar. She resembled a man more than the young woman who haunted his dreams, with broad shoulders and narrow hips, a prominent nose and hair hidden beneath a cap. Still, he wondered what might be concealed beneath her skirts, in that mysterious place where her legs came together. He pondered it for the space of two breaths before waving to her over his shoulder and striding out the door.

The sun had risen far enough over the horizon to chase the Small Gods away. Kuneprius stopped at the edge of the porch, staring up at a sky too light to be called night but not bright enough to warrant the name 'day'. Toward sunset, one final star yet gleamed— Rak'bana, the morningstar, the Small God who didn't belong amongst the Small Gods. The Small God who deserved no thanks.

No matter where he looked, the rest of the sky was a blank gray slate awaiting color. The first quarter moon hung stubbornly over the forest in which he'd left the clay man he insisted on calling Vesisdenperos, but not even the faintest of gods remained.

How do I give thanks?

He plodded down the steps to the beaten grass in front of the inn. A horse picketed out front lifted its head from munching what few blades it found and Kuneprius eyed it, wishing the priesthood had seen fit to give him a steed rather than making him walk.

"There isn't an animal big enough to carry around a block of clay the size of Ves," he mumbled as he passed the horse.

Across the dirt track in front of the inn—down which the town of Woodsel he wanted to avoid lay in one direction, sunset the other—he stopped in the middle of the yard. He spun in a tight circle, getting his bearings. There'd been no bowl to wash in, no water to capture his breath. The Small Gods had disappeared before he found himself under their broad sky. What chance of finding a suitable seed garden on an unlucky day such as this?

Of the four sunrises since they left Murtikara, this marked the second time he'd been without water upon waking, and the first time he was unable to give his thanks, but he'd found private gardens each of the other mornings. Though it wasn't always his seed he deposited, he was sure the Small Gods noticed his attempt.

Kuneprius' breath grew short and a thin sweat moistened his armpits beneath the binding shirt. He took three steps straight ahead toward the forest where the clay Vesisdenperos awaited him, but stopped. The night before, he'd come from that direction and seen no gardens. He amended his path and walked around the side of the inn, seeking fertile ground on which to lay his seed.

Tucked in behind the building, he found a herb garden.

He crept up on it like a hunter stalking prey, careful to move as quietly as wearing blocks of wood and chunks of dead animal on his feet allowed. As he neared it, he inhaled the aromas of basil and mint, saw green-gray sprigs of rosemary and wide bay leaves—a few of the same herbs growing in the seed garden at home.

Kuneprius stepped up to the garden's edge and fumbled with the buttons fastening the front of his breeches closed. The top one came open easily enough, but the second proved more difficult and a sliver of panic ignited in his stomach. What if he got trapped in these gods forsaken breeches? After a brief struggle, the second button finally popped free. He breathed a relieved sigh and pulled his manhood out of his trousers.

With the scents of fresh herbs filling his nostrils, Kuneprius allowed his eyelids to slide shut and his mind to wander to the curves hidden beneath the young girl's formless smock. His rod responded and he began to stroke.

Onetwothreefourfivesixseven.

He imagined reaching beneath the hem of the dress, touching the soft skin of her inner leg.

Twentytwotwentythreetwentyfour.

Both hands moved farther up her thighs, then stopped, unsure what to imagine he'd find where her legs came together, but he didn't let it deter his rhythm.

Fortyfortyonefortytwo.

Even with the aroma of mint strong in his nose, he imagined he tasted the saltiness of her skin on his tongue, heard her panting—

"Oy! What in the hell does you think you're doin'?"

Kuneprius snapped his eyes open and spun around, his manhood still in his hand, but the count lost. He'd seen the man before—he'd been pouring drinks behind the bar last night when he arrived, a cheerful smile on his innkeeper lips and a laugh ready on his tongue.

The barkeep was neither laughing nor smiling now. He must have risen early to split kindling for the fire, because he held a wood axe in his hands. His eyes went wide at the sight of Kuneprius with his cock out, but the look of surprise slipped readily back into an expression of anger.

"Get that thing away from my bay leaves." The man growled and brandished the axe.

Without a word of explanation or apology, Kuneprius bolted, attempting to tuck his erect-but-deflating manhood into his pants as he did. He got it stowed, but couldn't button his trousers while he ran, so he grabbed them by the waistband to hold them up.

His foot slipped as he rounded the corner at the end of the inn and he went to one knee. As he scrambled to regain his feet, the damned uneven boot heels slipped in the dewy grass. He stole a glimpse of the axe-wielding man bearing down on him.

Kuneprius jumped up, grabbed his breeches, and sprinted for the trees.

In his youth, he'd been one of the fastest runners in Murtikara, but the shirt binding his breath, the breeches sliding off his hips, and the boots turning his ankles all conspired to slow him. The footsteps of the man with the axe grew closer.

Kuneprius leaped over a fallen log, teetering but keeping his balance when he landed on the other side, and entered the coolness beneath the branches. The uneven boot heels scuffed through moss and desiccated leaves, leaving divots in the dirt. He ran past a few trees, dodged a stump bleached gray by seasons of weather, then dared a glance over his shoulder.

The axe man still pursued him.

"Ves," he cried out, voice shaking with the pounding of his feet. "Help me!"

Ahead of him, the forest floor climbed a short hill. He drove straight up it, but the soles of the unaccustomed boots slipped in the carpet of needles fallen from the trees above. Kuneprius hit the ground elbows first, saving himself from knocking the breath out of his chest. He scrambled to keep going, soles scuffling, and heard the axe man's steps take to the rise.

With nothing else to do, he flipped onto his back to face his death.

The man's face twisted with a rage that didn't befit catching a fellow who planned to leave a few drops of seed on his mint. Narrowed eyes glared from his reddened face; he gripped the axe handle in both hands in the manner of someone familiar with swinging it.

Kuneprius clambered farther up the hill using hands and feet, his ass dragging and his loose breeches sagging, scooping dirt and pine needles into his crack.

"You're the one," the man exclaimed. "Knew I'd catch you one day."

"I...I'm sorry. I meant no harm to your herb garden."

"Ain't my herb garden I care about, it's Ellie's lady garden. This ain't the first time you been by looking to pay a visit, is it?"

Kuneprius shook his head hard enough he couldn't keep count of the number of times he did. Four, he thought.

"It be the last time, dead right."

The man stepped up and raised the axe, gripping the knobbed end in both hands. Teeth gritted, arms tensed to swing, he stopped. His eyes opened wide and his face went slack.

A gray foot bigger than any boot could hold thumped the ground beside Kuneprius, sending fallen leaves skittering away.

"Ves. Thank the Small Gods."

The axe man seemed unsure what to do for an instant, but when the clay man took another step toward him, his indecision fled. The man jumped forward before Vesisdenperos had the chance to, and the axe head came down.

It entered the top of the golem's chest with a wet splat. Droplets of moist clay spattered across Kuneprius' cheek. He wiped at it, sickened as though he'd been splashed with his friend's blood, then the clay man's fingers found his attacker's throat.

"No." The word came out a whisper between Kuneprius' lips.

Muscles flexed beneath the smooth gray skin of the golem's forearm and the axe man's eyes bulged. Desperate hands released the axe handle to claw at the clay man's arms, but to no effect.

"Let him go." Kuneprius scrambled to his feet. "Please, Ves. Don't kill him."

An ugly choking cough found its way out of the axe man's mouth, and a spray of blood along with it. Kuneprius grabbed at Vesisdenperos' arm, but the big man shrugged him off. He could do nothing but watch as the clay monstrosity jerked his wrist and the axe man's neck broke with a sickening crack. He opened his hand and the dead innkeeper slumped to the ground.

The golem plucked the axe from his chest and stalked away, headed deeper into the forest and leaving Kuneprius standing over the corpse. He watched after his one-time friend, the gray flesh oblivious to the thorns and branches plucking at it, and wondered if any of Vesisdenperos remained inside the clay shell, or if believing so was a fantasy.

After a moment, he looked at the innkeeper's face, his tongue lolling out of the side of his mouth. The face of the young woman he'd killed flashed across his mind, the way it did when he first woke each morning, and he blinked to dispel it. Once, twice, three times.

"You didn't have to kill him, Ves," he said and followed the golem into the forest, picking clay out from under his nails as he walked. "You didn't have to."

XXIV Danya - Unmasked

Your brother is *not dead.*

The words haunted Danya during her stay in the small room overlooking the courtyard. She tossed and turned in the bed after the setting of the sun, she paced the thin carpet when it rose again. The need to get away and find him, or to let Trenan know he lived and to continue the search might have consumed her, but the strange feeling brought to her by the room, and her curiosity about everything she'd heard, kept her from leaving.

After her second sunrise in the room, she stood on the balcony staring at the patch of blank earth in the middle of the courtyard. No matter how she squinted and strained, she saw nothing but dirt and rocks—no tender sprout grew from the Seed of Life.

Mother of Death. Seed of Life. What does it mean?

The chamber door opened behind her, but she didn't turn to greet the person who entered. Without looking, she knew it would be Evalal in her drab green robe and wooden mask. No one else visited her despite the bustle of activity that occasionally emanated from the great room below. Evalal tended all her needs, from bringing her food to emptying her honey pot and teaching her the ways of the Goddess, but she had yet to see the girl's face.

"I'm not hungry yet," Danya said gazing out over the courtyard.

Evalal didn't respond. Footsteps whispered on the thin carpet as she entered the room, but she said nothing. Curiosity soon stole Danya's attention from the mound of dirt and the seed hidden beneath; she faced her keeper.

The girl standing in the middle of the room appeared to have seen the seasons turn ten or eleven times. The skin of her cheeks was smooth, her lips ready to smile, but it was her eyes which identified her.

"Evalal?" The princess stepped away from the balcony. "Is that you?"

The smile threatening on her lips broke across her face and she nodded. Danya took two quick steps into the room but then halted, quashing her urge to rush to the girl and embrace her. She didn't understand the Sisters well enough to know if the missing mask signified a good thing.

"Where is your mask?"

"I got my blood during the night."

Danya stared at her, uncomprehending. She wanted to smile along with the girl, but found herself unable. The princess raised a brow and shook her head.

"I don't understand."

The young girl's expression didn't falter at Danya's confusion. "In our order, initiates wear the mask until their blood comes. Today, I am no longer an initiate. Today, I am N'th Evalal."

"I see." Danya crossed the room to sit on the edge of the bed, indicated for Evalal to join her. "But I don't understand why the mask in the first place."

"There are no men here."

"None?"

Danya thought of the great room and the robed women working at their various tasks. She'd seen no men but had supposed them to be kept separate, somewhere else in the labyrinthine temple.

"None."

"And this is why you wear the masks? To look like men?"

"Initiates are given the tasks men might normally do."

Danya tilted her head. "Such as?"

"Going to market. Upkeep and repairs, that sort of thing."

"If no men reside in the temple, where do young ones come from?"

This time, Evalal appeared confused. "What do you mean?"

"Both a man and a woman are required to create life. How do your Mothers give birth without a man?"

"Our Mothers do not give birth," Evalal replied with a nervous chuckle. "The Goddess gives birth to initiates in other parts of the city, sometimes other parts of the kingdom. When people find them, they bring them to the temple and give them to the Mothers. Only the Mother of Death gives birth."

Danya recalled her trip to the temple, passing the brothels of Sunset on the way. She doubted the Goddess gave birth to the initiates any more than she did. The temple, it turned out, was a place for whores to dispose of their unwanted daughters.

Better than the alternative.

The princess tried not to think about what might happen to their sons. She forced a smile on her face and rubbed Evalal's arm.

"So this is a special day for you."

"Yes," she replied, nodding enthusiastically. "And for you, too."

"For me? How so?"

"Today is the day you take the Seed of Life from the earth."

XXV Trenan - Bloodhound

Trenan left Dansil standing by the tanner's front door in

case the woman and her son tried to escape through the cellar. He positioned Strylor at the far end of the alley and kept Osis with him as they headed toward the storeroom from the other end.

Godsbane in his hand, the master swordsman stalked along the alley, his boots sinking in detritus. The moon had turned through many seasons since he last spent much time in the outer city, but it seemed conditions had worsened. He didn't recall it being quite so dirty, so rough, so poor.

He shooed the thought aside to concentrate on his senses and the feel in his gut. Intuition told him they were on the right track, that this woman and her son had information to help them locate Teryk. No solid evidence supported the hunch, but his soldier's instinct had been piqued the moment he stood at the mouth of the alley gazing along its garbage-strewn length.

The door for which he searched should be the eighth from the corner, but the master swordsman determined which one it was long before he reached it.

Splintered boards hung at odd angles, protruding out into the alley, bent spikes jutting from them threatening any passers-by. Trenan gestured with his sword and Osis stood on his toes to see past. The sergeant nodded and the master swordsman put a finger to his lips, urging him to keep quiet.

When they reached the doorway, Trenan saw someone had done their best to replace the door in its jamb. It hung from one hinge, the other twisted and broken, the lintel shattered. Now they were so close, he realized the boards protruding into the alley had been nailed across the doorway, presumably to keep someone inside the storeroom.

Except someone had desperately wanted to get out.

Trenan banged Godsbane's pommel against the door, the weakened wood trembling with the impact.

"Open this door in the name of the king."

He stepped back, weapon at the ready. Nothing happened. The master swordsman hammered the door again.

"Open the door," he said, louder this time.

The sense of calm that always descended on him in violent or desperate situations fell over him, displacing any hint of fear or nervousness from his body. The only emotional reaction it failed to quell was his worry for Ishla and how all of this might affect the two of them. A moment later, the door hadn't opened, so Trenan stepped back, raised his foot, and set his boot heel against the wood.

The beleaguered hinge screeched as the remnants of the door exploded inward, boards breaking. Trenan rushed into the storeroom, Osis close behind.

Abandoned.

A table sat in the center of the small space, a bowl of dirty water on top of it; one chair, a crate, a couple of half-empty sacks of rice and flour, a dirty pile of hay, and an empty shelf mounted on the wall. Trenan stepped farther into the room, disappointed his instincts had proven wrong. Finding they were no closer to recovering the prince made his gut clench until he spied the trap door.

The cellar.

The worn and crushed thresh that covered the rest of the floor was absent from the top of the hatch, as though it had been recently opened. As if someone had climbed down, unable to replace the thresh.

"Have a look down there," Trenan said.

Unlike Dansil, Osis responded without protest—the reason Trenan chose the sergeant to accompany him into the storeroom instead of the queen's guard. In the master swordsman's opinion, watching a doorway was the best use of the big lout.

Osis gripped the ring in the trap door with one hand, his sword held ready in the other, then glanced up at Trenan. The swordmaster stepped up beside the sergeant with Godsbane poised to strike, then nodded. His companion pulled the door open, dropping it on the floor with a thud, but nothing emerged from the cellar's depths except the odors of stale urine and scat. Without a word, Osis descended the ladder, leading with the tip of his blade.

Trenan watched him go in the wan light spilling into the room from the shattered door. Normally, he'd have chosen to go himself, but navigating a ladder with one arm would require he put away his weapon, leaving him defenseless. The sergeant realized this and acted without needing to be told—another reason Trenan had chosen him over Dansil.

When Osis disappeared into the darkness under the floorboards, Trenan returned to the doorway and peered toward the far end of the alley. In the distance, Strylor leaned against the corner—nonchalant, but right where Trenan wanted him to be.

The master swordsman went back into the storeroom, making his way around its small and dim interior methodically. He paused by the table, peering into the dark and cloudy water filling the bowl set upon it. Lips pursed, he rested the crown blade against his thigh and plunged his hand in but came up with only a filthy rag.

Nothing but dirt and dust under the table and on the shelf. The amount of mouse shit he found in the rice as he sifted it through his fingers disgusted him; he squeezed the sack of flour, but it contained naught but flour. Finally, he crossed the room to the pile of dirty straw and kneeled beside it.

The pleasant scent of hay that usually reminded him of his youth in the country had long since disappeared from the sleeping area. Trenan's nostrils flared at the mixed odor of filth and sweat, but he inhaled deeply anyway. For his troubles, he caught a faint, coppery odor. He set his sword aside and leaned forward, picking through the pieces of straw until he found one spotted with brown. Raising it to his nose, he sniffed again.

Blood.

Anger and worry and guilt flooded the master swordsman's chest. He couldn't be sure to whom this blood belonged, but he knew it was Teryk's. The prince had been here, he was suddenly sure, but they'd missed him.

A crash from below the floorboards yanked Trenan from his thoughts. He snatched Godsbane from where it lay on the floor and jumped to his feet, hurrying across the room to the trap door.

"Osis," he called. "Are you all right?"

For a moment, the sergeant didn't respond. Trenan waited, breath controlled and sword gripped ready to strike. He opened his mouth to call out again, silently wishing he possessed two good arms to climb down the ladder to his companion's aid, but the shuffle of footsteps below stopped him. A few heartbeats passed, then a woman appeared at the bottom of the ladder. She tilted her head up toward Trenan; the light from the broken doorway cast shadows upon her face, giving her the appearance of having only one eye. An instant later, Osis was beside her.

"Up you go," he prompted.

The woman grasped the rungs and ascended the ladder.

"Please don't hurt me, sirs," the woman begged as she climbed. "Take whatever you want, but don't hurt me."

Trenan raised a brow. "We're men of the king," he said.

The woman reached the top and clambered

awkwardly into the storeroom. Now she was out of the cellar, the master swordsman saw her missing eye was no trick of the light. When she spoke, he realized her eye wasn't the only thing she lacked.

"I heard you say so when you knocked on my door. I ain't got much for you to take, and I'd gladly offer you my wares, if that be what you're looking for."

"Your wares?" Trenan tilted his head. Did she have something hidden below in the cellar?

The woman nodded and a sly smile crept across her face, clearly showing her two missing teeth. She grasped the front of her dress and lifted it, revealing to Trenan the tangle of graying hair between her legs. The master swordsman turned away. Anger flashed in him at the woman's assumption they'd come for that. Did other of the king's soldiers demand such services of her? The thought made him sick. He forced it from his mind, concentrating on why they were there and ignoring the implied misconduct by members of the army.

"Put your dress back down. That's not why we're here."

The woman did as Trenan said, then glanced from the master swordsman to Osis, who'd climbed out of the cellar behind her, and back again.

"Why else would two king's men visit if not for a roll?"

"We're looking for someone."

"Ain't no one here but me," she answered too quickly.

Trenan's eyes narrowed. "You haven't seen anyone out of the ordinary in these parts?"

She shook her head briskly.

"A young man? Twenty turns and dressed in a merchant's finery."

The woman's one-eyed gaze darted between Trenan and the door. When it returned to the master swordsman, she couldn't hold his stare and looked at his feet. Her hesitation in answering lengthened, and Trenan knew it meant the next words out of her mouth would be lies.

"I ain't seen no one."

"I see." Trenan stepped toward her and she raised her head. She took a step back, but Osis standing behind her prevented her from going far. "And where is your son?"

"My son? I don't have a son."

Trenan scowled and moved another step closer.

"The tanner told us he rents the storeroom out to a woman and her son," he said. The woman flinched as though he'd struck her. "Where is he?"

The woman's lips pressed tight together, the top one moving as she rubbed the space between her teeth with her tongue. Trenan resisted the urge to grab her by the throat and demand the whereabouts of the prince.

"He's out, is all. I sent him to market."

The thought of asking her why she'd lied occurred to Trenan, but he didn't bother. She lied because the prince had been here—he'd known so as soon as he found the bloody straw. He pursed his lips and glared into the woman's eye as he spoke to Osis.

"Go get the others," he said, his voice tight and controlled, full of menace. "We wait here until this woman's son returns."

XXVI Ailyssa - Reception

Ailyssa's disgust at the mention of what men did to her Daughter faded, dwarfed by Claris' loss and her suspicions.

Since her arrival, Ailyssa had heard babies crying in the third-floor nursery, calling for their Mothers' milk or the change of their underpants. But she hadn't realized the lack of small feet padding along hallways, the laughter of toddlers, the insolent tantrums of children.

There are none.

"No Daughter remains here beyond the first turn of the seasons," Claris said.

Ailyssa barely noticed her Daughter speaking, her mind twisted by the day's revelations—Claris loving a man, enjoying physical pleasure with them. Now, her Daughter's Daughters had been taken long before the start of their blood.

"Why? Why take them at such a young age?"

Fabric rustled as Claris shuffled closer to her Mother until their legs touched. When she spoke again, she had leaned in, moving her lips close to Ailyssa's ear.

"Some of the Sisters whisper that N'th Adenine Re'a has expanded the reach of Jubha Kyna, opened other temples."

"As has Olvana," Ailyssa replied, not grasping her Daughter's implication.

"Adenine does not do it to honor the Goddess."

Ailyssa faced Claris, raised her brows. "What do you mean?"

"It is not faith, but coin that drives her."

"What does that have to do with your Daughters?"

Claris hesitated before answering; Ailyssa felt her brisk breath against her neck.

"Some men are willing to pay a great deal for unspoiled flesh."

The skin on Ailyssa's arms went cold.

"They're..." Her voice caught in her throat and she swallowed. "They're babies."

"I've been told they take them early so they learn Adenine's way of life. How young they are...pressed into service, I don't know. I suppose it depends on how much money is offered."

Ailyssa's mouth opened and closed, opened and

closed. What could she say in the face of such atrocity? Beside her, Claris' breath shuddered. The older woman put her arm around her Daughter's shoulders, pulled her tight against her.

"I..." No other words came out.

"Others suspect, too," Claris said.

"Why doesn't someone do something about it?"

Claris shook her head against her shoulder. "Because we don't know where they are. If we did anything, what might happen to them?"

"This is terrible. How can the Goddess let this be?"

"Let what be?" The voice came from Ailyssa's left and the sound of it prompted Claris to her feet.

"N'th Adenine Re'a," she exclaimed.

Ailyssa's heart bounced in her chest and she pulled an unconscious gasp of air through her teeth. She stood unsteadily, arms reached out in front of her until a hand grasped hers.

"What can't the Goddess let be, N'th Ailyssa Ra?"

The hand squeezed and Ailyssa realized it was Adenine who gripped her. She considered pulling away, but what would that accomplish? Would she run blind through an unfamiliar garden? Gain her freedom by fighting? Despair and hopelessness weighed on her the way the man's body had pressed down on hers the night before. Maybe the Goddess let these things happen—as she'd let Ailyssa be cast out—because she didn't care.

"Well?"

The hand squeezed harder. Ailyssa ground her teeth, memories of her friend Adesi banishing her, of waking up unable to see, and of being forced to couple with no chance of honoring the Goddess boiling in her chest and up into her throat. She could hold it back no more.

"Where are the children?" she said through her teeth.

"The nursery is on the third floor. Didn't Creidra show—"

"Not the babies," Ailyssa snapped. "The children. Where are my Daughter's Daughters?"

Adenine hesitated three breaths before responding. "Daughter's Daughters?"

"Claris' girls."

"I see: Claris is your Daughter. What a wonderful...coincidence."

"You haven't answered my question."

The woman tugged on Ailyssa's hand, pulling her a couple of paces away from Claris. "They have been sent away for training. Does Olvana not separate Mothers and Daughters?"

"Not until their blood begins."

The hand holding Ailyssa's rose and fell as N'th Adenine Re'a shrugged. "So it is done differently at Jubha Kyna than in Olvana."

Ailyssa chewed her bottom lip, eyes darting, seeing nothing. "But Claris and some other Sisters think—"

"Were you upset when they required you to give up Claris?"

"Of course."

Adenine took Ailyssa's other hand in hers, stood facing her. Ailyssa wondered if she might be wearing a placating smile on her face or if she'd bother wasting the effort on a blind woman.

"That happens here, too," she whispered. "Any Mother is upset when her Daughter is taken, though she knows it to be the will of the Goddess."

Why does she keep her words from Claris?

"But they're so young."

"Things are different here, N'th Ailyssa Ra."

Ailyssa tilted her face away from Adenine's. The rage tightening her chest loosened. Could Claris be wrong? A Mother upset and worried over her children?

"If this is the case," Ailyssa said, the words drawn out as the thought formed. "Then let Claris see her

Daughters."

"That is not the Goddess' wish," Adenine said. "Did you see Claris after they took her to begin the rest of her life?"

Ailyssa's shoulders sagged as though the air had been let out of her body. Of course she hadn't seen her Daughter; she'd spent the last nineteen turns of the seasons wondering what had become of her. How much harder was it for Claris with her Daughters taken from her so much younger? Or was it easier?

"I didn't. I've known nothing of her until today," Ailyssa conceded.

"I know. Such is the way of the Goddess."

Adenine released her hold on Ailyssa's hands and her feet scuffled on the dirt path as she moved away a couple of paces. Without knowing where Claris stood— she hadn't made a sound while Adenine and Ailyssa spoke—an immense pressure of being alone rested on her shoulders.

"Claris," Adenine said.

"Yes, Mother of Mothers?" Claris said, shuffling forward.

"I have changed your schedule for today. Other Sisters will fulfill your appointments."

"Yes, N'th Adenine Re'a."

Relief flooded through Ailyssa. She'd worried that speaking out might end up in punishment for her—it certainly would have in Olvana. Instead, it appeared the Matron intended to grant her and Claris time to themselves. She parted her lips to thank Adenine, hoping to assuage the situation, but the Grand Matron spoke again before her tongue formed the words.

"You will come with me, Claris."

"Of course, N'th Adenine Re'a."

"Ailyssa, you shall wait here. I'll send Creidra for you. I think you are ready to experience a Reception."

The women walked away without another word, leaving Ailyssa feeling lost and alone in the middle of the prayer garden, birds twittering in the trees, water burbling close by. She carefully retraced her steps and slumped back on the bench, palm throbbing with pain unnoticed through her concern. She rubbed her hand on the front of her smock, nervousness growing as she wondered what a Reception was.

***

Other women milled about the reception hall, though Ailyssa couldn't have guessed how many. She picked out four or five distinct voices, perhaps more, and there may have been Sisters like her who chose not to speak.

She rubbed her cut hand on the front of her smock, felt the bandage binding it. Creidra had collected her and took the time to wash blood from her arm and hand, then dressed it and helped her change into a clean outfit, but the young woman had spoken little. Ailyssa's questions went unanswered as though they fell upon deaf ears. Creidra expressed concern about the cut on her hand, spoke of the lovely weather and the beauty of the gardens, but said not a word of this thing called a Reception.

But now Ailyssa sat in the hall, tense and worried as quiet conversations buzzed around her. Creidra had brought her, but left, so she knew no one else in the room, and they seemed happy enough to leave her on her own. Ailyssa wasn't sure if she was glad of that, or wished for the company.

Soon after her arrival in the reception hall, the door swung open and the conversations ceased.

"Hello, Sisters," N'th Adenine Re'a said from the doorway. "Is everyone ready?"

All around Ailyssa, disembodied voices confirmed they were, but she said nothing. Dread crept into her bones and she clasped her hands together tightly in her lap, shifting the bandage and causing pain in her palm. On the other side of the room, one of the other women squealed and clapped with excitement.

"Enter, gentlemen," Adenine said.

Boot heels thumped the stone floor—many of them, by Ailyssa's estimation—and the air in the room changed. It grew warmer and a musky odor crept in, usurping the pleasant aromas of scented oils wafting from the Sisters' freshly scrubbed bodies. Rose and jasmine and mint fell before the onslaught of dirt and sweat and lust.

This is my punishment.

The door closed again and the men's footsteps made their way around the room. A few of the Sisters began speaking again, but not to each other, and their voices took on different tones—higher pitched, with flavors of desire and beckoning.

"Hello," a woman to Ailyssa's right said. "You are a handsome fellow, aren't you? Big, too."

The man chuckled, a rough, low sound like the burble of a brook. "You're quite pretty yourself," he replied.

Ailyssa gulped—the Reception displayed the women for the men, no better than cattle at an auction.

"Come on," the man said, and the woman's skirts rustled as she stood.

"Where do you want to go?"

The man cleared his throat and when he spoke in a hushed voice, Ailyssa still heard his words. "Is there somewhere ye might tie me up?"

The Sister giggled. "Of course. Follow me."

They left and Ailyssa gripped the arms of the chair in which she sat. This process seemed worse than having a man sent to her chamber—these visitors wanted more.

Around her, people spoke and laughed as the women did their best to tempt the men and the visitors picked the woman who'd suit their peculiar needs. She caught snippets of hushed conversations with mentions of feathers, masks, and something called a dildo. Ailyssa had no idea what that was.

She fidgeted in her chair as more of the Sisters paired off with the visitors and took their leave from the reception hall. The few remaining men's boots scuffed on the floor as they made the circuit around the room from woman to woman. It didn't disappoint Ailyssa that they passed her by.

"What's wrong with this one?" a man she hadn't realized stood directly in front of her asked.

"She's blind." Adenine's voice.

"Blind, is she?"

Callused fingers gripped her chin, tilted her head back. Ailyssa gasped but didn't struggle. She stared into the hazy glow, hoping the man would find her lack of vision unsatisfactory and move on.

"I likes her short hair," he commented as he released her face. "Kinda makes her look like a man."

"Well, she's not, I assure you."

"Hmm," the man grunted. "Don't know about fucking a blind woman."

"It sounds as though you need an incentive," Adenine said. A second later, her voice dropped to a whisper. Ailyssa leaned forward, straining to hear, but couldn't.

"Really?" the man exclaimed, surprise in his tone. "You got yourself a deal."

"Excellent. I know you will enjoy yourself."

Ailyssa's eyes widened and she pushed herself back in the chair, head shaking.

"No," she said quietly. "Please, no."

"She's a feisty one, ain't she? All the better."

A hand gripped Ailyssa's upper arm and yanked her up out of the chair. She scrambled to pull free, but the man's grip was strong. Another hand touched her on the other arm; a mouth leaned close to her ear.

"Do not struggle," Adenine whispered. "For Claris' sake."

Her quiet threat prickled along Ailyssa's skin. She relented, allowing the man to lead her across the floor and out the door. Her heart beat heavy in her chest, its pounding echoing in her temples as they made their way along the hall and to a flight of stairs leading down from the temple's main floor—stairs she hadn't known existed. The odors of must and mold floated up from below.

"Where are you taking me?" she asked, fear making her voice flutter.

"The woman said I could take you for free," the man said, his tone suggesting a smile on his lips, "if I put you through your paces in the dungeon. The dungeon usually costs extra, so I couldn't say no to that."

Ailyssa let out a yowl and tried to dig her feet in, but they slid on the stone floor. Supporting her by the arm, the man dragged her down the steps.

XXVII Kuneprius - Down by the Creek

"You shouldn't have killed him."

The trees had thinned, the thick-trunked jackpines giving way to slender birches with leaves waiting to change color and fall when third season arrived. One full turn and a quarter moon were yet to pass before third season came, and the twilight sun warmed Kuneprius through the clothes he wore against his will.

"It's not what I taught you, Ves. Not how I raised you."

The clay man plodded on ahead without in any way

acting as though he heard or understood. Kuneprius wasn't sure the thing could hear at all.

It's not a thing. It's Vesisdenperos.

Part of him clung to the notion, but he also wanted it not to be true. If the golem acted on its own, or if the thoughts of some priest controlled him, then his friend wasn't responsible for the axe man's death. And if Ves wasn't responsible, neither was Kuneprius.

"Do you remember when you were in your twelfth turn of the seasons?" Kuneprius hurried his step to catch up. "The first day you modelled a man? You were so excited, you had trouble being still while I washed you."

The clay man's feet crunched through the undergrowth, unslowed by the creepers and twisted roots impeding Kuneprius. The living sculpture stepped over a fallen tree without adjusting his pace.

"That day, I guessed the destiny awaiting you. Certainly, other sculptors came before you, but none who moved so quickly beyond bowls and shapes to using their skills for molding a man."

Kuneprius peered up through the leaves at the darkening sky. Soon, Ine'vesi—the evenstar—would appear, and the other Small Gods after that. Their appearance signaled time to stop for the night and offer vespers; since he'd missed his morning thanks, he couldn't skip the evensong.

"Remember when you sculpted a statue of me?"

He glanced sideways, tilting his head back to watch for a flicker of recognition on the clay man's brow. The unchanged expression left him disappointed. Kuneprius stared at his feet, carefully avoiding snags and ruts.

"I'm glad they allowed you to show me before they destroyed it."

In the branches overhead, a nightjar sang, proclaiming the approach of sunset. The bird paused, the world holding its breath along with it, until another answered somewhere ahead. Wings beat, leaves fluttered, and the bird left Kuneprius alone with the living clay statue.

They continued in silence. Every ten paces, Kuneprius raised his eyes toward the sky, watching for Ine'vesi to show his twinkling face. Given they'd reached the eighth moon, the evenstar should show up overhead. Ten paces, glance up. Ten paces, glance up.

Between peering skyward through the branches and leaves in search of an excuse to stop for the night, Kuneprius rubbed his face with his hands. Each particle of dirt scraped on his flesh; his cheeks ached to be washed. With night so close to falling, it appeared he'd spend the night outdoors with the clay man for the first time since they left Murtikara—no roof over his head and no chance for a bowl full of water. He hoped they'd find a pond or stream nearby.

Two sunrises hadn't passed without washing since the night he killed the girl, and still he couldn't lave her blood from his cheeks.

His fingernails scraped along his jawbone, desperate to relieve the itch of her life dried on his skin. In doing so, he lost count of his steps. He stopped, let his arm fall to his side, and tilted his head back.

A smudge of gray crept across the sky from the direction of sunrise, but the leaves rustling in the gentle twilight wind obscured his view, and Ine'vesi remained hidden. The crackle and crunch of the clay man's footsteps continued as Kuneprius stared up but, after a moment, they stopped, too, leaving only the whisper of the breeze to break the silence.

Kuneprius' gaze flitted between the brief spaces that flashed when leaves shifted and allowed him a glimpse of the sky. He leaned one way, then the other, searching for the evenstar, when a thought occurred to him:

Why did Ves stop?

A finger of panic leaped into his chest and he tore his gaze away from the branches overhead to scan the sparse forest. He easily spied the clay man's broad gray back fifteen paces ahead but, in the gathering dim, Kuneprius couldn't see why he'd halted.

Unevenly heeled boots scuffing along the ground, he hurried to catch up. The living sculpture didn't move and, for a moment, Kuneprius worried he might no longer be alive. Both sadness and relief flashed through him at the thought but, as he came up beside the golem, he saw this wasn't the reason he'd halted.

Thirty paces ahead, at the bottom of the shallow rise on top of which they stood, a creak cut through the forest, its fast-running water burbling over stones worn smooth by time. With the dip in the ground and the wind in the trees, its gurgle had been hidden until they were nearly upon it.

The sight of the stream invigorated Kuneprius, sending energy coursing through his limbs. He might have rushed forward to plunge his face into the swift coolness, joyously counting how long he held his breath, but the same thing which halted the clay man froze his steps, too.

Beside the creek, two children kneeled, staring up the hill at the blank-eyed, clay-skinned man.

Neither of them moved and, were he closer, Kuneprius suspected he'd have found they held in their air, as did he. The entire forest went quiet, save for the burble of the stream. If he listened close enough, Kuneprius thought he might have counted the worms slithering through the dirt, detected the tiptoe steps of spiders, discovered whether the clay man possessed a heart.

One of the children—a girl who hadn't seen the seasons turn more than seven times—stood, arms dangling at her sides, a short stick caked with mud on one end held in her hand.

At her movement, the clay man took a step toward them.

Kuneprius' heart jumped against his ribs and he forgot about worms and spiders, water and ages-old blood. A chill crept across his cheeks and he clutched at the clay man's arm.

"No," he said, breathless.

The golem's head twisted toward him, as though he heard his words for the first time since they'd departed Murtikara. Dull gray lids scarped across lifeless dun-colored eyes. For an instant, Kuneprius thought the clay man understood, then the boy, who had remained kneeling, stood.

The clay Vesisdenperos' head jerked in the direction of the children and panic flared in Kuneprius again. He raised his hand toward the boy and girl staring up the hill at them.

"Get away! Run!"

He'd made the gesture before he realized what a mistake it was.

The girl dropped the mud-caked stick and grabbed the boy's sleeve, pulling him away from the flattened bank where they'd been playing by the creek. Small feet beat the firm ground, leaping over rocks with the certainty of those who'd walked the same path many times.

The clay man hesitated one heartbeat before bounding down the hill after them.

"No!"

***

The stream burbled. Wind rustled the leaves. Overhead, darkness had overtaken the day and the Small Gods twinkled and winked from their prison in the sky.

Wet mud soaked the knees and backside of Kuneprius' breeches, but he neither noticed nor cared.

He felt no urge to dunk his face in the rushing water, nor did he notice the tightness of old, imagined blood drying on his cheeks.

Fresh blood on his hands usurped his attention.

The young girl's head lay on his lap, eyes closed, broken body still and quiet. She was much younger than the woman he'd killed long ago. This time, it hadn't been his hands that brought her death, but it did nothing to ease the pain in his heart. Responsibility still belonged to him.

Kuneprius brushed hair off her forehead, a few strands sticking in her crusted blood. The boy—her younger brother, he suspected—lay in the mud five paces away, his body twisted, his sightless eyes staring at Kuneprius, accusing.

"I'm sorry," he whispered and brushed his fingers along her cheek. Her skin was already cold. "I'm so sorry."

Kuneprius raised his head and glared at the clay man sitting on a log at the bottom of the rise. The statue stared straight ahead, his sleek skin glistening in the moonlight, and paying no attention to his companion sent to ensure he returned with a Small God of the Green. Kuneprius trembled—with anger, with hatred, with fear and despair.

How had this happened to his friend? To either of them?

He squeezed his eyes closed and bowed his head toward the girl, wanting to ask the Small Gods to care for her in death, but how could he do so when it was their fault her life had come to its end?

Tears rolled down his cheeks. He inhaled a shaking breath, the stink of water and mud and clay scraping the insides of his nostrils raw. If he never inhaled their scent again, it might be too soon. But what was he to do?

He opened his eyes, blinked three times to clear his

vision, and gazed at the girl's face again. She was pretty, as young children always are, but he thought there'd been a glow about her as she kneeled beside the stream, the muddy stick in her hand. The golem's thick fingers had crushed the glow, extinguished it before given the chance to blossom and grow.

Nightjars twittered and sang in the trees. Kuneprius tilted his head back and saw them flit through the sky, tiny shadows across the sky vanishing as quickly as they appeared. A corona of mist surrounded the moon, obscuring the Small Gods perched around it in tribute, but one shone through, larger and brighter than the others.

Ine'vesi, the evenstar.

Kuneprius turned his head away and wept.

XXVIII Danya - Seed of Life

Despite the warm sun shining into the courtyard, the stone floor chilled the soles of Danya's feet. She waited inside the doorway, not knowing what to do or what to expect. A thin sheen of perspiration covered her palms and she resisted the urge to wipe it on the front of the vibrant green smock Evalal had dressed her in.

"Are you all right?" the girl asked standing behind her.

"Yes. I think so."

The princess stared straight ahead, eyes fixed on the slivers of dark earth in the center of the courtyard she glimpsed between jagged rocks. Beyond, figures lined the far wall, some wearing painted masks, others with bare faces allowing her to see women of all ages watching, waiting.

"What am I supposed to do?"

"Get the seed of life."

"How? When?"

The girl's gentle touch on her back startled Danya. "You will know."

The princess shook her head. "But I don't."

"The Mother of Death said you will."

Danya suppressed a shiver. The thought of N'th Sylla Re'a Shi with her wizened skin and pregnant belly made nausea rise in her throat, adding discomfort to the nerves churning her gut. How could a woman of such age give birth, alive or dead? More importantly, with no men in the temple...

"Take your time," Evalal said. Danya heard her feet shuffle, carrying her away.

The princess inhaled deeply through her nose and scented the aroma of the moist earth. Her gaze darted from the dirt to the girls and women standing against the far wall, then to the line of sharp rocks ringing the tiny garden. Now she stood near them rather than staring at them from above, it became obvious they'd been chosen and placed to protect the garden's treasure.

With a loud exhalation, Danya stepped across the threshold and into the sun. Once through the doorway, she saw that Mothers and Daughters were lined up against the wall all the way around the courtyard. They stood on a narrow strip of ground between the temple wall and the jagged rocks. Each woman and child watched her.

"Evalal, I—"

Danya turned back, doubting her task, but the hallway behind her lay empty. A shroud of dread fell across her, blurring her vision, until she recalled the reason she was doing this and her senses returned.

For you, Teryk. Wherever you are.

The princess faced the garden again and stepped up to the edge of the rocks. The one closest to her stood as high as her knee, but others even larger stood between her and the garden mound in the middle of the rocky ring. She placed her hand atop the nearest stone and leaned over, surveying the best path to take. Precarious, but she'd spent her life looking for adventures, small and large. Here was a small adventure poised to lead her to the biggest one she'd ever know.

Danya set her foot on a low rock, its rough surface warmed by the sun. Coarseness scoured the sole of her foot as she put her weight on it. She stepped up, placing her other foot on the rock beside the first, balancing between the two.

Pain lanced up Danya's leg and breath hissed in through her teeth. She waved her arms to maintain balance and peered down to see a thin line of blood trickling along the side of the rock. She shifted, relieving the pain, and raised her gaze toward her goal which seemed farther away than before. The eyes of the Mothers and Daughters bore down on her and she wondered what they'd do if she chose to climb down off the rocks and leave.

I'd never find my way out.

She imagined herself wandering the labyrinthine temple, lost and alone, until hunger and despair finally took her. That was no solution.

Danya moved her wounded foot, a drop of blood spattering on the sharp edge of another stone. Carefully, she eased forward, setting the ball of her foot on the flat surface of the next before following up with her trailing foot. Pause, choose her next step, continue. She considered stepping between the rocks, but not a hint of ground showed among them and she worried she'd be trapped.

Halfway across the ring of stones, Danya's thighs burned and blood ran from the bottoms of both feet, each step leaving a bloody footprint in its wake. She struggled to remain focused, distracted by the pain and by wondering who'd set these stones here, how, and why.

The sun seemed to have grown hotter, glaring on her with an intensity approaching hatred that brought sweat to her brow. Perspiration ran down her temples, caught in her hair, and stung her eyes; it moistened the smock Evalal had made her wear, sticking the rough cloth to her skin. She wished for the sun and its unbearable heat to leave her alone.

Danya raised her head and looked across the stretch of rocks at the patch of dark soil. Close as she'd come, she still observed no sign of a seed planted in the garden—not so much as a weed disturbing the earth.

Blood squelched beneath her foot as she took another step. She lifted the other to move forward and the wetness of her foot and the rock's smooth surface conspired to make her slip.

Danya gasped as her foot went out from under her. She sprawled forward, knees scraping down the side of a rock. Her hands flashed out, grasping for something to catch herself on and finding sharp edges. She jammed her finger, sliced her palm, but stopped herself, her eye a finger's-width away from a jagged point.

The muscles in her arms and shoulders knotting, the princess held herself for a moment, staring at the rock's sharp edge. Time had shaped it to an edge worthy of a weapon, but in its lines and contours, she glimpsed shapes and figures; tiny people stacked in heaps. Danya blinked hard and they disappeared.

A shuddering breath helped her regain her equilibrium and she carefully found her way back to her feet. She stood teetering and glanced at the rock that had cut her palm, saw her blood glistening on its surface. As she watched, it sizzled and dried, as though the rock sat in the bottom of a fire pit, though she knew it was not hot.

Danya raised her head, fixing her gaze on the patch of dark earth ahead.

"I wish you were here, Teryk," she whispered.

After wiping her hand on the front of her smock and smearing it with blood, she set out again, stepping gingerly from one stone to the next. The soles of her feet ached, the flesh shredded with lacerations. A few more steps and she peered back over her shoulder at the trail of bloody footprints marking her path across the bed of rocks.

Concentrate.

She returned her attention to the precarious way ahead instead of what she'd left behind, her eyes searching out the best spots to place her feet. The muscles in her thighs and backside felt as though they'd been transformed into hot steel, burning away the flesh covering them. Cold sweat covered her as she pressed on, picking her way rock to rock, pausing before each step to ensure she didn't stumble again—doing so might be the end of her.

When Danya next looked up, she found but one more step separating her from the round patch of moist soil. She stopped and stared at it, inhaled its earthy odor. Silence clogged the air around her, free of the calls of birds, the rustle of wind, the breath of the Mothers and Daughters she knew ringed the courtyard. Concentration reduced the world to her sore feet on the rocks, her pulse beating in her temples, and the impossibly rich-looking soil.

She stepped up onto the last rock and hesitated, the blood on her soles making the hard stone slick. If she trod upon the garden, the dirt would penetrate her cuts, and might lead to infection. Did the temple house a medical practitioner? They must, but it didn't matter. The members of the temple believed the garden contained the Seed of Life, and she suspected it may be the key to finding her brother.

Danya lifted her right foot off the rock and held it over the soil without setting it down. A drop of blood ran along her sole to her heel, dangled there before plummeting to the garden. The droplet indented a tiny divot into the earth and an instant later, a tender green shoot sprang up.

Breath held, the princess took a step, guiding her foot past the unbelievable new growth, and her toes sank into the cool soil. Its touch soothed her and relieved her pain. She stood for a few heartbeats, relishing the sensation in her feet as it snaked up her legs, unknotting her muscles. It climbed through her belly into her chest, easing her unrest. It touched her mind, calmed her thoughts, and Danya fell to her knees.

She dug into the garden with her bare hands, knowing neither where to search for the Seed of Life nor how it appeared. Dark earth clogged the space under her fingernails as she pushed dirt aside, striving to find it, ignoring thoughts of her dreaded return trip across the treacherous rocks.

With the hole as deep as her wrists, the princess thought to give up on the spot and try another, but her fingertip brushed a hard, smooth surface. She stopped digging and rocked back, staring into the hole. In the darkness of the soil, she spied something darker still.

Sunlight gleamed on the sliver of black at the bottom of the hollow. It might have been a rock, or the carapace of a huge beetle, but Danya knew neither to be true. This was what she'd been seeking.

The Seed of Life.

She leaned forward again and reached into the hole, gently pushing soil away from the dark shape until its curve became apparent. Danya noticed the stillness and silence around her as she pressed her fingers into the rich earth, inserting them around and under the seed until she cradled it in her grip.

She lifted it carefully out of the garden.

The seed was oval and big enough to fill her palm, its veneer black and smooth. No fissures out of which might grow roots or shoots marred its surface, no cracks to allow in water or light. How any life might spring from this, the princess didn't know; it appeared no more capable of bringing forth life than the rocks that had cut her feet, or the Mother of Death.

Danya lifted the seed, supporting it in both hands; a rustling of cloth broke the silence. She thought to seek out the source of the sound, but the black oval in her hands held her mesmerized. She closed her palms around it, polishing away the dirt stuck to its surface and another noise startled her—the grate of stone rubbing against stone.

The princess blinked and shook her head, breaking the seed's spell, and climbed to her feet. Her body felt refreshed and rejuvenated, better than it had since she and Trenan left Draekfarren in search of Teryk. She pulled her gaze away from the dark seed resting in her cupped palms and noticed the Mothers and Daughters who'd lined the wall of the courtyard had fallen to their knees. Each one of them—bare-faced Mothers and mask-wearing Daughters alike—leaned forward until their foreheads touched the ground, their arms stretched out in front of them. Danya regarded them, her breath easing, until she realized what else had changed.

Between her and the Mothers and Daughters, the garden of stones had disappeared. In its place grew colorful flowers and emerald grass, leaves and blades waving in a gentle breeze that brought their delicate fragrances to Danya's nose.

She inhaled deeply, and the scent of new life breathed hope into her heart.

XXIX Trenan - Tracking Teryk

The point of the sword hovered an arm's length from the big man's throat, Trenan's weapon as rigid as his expression. The sound of his words died away, leaving the room in silence as the gaze of the woman's son darted around the room, hesitating upon reaching his mother.

Out of the corner of his eye, the master swordsman saw her head move almost imperceptibly as she discouraged her mammoth progeny from revealing the truth.

"Don't know what you're talking about," the man said. "What's a Prince Teryk?"

Trenan surveyed the man—bigger than average; well-muscled from physical work, but carrying the paunch of too much drink; one arm ended in a stump covered with a smooth, pink scar. His eyes glittered with the nervous excitement of a poor liar on the precipice of doing something stupid.

"Dansil," Trenan said and tilted his head toward the woman without removing his gaze from her son.

The queen's guard crossed to the woman in two strides and raised his axe, its sharp and gleaming edge touching the flesh of her throat. The woman—Bieta was her name—sucked a whistling breath through the gap in her front teeth.

The man—Stirk, she'd told them—tensed. His remaining hand clenched into a fist and the muscles in his jaw flexed as he bit hard on his back teeth. The nervous glimmer in his eyes disappeared, replaced by a flare of anger and fear. Trenan watched the cords in his neck tighten and recognized this fellow intended to leap forward to aid his mother. He wouldn't stand a chance against the four soldiers, but any information he might provide about Teryk would die along with him.

Trenan stepped forward until Godsbane's tip floated a hand's breadth from Stirk's neck. The man diverted his gaze back to Trenan and swallowed hard, the lump in his throat rising and falling.

"Do you know who I am?" Trenan asked.

The big man shook his head once, like a horse shooing a fly.

"I am called Trenan, the king's master swordsman. Do you know what that means?"

Stirk shook his head again, the muscles in his neck and shoulders loosening as though he might have some sense of what it meant, but Trenan wanted to be sure he understood.

"It means I could kill you before you moved."

Light shining through the doorway behind Stirk flashed on Godsbane's blade as the tip flickered through the air with a dangerous whistle. A lock of the big man's hair fluttered across his shoulder on its way to the floor. The sword returned to its threatening position before Stirk realized it had moved. He jerked back.

A smile tugged at the corner of Trenan's mouth.

"I'll ask you once more: where is Prince Teryk?"

Stirk leaned away, his angry posture easing into fearful uncertainty. His gaze flickered toward Bieta again, but Trenan raised Godsbane, using the broad steel blade to block his line of sight.

"Don't look at her. Look at me."

Stirk did. He sucked his bottom lip into his mouth, chewing it as he rubbed the smooth end of his arm against the thigh of his breeches.

"Where is the prince?"

"I..." Stirk hesitated, licked his lips, took a peek at his mother again. "I got rid of him."

Trenan's heart jumped in his chest. Did he mean he'd slain the prince? Despair threatened at the back of his mind as he imagined his love's grief, the thought of her pain seeping into him. He gritted his teeth to hide his emotions and stepped forward, the tip of the sword dangerously close to Stirk's throat.

"Where?"

Stirk shrugged. "Somewhere near the water, I guess."

The big man's lips quivered as though he suppressed a smile, a sliver of confidence finding its way into his demeanor. Perhaps he realized Trenan wouldn't kill him as long as he didn't reveal the prince's location. It made the swordmaster want to grip his windpipe and pull it out.

"Where?" Trenan said again through clenched teeth.

"Don't know what they call the place."

"Then you'll take us." Trenan tilted his head. "Bring her."

Dansil removed his axe from Bieta's neck and Osis and Strylor dragged her toward the door. Stirk looked as though he might reach out to grab her, but Trenan flicked Godsbane, touching the man's cheek with the flat of the blade and freezing him in place. After the others escorted the woman out, Trenan leaned closer to the man, glowered at him.

"If we don't find the prince," he said, his whispered words dripping more threat than if he'd yelled, "the crown sword will taste your blood. And your mother's."

***

Stirk glanced at the door of the whore house where he'd stopped to quench his manly needs with the tiny woman on the way home, regretting he'd chosen to do so. If not, he might have made it before the one-armed man and his fellows arrived. They might have gotten away. Then they could've come back for the prince and still had a chance at getting a ransom. Now, he didn't expect they'd escape with their lives.

A block farther ahead, the warehouses of waterside began, and not far beyond they'd find the crate in which he'd dumped the kingdom's heir. The one-armed man had said what he'd do if they didn't find the prince, but what if they did?

Instead of continuing straight along the avenue, Stirk went right at the next street, sticking to areas with which he was somewhat familiar. He'd been here before, not just to visit the bordello, but to acquire sour mash or try his hand at gambling the odd time he found a coin in his pocket—a rarity, and usually only after he'd taken it by force out of someone else's.

They passed a woman crumpled in a doorway, her eyes closed and dress hiked up to mid-thigh, one nipple showing through her ripped bodice. Stirk might have wondered whether she was alive or dead if he cared. He didn't.

Half a block farther along, he turned the party into an alley wide enough for them to walk two abreast, but he knew it opened into a small courtyard. This was where the denizens of Sunset came to gamble, and their blades were always ready.

"A little farther," Stirk said keeping his voice low. The one-armed man beside and one step behind him said nothing, but one of the other armored men farther back grunted.

As they neared where the alley spread out into the courtyard, sounds carried along the mud and brick walls—laughter and grumbling as gamblers won or lost their bets. Stirk stepped out of the lane into the wider area and saw nine men in the courtyard. Some knelt over circles strewn with shaking bones while others sat on crates at makeshift tables made of barrels as they flipped cards and traded insults.

Stirk halted, his tongue tingling with anticipation. If

he'd read the king's master swordsman right, he wouldn't kill them without finding the prince first. Now was the time to take a risk.

Stirk cleared his throat and the closest gambler looked up from his game. The big-bellied man's eyes widened when he saw the armored men. He took to his feet, hand reaching for the hilt of the sword dangling at his wide, round waist.

"What's this?" he said loud enough for the other gamblers to hear. They paused in their games and stood, too.

Beside him, Stirk felt the one-armed man tense, his attention fixed on the group of brigands in the courtyard. There'd never be a good time to defy the man, but if there was a best time, this was it. Stirk jerked his elbow toward the master swordsman's face while grabbing his mother's sleeve and jerking her forward, away from the others.

Stirk and Bieta bumbled into the courtyard, stumbling and surprised the four soldiers let them go so easily.

"They're men of the king," Stirk hollered, yanking his mother aside. "They made me bring them here to kill you all."

"Did they, now?" the big-bellied man said and pulled his steel, the blade hissing out of its scabbard. The other gamblers followed his lead, pulling swords and axes, maces and war hammers.

"We have no quarrel with you," Trenan said, his narrowed gaze flickering from one gambler to the next, sizing them up. "We've come in search of someone other than yourselves."

"You may have no quarrel with us," one of the gamblers said, tapping a club on his palm, "but you be trespassing. Ain't none of us invited you here."

Stirk backed away toward the courtyard's farthest corner, ushering Bieta along behind his back. A satisfied smile crept across his face. Not many people considered him smart or crafty, but it seemed he'd gotten the better of four men of the king, by God.

Tense silence fell in the courtyard, the air heavy with impending violence. The gamblers glowered at the king's men and the soldiers glared back. Stirk watched and noticed the faces of the armored men lacked the slightest hint of fear, while the gamblers' showed twitching lips and darting eyes. A chill crawled up his spine when he saw the grin on the face of the big soldier holding the wide-headed axe.

"Give the two kidnappers back to us and we'll be on our way," Trenan said nodding in Stirk an Bieta's direction. "Do it and no one gets hurt."

The fat gambler barked a laugh that echoed against the walls surrounding them and bounced away down the alley. Deep-throated chuckles rumbled in the chests of his compatriots.

"Come on, boys," he said waving his hand. "Let's rid us of some trespassers."

The gamblers moved toward the soldiers brandishing their weapons but, before they'd gone a full pace, the king's men fell on them. Stirk hadn't seen or heard the one-armed swordsman give the command to attack, but they moved as though he had.

Swords flickered and the heavy axe rose and fell. The big-bellied gambler crumpled, innards spilling out of his sliced-open gut; the man with the club's war cry got cut short when the axe split his head. It took the space of fewer than ten breaths before every one of the evil-meaning gamblers lay on the dirty ground, dead or dying, clutching their wounds as they writhed atop their gambling bones and blood-soaked cards. Stirk gaped, disbelieving the efficiency with which the soldiers dispatched them. His mouth still hung agape when the edge of Trenan's fancy sword found his throat, touching hard enough to break the skin. He swallowed hard, a drop of blood trickling toward his chest.

Trenan leaned in until his nose nearly touched Stirk's.

"I should kill you right now," he hissed.

Stirk stared at him, sensed his mother quivering against his back. He didn't move or breathe, didn't even dare risk gulping down the fearful saliva threatening to spill out of his mouth.

"Kill him anyway," the big soldier said wiping blood from the face of his axe on the fat gambler's shirt. "The prince is around here somewhere. We'll find him without this asshole."

Trenan's gaze flickered toward the small square of sky visible above, then came back to find Stirk's wide eyes.

"If we haven't found the prince by the time the sun is three quarters across the sky, your lives will be worth nothing."

He backed away a step and lowered his sword. Stirk swallowed, saliva spilling from the corner of his mouth.

"Bind them," Trenan said slipping the fancy sword back into its sheath. "They are now prisoners of the king."

* * *

They looked down at the empty space on the wharf, staring at nothing but oiled wood. The area was big enough a crate the size of a man might have occupied it—several of them, actually—but none remained.

Stirk stirred, shifting one foot to the other, and Trenan's hand fell to Godsbane's hilt in case the big man decided to make a run for it. He didn't, obviously thinking better of it after seeing how the soldiers dispatched the gamblers in the alley. Instead, he raised his head and turned his gaze upon the master swordsman.

"This is where I left him," Stirk said, eyes watery and lip trembling. "I swear."

Trenan glanced at the woman. She'd said not a word since they left the storeroom, and now stood staring at her feet. Her lips moved as she ran her tongue in and out over the space where she'd once had front teeth, but she otherwise neither moved nor spoke.

Has she accepted her fate?

"Have a look around," Trenan said, nodding toward the dock. "It might have been moved. I'll watch these two."

Dansil grunted, then he, Strylor, and Osis fanned out, peering behind coils of hawsers and into crates and barrels. Trenan watched them before returning his attention to the woman and her son.

"Why?" He looked at Stirk, realized the man couldn't have been the brains behind the abduction, but he didn't think Bieta could be, either. "Why did you do it? Did you think you'd get away with kidnapping the heir to the throne?"

"It wasn't like that," Stirk replied, his voice squeaking through his tight throat.

Trenan waited for him to say more, but he stopped speaking and his gaze fell to the worn boards of the wharf. A moment later, his shoulders shook with sobs. The master swordsman sighed and shook his head.

"We saved him."

Hearing the woman's voice caught Trenan off guard. He pivoted to face her, watching the big man out of the corner of his eye.

"What do you mean?"

"He jumped into something he shouldn't've. Got between me and Teth when Teth wanted a freebie. The prince thought he was helping me out, bless him."

Trenan pressed his lips together and glared at her, remembering the men in the tavern.

"And this Teth hurt him?"

"Not right away. The prince embarrassed him...by accident. He brought back some of his pals. They beat the lad within a finger's breadth of his life and ran him through. Me and Stirk found him and took him back to our place."

"We were just trying to make him better," Stirk blurted, saliva spraying from his lips. A string of snot dangled out of his nose.

"He was in bad shape," Bieta agreed. "We got the horse doctor to look at him, but he couldn't do nothing, so he brought in a healer."

"That's why I ain't got no hand no more."

Stirk raised his arm and waved the shiny stump in front of his tear-streaked face. Trenan took a half-step back, sword poised, but he didn't think Stirk was stupid enough to jump him.

A chill crawled across the master swordsman's flesh as he considered what he'd heard. First, his suspicion about the horse doctor had been correct, but they'd also involved a healer. While Trenan suspected many of the healers who charged for their services were nothing but a sham, he couldn't deny Stirk's hand had been removed in some way other than by force.

They'd exposed the prince to dark arts.

Trenan suppressed a shudder. First the scroll, now the healer. What effect would being in contact with magic twice have on the prince? Anger swirled into the bottom of his gut.

"Why didn't you tell someone?"

"We didn't realize who he was until Enin came and told us the king's men were out looking," Bieta said. Her head swung side to side as though she thought denying things might yet save her. "And we needed him to be better. He might've died."

"We weren't gonna keep him and ask for ransom,"

Stirk blubbered.

"Shut up," the woman snapped.

Trenan stepped up in front of the woman, peered into her one eye. Her eyelid fluttered, but she didn't wilt under his glare. He pursed his lips and swallowed, concentrating on containing his temper.

"If all this is true," Trenan said, drawing out his words and glancing sideways at Stirk. "Why did you hide him when you knew we searched for him?"

Bieta dropped her gaze and he put the hilt of his sword under her chin, raised her face. Stirk shifted as though he might take exception, but Trenan shot him a threatening glare and the big man wiped tears and snot from his face on his sleeve, holding his ground. The soldier returned his attention to the woman.

"Why. Did. You. Hide. Him?"

The woman stared, lips moving as her tongue worked her gums behind them, but she said nothing. Trenan's pressed harder against chin, soliciting a squeak from the back of her throat.

"We didn't find anything," Osis said, returning from the search with Strylor and Dansil trailing behind him. "If the prince was here, he's gone now."

Trenan glanced at the sergeant, then back at the woman, his expression hard. His gut churned with anger and worry—for Teryk's safety and for how the queen would take the news. He glared at her for a time, jaw flexing and releasing as he ground his back teeth, barely keeping himself from jerking his arm away and slicing her throat. Finally, he took a step away.

The swordmaster raised his gaze, glancing out toward the sea at a sail in the distance. What happened to the prince? Did he come to his senses and wander off, either headed home or to embark on his journey? Did the magic befuddle him? If so, he might have plunged off the end of the pier and into the ocean to be carried away by the tide. Or maybe another brigand set on making a ransom had found him and stolen him away.

Trenan lowered his eyes and shook his head. The search must continue.

"Bring them," he said, pivoting to head back the way they'd come. "They're enemies of the king and they must be made an example of."

"No," Stirk cried. "It wasn't like that. We was trying to help."

"And shut him up."

Trenan walked away, the meaty sound of a fist contacting the side of Stirk's head in his ears and the taste of bile on his tongue. Today, he'd take the heads of Bieta and Stirk for what they'd done. And the horse doctor's, too.

Would the king take his when he found out the prince was lost?

XXX Juddah - Going on a Trip

Juddah woke with a start, snorting air and mustache hair in through his nose. He shifted his ass on the uncomfortable chair of driftwood he'd built himself, its seat fitted with a cushion made out of a sack stuffed with duck feathers. A pleasant sensation quivered in his belly and he found he'd awakened with a bulge in his britches.

"Must've been a good dream, Juddah," he said to the empty room, rubbing his palm over the top of the mound hidden in his overalls. The touch sent a shiver up his spine.

"It's been too long, ain't it?" he said peering at his crotch. "Gonna have to take care of you right quick, aren't we?"

He pushed himself up out of the chair, struggling his

bulk to his feet with the dubious support of the chair's bent driftwood arm. When he made it upright, he glanced across the room. Dim light still squeezed through the space between the shutters. It shone across the dog's dark pelt where he lay on a straw-stuffed sack on the other side of the room, watching his master expectantly. The quality of the line of sunlight illuminating the dog's hindquarters suggested the approach of sunset. Juddah stretched his arms above his head and broke wind.

"Woo," he exclaimed, waving his hand in front of his face. "What've you been eatin', Kooj?"

The dog lifted his head at the sound of his name, heavy tail thumping the floor.

Nostrils flared, Juddah crossed the room to the window, scratching his sack through his britches, but being careful not to further excite his shrinking manhood. He pushed open the shutter and gazed out at the man in the white shirt and red breeches.

"Forgot about you."

The man stared into the forest instead of digging the well, the shovel's blade stuck in the dirt while he leaned on the handle. Juddah sucked on the stray mustache hairs hanging over his lip and leaned forward, readying to give a good shout, but he pulled up short, wondering what the man found so interesting out amongst the trees.

"Maybe a rabbit. Or a deer," he muttered. His gut rumbled in response.

Wiping the last of his nap out of his eyes, he rushed to the door, the loose heel of his boot clomping against his foot.

"Come on, Kooj."

The dog padded across the room and waited at his master's side while he opened the door carefully instead of throwing it open in anger the way he wanted. With the door left ajar, he stepped off the uneven porch into the knee-high grass and bulled his way through the yellowed blades toward the idle man.

"Psst," he hissed to gain the fellow's attention. The man didn't look, so he repeated the sound, louder this time. "Psst."

The fellow squinted toward him and Juddah raised his hands questioningly, not expecting him to understand; the man pointed into the forest.

Juddah amended his path, moving toward the tree line, and saw movement. Leaves rustled, a branch snapped. A flash of dark fabric between the foliage and tree trunks told Juddah it wasn't an animal creeping up on his property. His stomach gurgled in disappointment, but his throat growled angrily.

"Birk! Is that you?" He stopped and grabbed a stone big enough to fill his wide palm off the pile of dirt the stranger had created. "I told you to stay off my land, fucker!"

Juddah heaved the rock into the trees. It crashed through foliage, setting bushes and limbs shuddering, but thumped to the ground without a pained cry from the mouth of a man.

"Get him, Kooj."

The dog launched into the scrub, his broad shoulder crashing through leaves and branches, wide paws thumping the ground. Juddah stood up on his toes, stretching to peek over or through the curtain of green, but he saw nothing except shivering brush. Kooj growled, barked; a man cried out, the dog yelped.

Silence.

Concern leaped into Juddah's chest. "Kooj!" No sound. "Kooj! To me!"

Nothing happened for a moment, then the bushes shuddered. Juddah tensed, hands clenched into fists until the dog bounded out of the forest. Relief eased his worry, but the indignation at the intrusion on his land remained.

Juddah raised his fist and shook it in the air.

"Don't you come back, neither. If I catch you here again, I'll kill you."

He stared into the trees, teeth clenched along with his fist, his breath short and hard as though he'd run a long distance. Nothing moved until a bird flitted out of a bush. Juddah lowered his arm.

"And don't come back, you bastard."

Hand resting on Kooj's head, he surveyed the forest for a half dozen heartbeats until he heard the soft clink of metal behind him and remembered the stranger—the stranger holding a spade suitable for cracking open a man's skull.

Juddah jumped away and spun around, arms raised to catch the shovel before the blade bit into his head. To his surprise, the stranger continued leaning on the handle, watching his captor.

"Give me that," Juddah demanded, hand held out to receive the tool. The man didn't move. Juddah sighed, annoyed. This saying everything twice thing was wearing thin quick. "Give me the spade."

Kooj growled and the stranger leaned back to consider the tool, then pulled it free from the ground and held it out, handle first. Juddah snatched it out of his grasp.

"Enough digging for today," he muttered and surveyed the hole the stranger had made.

He estimated it to be twelve handspans wide and the same in depth. A good amount of work accomplished; not quite a well yet, but heading the right direction. Satisfied, Juddah nodded, then gestured for the man to step back. To his surprise, the stranger complied without him having to repeat himself.

"You don't get my words, but you're okay at understanding signals, I guess. Kind of like Kooj." He glanced at the dog, held his hand out palm up, then flipped it over. The dog sat.

Juddah kneeled beside the stake and fished in his pocket for the key, his gaze fixed on the stranger. He hadn't taken the opportunity to club him over the head with the spade, but it didn't mean he could be trusted.

"I found Kooj same way I found you, you know." The lock clicked open and he pulled both it and the chain off the stake. "He was a damn bit more aggressive than you've been so far though, weren't you, Kooj?"

The dog bounced forward on its ass, tongue hanging. When his master didn't admonish him for the movement, he trotted to Juddah's side and dragged his tongue across his master's cheek, saliva sticking in long whiskers. Juddah laughed, pushed the dog's snout away and stood, chain in hand.

The stranger stared, expressionless except for the shine of confusion in his eyes. Juddah yanked the chain, pulling the stranger in the direction of the barn, the shaggy dog up and trotting along beside him.

"Yep, I found him and added him to my collection, just like I did you," Juddah mused aloud despite knowing his companion didn't understand any more words than the dog. "Same as everything in the barn and my shack. Even the cow." He chuckled to himself. "Found her at Birk's place. Might be why he's creeping around in the forest."

He jerked the door open, setting the birds in the rafters fluttering, and ushered the stranger through the door ahead of him. The man obliged without resistance.

"Go stand yourself over by the sacks," Juddah said, but didn't gesture. Sure enough, the man did nothing but gaze at him blankly, proving Juddah's suspicions. He waved his hand in the direction of the stack of burlap bags. "Get over there."

The man obeyed this time and satisfaction at figuring

him out washed over the stocky man. He didn't much enjoy being around other people—except on the odd occasion he woke with a tent pitched in his britches and decided to take care of it, maybe—but he began thinking it might be handy keeping this fellow around. At the very least, he'd get the well dug. Who knew what might happen afterward? He might prove good at repairing the roof. Or his bones might eventually end up in one of the burlap sacks, like the others.

Juddah attached the chain to the stake then backed toward the door, Kooj at his side the entire time. He stopped in the doorway and crossed his arms in front of his barrel chest. The stranger staggered to the pile of hay gathered against the far wall and lowered himself down. When he'd settled, he held his hands out toward Juddah, palms turned upward. The stocky man leaned forward to get a peek.

Blood smeared one of his palms where a blister from shoveling had burst and the handle rubbed through. Angry redness covered his other hand, the white skin of blisters that had made it through the digging without bursting standing out against the raw background.

"Can't do much about them." Juddah shook his head. "I'll get you water, though. Some to drink, some for washing up. Other than that, you're on your own. I'm going out tonight to take care of my boy."

***

Jud-dah stood in the doorway, peering at the man's chewed-up hands and speaking his nonsensical words. He seemed pleased with himself, but the man didn't know why. All he really wanted was food and drink; the day's work had highlighted how long it had been since he'd had either.

After a while, Jud-dah left, though not much time passed before he returned with a small pitcher of water. He set it on the ground between them, one hand held up with a finger pointing upward. The man guessed it meant he should wait, so he did, his mouth flooding with sour saliva at the sight of water sloshing around within the ewer. When Jud-dah disappeared through the door again, the man crawled across the dirt floor and gripped the jug's handle in his tender hands.

A pained breath whistled between his teeth and he bobbled the container of precious, replenishing liquid. Instead of drinking immediately, he splashed water over the edge onto his hands, rubbed his palms lightly together to wash away the blood and dirt ground into the lines. The flesh beneath was raw and torn on one hand, red and sore on the other. He clenched his jaw and clasped the jug in both hands. His arms shook with exhaustion, but he raised it to his lips, a wave of the fluid spilling over the edge and muddying the dirt floor where it landed.

He filled his mouth, held the liquid in his cheeks for a few seconds, then choked and spit it out. The man gasped for breath and peered into the pitcher at bits of dirt, bark, and hair floating in the water. He spit a chunk of unknown detritus out onto the ground.

Despair knotted his chest and he thumped the jug on the ground, slopping more water over the edge. Was he supposed to drink this? Survive on this vile fluid?

What choice do I have?

Despite the foul taste of the water, his mouth filled with saliva, his throat ached for whatever refreshment it might provide. He sighed and raised the container to his lips again, this time sucking the fluid slowly through his teeth, using them to filter out the detritus. He swallowed, spit debris out, then repeated the procedure.

Jud-dah returned leading the cow by a short rope. He tethered the animal to a ring beside the door that didn't appear solid enough to keep one of the rafter birds from taking flight if they were tied to it. Task complete, Juddah faced the man, one arm leaning against the cow's shoulder.

"Gudinninit?"

The man watched him in silence, the pitcher's cool clay surface soothing his palms. The cow lifted its tail and let go a stream of greenish-brown chunks of manure. Jud-dah slapped the animal on the back and laughed.

"Thatsincaze yagetungree."

He canted his head and whistled through his teeth. Two heartbeats passed, then Kooj came trotting through the door, tongue lolling, and took a seat at his master's feet.

"Koojelsleeperetanite," Jud-dah said scratching the dog behind the ears. "Beehaver hillbiteov yercawk."

He laughed again and pointed at a sack beside the door, opposite where he'd tied the cow. "Lied owan, Kooj."

The dog sauntered to the sack, spun two tight circles and settled. Jud-dah directed his gaze to the man, his eyes stern, and jabbed his finger toward him threateningly. He didn't know what the stocky man meant—perhaps that he shouldn't leave—but chained to the floor with a dog watching him, he didn't have any other choice.

"Elbeebak innacubla dazeboy."

Jud-dah scratched the dog behind the ears once more, then exited the barn, slamming the door behind him. It rattled briefly—a latch being set—then all fell quiet.

Pitcher in hand, the man scrambled back to his pile of straw, putting as much distance between himself and the dog as the room and the chain allowed. The animal eyed him—hungrily, he thought.

Overhead, the rafter birds settled in for the night. The light shining through the cracks between the boards glowed orange and red with the setting of the sun. The man set the pitcher of water aside and leaned back against the wall, his gaze flitting from the dog, to the door, to the row of tools. Another time, he might have devised a way to escape, but the exhaustion in his arms left them unable to do more than sag by his side, hands throbbing. He sighed a long breath, hoping for sleep to take him quickly and relieve his aches and pains, though he knew both hunger and the discomfort would remain when he awoke.

He closed his eyes. In the dim barn, another load of manure thumped to the floor.

***

Juddah tossed aside the comb, its broken teeth proving useless for removing knots from his hair. To tame his mane, he dipped his fingers in the jar of fat he'd drained from the morning's slice of pig and smoothed stray strands away from his face with it. He gazed at himself in a polished piece of tin, flattened a chunk of hair sticking up, then nodded.

"You look fine, Juddah," he said.

He wiped the grease off his hands on the thighs of his overalls, already stiff with grime, and brushed the crumbs of dinner out of his beard. Two days and two nights for the trip—including the night spent enjoying himself. The cow had plenty of hay, and the stranger the pitcher of water, but Juddah worried about Kooj feeding himself. He'd find a few scraps around the barn, not to mention rats and mice, but would it be enough? The possibility existed Juddah might return and discover the stranger gone and the dog with a pot belly.

"As long as he don't eat the cow," Juddah said aloud. He pulled his hat on over his greased-back hair and exited the shack.

He rounded the barn to the lean-to where he kept the horse he'd collected from wandering the woods, complete with saddle, bridle, sword, and a dead man to go with it. The beast ignored him, lazily chewing hay as he set the saddle in place and tied it on. The munching stopped only when Juddah slipped the bit into its mouth, then the horse shook its head and returned to its meal.

Juddah struggled his left foot into the stirrup and hauled his bulk up into the seat. The horse took a step back and whinnied, slapped its tail against its hindquarters.

"Whoa. Don't worry, now, I won't make you go too fast," Juddah said, but the thought of his destination started a stirring in his britches. He pulled the reins and pointed the animal away from the barn, dug his heels into its sides.

"Jubha Kyna, here we come."

XXXI Horace - Haven

Horace gaped at the greenness o' the grassy field. It stretched from the brush where they hid to the town lyin' in the distance. Greener'n any grass the ol' sailor thought he'd ever seen in his life. It weren't sayin' much, given he'd spent most o' near thirty-five turns o' the seasons with his feet on a ship's deck, but he'd experienced his share. Nothin' lay upon the emerald field—no buildin's, no towers nor wells nor animals, and no people. Green and more green right the way to town.

"Whatcha think?" Horace said without removin' his gaze from the field. A breeze rippled through the grass, spreadin' a wave across its tips.

"Thorn thinks it's a camp."

"Out here, we call it a town."

"Town," Thorn repeated, fittin' the word to his mouth. "There will be people in this town?"

"Mmm hmm."

They was too far away to make out much other'n a few buildin's shapes. It weren't a big town, from what he spied, and Horace found himself wishin' for one o' them longeyes they used on the boat for keepin' an eye out for the watery god what ate him. Ships was awful places, but they kept a few handy tools on them.

Thorn jumped to his feet and took a step out o' the brush. Horace caught him by the forearm, stoppin' him, then jerked his hand away before the little feller had the chance to see anythin' more 'bout his past.

"Where you goin'?"

The gray man lifted his arm and pointed at the group o' buildin's. "To the town."

Horace shook his head. "I think we should avoid it."

"Thorn has heard the sounds made by your stomach, Horace Seaman."

"Don't call me that," Horace said through clenched teeth. His gut rumbled on cue. "Just Horace."

"Just Horace."

"It might not be safe."

"True, but Thorn is hungry, too." He rubbed his palm on his flat belly. "More pig leg would taste good."

Horace sighed heavily, his shoulders risin' and fallin' with the breath. They'd seen two sunsets since Thorn stole his britches, but nothin' what might've served to feed them well. The berries they'd found, Horace were hesitant to pop in his mouth because berries'd made him sick before and he weren't willin' to fall for it again. Thorn'd munched on roots and shoots, but Horace couldn't imagine himself developin' an appetite for them.

"All right," he said finally. "I guess I'll go into town and see what I can find. You'll have to stay here."

He took a step into the impossibly green grass; this time it were Thorn's hand on ol' Horace's arm stoppin' him. He spun 'round toward the little feller, pullin' away when he did.

"Thorn goes, too."

A grasshopper flitted past Horace's nose, its wings clickin'. "You can't go."

"Why not?"

"Why not? Take a look at you, then me. You thinkin' ain't no one gonna notice any difference?"

Thorn raised his arm to regard his gray skin, then directed his gaze to Horace. An instant later, his flesh shifted to the same hue as the sailor's. He tilted his head back and smiled up at his companion.

"Better?"

Horace shook his head. "It ain't just the color o' your skin, little feller." He waved his hand before his face. "You don't look too similar to me, do you?"

Thorn's lips extended in an exaggerated pout and the place on his forehead where a man'd have eyebrows dipped toward the bridge o' his broad nose. His eyes narrowed and the muscles in his jaw bulged. A wave o' panic flowed through Horace's chest, but shock overwhelmed it when hairs started sproutin' on The Small God where them brows should've been.

The shape o' Thorn's nose changed. His full mouth shrank, and stubbly whiskers sprouted on his cheek and his lip below his nose. By the time his jaw relaxed and a smile crossed his now-pink lips, Horace were peerin' wide-eyed at a tinier version o' himself.

The ol' sailor shook his head hard enough to make it hurt and blinked fast. It didn't stop Thorn lookin' like Horace.

"We don't all have the same face, you know," Horace exclaimed, the muscles in his legs feelin' a might watery seein' the gray man wearin' his face. "That won't help."

Thorn shrugged and closed his eyes. The stubble faded from his skin, the shape o' his nose and cheek bones shifted. When his lids opened, his appearance were different enough no one'd mistake the two o' them for twins, but similar enough they might've been thought father and son.

The ol' sailor gulped hard; it were as if the years'd rolled backward and a youthful Rilum Seaman stood before him. Did Thorn pluck his boy's memory from his head, or did Rilum appear so similar to Horace he were mistakin' the young himself for his son?

Horace sucked on his bottom lip, thinkin' 'bout what to do. The feller looked mostly like any other boy, without much aspect belongin' to a Small God from outta the Green.

"Are you gonna be able to stay like that, or will I be carryin' you after a while?"

"Thorn will be fine," the gray-but-no-longer-gray man said. "Thorn feels stronger. He must be closer to home."

The words caused an involuntary shiver through Horace's shoulders and his mind started attemptin' to cook up ways to keep from havin' to go farther. No excuses came to him, and the part inside what wanted to get Thorn safely back where he came from seemed to be growin'—in the way o' fungus when you're stuck on a boat too long and don't have the chance to wash your feet.

"All right," Horace conceded. "But if you're gettin' to feelin' wobbly again, you let me know. Better we leave than the nice folk o' this hamlet get a peek at your real face."

"Agreed."

They stood lookin' at each other for a bit for no good reason. For Horace's part, he had trouble takin' his eyes offa the little feller what looked so much like his son, but he weren't sure why Thorn kept starin'. Prob'ly he wanted Horace to take the lead. It took some convincin' in his own head, but the ol' sailor eventually did exactly that.

The greener'n green grass stood taller'n Horace's knee—high enough to tickle Thorn's waist. The little man hummed in the back o' his throat as they strode toward the village, though it weren't no tune Horace'd ever recognize. He'd never been much for music, anyways. Once, he'd been aship with a feller what used to scratch out tunes on a fiddle, but the scraggly notes made Horace's teeth tingle, and not in a good way. On the nights the instrument emerged, he hit his bunk early rather'n dancin' 'round all foolish the way some o' the crew did—the ones what didn't mind a poke in the porthole, he always thought.

"Keep quiet," Horace growled, more because it made him think 'bout the fiddle'n because Thorn's tune were unpleasant. Either way, the little man fell silent.

Their feet rustled in the grass, stirrin' up odors that excited Horace's nose. He sniffed deeply, inhalin' the scent o' dirt and the hayish perfume o' the blades themselves. Mixed in with it was the aromas o' bugs layin' eggs, and pollen makin' new flowers, bird shit dried in the sun, and the fur o' tiny voles what stood still as stone while they passed.

But none o' those was what made Horace come to a halt, one foot held up in the air. Beneath them, his nose detected a stink what had no right bein' found in a field o' the greenest grass: salty water.

The sea.

"What is it?" Thorn asked, noticin' his companion had stopped with his foot halfway done a step.

"We're nearin' the ocean," Horace said, starin' off toward the village ahead, narrowin' his eyes for a glimpse o' the sun glimmerin' on waves. He didn't spy nothin' but grass and buildin's, now loomin' a little closer'n they did before.

"How do you know?"

"I can sniff it." He drew his tongue across his lips, detected the vaguest hint o' brine. "And taste it."

"Good. The shore will lead back to Thorn's home."

Horace set down the foot what he'd left hangin' in the air and continued starin' straight ahead. Aware o' Thorn's gaze upon him, he didn't pay it no mind; the thought o' the sea kept him too busy preventin' his stomach from turnin' to care much what the little feller gawked at.

"Come on," Thorn said, wavin' his hand. When Horace didn't move, he retraced the three steps he'd gone before realizin' the ol' sailor'd halted. "What's wrong?"

"Don't like the sea."

"Horace Seaman don't like the sea?" Thorn mimicked Horace's voice.

Horace frowned. "He don't. And I told you—"

"Just Horace, Thorn knows. Not liking the sea explains why you only want to be called Horace."

The sea-hatin' sailor sucked his bottom lip hard enough to make it hurt, the buzz o' flies and hiss o' wind in the grass markin' the passage o' time. Thorn waited, crossin' and uncrossin' his arms, rockin' back and forth on his feet, before Horace gave in and began walkin' again.

"We ain't goin' nowhere near the sea," he said.

***

They approached the village from the sunrise end. No road headed into the place, only grass as far as you could see until the trees took over, and they did so all 'round, but for the windward side. That direction, high in the sky, he thought he spied gulls wheelin', and where you found gulls, you found the sea.

A dirt track finally began just outside where the buildin's started. Though no weeds or grass poked through it, Horace didn't think no wagon wheels or horses' hooves'd touched the road, least not in a long time. And the buildin's he saw—he lost count after ten, because he didn't usually have no reason to count any higher'n that—appeared either freshly painted or newly built.

Ev'ry one o' them.

They trod onto the track, Horace walkin' a pace in front o' Thorn the way someone might've expected a pa to walk before his boy. He didn't sense no one watchin'. Pebbles crunched beneath the sole o' the boot what were pinchin' Horace's foot; Thorn's steps—made by feet he forgot wasn't wearin' no shoes—made not a sound.

Birds Horace couldn't lay eyes on twittered in hidden nests built in the eaves o' the closest buildin'. He directed his gaze toward the sound, squintin' against the bright sun shinin' on him. The sing-song stopped. Horace scratched his cheek, fingernails what were in need o' trimmin' scrapin' against his coarse whiskers. He kept starin' up until he felt a tug on his sleeve. When he looked at Thorn yankin' at him, the little feller's other arm were pointin' at somethin' in front o' them.

The boy appeared to have seen the seasons turn eight or ten times. He stood similar in height to Thorn, though his cheeks showed more o' the childlike glow expected in a child o' that age, an aspect the Small God hadn't captured in his youthful approximation.

This boy what came outta nowhere watched them and did a helluva good imitation o' a figurehead like they put on the prow o' those fancy ships the king sailed on himself. Horace stared back, unsure how to proceed, and Thorn were lettin' him be the one what made the decision. The ol' sailor moved them forward a few paces in order not to have to shout.

"Hello," he said, raisin' his hand in a friendly greetin' gesture.

The boy nodded in return, his eyes dartin' between Horace and his companion. Horace fought to keep from glancin' at the gray man to ensure he hadn't reverted back to bein' a gray man.

"What's the name o' this place?"

The boy's gaze came to rest on Horace. He squinted. "Haven."

Haven. That sounded good to Horace. "There be anyone else 'round?"

In answer, the boy turned tail and ran for a buildin' across the little square in the town's center. Seein' the feller's shoes kickin' up dust as he ran through the middle o' town started an uneasy rumble at the bottom o' Horace's gut. He let his eyes search 'round, squinty and suspicious, at the other buildin's, but he didn't see nobody just then. He took hold o' Thorn's arm and began leadin' him toward the far end o' the village.

"I ain't feelin' too good 'bout this place," he said. "And I don't appreciate the way the air smells all briny."

"Thorn thinks the town seems nice."

They got near to the center o' the village square when people started emergin' from the doorways o' the buildin's surroundin' the common area. Each door spewed out four or five stony-faced adults, spillin' them down short sets o' stairs and across porches out into the village green.

Horace drew up at the center o' the square, draggin' Thorn to a halt beside him, and spun a tight little circle, peerin' at them faces. None o' them held the aspect o' friendliness one might want to find upon visitin' a new village. The ol' sailor fought back a shiver and squeezed Thorn's shoulder.

"Sorry, little feller. It don't appear you're gonna be headin' home."

XXXII Danya - A Public Execution

The princess barely found a wink of sleep the night after digging up the seed. She'd been allowed to keep it with her, perched on a table beside her bed at eye level, and she'd spent most of the night staring at the dim light reflecting in its dark surface. She imagined shapes and faces in it—Teryk, Trenan, a child with gray skin, a woman with her hair cut close to her scalp, and what appeared to be a living statue. When first the image of her brother and the master swordsman showed themselves, she assumed the visions to be figments of her imagination, but she'd never seen the others who appeared in the dark surface.

The next morning, Evalal gathered the princess, clothed her in a red robe over her armor and weapons, and led her from her room. No one else accompanied her and the girl who wore a constant smile on her unmasked face, a pouch hanging at the princess' waist the only other item they took. It bounced against her hip as they walked, the Seed of Life's smooth oval hidden within.

Danya didn't bother asking Evalal where they were going; they were seeking the barren Mother—she who'd bear the fruit of the Seed of Life. Where they might find her, neither of them knew, but it was the task laid before them.

The path out of the temple seemed too quick and uncomplicated. After the circuitous path they'd followed to arrive at the Mother of Death's room, then the room overlooking the courtyard, she presumed half a day's travel to find their way through the temple's knotted maze.

Two turns and a long hallway ending in an

unassuming door led them out.

They passed across the threshold and—impossibly by Danya's estimation—into the same alley which they'd followed to enter the temple. The princess stopped and stared back at the door.

"How is this possible?"

Evalal pulled the painted mask she'd worn before from under her robe and glared at it in her hand, the smile disappearing from her lips. Danya thought she hadn't heard her question, but she didn't ask it again. The girl raised the mask toward her face but paused before pulling it on.

"Put your hood up," she said. "There may be watchers."

Danya nodded and pulled the cowl of the red robe onto her head as Evalal donned the painted face. The princess realized the girl hated having to wear it but made the sacrifice for the greater good.

"What are watchers?"

"People who don't agree with what the Goddess stands for," she said, voice muffled behind the wooden mask.

"And what's that?"

"Preventing the return of the Small Gods."

Evalal headed up the alley leaving Danya to follow.

***

Danya thought the red robe the Mothers provided her as a disguise might be the worst possible garment for avoiding attention. Anyone watching could easily pick her out of a crowd—precisely why they'd chosen it.

"The red robe is worn by members of the temple who are deathly ill," Evalal explained through the red-painted smiling lips when Danya asked. "They are escorted from the temple to keep others from falling ill, too. The red robe warns people to stay away."

"And where are the sick taken?"

Evalal answered the question with a silence that made the hairs on the back of Danya's neck quiver.

The girl led her along streets and avenues she'd never seen before and, without exception, everyone they encountered gave the red robe a wide berth. Evalal kept them to the sparingly used lanes, but they encountered many citizens about at this time of the day.

And they all seem to be going the same direction we are.

They didn't veer from their path, following along with the crowd flowing through the streets, their numbers swelling as they went. Ahead, the narrow street widened into a small square jammed with people. Evalal didn't stop when they reached it, but the princess did. She stood on her toes to peek over the sea of bodies crowding the open area in front of her. The girl stopped when she realized Danya had.

The princess stood straight, the thongs fastening her sword's scabbard to her leg beneath the robe digging into her thigh as the muscle flexed with the effort. At first, she saw nothing, and a knot threatened in her calf, so she lowered herself again. She looked to Evalal, who shot her a disapproving expression, then bounced up onto her toes once more. This time, she spied a wooden platform through the crowd, the kind one might stand upon to make a speech. She wondered who the orator might be.

They didn't need to wait long to find out.

An armored man vaguely familiar to Danya walked up the steps onto the platform, a length of rope trailing from his hand. A woman who looked as though she'd seen better days followed, her wrists bound. Behind her, a large man made his way up the stairs, a scowl on his face and the rope tied awkwardly around his forearms. Danya stretched farther and realized it was because he had only one hand.

"What's happening?" the princess asked.

Evalal came back to stand beside her, but made no attempt to see past the press of bodies crowding the square. She grabbed Danya's sleeve and tugged, attempting to get her moving again.

Before the girl answered, another man climbed the stairs onto the platform, and this one Danya recognized as one of her mother's personal guards. She didn't know his name, but she'd never liked the man. The princess' brow dipped.

What is he doing here?

Her gaze swept across the front of the crowd. Did his presence indicate the queen might be here? Surely not; Danya couldn't imagine her mother coming to Sunset. Jeering men made up the crowd's front line, their fists raised and shaking. The queen wasn't present, and the princess was about to settle back and allow Evalal to lead her away when her eyes found a one-armed man she'd recognize anywhere.

Trenan.

The master swordsman climbed onto the crowded platform, a steely expression pressing his lips tight. She'd seen him angry before, but nothing like this. The glint in his eye reminded her of the way he'd looked the night in the tavern.

"Evalal," Danya said without removing her gaze, her voice quiet. "What is going on here?"

This time, the girl let her hand drop away. Danya glanced at the painted mask with its inane expression but perceived something else in the young girl's eyes.

"An execution."

A chill finger touched the nape of Danya's neck, sending goose bumps racing along her arms and bitter saliva flooding her mouth. She looked hurriedly at the group standing on the platform, saw the way the woman hung her head and realized tears dampened the one-handed man's cheeks.

"Impossible," she said, looking back to the girl. "No one has been executed in the kingdom since before my birth. My father has forbidden it."

Evalal shook her head. Danya's mouth went dry and she resisted the urge to lick her lips. Though the crowd did their best to keep their distance from the red robe, the sharp tang of their unwashed bodies penetrated her nostrils and threatened to roil her stomach.

"It can't be."

Danya glared back at the platform and noticed the guard who served her mother had forced the woman to her knees, hiding her behind the crowd of bodies. With a crooked smile on his face, the soldier pulled his axe from its sling, raised it above her. The buzz running through the crowd hushed to a murmur and the air grew heavy with anticipation.

"By order of the king, these two kidnappers are to be punished," Trenan said, his voice clear and hard. "They are to pay with their lives."

The last of the murmurs died and the crowd went silent. Trenan faced the guard and nodded. His blade fell, sunlight catching its edge, the faint whistle of steel cutting the air and a frightened sob from the one-handed man the final sounds Danya heard before the crowd erupted in cheers.

Though she didn't see the result, the thought of what happened brought a bile-flavored knot to the back of the princess' throat. Its pressure increased when her mother's guard raised the blade, showing the blood on its edge to the frenzied mob.

The crowd in front of her waved their arms, obstructing her view. Evalal took the opportunity to grab her arm and pull her away. This time, Danya allowed herself to be led but kept glancing back. They'd gone five paces when the crowd lowered their arms again and she glimpsed the platform once more. The man had disappeared, presumably forced to kneel as the woman had been before her.

Trenan held Godsbane in his hand.

Danya's heart jumped as he raised the blade and the crowd hushed again. The master swordsman's face bore no sign of a smile as had the guard's. Instead, his expression was grim—the aspect of a man who had no relish for what he must do. The cords in his neck stood out as he prepared to strike the killing blow.

"Trenan! No!"

The words escaped Danya's lips before she had time to decide if speaking them was the best course of action. The master swordsman's head snapped toward her, eyes searching the crowd. She froze, knowing the red robe's cowl would hide her face, but wanting to raise her hand and let him know she was there.

Trenan lowered his blade and jumped from the edge of the platform into the crowd. The people at the front fell over each other hurrying out of the grim-faced soldier's way.

Evalal's grip on Danya's forearm tightened to the point of pain.

"Hurry," she said, tugging on the princess to follow. "He must not stop us from finding the barren Mother."

Danya's mind raced. Trenan would help, wouldn't he? His duty had always been to give Danya and Teryk whatever they needed, to support them and teach them. If ever Danya needed him, this was the time.

But that wasn't the whole truth. The master swordsman worked for the king, not the prince and princess. If Teryk was dead, or alive and missing, their parents would want their children returned to them, not left to wander the land in search of phantoms and legends. Finding them and returning them would be Trenan's duty.

With a breath tasting of despair, Danya hurried after the girl, fleeing from the one man who might be able to aid her in her search for a woman she couldn't be sure existed.

XXXIII Horace - Gettin' Out

The circle made outta people cinched tighter 'round Horace and Thorn. The ol' sailor moved the two o' them back a step, but it weren't no good with more town folk directly behind them, too.

Horace's gaze flickered from person to person and found a smatterin' o' women amongst the men, but only the boy what they'd come upon first. No babes-in-arms, no little ones toddlin' 'round or pickin' up clods o' dirt and tryin' to eat them, just the one boy o' eight or ten turns and a bunch o' grown-ups what, upon closer inspection, bore a strikin' resemblance to each other. Horace dragged the back o' his hand across his lips, wipin' away nervous spit what made its way out.

"We don't mean no harm," he said, disappointed with himself at a waverin' in his tone. "We didn't intend on visitin' your little town. Found ourselves here, is all."

One man standin' right in front stepped forward, away from the others. Horace's muscles went tense, readyin' to defend if necess'ry, but he weren't sure what they'd use for the purpose. Neither he nor Thorn had no weapons, and near thirty-five turns o' the seasons aboard one ship and another never did nothin' to improve his fightin' skills. He curled his fingers up into fists, anyways—sometimes you get lucky when you take a swing.

The feller stopped before he got close enough to throw a punch; he didn't have a weapon in his hand nor carry any at his waist, neither, so far as the ol' sailor saw. He stood a couple hairs taller'n the other fellers— same height as Horace—and wore his face shaved clean the way all o' them did. His breeches was black, his shirt white, and they both looked as shiny and new as the buildin's ringin' the town square. Horace's gaze moved to the next feller, then back, then to the man on the other side before returnin' to the stepped-forward one. The three fellers might've been brothers.

"Mister," Horace said, raisin' his hands defensively. "We ain't—"

"Who are you?" The man's voice came out flat, emotionless.

Horace touched his hand to his chest. "My name is Horace. And this is..." He hesitated, gulped back saliva flavored with nerves. "My son, Rilum."

Horace didn't need to glance at Thorn to know the little man were smilin' up at him; the gleam o' sunlight reflectin' offa his teeth practically blinded him. It did nothin' to ease his concern o'er their current situation.

"You are not of Haven," the monotone voice said.

"No." Horace considered the statement a might curious. He'd only have to count his fingers five, maybe six times and he'd have the number o' people in the circle 'round them accounted. "I...we're from the Horseshoe."

The stepped-forward man's head tilted and a brow moved up his forehead in the direction o' his dark hair what were the same color as all the others gathered 'round.

"Horseshoe?"

Horace raised his own brow in return. "The Horseshoe. You know: where the king o' the Windward kingdom sits on his throne."

The man didn't untilt his head. Were it possible they'd come so far that these people didn't know 'bout the Horseshoe? No, weren't no way. Couldn't live Windward and not have the taxman from the Horseshoe pay a visit. Horace'd crewed a few ships what'd transported them bloodsuckers along the coast, takin' whatever coin they could get from people what worked hard for it and couldn't afford to give it up.

"You don't know 'bout the Horseshoe?" Horace did his best not to sound disbelievin', but didn't think he'd done a very good job, so he decided to try somethin' else. "The last place we was at were called Millstream. It's 'bout eight sunrises walk from here."

The man shook his head. Beside Horace, Thorn rocked back and forth the way a little one might when needin' to make water soon or it'd be runnin' along the inside o' his pant leg. The ol' sailor resisted the impulse to direct his gaze toward him to see what were goin' on.

"Nobody has ever come to Haven." The man's unemotional voice came out a drone.

"But don't you go to nearby towns? To trade, and such?" Horace recalled the shack in the woods where Thorn acquired his britches.

"Nobody has ever left Haven."

A murmur spread through the gatherin', whisperin' from lips to ears and spreadin' quick as the tide fillin' a hole in the sand. Horace surveyed their faces, each o' them so similar to the last, and found most starin' at Thorn. He clamped his teeth together tight to keep them from chatterin' with a fearful shiver and looked at the little feller.

Thorn's nose'd gone a little flatter and wider, back more toward it's reg'lar shape, and an eyebrow were missin'. A streak o' gray across one cheek akin to a smudge o' ash stirred up panic in Horace's chest. He raised his head, ready to make excuses why he and his son needed to get right back outta Haven this instant and found the stepped-forward man with a smile across his face what didn't appear altogether natural. He spread his arms wide and said:

"Welcome. Welcome to Haven."

Welcome weren't exactly what Horace experienced—scared outta his drawers, maybe, but not welcome.

***

After havin' time to sit, Thorn grew back his brow and glossed o'er the mark on his cheek, though it still looked like he carried a faded scar. His nose refused to go back to the way it were when he first took on his disguise, but Horace didn't mind—the little feller looked less like Rilum this way, and the ol' sailor didn't need remindin' o' the son he hadn't seen in more seasons'n he remembered.

The buildin' the crowd o' town folk'd taken them too were one big room with a churchy atmosphere to it, though it didn't hold no idols or worshippy things nowhere inside. Horace guessed that made it more meetin' hall than worshipful place; he were thankful for its chairs for Thorn to sit and get a little rest.

The whole town crammed in with them, ev'ry set o' eyes on them as a few women—most o' them what looked far too much like the men—brought him and Thorn food for nibblin'. It tasted good, but they served snacks what Horace didn't recognize.

They munched on what might've been cheese but for bein' flavored o' roses and honey, and bread thick and heavy enough to've been meat. A bowl carved outta wood contained pinkish-white meat, too, what the ol' sailor would've guessed to be crab, but it didn't have the flavor o' crab. Truthfully, he couldn't've said exactly what its taste were but, after a few sunrises in a row puttin' twigs and leaves and nothin' more in his belly, he were glad to have it. Thorn sittin' beside acted pleased, too.

Ev'ryone watched them while they ate, makin' Horace nervous and wonderin' if some food'd got caught in his whiskers what were longer'n what he were used to sportin'. He paused in chewin' and wiped a hand across his mouth, just in case. Weren't nothin' there, but his discomfort at bein' stared at carried on.

When they finished, the man stepped forward again. At least, Horace thought him to be the same man.

"Have you eaten enough?" His voice held some expression this time. Not much, but more'n before.

"Mmm hmm," Horace said, chewin' on the last mouthful.

"Excellent. Now we shall find a place for you to make your beds."

He clapped his hands twice and 'bout as many people as Horace had fingers left the buildin'. At the same time, Thorn reached o'er and tugged on the ol' sailor's sleeve. Horace leaned toward him.

"Thorn can't stay here," the little feller what looked only a bit like Rilum whispered. He waved his hand in front o' his face. "This will disappear in my sleep."

Horace nodded, sat straight in his chair, and cleared his throat.

"We thank you for your hosp...your hospi...your kind offerin', but we have to be goin'."

He rose outta his seat and the man took a stutterin' step back, wearin' an expression as though Horace'd spit at him, his head swingin' side to side. The shocked aspect got passed to the others gathered in the big, open room.

"There is nowhere to go." A tone o' non-understandin' made his monotone voice come to life. "Nobody has ever left Haven."

A chill crawled along Horace's skin, pricklin' the hair at the back o' his neck and makin' his staff shrink up toward him as if he were sailin' too close to the

Green. At that instant, his situation's perilous nature struck him—he were either gonna be stuck in a picturesque but unusual little village, or continue on in his trek toward a place what gave him nightmares. Standin' there in the churchy meetin' hall with them people starin' at him, it didn't seem like muchuva choice.

"Horace," Thorn wheezed, and for the space no longer'n an eye blink, the word reminded the ol' sailor an awful lot o' how Dunal's voice'd sounded with his fingers wrapped 'round the big oaf's throat.

Horace chewed on his bottom lip and rubbed his fingernails in his scratchy beard, the lower portion o' his gut startin' to go watery. His gaze flickered to Thorn, who stared up at him with a desperate expression in them eyes what resembled his son's, then at the stepped-forward man. The tautness in his lips or the tilt o' his brow didn't hold nothin' sinister, but Horace wondered if a threat might be meant by what he spoke. The ol' sailor's belly grumbled 'round the tasty food inside it and he sighed—he'd told Thorn he'd get him home. A promise made should be a promise kept.

"We do appreciate what you've done for us," Horace said, drawin' his words out like he didn't know if he were makin' a statement or askin' a question, "but we gotta be goin'. My son's got a...condition."

He edged toward the door, peerin' from one friendly-seemin' person to the next and wonderin' which might be the one to jump out and stop them leavin'. Thorn held onto the back o' his shirt, hidin' himself behind Horace's back. Whether he did so to keep up his childlike charade or because his disguise were beginnin' to fade again, Horace weren't sure.

They crossed the threshold and warm sun prickled on Horace's neck. He backed them away slowly, so as not to make anyone upset, but Horace'd forgotten 'bout the two steps leadin' to the door, and they tumbled into the grass.

The ol' sailor came down heavily on his companion, forcin' a woof from his own lungs and jabbin' them with that broken rib what he'd nearly forgot. They rolled over, both o' them scramblin' to get to their feet. Horace made it up first and grabbed Thorn by the arm to help him.

His gray arm.

Horace glanced at the little feller and saw streaks o' gray showin' through on his cheeks, and the color gone completely from the one arm. His hand threatin' to tremble, the one-time sailor moved his gaze to the door to find it jammed with people gawkin' at the sight. Horace remembered havin' done the same thin' himself.

"We gotta get outta here," he gasped, pain throbbin' in his chest, and pulled on Thorn's arm.

He lurched away, draggin' the half-gray, half-pinkish Small God behind him. Thorn's feet wasn't workin' so well, stumblin' and scuffin' along the ground. They got to the dirt track runnin' through the middle o' the square before Horace looked back.

Not a soul'd taken a single step outta the buildin', but the ol' sailor didn't let the fact slow him.

He directed them toward the far end o' town, opposite where they'd come in. That end didn't look no different from the other—same tidy white buildin's and unbelievably green grass—but it seemed to Horace the best direction to head if they intended on gettin' Thorn home.

The little feller's feet kicked up dust as they shuffled along the dirt track. They was most o' the way to the edge o' the village when them people finally got themselves together and came boilin' outta the meetin' hall. The stepped-forward man jumped down the stairs and hit the ground runnin', a bunch o' the other fellers what looked so much like him followin' close behind.

"Fuck me dead," Horace breathed. "Come on, Thorn. You gotta help me or you ain't gettin' home."

The splotchy-skinned little man peered o'er his shoulder and saw what Horace'd already seen. Bein' chased gave him extra energy, and he got his feet under him and began runnin' faster'n Horace, leavin' him behind. The ol' sailor's heart did a lurch and he made his own feet go faster.

The sound o' runnin' steps got closer behind them, drownin' out the singin' grasshoppers and the chirpin' birds tryin' to eat them bugs. Thorn were gettin' farther ahead o' Horace, the muscles in his half-gray back flexin' as he swung his arms runnin', so the sailor pushed himself harder. His broken rib flared pain in his chest; sweat rolled offa his forehead and into his peepers, stingin' them with salty water.

The villagers' runnin' steps was even closer behind them, close enough Horace expected to feel breath on his neck or a hand on his shoulder. A few paces ahead, Thorn came to the edge o' the village, where the dirt track ended as abruptly as it began. The little man sprinted into the grass, his legs cuttin' a swath through the tall blades, and Horace followed him into the meadow four fast heartbeats later.

They kept runnin', the swish and whisper o' the slender-bladed grass floatin' up from Horace's thighs to his ears. It took more'n five runnin' strides before he realized it were the only sound he heard—no more rumble o' feet thumpin' on the ground behind them.

Still runnin', Horace cranked his head 'round to peek back and nearly tripped o'er his own feet. His hammerin' heart jumped, but he kept his balance and glanced back. His peepers refused to believe what they was seein'.

The villagers'd stopped at the end o' the dirt track,

watchin' after them with confused looks on their gobs what would've been at home on Dunal's kisser. Horace slowed some before stoppin' to stare back at the disenchanted mob.

"Hold up, Thorn," he called over his shoulder. "Take a peek at this."

Horace stood watchin' them people what looked too much alike for comfort until grass rustled and Thorn pulled up beside him. Horace regarded the little feller, annoyed he weren't even breathin' hard.

"What d'you think's goin' on?"

"Nobody leaves Haven," Thorn said.

Horace redirected his gaze to the villagers, a few at the back o' the crowd wanderin' off toward the heart o' the village like they forgot why they was standin' there.

"Nobody but us."

The ol' sailor and the mostly-gray man faced their backs to the village o' Haven and didn't stop runnin' until they reached the trees what lay ahead.

XXXIV Ailyssa - Given a Chance

To Ailyssa, the soft mattress had become a bed of nails, each of the feathers jabbing into her soul as she perched on the edge of the bed. She rearranged herself, searching for comfort, but the new position put pressure on the fresh bruise on her thigh. Another shift, another pain.

She considered getting to her feet, but the blinding haze hanging before her vision made her fearful of walking into a table or knocking over a lantern. Perhaps setting the temple alight and burning might alleviate the soreness two days and five men had left pulsing between her legs, but it wouldn't dispel the worry for Claris unless the blaze took her life.

Ailyssa rubbed her sleeve over her face, wishing for the fabric to remove the thick layer of grime she imagined covering her, inside and out. She still felt the weight of the last man's member in her mouth, tasted his viscous expulsion. How could these women justify doing this in service of the Goddess? Surely the Goddess planned to descend on Jubha Kyna one day and expel them from the world for their sins the way the Small Gods had been cast out so long ago.

The bright blur faded slightly as Ailyssa closed her eyes. Why did the Goddess do this? Would dying blind and alone in the woods not have been discipline enough for failing to honor her with Daughters and Daughters' Daughters? Did she do something else to deserve being brought here and punished by a parade of men, day after day? To have her Daughter taken from her again?

Ailyssa leaned forward, elbows on knees, head held in her hands. A pain twinged along her spine, but she disregarded it. Her brain throbbed inside her skull, growing too large and pushing against the bone, then shrinking back and squeezing in on itself. She wished she'd tried harder to have more Daughters, wished she didn't stop making the Goddess' marks on the wall, and that Claris hadn't fallen in love.

Wished to be anywhere but in Jubha Kyna.

The door latch rattled, hinges creaked.

"N'th Ailyssa Ra?"

Ailyssa pulled her face out of her hands, leaned back, spoke in a flat tone. "Creidra."

"Are you all right?"

The blind woman sucked a breath through her nose, let it out her mouth, the air shuddering through her lips. What did the young woman expect her to say? Didn't she realize what was going on here?

Is she more blind than me?

Ailyssa's shoulders sagged. "Fine, N'th Creidra.

Tired."

Footsteps whispered in the deep carpet and a weight pressed on the mattress. An effort kept her from flinching away when Creidra's hand fell on her thigh.

"One more today, Mother, then bath and sleep. N'th Adnine Re'a said you should take the morrow to rest. A woman of your age requires time to recuperate."

My age? A woman of my age shouldn't be doing such things at all.

The words rang in her head, but didn't reach her lips. She didn't trust Creidra, but she depended on her for food and aid; without her, she couldn't climb the stairs or locate the honey pot to tend to her bodily needs. She'd been condemned to a prison without bars, her own eyes providing the cell.

"This man has been here before," Creidra said. Ailyssa suspected she may have said more, but she didn't hear. "...from the shore. A large but gentle man."

The word large shot a pang through Ailyssa's groin and she winced. The first man of the day had been large—larger than she'd ever dreamed possible. She didn't look forward to another endowed with a similar cursed gift.

"Are you ready?"

Ailyssa stared straight ahead at blank nothingness and nodded, hating herself for it, but what else could she do? If she didn't do as they said, she stood no chance of finding Claris.

Creidra squeezed her thigh, fingertips digging into the bruise on Ailyssa's leg, making her tense. "I will get him."

The young woman rose from the bed and padded across the room, leaving the door ajar as she exited, and Ailyssa clasped her hands together in her lap. A lump clogged her throat at the thought of another man and what he might do to her, but she had no choice. If she didn't, they might hurt Claris. How was she going to find her Daughter, ensure she was all right? Without her sight, she couldn't even see to find a way to take her own life and end this misery.

***

Juddah sat on a chair with a high back and a thick cushion on the seat, his hat in his hands, turning the brim through his fingers as he waited. As always, the thought of visiting the Sisters of Jubha Kyna seemed a good idea while in the comfort of his own shack, an erection straining the fabric of his overalls. As always, nerves rose to the surface upon approaching the temple. Now, waiting in the reception hall, fidgeting with his head wear and wondering if his cock would do him the favor of not curling up and hiding like a hibernating bear, he regretted making the trip.

A thin sheen of sweat stuck a few strands of hair that had escaped the pig fat to his forehead. He wiped at it with his sleeve and huffed a breath.

Ain't too late. Still could get up and leave.

No one would judge him for it, at least not until he made the mistake of returning.

He shuffled his feet, readying himself to follow through on the thought, when the young woman returned. The wide smile on her lips pushed him back onto the chair, froze the hat in his hands.

"Ready," she said.

Juddah licked his lips—the action hidden beneath his mustache—and raised his brows in an expression that might have been considered either questioning or surprised.

"It...it ain't you I'm seeing. Is it?"

On another visit, a younger initiate had left him embarrassed about his...challenge...so he'd requested one of the older Sisters. Experience told him the mature ones managed more understanding of such things.

"No, sir. A new Sister is waiting for you."

"New? You mean young, like you?"

The young woman—hardly old enough to be called a woman—shook her head. "No. She is a Mother who's seen many seasons, as requested."

Juddah raised his hand to his face, inserted a finger through the forest of facial hair, and chewed the corner of his fingernail. The digit tasted of pig fat.

"Not too old, though."

"Come."

She gestured with her fingers, smile sticking stubbornly on her lips, eyes shining. A piece of dyed leather held her long auburn hair off her face, accenting sculpted cheekbones and upward tilted nose. A beautiful girl. When she came across the hall toward him, Juddah's staff shrank a little more.

"Will—"

"Come, sir. I'll take you to her room and, if you are dissatisfied with the selection, we will find another sister who better suits you." She offered a hand like she meant to help him stand. "Perhaps you'll choose me if she doesn't meet your needs."

One glimmering brown eye winked at him and Juddah gulped down a mouthful of saliva that might have been rocks. Without another word, he climbed out of the chair, refusing to accept her hand. The young woman didn't appear to take offense at his refusal of assistance, his avoidance of her touch, and led him toward the stairs to the second floor.

They ascended the steps in silence, the girl with her head up and her back straight, Juddah slumping his shoulders and watching his boots instead of the shape of her hips in the form-hugging smock. Gawking at her would increase his nerves and make things worse, he knew.

After passing a landing, they reached the top of the

stairs and continued along the hall to a door standing half open. The young woman pushed it the rest of the way and stood aside, motioning for Juddah to enter. He stepped into the doorway and paused.

The woman sitting on the edge of the bed was certainly older than the Sister who'd led him up the stairs. Her dark hair cropped close to her skull showed flecks of gray and, even from across the room, Juddah saw shallow lines beside her eyes. Wisdom lines, his mother had called them. She sat straight and erect enough to give the impression of tension filling her limbs. Juddah's nerves eased, his staff emerged from its den.

He faced the younger woman and found her peering at him, brow raised in silent question. Juddah nodded in response and she ushered him across the threshold. He obliged and she shut the door behind him, the latch catching with a soft click.

The woman on the bed didn't move. She stared at the wall, as though looking through it rather than at it, the wavering light of the oil lamp on the dresser reflected in her unblinking eyes. Juddah fidgeted foot to foot, resisting the urge to chew his nails as he awaited her invitation to enter.

After a short while in which Juddah wiped sweat off his palms on the stiff front of his pants legs, ran his fingertips completely around the outside edge of his hat, and chewed on over-long mustache hairs, the woman finally shifted.

"Hello?" she said, head tilted more toward Juddah; her gaze didn't settle on him.

"Erm...hello."

Finger to his mouth, he nibbled the nail. She moved on the bed again, but still didn't look at him.

"Are you..." She paused and sighed deeply, as though she'd lost her wind mid-sentence. A faint smile appeared on her lips, but Juddah suspected it wasn't real. "Are you just going to stand by the door or are you coming in?"

"N—no, Ma'am. I mean, yes, Ma'am."

Juddah crossed toward the bed, loose boot heel scuffing in carpet deeper than he'd ever seen. Someone had gone overboard on it, really. His eyes flickered to the dresser, then the bedside table, watching for things he might add to his collection that this woman wouldn't miss. A brush with an ivory handle sitting on the dresser beside the oil lamp caught his attention, but he already had brushes. A tiny silver bell on the bedside table caught his eye.

Juddah stopped in front of the woman, looking down at her. She turned her head, eyes still staring off at something other than him, but he barely noticed as he directed his own gaze to his feet.

"What's your name?" she asked.

"J—Juddah."

His staff shrank up and the sweat he'd wiped off his palms came back. His hands ached to wipe the perspiration away again, but he resisted the urge. Realization his trip to Jubha Kyna might've been a bad idea rose up in his mind, but how to get out of it now? He'd paid his coin and he stood before this beautiful woman who had an expectation of him satisfying her. What would she do when he gave her only disappointment? Laugh?

The brim of his hat crimped in his grip.

"Creidra said you live near the shore, Juddah."

"Yes, Ma'am."

"I have never been to the shore. Tell me what it's like."

Juddah raised his eyes, confused. In all his misguided visits to the temple, none of the women had ever asked anything more than how he wanted to be pleasured. His gaze trailed up her gray smock that didn't fit her so tight as the younger woman's. Her disinterest continued, staring off to the left of him, and he noticed a thin white film clouding her eyes. He raised a hand, waved it in front of her face. No reaction.

"Can't you see?"

The woman's expression fell. Her lips quivered like her mouth wanted to speak but didn't know how. He waited.

"Creidra didn't tell you?"

The long whiskers of his beard scraped against the front of his overalls with the shake of his head. When she didn't react, he realized his mistake.

"No. Didn't say anything."

"I can have Creidra get another Sister, if you want." Strangely, her mood seemed to brighten. "It isn't a bother."

"It's fine."

Her head tilted and her unseeing eyes finally found his, the cloudiness making their natural brown fade to a stale shade of gray similar to her smock. What might have been tears shimmered around their edges.

"You can't see anything at all?" Juddah asked, his gaze flickering to the silver bell on the table beside the bed, then back to her.

"No. I'm sorry." Despair choked her words. "Nothing at all."

Juddah sat on the bed to her right, positioning himself between the woman and the table. He glanced at the bell and back.

"How long've you been without your sight? Born that way?"

"No." Her chin drooped forward, nearly touching her chest. "I...I don't belong here."

Her shoulders rose and fell with a sob she'd tried to contain but failed. Juddah stared, unsure what to do. This wasn't at all what he expected from a visit to the Sisters of Jubha Kyna; his staff quivered in his drawers, surprising him.

"You're not one of the Goddess' wh..." He hesitated.

"One of the Goddess' whores? No." She covered her mouth, holding in another sob. "Home is a long way from here."

Juddah put his hat on the bedside table, concealing the shiny silver bell beneath, and raised his hand toward the woman. Pausing before he touched her, he saw his hand tremoring. The Juddah who normally visited Jubha Kyna would have stopped short, worried about the inadequacy of any stimulation he offered, but in this woman he sensed a difference from the others, a wonderfulness he'd never noticed in a woman before. He rested his fingers on her shoulder and his manhood expanded, a tortoise emerging from its shell.

"We don't have to do this," he said, staring at his hand on her, hoping she'd agree.

She sniffed hard. "We don't?"

"No. Don't really seem like your thing." Relief flooded through Juddah and his staff grew in response. His gaze flickered to his crotch.

"It's not," the woman said, her words a half-laugh, half-sob that became outright tears an instant later. "I don't want to be here."

Juddah's eyes widened, the bell hidden beneath his hat forgotten. His mind flashed to his barn, built of salvaged materials, its sundry contents he'd procured over the years. The horse and gear he'd found wandering in the woods with a dead man hanging in the saddle. The cow he'd come across right outside Birk's fence—fair game for any collector. Kooj who'd wandered onto his land, limping on a broken leg.

And the man he'd discovered near-drowned on his beach.

Juddah put his finger to his mouth, gnawed the corner

of his nail, the movement in his britches growing into a modest bulge.

"You can come with me."

***

Ailyssa stood in front of the open window she hadn't realized was beside the bed. Only a short time had passed since Juddah pried it open and levered himself out through it. Headword by the grunting and panting, Ailyssa guessed that when Creidra referred to him as a large man, she'd meant he was bulky. He'd dangled from the windowsill for a moment, getting ready before letting go and tumbling to the ground with a thump and a woof of air. Ailyssa held her hand to her mouth, leaning out the window as though she might see him. After a brief pause, he caught his breath and called up to her that he was all right and he'd be right back for her.

Unbelievably, Juddah had offered not only to help her escape, but to aid in finding Claris, too. Ailyssa hugged herself, protecting her body from the slight breeze blowing through the open window while trying to calm the bundled nerves firing through her. Just when she thought things their darkest, this man showed up to rescue her. She should be overjoyed, spilling over with relief, but trepidation coiled in her belly. Hadn't she thought herself saved from starvation and a lonely death when Creidra found her? That salvation had turned into a nightmare. She shivered and thought of the Goddess' teachings:

An unfortunate past does not predict a terrible fate. Live in the now, not the then or the yet to come.

The words had provided comfort when she needed it before—when she lamented her Mother, when Claris and her sons were taken—and she wished for them to do the same now, but her heart resisted. If the Goddess had deserted her, she'd be unlikely to return.

Ailyssa sighed and shifted, her thigh bumping the

edge of the bedside table. She froze, worried she'd knock over the bell intended to call for help if she needed it. The tiny clapper didn't jingle. She released her breath and reached out for the bell's handle, intending to put it on the bed, place a pillow over it, and ensure its silence, but didn't find it. She bent and brushed her hand over the top of the table.

It's gone.

Though she had no need of it, she wondered what had happened. Had she used it once too often and Creidra took it away? No matter, she wouldn't be requiring it again.

"Ailyssa."

The word floated up from below on a hoarse whisper. She grasped the lintel and leaned out for him to see her.

"I'm here. Right below the window."

Ailyssa nodded. "How will you get me?"

"You have to jump."

The words chilled the blood flowing through Ailyssa's veins. "Jump?" she squeaked.

"Ain't no other way."

"But we have to find Claris."

"We'll do that once you're out. Jump."

"I can't."

"You have to. I'll catch you."

She shook her head. "I can't."

Silence hung in the air, disturbed only by a bird chirping its chicks to sleep in a nest built in the overhang of the roof.

"Do you want to stay here?"

Nausea roiled in Ailyssa's belly as she remembered the things the other men before Juddah made her do. She thought of the dungeon room with its chains and whips and things she couldn't begin to put name to. Bitter saliva spilled into her mouth, reminding her of what the last man filled it with. She covered her lips to make sure she didn't vomit out the window on her would-be rescuer.

"No," she said after swallowing hateful bile. "I don't want to stay."

"Put your legs out through the window. Hang down far as you can. Let go when I say. I'll catch you."

She responded with a nod and leaned away from the window, rubbing her palms together, feeling the bandage protecting her right hand. The toe of her sandal brushed up the wall, finding its way to the window in the bright glare of her blindness. When she'd gotten it through, the other leg followed, leaving her hanging over the sill, the top of her body inside the room, her legs dangling outside. It occurred to her that Juddah could see up the skirt of her smock and that she wore no underpants. Still preferable to what might have happened had he been the same as the other men.

"Lower yourself down," he whispered.

Ailyssa did, her stomach scraping against the wall below the window. She winced, gritted her teeth, and continued. A moment later, she dangled from the sill, panting with fear and exertion.

"Okay. Let go."

She didn't, choosing to hang instead, scared for her life. Scared of her life. What if he didn't catch her and she broke her leg? Would he still take her with him, or would she become a blind and crippled whore?

How did I end up here?

Her fingers slipped and Ailyssa let out a squawk.

"Sshh," Juddah hissed. "Just let go."

Ailyssa closed her eyes, muting the blinding glare of her sight, and imagined her life if she remained at Jubha Kyna—the pain, the embarrassment, the shame. She released her grip on the sill.

Air rushed around her, then she thumped into something soft yet sturdy. A tiny jingle and a grunt

291

sounded and she knew Juddah had caught her, as he'd promised. She threw her arms around his neck and held on tight, her heart racing, breath panting in and out of her throat.

"I got ya," he said. They stood for a moment before another voice called out.

"Hey!" The man's voice yelled. "Hey you! What're you doing?"

"Shee-it."

Juddah spun away from the wall and loped across the ground, Ailyssa bouncing in his arms. Pain shot through her bruises and scrapes, but the adrenaline of jumping out of the window and being pursued blurred it into a pulse of fear and excitement coursing along the surface of her skin.

The man carrying her pulled up and the scent of horse sweat wafted to Ailyssa's nostrils. With a grunt of effort, Juddah hefted her up, throwing her across the horse's hindquarters, then he followed her up to sit in the saddle.

"Hold on," he said and snapped the reins.

The steed leaped forward, nearly tossing Ailyssa off the back. She jammed her fingers under the saddle's belly strap and curled her hand closed around it.

"Hey!" the voice called again, smaller with more distance between them.

"Claris," Ailyssa said, struggling to hold on while making herself heard above the pounding of hooves on dirt road. "We have to go back and get my Daughter."

"Can't," Juddah said over his shoulder. "Someone saw. They'll be after us in no time."

"But Claris."

She craned her head around, looking back where they'd left, though her blind eyes saw nothing but the hazy mist. In her mind, she saw her Daughter—a girl of only fifteen turns—shrinking in the distance, lost to her once more.

XXXV Horace - Demise

It all seemed very familiar to Horace: the bushes hidin' them, the tang o' brine in the air, the wavy meadow leadin' to the village what popped up outta nowhere. Made the ol' sailor twitchy and right uncomfortable in his own britches.

As much as it were the same, though, it were different, too. Wilty leaves hung on the bushes; the wavin' grass weren't emerald, but yellowy-brown; instead o' lookin' like they'd been recently built, the buildin's might've been standin' since Thorn's kind went hidin' in the Green.

"How can there be another village?" Horace said, not expectin' an answer. He peered back over his shoulder into the stand o' trees what hadn't taken them so long to walk through when they left Haven behind. "That feller said there weren't no other people. Said they ain't never seen anyone but us."

"Thorn doesn't understand, either. They have neighbors."

Horace fidgeted, the discomfort in his britches spreadin' through the rest o' him. Even though they'd been runnin', his legs vibrated with energy wantin' to spill out. He curled his fingers into tight fists and let them go again, flexin' his hands.

"I don't like this."

"Neither does Thorn. But maybe they can direct us to the veil."

Horace tilted his face toward the gray man and found the little feller lookin' at him with pleadin' eyes. The ol' sailor raised one brow and looked him up and down.

"You're all gray."

Thorn's eyes narrowed and a pink hue crawled across his flesh. Sparse brows sprouted above his eyes; his nose and cheeks didn't change.

Not so much like Rilum this time. A familiar seemin' grasshopper flitted by Horace's face.

"Still think it's a bad idea," he said, rubbin' his stubbly chin. "Didn't go so well in Haven, and it appeared a nice place."

"There probably isn't anyone here," Thorn said, wavin' in the direction o' the dirty-lookin', lopsided buildin's. "But we have to try."

"We can keep headin' toward sunset. If we—"

"Horace." Thorn rested his hand on the ol' sailor's forearm and the energy feelin' pulsin' in him grew. "Thorn needs to get back soon."

"What're you—"

The pinky shade faded from the little feller's face, leavin' it a gray that looked sickly even on a man what normally wore the shade. Bags formed under his eyes and the skin on his cheeks sagged toward his chin as though it might slide right off. Horace gasped and swallowed to keep nausea outta his throat.

"I thought you said you was feelin' stronger."

The small man shrugged. "Thorn must get back soon."

Horace glanced from the sallow Small God to the woebegone village and back again. If anythin', in his state, he looked as though he might fit in pretty good. Against his better judgment, Horace nodded his agreement. Better judgment were an unusual thin' for him to have, anyway.

"Fine," Horace said, standin' straight. "Let's get on with it."

They set out across the field o' yellowed blades, a feelin' o' havin' done this before sittin' on Horace's shoulders like he were wearin' a jerkin made outta it.

The smell o' dyin' grass and a whiff o' the sea filled Horace's nostrils while wadin' through the dried-out meadow, right up until they approached the village's edge. They stopped when they got there, starin' at the dirt track what started right where the buildin's did, too.

"Somethin's wrong here," Horace whispered directin' his gaze sideways at his companion.

Thorn peered back with glazed eyes. The pink o' his skin pulsed and faded, pulsed and faded. The ol' sailor sighed heavily because he didn't enjoy seein' the little feller lookin' this way.

"Come on," he said and plodded out o' the grass, Thorn followin' close behind.

They entered the village from the sunrise end, walkin' out onto the dirt track the way they'd done at Haven. The buildin's was the same, 'cept for their appearance o' havin' seen season after season o' harsh weather and neglect. Paint chipped and faded; shutters hung askew; moss growin' on roofs. Made Horace a might nervous, right down to an unseen bird twitterin' up underneath the eaves o' the closest buildin'. Horace tilted his head back for a peek, squintin' against the sun until a cloudy wisp crept across it, throwin' them into shade. But the chill didn't rattle its way up his spine until Thorn jerked on his sleeve. He lowered his gaze and saw the boy.

The feller appeared to have seen the seasons turn eight or ten times and stood a similar height to Thorn, same as the boy at Haven. This young one were different too, though, in the same way o' the buildin's and the grass. His countenance didn't shine with no childlike glow, and dirt were smeared on his cheeks. He leaned to one side, like many o' the village's structures, and when Horace glanced down, he saw he possessed but one leg and supported himself with a crutch on the side where it were missin'.

This broken-down boy what appeared outta nowhere stood watchin' without movin', his presence callin' nervous sweat to Horace's brow. The ol' sailor's pulse raced, thumpin' in his ears, and he sensed Thorn standin' beside him, starin' at the boy along with him. They didn't move forward a few paces this time. Horace cleared his throat.

"Hello," he said, raisin' his hand the same way he'd done before.

The boy continued starin', mouth pulled into a frown and his gaze dartin' between Horace and Thorn.

"What's the name o' this place?"

The boy's gaze rested on Horace. He squinted. "Demise."

Demise.

The same chill what he had upon seein' the boy came back and perched itself in Horace's spine. He swallowed hard, shivered, and took a shuddery breath before askin': "There be anyone else 'round?"

The boy kept starin', his empty gaze makin' Horace feel like sea water were pumpin' through his veins instead o' nice, warm blood. Finally, he pivoted on his one leg and hobbled toward the square at the middle o' the village.

"Fuck me dead," Horace said. "We gotta get out o' here."

He spun to take off back the way they'd come, but Thorn holdin' onto his sleeve wouldn't let him. The ol' sailor glared at the little feller, energy pumpin' through him and promptin' him to get runnin'. The thought o' pickin' up the Small God and carryin' him entered his consideration, but the faded glow in Thorn's eyes stopped him.

"This way," Thorn said soundin' outta breath.

He pointed across the village with the ominous name o' Demise, toward the field o' yellow grass on the far end, and the brace o' trees beyond. It were the shortest way to get past the place without goin' back, Horace had to admit.

But it's a place named Demise.

Horace huffed, disbelievin' he were 'bout to do this, and caught sight o' the youngster disappearin' into what would've been the meetin' hall if they was in Haven instead o' here. Time were runnin' short.

After a peek at his companion in which he noticed Thorn'd given up the appearance o' bein' anythin' but a small gray man, Horace let his achin' legs get movin'. His feet tromped on the dirt track, the too-tight boots pinchin', his broken rib pokin', and Thorn keepin' up the pace. Halfway across the square, the crowd began comin' outta the buildin' and rain started to fall.

Drops plunked on top o' the heads o' men and women what looked like the ones they'd left behind in Haven, 'cept for their tattered clothes and dirty faces. The men wore scraggly beards instead o' bein' clean-shaved, but there weren't no mistakin' their eyes. The women was unkempt, with locks stickin' out and empty gazes starin', but they might've been the same bunch. And Horace didn't see no more because he lowered his head and ran.

The rain fell hard, plasterin' what hair the ol' sailor had to his scalp in no time. The dirt track turned to slop under their feet, the thump o' runnin' steps hurryin' up behind them becomin' splashes instead. He raised his gaze, fightin' against the urge to peer back at the pursuin' throng, and saw they was gettin' near the sunset edge o' Demise.

Horace and Thorn leaped from the muddy track into the tall grass, wet blades *thwappin'* against their legs. No sooner'd they made it outta the village than the sound o' pursuit stopped. The ol' sailor glanced back, came close to losin' his footin' before skiddin' to a halt to turn back.

Sure enough, the angry-lookin' mob stood at the edge o' Demise as though held back by a wall what couldn't be seen.

"I guess no one ever leaves Demise, either," Horace said.

They turned their backs on the tumbledown village and ran through the field into the woods, runnin' until the trees and rain both stopped. The last clump o' brush parted and they emerged on the edge o' a greener'n green field with the village o' Haven in the distance, shinin' in the sun.

XXXVI Kuneprius - The Small God

One hundred seventy-eight. *One hundred seventy-nine. One hundred eighty.*

Kuneprius blinked. The saltwater felt different against his eyes than the fresh water drawn from a well to which he'd become accustomed—more natural. A crab no bigger than his thumbnail scuttled across the bottom of the tidal pool, its tiny legs disturbing individual grains of sand as it scuffled its way to hide beneath a stone.

One hundred ninety-three. One hundred ninety-four. One hundred ninety-five.

He wanted to be excited at eclipsing the highest number he'd ever counted with his face in the water, but he couldn't. A piece inside him had broken, leaving shards of anger and despair embedded in his chest, working themselves into his belly, his heart.

A fish tinier than the crab wriggled past his nose— he'd never have seen it if he hadn't plunged his face below the surface of the tidal pool. He blinked again; his lungs ached.

Two hundred.

Kuneprius pulled his face and hands out of the water, leaning over the pool to allow the liquid to stream out of his nose and ears, from out of his hair and off his eyelashes. The falling drops stirred the pool and he imagined the fish fleeing, the crab jamming itself deeper into the sand under the rock.

He wished to do the same.

A bird squawked overhead—a crow, by the harshness of its voice—and Kuneprius raised his eyes, but the sky lay empty except for the endless blue. He waved his hands, drying them, and wiped his face on his sleeve, then inhaled the salty air. His stomach clenched at the hint of clay lurking beneath the brine and the ghost of old blood clinging to his cheeks, the new blood soiling his fingers.

"How long this time?"

Kuneprius didn't reply. He knew it wasn't the golem who'd asked, but a memory of the way things had been, the way he wanted them to be again. It seemed far too late for that.

He peered along the shore and it took a moment to identify the clay man seated amongst the rocks. The color difference between him and the boulders strewn across the seashore was subtle, and he'd curled his knees up to his chest, wrapped his arms around them so his appearance varied little from his surroundings.

The waves washed against the rocks, filling Kuneprius' ears with the tumbling roil of water as he picked his way across the beach. His boots lay discarded on the verge between forest and shoreline, tossed aside in favor of navigating the shore with his bare soles, allowing the sea to kiss his toes. It pleased him for having done so, but like everything else in the days since they'd left two young and broken bodies lying in the mud beside a creek, a shadow hung over the little pleasure it gave him, painting it black.

Pebbles shifted and crunched under his feet as he came to stand in front of the clay man. The living statue didn't move. Kuneprius glared at the thing's muscles bulging beneath its smooth skin, its aquiline nose and symmetrical features, its face looking so perfectly...

Sculpted.

A splinter of pride wedged itself between the anger and sadness gripping his soul. No matter what this thing was crouched before him, or what it had done or might do, Vesisdenperos made it. The same Vesisdenperos whom Kuneprius had killed for to liberate from the Goddess' caravan. The same Vesisdenperos whom Kuneprius raised and cared for from that moment on.

The same Vesisdenperos who gave his life to and for the Small Gods.

Did he?

"Two hundred," Kuneprius said, his gazed fixed on the clay man's expressionless face. "I counted to two hundred this time—the most ever."

The thing's head tilted back, its eyes flickering up and finding Kuneprius'. Their gazes met for an instant and a spark of hope leaped into the older man's chest.

"Ves? Are you in there?"

The moment passed as quickly as it had come. The clay man's head settled back, his eyes staring ahead at nothing, or everything—at things Kuneprius could never fathom and didn't care that he never would.

Kuneprius let go a sigh and wiped away sea water running down his face from his hair. The flash of connection, of potential communication, disappeared, and he held no desire to be around the aberrant behemoth.

He trudged away from the living statue, the soles of his bare feet crunching in the pebbles of the shore.

***

Every time Kuneprius inadvertently trod upon a thorn, he whispered small thanks he'd thought to put his boots on again—the only thanks he'd offered since what happened to the children. Much as he hated the footwear, he appreciated the protection the boots offered, and the forest beside the shore was full of prickles.

He passed thin-trunked birch trees that reminded him too much of the ones near the creek, and a red and peeling arbutus that made him wish for home.

Will I ever see it again?

Doubtful. The plain huts, the seed garden, the courtyard—it was all so far away, both physically and emotionally. He shook his head thinking about it. After what he'd witnessed the Small Gods allow to happen, did he want to go back?

His legs thrashed through the brush, uncaring of the racket he created. Two sunrises had passed since they last encountered anyone—and he was glad of that—so he didn't imagine he'd find people so near the shore. If they were going to find a fishing village, they'd have stumbled upon it by now.

Ahead, the trees thinned further and the underbrush gave way to shrubs and bushes that stood as high as his head. Kuneprius pulled the edge of his vest up to protect his face from thorns and brambles and pushed his way through.

Wide green leaves slapped his ears. He turned his head away, leaned forward. His boot caught in a creeper, tangling his foot, and he stumbled, falling and catching himself on his hands before his chest hit the ground.

He lay still, breathing heavily but happy not to be moving. Around him, the brush had fallen away and his face was in grass growing far above his head. Without meaning it to, a chuckle burbled in the back of his throat.

Grasshoppers hidden amongst the blades chirruped along with him.

When the unbidden mirth ended, Kuneprius stay where he'd landed, inhaling through his nose, sucking in the scent of the grass, the earth—each breath blissfully free of the stink of clay. For the first time since they left the creek, the pain in his heart eased.

Then he heard the voices.

Small and distant—impossible for him to distinguish their number or the words spoken. He ceased breathing in favor of listening, his pulse beating faster. Whoever they were, he needed to be sure they didn't head for the shore—if they stumbled upon the clay man, it would be the death of them.

Kuneprius climbed to his knees, peering over the top of the thigh-high grass into the meadow. Though he intended to follow the same path he and Vesisdenperos had taken on their way to the shore, they hadn't passed through the field. Somewhere along the way, he must have gotten turned about.

The green grass stood a uniform height, as though trimmed by the hand of a god. The tall blades undulated in the soft breeze, each gentle gust sending a wave across the field the way it might disturb a lake.

For a moment, Kuneprius experienced nothing but the breathtaking sight of the meadow, its color and movement calming him. It drew him to his feet. He stared out at the field, longing to strip and dive into it, allow the blades to caress his skin as he swam amongst them. He imagined taking the rest of his lifetime to count them, but then a movement jarred him from his reverie.

A head bobbed amongst the grass.

No. Two.

Kuneprius remembered the voices, and his heart sank as he crouched, hiding behind radiant green blades to spy on the bobbing heads.

The distance between him and the figures striding through the grass was not as great as the quietness of their voices suggested. He saw it was a man and a boy, though they were yet too far for him to make out their features. They spoke as they walked, but their gait held a hesitancy, as did their speech. To Kuneprius' relief, their path carried them across the field, parallel to the shore.

He shifted his feet and settled in, waiting for them to pass out of the meadow and allow him to return to enjoying the way the blades shivered in the breeze. They approached the far end of the expanse and Kuneprius' heart pounded—once they left, they'd be safe and he'd be alone. As he readied himself to stand and plunge into the sea of grass, the two figures stopped, turned, and hurried back into the meadow. Confused, Kuneprius returned to his crouch.

The man and boy traversed the meadow again, following precisely the path they'd taken the first time, but in the opposite direction. They moved more quickly this time, and soon reached the other end. Kuneprius held his breath, waiting for them to cross the verge and enter the forest.

They didn't.

Curiously, they reversed course again and hurried across the field a third time. Kuneprius furrowed his brow and pressed a knuckle to his lips. Were they searching for something? If so, they moved too quickly to be effective. He resisted the urge to jump up and tell them so, to direct them to take more time and care lest they walk right past whatever they hunted for.

The thought struck a chord in Kuneprius.

What if they're searching for Vesisdenperos?

He'd put little thought to the golem since happening upon the field of green, but now he craned his neck, peering back through the tangle of brush. Surely, he didn't need to see the living sculpture to know of his approach—the clay man had yet to act as though he cared if anyone heard him coming.

Instead of hearing clay feet beating through the brush, the harsh call of the crow he'd heard earlier reached his ears. Kuneprius directed his gaze toward the sky, and this time he spied the bird.

Not a crow...a raven.

Feathers black as a moonless sky covered its enormous wingspan. The bird glided through the sky with authority and effortless ease, adjusting its wings and tail to circle back over the clearing as though aiding the man and boy in their search.

Kuneprius watched, his mouth fallen open with the feeling he'd stumbled upon a land of wonders—the remarkable field, the awe-inspiring raven. What other surprises did it hold?

The raven wheeled, heading toward the sea, and Kuneprius pulled himself out of its spell to return his gaze to the man and the boy. For a moment, he didn't find them. Joy flashed through him that they'd likely disappeared into the forest, but then panic echoed through his chest when he considered they might have slipped by him on their way to the shore. Three stuttering heartbeats later, he located the man still following the same path through the field. Alone.

Where is the boy?

Kuneprius stretched up to peer over the tips of the grass, scanning the field. His breath came in short gasps as his concern grew. Surely, in the time the bird distracted him, the boy couldn't have gotten far.

The lad had split off from the man and trod a fresh path through the grass. Kuneprius watched with alarm as the boy headed toward the shore where the clay man waited. He opened his mouth to call out a warning, but something inexplicable stayed his tongue. Instead, he narrowed his eyes, watching the boy come closer to his hiding place.

One. Two. Three.

Kuneprius counted the beats of his heart. As the distance between him and the boy narrowed, it sped up.

Eightnineteneleven.

The boy stopped and directed his gaze toward the sky and the raven now hidden from Kuneprius by the trees. The lad's head pivoted side to side as the great bird circled, and it gave the observer his first opportunity to view the boy clearly.

Broad nose, gray skin.

For an instant, Kuneprius thought he was seeing a boy made of clay—like Vesisdenperos whom he'd left hidden amongst the rocks by the shore—but then the truth of it came to him.

This is the Small God we search for.

His eyes widened, the two children left broken beside a creek forgotten. Here before him was the reason he'd been torn from his home and sent on this terrible journey, the reason his friend had given his life. Here was the opportunity to make the loss and the pain worthwhile.

Still crouching, Kuneprius pivoted on one uneven boot heel and plunged back through the tangle of bushes and brambles, creepers and thorns, to hurry his way back to the shore.

To tell the clay man he'd found the Small God from the Green.

XXXVII Horace - The Towns

"Must've got turned 'round."

Horace dragged the back o' his hand across his

forehead, wipin' away the rain drippin' outta his bedraggled hair. He stared at the village, recognizin' its new-lookin' buildin's, then pivoted to glare at the forest like it were the trees' fault they found themselves here again.

"We are near Thorn's home." Since the little feller stopped makin' himself appear as somethin' he weren't, the proper gray color'd returned to his cheeks and his skin tightened up again. "The veil is keeping us away."

"What? Can't be. It's just a place."

"But not like any other. Have you ever heard of any man crossing the veil? Entering what you call the Green?"

Horace put his hands on his hips and felt the wetness o' his shirt and breeches. After posin' that way for the space o' four or five breaths, he scratched his head, not rememberin' anyone ever bein' in the Green and tellin' Thorn so.

"But I know 'bout the Green," he added. "I seen it dozens o' times."

"But the veil has kept you and others of your kind..."

Thorn's voice trailed off, his mouth hangin' open and his eyes starin' up into the sky. Horace swung 'round to find out what he were gawkin' at. The sun got him right in the peepers, so he didn't spy nothin' at first, but then a black shape crossed the glowin' disk.

"Don't know what you got in mind," Horace said, squintin' up into the sky. "But I ain't goin' back into that Haven place."

"Father Raven," Thorn said in a whispery voice like he didn't listen to any o' the ol' sailor's words. "Come with Thorn."

The Small God took Horace by the sleeve and led him into the meadow. The clouds what'd soaked them durin' their flight from Demise'd burned away, leavin' the sun shinin' down to dry them out. As it did, Horace caught a whiff o' how long it'd been since he'd put on a fresh shirt and wrinkled his nose. O'er all them turns o' the seasons, he'd grown accustomed to bein' asea for long stretches, but he'd always been one o' the fellers what did his best to stay clean.

The ol' sailor shook his head, dispellin' the odor what the rain'd brought to the surface, and looked 'round at where Thorn were leadin' him. Turned out the little feller were followin' the tree line, headin' windward and skirtin' the village o' Haven with his gaze directed up at the black-winged bird wheelin' through the sky. Missin' the creepy little town suited Horace fine, but only one thin' lay windward from where they was, and it carried with it a briny stink.

"Hold on," Horace said, diggin' in his heels and carvin' ruts in the dirt. "Where do you think you're takin' me?"

Thorn faced him, fingers still grippin' the ol' sailor's sleeve, and pointed toward the sky.

"Father Raven brought Thorn over the veil. He can take Thorn back."

"But the ocean's o'er there. Told you I ain't goin' anywhere near the sea."

"It's the only way."

Horace jerked a thumb backward o'er his shoulder without lookin' that direction. "If we head leeward, we can get 'round Haven and Demise, through the forest, find your veil."

"Thorn would have no way through. Over is how he must go."

The little feller released his grip on Horace's sleeve and hurried his feet in a straight line toward where the shore'd be, eyes scannin' the sky until they found the bird again. His pace picked up from a fast walk to a trot to a gallop. Horace stood watchin'.

"I ain't goin' nowhere near the sea!"

Thorn didn't look back.

The tall blades o' grass whipped 'round the gray man's waist as he shrank with the distance he were puttin' between himself and the ol' sailor. Horace's heart wanted his feet to go after the gray man, but his body what hated the sea, and his mind what remembered how it near took his life, weren't up to it. His boots stayed where they was, leavin' him nothin' to do but hope Thorn'd realize his mistake and reverse course.

He didn't.

After a while what saw the little feller shrink to nothin' but a dot headin' for the horizon, Horace finally heaved a sigh and got himself turned 'round. No idea occurred to him where he should be headed, but somethin' made him think that, since he'd gotten this far, he should at least see the place what Thorn'd called the land behind the veil, even if he did so through a magical green mist. He didn't think he wanted to set foot in it, anyways.

Horace trudged through the tall grass, his mood addin' weight to his steps. Stickin' to the verge at the forest's edge, he hoped to skirt his way past Haven like he'd suggested to Thorn, and then do the same with that Demise place, too.

The ol' sailor walked for a while, his mind thinkin' 'bout how it'd been but a few sunrises since the same bird what Thorn were chasin' had dropped the little feller on top o' Horace. Head shakin', he chuckled while rememberin' how he'd been so scared he shat in his britches. Doin' so made him recall Thorn stealin' his breeches off the line outside the shack in the woods, then he thought o' what he'd said 'bout Rilum. Them thoughts made the ol' sailor's chest tighten, but not because o' his hurtin' rib. It tightened in a way what made breathin' hard and caused an ache right to his belly.

Horace stopped and glanced back the way Thorn'd gone. The little feller'd disappeared. His gaze dragged o'er the field o' green grass, wavin' 'round in the slight breeze and practically gleamin' in the sun, just like the buildin's o' Haven.

The village sat quiet and unmovin' in the middle o' the meadow, lookin' like it should be a pleasant little place to call home. If them men and women what looked too much like one another hadn't chased him out, it might've been the kind o' place he'd've settled. That, and if it weren't so near to the sea.

As he walked, Horace gazed at the boots what Birk'd given him, their narrow ends pinchin' his toes. It seemed like so long since he'd been at the inn run by the big man they called Krin, enjoyin' stew and ale and thinkin' he'd been saved. But like Dunal'd been the one what put him in the drink to begin with, he'd also been the one what made it so he found himself doin' his best to avoid a couple o' bewitched villages. Made him wish he either didn't wrap his fingers 'round the oaf's throat or he'd taken the time to choke the life outta him long ago.

The black boots trod upon the long grass, bendin' it and breakin' it under his steps. Horace watched the blades crushed under their soles, usin' the gentle sound to distract him from memories o' killin' Dunal, and from knowin' Thorn were gone—left him behind without a so long.

When the grass ended and Horace found himself standin' on a patch o' dirt, he stopped and stared at the puff o' dust his last step kicked up. It rose a handspan and dispersed into the air. Horace raised his head to find the buildin's o' Haven standin' directly before him.

The ol' sailor's breath caught up in his throat and he jerked his head 'round to peek behind him. A stretch o' grass, then the forest.

How can I be here?

The last he'd looked, he'd been walkin' alongside the village as he followed the tree line. It weren't possible for him to finish up standin' at the sunrise end o' the place, the way he and Thorn'd done when they first arrived. His head made its way back to gazin' at the new-lookin' buildin's and he detected the twitterin' o' baby birds hidin' in a nest. Two breaths later, he caught sight o' a boy aged between eight and ten turns.

Horace didn't need no more promptin'.

He turned tail and ran toward sunrise, not carin' no more 'bout seein' Thorn's veil nor the Green hidden behind it. He cared 'bout nothin' but gettin' as far away from the town called Haven as his feet'd take him.

His too-small boots hammered the ground and his breath shortened into pants as he ran, but the forest didn't appear to be comin' no closer. He kept his tired legs pushin' him forward, anyways. Each breath became a labor, his broken rib rubbin' and shootin' pain through him. He glanced sideways, half expectin' Thorn to be runnin' alongside, his breathin' easy and gray skin showin' no signs o' the sweat spreadin' under Horace's own armpits.

Course, Thorn weren't there. He'd gone chasin' birds rather'n stayin' with his friend.

His gait slowin' up with fatigue, the ol' sailor craned his neck 'round to peer back over his shoulder, thinkin' he'd find Haven keepin' pace behind him. It weren't. Instead, a patch o' grass separated him from a stand o' jackpines.

I didn't go through no forest.

Horace slowed to a stop and bent at the waist, eyes closed tight and hands planted on his knees as he gulped mouthfuls o' air into his chest. The rib begged him to stop, but his lungs insisted he keep on gulpin'. When he finally suspected he might be able to return his breathin' to somethin' near its normal, he opened his eyes. As soon as he did, he wished he hadn't.

His feet was standin' on a patch o' dirt, and he'd seen but one place with a patch o' dirt to trod upon.

Horace raised his head, peekin' out ahead o' him, but saw nothin' besides yellow grass leadin' to a stand o' trees. His brows wrinkled. Shouldn't be no dirty patch in the middle o' the meadow on the way to the forest.

The ol' sailor rubbed his stubbly chin with his fingers, strugglin' to make sense o' his current predicament. A stretch o' field and a bit o' trees behind him, the same thin' before him, and a patch o' dirt under his feet. Might be he'd've shrugged and kept on his way if not for the creepin' shiver what crawled up his spine and made him spin himself 'round.

He were standin' at the sunrise edge o' the town called Demise, a one-legged boy with a stick for a crutch frownin' at him. A cloud crossed the sun and a drop o' rain landed on Horace's nose.

For the second time in a short while, Horace thought he might be leavin' a brick-shaped shit in his britches. He faced back toward the trees and got to runnin' again before it squeezed outta his porthole.

He ran as many paces as he possessed fingers and toes before the cloud passed from in front o' the sun and he realized there wasn't no trees ahead. Where they'd been a moment before stood a shiny, white town what he knew without gettin' no closer to be called Haven. He stopped again, surprised at the gratin' sound o' footwear in dry dirt.

Confused and worried his frightened heart might beat right outta his chest, Horace gazed at his boots and the patch o' dirt on which they rested.

"No," the ol' sailor breathed.

He raised his head and found the town what were sittin' before him a few quick heartbeats ago were gone. A stretch o' green grass and a patch o' trees replaced it;

he figured he knew where to find the village what he lost.

Horace whirled 'round, the tiny chirps o' baby birds already findin' his ears. Freshly painted-lookin' buildin's loomed on both sides and a boy at least eight turns but no more'n ten stood exactly where Horace expected him to be. One thin' were different 'bout the town o' Haven this time: the big group o' men and women what looked too much like each other standin' behind the boy, glarin' at Horace.

The ol' sailor didn't wait to find out what the mob'd do, nor did he set out for the trees, already knowin' he'd somehow find himself standin' on the town o' Demise's doorstep. This time, Horace lit out the direction he'd watched Thorn go chasin' after the raven.

The ol' sailor's feet cut through tall grass, carryin' him toward the sea.

XXXVIII Teryk - Awakening

A splinter of light shone through the impenetrable blackness. Teryk focused on it, waiting for his surroundings to resolve into something recognizable, something other than darkness and nothing.

An odor came to him, salty and sharp, then a sound.

He didn't recognize it at first, but it became the creak of boards. The noise came from under him, all around him. Air entered his lungs, brushing across his lips, cooling his tongue on its way through his mouth. Hardness pressed against his left shoulder and arm, his hip, his leg.

I'm alive.

He stretched out, but his foot stopped after moving less than a hand's breadth as it hit something solid with a gentle thump. Teryk closed his eyes and the sliver of light—the shred of hope—disappeared. Mind straining, he attempted to remember where he might be and how he got here, but came up empty. Vague and fleeting impressions came to him—memories, perhaps—but each fled before his precarious awareness grasped them.

He shifted and his head brushed a hard, flat surface. He stretched his hand straight up, but it caught in a rough fabric. After a moment's struggle, he freed it and his fingers encountered another surface the same as the ones restricting his head and feet.

A coffin. I'm in a coffin.

His eyes snapped open and his stomach seized when he couldn't find the thin fragment of light again. Heart racing, his gaze darted in the dark until he located it and released his held breath into the enclosed space. His exhalation pressed on him as though weights held the air around the edges like a fisherman's net.

Teryk jerked, thumping his head and feet against the ends of the coffin.

"Help," he croaked, his parched throat unable to create meaningful sound.

The muscles in his arms and chest ached, twisted in painful knots as though he'd spent a day training with Trenan and the master swordsman had pushed him beyond his limits. The thought of his mentor brought memories along with it: Godsbane, a man in an alley, a woman missing an eye and her teeth. His gut lurched as he recalled being skewered on his own blade.

Maybe I'm not alive and this is what it's like to be dead.

"No."

The word scarped his throat and he reached up and rested his hand on the board above him, measuring the distance. More space lay between himself and the lid of the coffin than between his feet or head and the ends. But enough?

Teryk shifted himself to lie flat on his back, the muscles along his spine unimpressed with the effort. Panting, he waited for his tortured sinews to recover. His pulse beat in his ears, whooshing through his head like waves washing against the shore. He closed his eyes again and took control of his breath, inhaling deeply, filling his chest until his ribs ached, then letting the air go. His racing heart slowed.

This time, he found the dim line of light easily, and let it encourage him. He may be in a coffin, but if light shone in, he wasn't buried in the ground, and hope remained.

He cocked back both arms, resting his elbows on the wooden bottom of his prison, and drew another breath in through his nose. The salty aroma tickled his nostrils, but he detected the scent of wood and dirty straw, animal fur and feces, too.

Where am I?

Hands stretched open and palms flat, Teryk extended his arms with all the strength he could muster. The heels of his hands slammed against the wood above him, pain shooting along his body, but nails screeched in the shifting wood, and the sound energized him.

Teeth clenched, he repeated the action. The thin line of light widened, his hope growing along with it. He hit it again. Again.

Man from across the sea.

These words flashed across Teryk's mind unbidden, stopping him before he struck the board again. The light coming through the widening gap flickered and cast shadows into his prison which he now recognized as a crate, not a coffin.

The scroll.

Memories flooded back to the prince—getting caught beneath the grate in the river under Draekfarren; finding the parchment; his father taking it, burning it; sneaking out of the inner city. He remembered the deadly encounter with the brigand and had vague recollection of being rescued, cared for, but then a gap.

A gap ending with him in a crate.

He hit the top of the crate again and nails squealed, the space wide enough to allow his fingers to poke through. Heart pulsing with frightened excitement, he scrambled to a crouching position, fighting to tear himself out of the fabric tangled about him. Head bent and shoulder pressed against the wooden lid, he lifted with his aching legs, pushing the crate's top free.

The lid tumbled off, the jagged end of a nail or piece of broken wood scratching his cheek. Teryk threw the top aside with one hand and brought his other to the scrape, felt the warmth of blood flowing from his face. He cursed under his breath and straightened creakily, his spine resistant to the efforts.

A lantern hung from a hook affixed to a post, its light flickering across a host of crates of similar size and shape to the one imprisoning the prince. When his bare foot touched the wooden floorboards, he realized he wore only his undergarments. He gazed at the dark patch on the front of his shirt, touched it and found it hard with dried blood.

Panic flooded through him, filling his mouth and clamping around his lungs. He clawed desperately at his shirt, pulling it up to see his abdomen. Dark blood covered it, flaking away at his touch, but he found no wound beneath, no gash or hole, no sign of the stabbing he now clearly remembered.

Teryk stared at his dirty stomach for too long, forgetting his situation as he attempted sorting through his memories and the reality before him. Had so much time passed for him to heal? Or did he misremember the events leading here?

A sound above his head yanked him out of his thoughts. He looked up at the wooden ceiling and discovered more light seeping through cracks between the boards. He waited, listening.

Footsteps.

The sound shifted away, but Teryk didn't doubt it was the clomp of boot heels on wood. He let the stiff fabric of his shirt fall back over his dirty but uninjured belly. After the sounds moved far enough away Teryk could no longer detect them, he surveyed the room. His gaze fell across crates, sealed barrels, and finally a ladder leading up to a hatch. He stepped furtively across the floor and paused at the bottom.

Standing with his hand on one of the ladder's rungs, Teryk stared up at the trapdoor, brow furrowed. What sort of place had a floor and walls of wood and a hatch overhead? As he pondered his situation and the wisdom of climbing the ladder and through a door into the unknown, he felt the floor shift ever so slightly beneath him. The prince grabbed the rung tighter.

It's in my head.

Amongst his memories, he recalled the beating given him before the brigand ran him through with his own sword. The thought made him cringe. He knew he should be thankful for being alive, but how when he didn't know where he was or why?

One way to find out.

Teryk set his foot on the bottom rung and stepped up

onto the ladder, then reached higher with his hand. He paused when he noticed it tremor and curled his fingers into a tight fist, willing it to stop. His entire life, he'd let his sister take the lead when he wanted nothing more than to be the one being followed. Now, standing at the bottom of a ladder staring up into the unknown, he wished for Danya to be there to encourage him and give him strength.

The prince shook his head, loosening the thought. He was his own man and didn't need the princess' help. Let her sit in her chamber, safe at Draekfarren while he set out to save the world—that was what he'd wanted from the beginning.

An opportunity to prove himself.

He climbed the ladder, pausing between each step to listen for footsteps from the room overhead, but he heard none. Upon reaching the top, he stopped again, examining around the edge of the hatch in the dim light thrown over his shoulder by the lantern hanging behind and below him. He saw no latch meant to hold him in or keep anyone else out.

Teryk licked his lips, tasted dirt, and reached his arm over his head, joints aching as his fingers touched the hatch's smooth, painted wood.

A hinge creaked quietly as he lifted the trap door, inching it open a crack to peer through. He climbed one more rung, bringing his eyes up to the opening. Teryk saw little beyond the narrow opening; bright sun found his eyes, blinding him to his surroundings, but telling him more than he'd known.

Outside. I was being kept in some sort of dungeon.

The sun's warmth and brightness fortified him as he pushed the hatch open farther. His head passed the level of the hatch, extended up into the open.

A salty breeze touched the prince's cheeks and the briny scent found its way into his lungs with his next breath. Once, in his youth, his father had taken him and Danya on the maiden voyage of his flagship, the *Devil of the Deep*. The scent of the ocean had stuck with him, and he'd longed to experience it again but never had the opportunity; he recognized it instantly now. It drew him out, encouraging his legs to climb the rest of the way up the ladder and out of his prison.

Gulls wheeled overhead, the beat of their wings mingling with the wash of sea against the side of the boat, a sound which attracted Teryk. His bare feet padded on warm, oiled boards as he lurched across the deck toward the wale, oblivious to everything around him. As he approached, he spied the ocean over the side, modest waves topped with white foam.

He increased his pace, hurrying to lean against the rail and peer out across the water, his breath sticking in his throat.

The spires of Draekfarren and the inner city were still visible, but the haze of distance blurred the docks and fishing wharves along the shoreline. He didn't know how he'd ended up on the boat, but it appeared he'd been on it for the better part of a day.

The tang of the ocean air invigorated him, but the sensation was short lived, his thoughts returning to the scroll and the reason he'd left the inner city in the first place.

The man from across the sea.

Was this ship taking him away from his quest, or had the fates intervened to carry him closer to his destination? Fingernails dug into the painted wood as his fingers gripped the railing tight.

Am I the man from across the sea?

The thought left him chilled, but it was a familiar sound behind him that froze the prince.

The steely song of a blade pulled from its scabbard.

Teryk released his grip and raised his hands, turning

to face a man who held his sword extended level with the prince's throat. A ponytail held the sailor's brown hair back from his face, and a long mustache waxed into curled ends perched atop his lip. A group of men milling behind him eyed Teryk, their hands hovering near their weapons.

"What have we here?" the mustachioed man asked. "A stowaway, it seems."

The sailors grumbled and scowled; he waved his free hand, silencing them.

"Do you know what happens to stowaways, lad?"

Teryk looked at the man but didn't answer. A smile tilted his lips beneath his coiffed facial hair and he stepped forward until the tip of his blade touched the prince's throat. Teryk leaned back to get away, but the wale pressed against this back, keeping him from moving as the cold steel caressed his flesh.

"Feed 'em to the sharks and honor the God of the Deep, they do. Ever thought your fate'd be to feed a god?"

The salty air Teryk drew into through his mouth no longer tasted so sweet.

XXXIX Teryk - Back to the Sea

Each step made the scent o' brine in Horace's nose stronger, and his wish to turn himself 'round and run the other way grew along with it. But he'd already experienced what lay that direction: Haven and Demise, though he'd started to think o' the twin creepy villages as Death and Demise. Suited them better, he figured.

Ahead, a line o' shrubs and sparse trees loomed, but they didn't look like the bushes and jackpines what'd tempted him into thinkin' he were gettin' away from them towns before. The shrubs grew lower and more tangly, and the trees thin and tall with leaves what'd turn colors and fall off when third season came. And better'n that, he actually got closer and closer to them as he trudged along on legs beggin' for a rest.

A breeze he recognized for seawind rustled through them leaves and set the grass to wavin'. Horace pressed on, tellin' his legs they'd have to wait before they got some respite because if they didn't keep goin', he might end up dead, and then they'd get nothin' but rest. But the thought o' death were only one part o' what kept him trompin' on, he had to admit. He also desired to find a little gray man—his only hope for gettin' outta this accursed place.

Horace waded into the shrubs, the breeze blowin' stiffer as he got nearer to the shore. Amongst the shoosh o' the wind through the trees and his feet disturbin' bushes, he detected the rush o' waves breakin' against rocks. Judgin' by the sound, they wasn't big swells, but they was gettin' closer. Knowin' so gave the ol' sailor a shudder.

Bushes with pointy thorns plucked at Horace's sleeves and pant legs, and he wondered if a feller named Thorn worried 'bout the same thin' happenin' to him. Prob'bly he did—a name didn't mean much to the world...though given the moniker o' Seaman'd condemned Horace to a life on the water.

The shrubs thinned and Horace lurched though the trees. Ahead, beyond another stretch o' tangled bushes and brambles, rocks scattered across a wide shore, and then came the sea. He stopped in his tracks, suddenly findin' difficulty in pullin' air into his chest.

Horace stood for the space o' as many breaths as he had fingers, his hands restin' on his hips, his head not wantin' him to go any nearer to the briny deep.

"I ain't goin' in it," he said aloud as if doin' so might

convince him to keep goin'. "Just lookin' for the little gray feller, is all."

He attempted a step toward the shore, but his foot hesitated and it only ended up goin' a half-step. Horace glared at it like it were a beast with its own mind what weren't doin' what he wanted it to.

"Ain't no gettin' outta here without Thorn." He figured it may or may not be true, but he'd found out the hard way he weren't goin' nowhere alone. "One quick peek and if he ain't 'round, I'll hightail it away from the shore."

Lyin' to himself did the trick. His achin' legs made his stubborn feet move, carryin' him between the thin trees with their peelin' white bark. His stomach continued flippin' 'round at the smell o' the salty sea, but he kept it under control and didn't puke out the unusual yet tasty snacks they'd given him in Haven.

Horace got to the next line o' shrubs and stopped, stretchin' up on his toes to catch a glimpse past them. Driftwood and seaweed littered the rocky shore in the manner o' most ev'ry beach he'd seen. Just beside where Horace were comin' out o' the shrubs, a short bay cut itself into the shoreline. On the other side, a point jutted out into the water. At the end o' that, a small gray man stood atop a big rock, his hands stretchin' toward the sky.

A sense o' relief washed into the ol' sailor, rinsin' away some o' the trepidation bein' near the sea'd put inside him. The watery feelin' in his arms and legs solidified, givin' him more energy, and a smile tugged at the corners o' his mouth. He pushed through the brush, ignorin' the thorns tuggin' at his arms as he moved toward the one tuggin' at his heart.

I ain't alone no more.

He emerged from the bushes onto the beach, feet crunchin' on its rocky edge. The briny wind blew through his thin hair and tickled the scrubby whiskers on his cheeks. He breathed through his mouth, attemptin' to avoid smellin' the stink o' the ocean and the dried-up seaweed it'd cast aside. Though he hated it, the sea's familiarity calmed him more'n he'd been since he and Thorn set foot in Haven.

Horace picked his way a few steps over the rocky terrain, intendin' to skirt the small bay and head for his wayward companion standin' at the end o' the point. The ol' sailor stopped and tilted his head back, lookin' up into the sky at what Thorn were stretchin' his arms out toward, expectin' what he found.

The bird Thorn'd called Father Raven circled high over the gray man's head, spiralin' closer to the ground with each successive turn. Seein' it comin' down and down, Horace realized what Thorn were attemptin'.

He's usin' magic to call him.

The ol' sailor watched, his insides twistin' and fightin' at the thought. He'd be happy the little feller found his way home, but he'd miss him, too. Back when he'd set his feet on the deck o' the Devil, who'd've thought he'd end up meetin' a Small God from the Green, never mind missin' him when he'd gone?

Life sure feeds you some funny meals.

Horace lowered his head and took one more step before holdin' up again. He squinted and leaned forward, peerin' not at Thorn stretchin' his arms and callin' Father Raven, but at the rocks behind him. It were hard to make anythin' out from a distance, but it seemed to Horace somethin'd moved.

He held his breath, watchin' and waitin', until it happened again. When it did, he realized why it'd been so difficult for him to see.

The man were pretty near the same color as the rocks.

***

The sun on Thorn's cheeks fed him, though not

322

enough to compensate for the energy he expended. Masquerading as a human had drained him, but seeing Father Raven prompted him into drawing on what power he had left to control the bird, use him to return behind the veil. At home, he'd never come close to depletion, so he didn't know how much more remained to give, but it wouldn't matter once he made it back. When Father Raven carried him over the veil, all the magic in the world would belong to him again.

Eyes closed, he stood up on his toes, stretching his body as high toward the sky as his small stature allowed. In his mind, he pictured his energy extending upward, felt it brush the raven's feathers as though he touched them with his own fingertips. The hold he gained on the bird was tenuous, but he had it.

If he kept concentrating, if his power held, he'd be home soon.

The sea breeze caressed his face, whistled gently in his ears. He breathed in the saltiness Horace despised so much, the scent of fish swimming in the sea, of sun on stone, bird droppings baking in the heat, and the distinct aroma of clay.

Father Raven spiraled closer and Thorn nearly lost concentration as he wondered what had become of Horace Seaman, his mind hearing a phantom of the man calling his name. He quickly refocused before his grip on the bird slipped. The old sailor had survived a long time before he met Thorn; he'd survive a good while after the Small God was gone.

Thorn's energy lagged, but the bird had come close enough he needed to expend less to hold him in his thrall. His heart swelled with bliss at the thought of returning home—for himself and to restore glorious Father Raven to his rightful place.

"Thorn!"

The Small God's eyes snapped open. No mistaking it:

the voice belonged to the real Horace Seaman, not a memory or his fatigued mind playing tricks. His hold on the raven slipped.

"Behind you!"

For an instant, Thorn considered ignoring the old sailor's warning, but the tone of his voice convinced him something was amiss. The gray man pivoted his body and lowered his arms, releasing some of his influence on Father Raven. He glanced across the small bay at Horace splashing through the water and waving his arms over his head. The comical sight might have brought a smile to Thorn's lips had there not been another man racing through the sea, chasing his friend.

It didn't seem to Thorn that Horace realized his pursuer's presence.

The Small God inhaled a breath, intending to call out a warning. The scent of clay filled the air he drew, overpowering everything else.

Powerful limbs encircled Thorn, pinning his arms to his side and squeezing the air from his lungs. Sea and sky wavered before his eyes and his hold on Father Raven was severed. The gray man wrenched his gaze over his shoulder and saw angry eyes, flared nostrils, cheeks the color of clay.

Beyond, the black bird rose into the sky, then the world faded into darkness.

***

"Thorn!"

Horace waved his hands o'er his head, desperate to attract the little feller's attention. Salty water splashed up 'round him, drops landin' on his lips and spillin' the briny flavor into his mouth, threatenin' to turn his stomach. He ignored it.

"Behind you!"

Thorn faced Horace, but it were too late. The giant feller grabbed him 'round the middle and the gray man went stiff first, then sagged in his grip. Outta the corner o' his eye, Horace spied someone else splashin' through the bay, but it were too late for him, too. The man jumped across the last bit o' space between them, tacklin' Horace and draggin' him into the water.

Salty fluid filled his eyes and found its way into his mouth. A silvery flash o' fish scales fleein' the scene went past his head, but he didn't think nothin' 'bout it while he tried to keep from swallowin' the ocean what experience told him'd mean unpleasant thin's for him.

The weight o' the man what tackled him held Horace under. He worried the feller'd wrap his fingers 'round his neck the way he'd done to Dunal, but if he didn't get his face outta the sea to get himself a breath, it wouldn't matter 'bout squeezin' his throat, anyways. Horace thrashed like when he thought the God o' the Deep'd drag him to the ocean's depths, fightin' for his life. This time, at least he understood what it were wantin' to end his days, even if he didn't grasp the stranger's reasonin'.

The ol' sailor twisted and got one shoulder out from under the other feller. It gave Horace enough leverage to lift his face outta the water for an instant and suck a hurried breath, but sea water went in with it, makin' him cough. He glimpsed the face o' the man holdin' him, fear in his eyes and his lips movin' as he counted off numbers out loud.

An instant later, Horace's head were back under again. He struggled and writhed, but the man on top o' him had a better grip and he held him from gettin' free.

Death'd soon be his and, even worse, he did a shit job o' warnin' Thorn 'bout the man creepin' up on him. As the air in Horace's lungs began to burn, he wished he'd never've let the little feller go off on his own. If they'd stayed together, maybe thin's might've turned out different'n both o' them endin' up dead.

Horace closed his eyes, awaitin' his end to come,

when the hands holdin' him under jerked him up. His head broke the surface, the briny sea runnin' outta his hair and offa his cheeks, and for the second time in his life, the ol' sailor gasped a breath he weren't never expectin' to take. He blinked hard a bunch o' times to clear the ocean outta his eyes and breathed as many times as he could, thinkin' he'd get submerged again.

He didn't.

"I can't do it," the man holdin' onto him said.

The feller appeared to be younger'n Horace himself and didn't look no different'n anyone else. His face didn't hold no monstrous aspect—no deep scar, no nasty-lookin' eyes like Horace might've expected from a man meanin' to kill him.

The same might not be said o' the giant loomin' behind him.

The man—if he were a man—didn't respond to his companion. The skin on his muddy-brown forehead wrinkled as though he didn't appreciate what the feller had to say. He blinked his muddy-brown eyes once and straightened, adjusted Thorn's limp body what he carried thrown over one shoulder.

Horace opened and closed his mouth a couple o' times. His brain told him he should do somethin'—fight or try to escape—but his muscles'd gone as liquidy as the sea lappin' 'round his ball sack what was tryin' to crawl back up inside him. He'd nothin' to do other'n suck air into his chest and consider beggin' for his life, but his lungs never got full enough for his mouth to consider makin' sounds.

The giant took a step back and gestured with his free hand for his companion to stand Horace up. The tiniest spark o' hope flashed to life deep inside the ol' sailor—did this mean they was fixin' to let him go? Maybe, but they wasn't seemin' they'd do the same for Thorn.

The man who'd tackled Horace shifted himself

'round behind the ol' sailor, grabbin' his arms and holdin' him upright, fully exposin' him to the giant standin' before him.

The big feller were the same muddy-brown all o'er, as though he'd fallen in a dirty puddle after a hard rain and never bothered washin' himself. Sunlight glistened on his smooth skin, accentin' muscles what looked sculpted rather'n grown. Not that he cared 'bout such thin's, but danglin' between his legs, the man had the biggest cock the ol' sailor'd ever seen.

Horace shook his head and finally found his voice.

"Let Thorn go," he wheezed.

The big feller didn't act as though he heard, but the man holdin' Horace leaned his lips in close to his ear and spoke: "A Small God shall fall so the Small Gods might rise."

A mighty shiver found its way along Horace's limbs, one not caused by the sea breeze blowin' on his wet self. The big feller standin' in front o' him raised his arm and extended a finger toward Horace's chest.

"Don't kill him, Ves," the man at Horace's back said. "You don't need to kill him."

The clay-lookin' man hesitated, his big, brownish finger hoverin' in the air a few handspans from Horace. The ol' sailor stared at it hangin' there and the world 'round him became more clear. Waves washed up against his legs, movin' his breeches; gulls cried out o'erhead, their calls near drowned by the splash o' the ocean rollin' onto the shore; he caught a whiff o' clay and knew the thin' weren't no man.

"Please," Horace squeaked before the muddy-brown fingertip touched his breastbone.

It didn't hurt. It didn't feel like nothin'. The cold o' the sea water soakin' his clothes went away. The achy exhaustion in his limbs disappeared. The painful rib pokin' him stopped hurtin'. He stared at the man standin' in front o' him and sensed the one holdin' him from behind; he heard the waves lappin' 'round their legs, but there weren't a thin' he felt, inside or out.

The big feller nodded and then Horace were fallin' backward because the man what'd been grabbin' him let go. The ol' sailor hauled a breath in before his head went back under, the sea rushin' in 'round his face, though he couldn't feel its chilly salt fingers. A few skippin' heartbeats later, Horace bobbed to the surface, floatin' on his back. Water ran outta eyes he were unable to blink and he stared straight up into the sky.

Horace attempted speakin', but his mouth and tongue and throat refused to work for nothin' but takin' breaths. Weren't nothin' movin' on the ol' sailor, though the splashin' o' the two men wadin' back to shore reached his ears as they carried his friend Thorn away.

They mean to kill him.

He didn't understand what the feller meant 'bout Small Gods risin'—it didn't sound too good to Horace—but there weren't nothin' to do right then. After near thirty-five turns o' the seasons with his feet on the deck o' one ship and another, Horace knew enough to realize the tide were ebbin' and the current were goin' to carry him out with it.

High o'erhead, the black bird Thorn'd called Father Raven circled once, twice, then straightened his course, flyin' in the direction o' sunrise and leavin' Horace alone with the sea.

ABOUT THE AUTHOR

Bruce Blake lives on Vancouver Island in British Columbia, Canada. When pressing issues like shovelling snow and building igloos don't take up his spare time, Bruce can be found taking the dog sled to the nearest coffee shop to work on his short stories and novels.

Actually, Victoria, B.C. is only a couple hours north of Seattle, Wash., where more rain is seen than snow. Since snow isn't really a pressing issue, Bruce spends more time trying to remember to leave the "u" out of words like "colour" and "neighbour" then he does shovelling. The father of two, Bruce was once the trophy husband of burlesque diva..not so much any more, but they remain friends.

Bruce has been writing since grade school but it wasn't until the mid-2000's he set his sights on becoming a full-time writer. Since then, his first short story, "Another Man's Shoes" was published in the Winter 2008 edition of *Cemetery Moon*, another short, "Yardwork",was made into a podcast in Oct., 2011 by *Pseudopod.* Since then, he has concentrated on writing novels, publishing the Khirro's Journey trilogy (Blood of the King, Spirit of the King, and Heart of the King), three books in the ongoing Icarus Fell urban fantasy series (On Unfaithful Wings, All Who Wander are Lost, and Secrets of the Hanged Man), and the Books of the Small Gods series (When Shadows Fall, The Darkness Comes, And Night Descends, When Ravens Call, The Twilight Fades, and And Kingdoms End). Bruce has many more projects simmering on the back burner, so stay tuned.

Blood of the King (Khirro's Journey Book 1)

A kingdom torn by war. A curse whispered by dying lips. A hero born against his will.

Khirro never wanted to be anything more than the farmer he was born to be, but a Shaman's curse binds him to the fallen king and his life changes forever.

Driven by the Shaman's dying words, Khirro's journey pits him against an army of the dead, sends him through haunted lands, and thrusts him into the jaws of beasts he wouldn't have believed existed. In one hand he carries the Shaman's enchanted sword, a weapon he can barely use; in the other he holds a vial of the king's blood, the hope of the kingdom. His destination: the Necromancer's keep in the cursed land of Lakesh. Only the mysterious outlaw magician can raise the king from the dead to save them all from the undead invasion, but can Khirro live long enough to deliver the vial?

Can a coward save a kingdom?

"Blood of the King is a masterpiece. It is as close to perfection as I would consider a book to be."- Ella Medler, author of *Blood is Heavier*

"Blake has a knack for bringing you into the story"

"Mr. Blake's writing is masterful and clear, he draws you into his story and when it's finished you feel like you're leaving an old friend."

On Unfaithful Wings (Icarus Fell #1)

To some, death is the end; to others, a beginning. To Icarus Fell, it should have been a relief from a life gone seriously awry.

But death had other plans.

Icarus doesn't believe that the man awaiting him when he wakes up in a cheap motel room is really the archangel Michael, or that God's right hand wants him to help souls on their way to Heaven. Icarus doesn't believe there's a Heaven, so why should they want his help?

But the man claiming to be the archangel tempts him with an offer he can't ignore--harvest enough souls and get back the life he wished he'd had.

It seems Icarus has nothing to lose, until he botches a harvest and the soul that went to Hell instead of Heaven comes back to make him pay by threatening to take away the life he hoped to win back.

To save the wife and son he already lost once, Icarus will have to become the man he never was. Somehow, he will have to learn to believe.

"The next book in this series cannot come out soon enough for this reader. Not just my favorite Kindle book of the year, but one of my favorite books ever."

"I loved this book."

"Bruce Blake's On Unfaithful Wings is a great urban fantasy novel. I love good character development in a story's protagonist and Blake nails it with Icarus Fell. I found myself rooting for him from the get-go and laughing out loud at some of his observations."

"On Unfaithful Wings was an impressive first novel. All of the characters were interesting and engaging, but in particular the main character and his struggle to reconcile with his new identity/job. This is one of those stories that stays with me long after I read it and I'll be on the lookout for more from this author."